DEDICATION

*This is for all my readers! I love you, guys!
You guys already know there is sex in the
first chapter. I wouldn't be me if
I didn't.*

*I've also been told to add the warning that
you may need a pair of clean panties handy (thanks
Kelly!)*

Happy reading!

ALL I HAVE

PART ONE

ABBS VALLEY SERIES

AMES MILLS

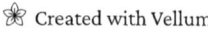 Created with Vellum

AUTHORS NOTE

Welcome back to Abbs Valley! Abbs Valley is a fictional place in sunny California. So much happens here!

WARNINGS

Content and triggers warnings include: Mentions of domestic abuse, sexual assault, stalking, explicit language, explicit sex scenes, explicit group sex scenes, breath play, exploration of kinks, sex club, voyeurism, first time orgasms, orgasm denial, forced orgasms, rough sex, mm, mmf, mmmfmm, mfm

If any of this triggers you or if it's not something that catches your eye...turn back now.

P.S. No, mom. You shouldn't read this one either.

PROLOGUE

MICAH

SIX MONTHS AGO

"Are you going to pout because Les sent you with me?" Evander asks, looking at me from the driver's seat. I understand why Les did it. She and the guys are on the run until this sick fucker Jay is caught, leaving me nowhere to go since I can't stay alone. Getting shot sucks, but I'll wear this bullet wound proudly since it means Viktor is finally dead.

"I'm not fucking pouting," I answer. It hurt to be in the car with him. Everything that went down with us had me so damn confused, and by the time I figured it out, he was done with my shit.

"Sure looks like it to me," Evander replies. "Don't worry; when we get to the house, I'll make sure I don't show my face."

"It has nothing to do with that, Van," I say with a sigh. "I know you don't want me here."

Evander pulls into the garage at his house and puts his BMW Alpina into park before turning to me. "Is that what you think? I wouldn't have told her you could if I didn't." Before I can answer, he's already out of the car, on his way to my side. He pulls my door open and, without a word, starts helping me get out of the car.

1

"I can do it myself," I grouch. He rolls his eyes, pulls my arm over his shoulder, and helps me stand. I can't control the shudder that rolls through my body at his touch. I haven't touched him since I kissed him at Les' house, and he pushed me away.

Evander gets me into the house, leading me down a short hallway to a bedroom right off the living room. He gets me into the bed, propping my leg up, and turns toward the door. "Van," I say. "Are we ever going to talk about it?"

"Talk about what, Micah?" he asks, turning around to face me. "You wanted to pretend we had nothing." He shrugs. "I don't see what we have to talk about."

I lay my head back on the pillows, staring at the ceiling. "I tried to apologize for that."

"No," Evander says harshly. "You wanted to blame it on every fucking body else. You thought one conversation would have me falling at your damn feet again."

"I want to make this right," I tell him honestly.

When Van and I started fooling around, we thought it would be an experiment to see why we felt attracted to each other; neither of us had been attracted to another man. It turned into something way more than either of us bargained for, then ended just as quickly because I don't do feelings. I did nothing other than casual sex until Evander.

"I gave you a chance, Micah." He sighs, running his fingers through his brown hair. "We both need to move on; go back to being friends," he says and turns back towards the door.

Is he serious right now? "Friends? After everything between us, you want to be...friends?"

Evander whirls back around. "What do you want from me?" he growls, taking a step back toward the bed. "I laid it all out on the line, and you slammed a door in my face after saying we had *nothing*."

"I'm sorry, Van," I say miserably. "I never wanted to hurt you."

"Well, you did." He shakes his head. "It doesn't matter, anyway. I'm going to get your meds." He spins on his heel and is gone before I can argue, returning minutes later, thrusting a bottle of water and two pills into my hands. "Take these and get some rest."

2

I take them without complaint, sit the water bottle on the bedside table, and grab his arm before he can walk away again. "I don't want to be just friends, Van."

Evander sits on the side of the bed with a sigh. "That's all I can give you right now, Micah."

"You don't feel this between us?" I ask, running my hand down his leg—Evander's whole-body tenses at my touch.

"Of course, I feel it."

"Then why fight it?" I retort, sliding my hand to the inside of his thigh, right above his knee. I keep going when he doesn't stop me, but when my fingers brush his cock, he grabs my wrist. I think he's going to push me away, but he twists on the bed, positions himself between my thighs, careful with the brace on my leg, and leans down until his lips hover over mine. Both our breaths are coming in short, little pants just from being this close to each other.

"You know what I feel, Micah?" he whispers against my lips, then drops his hips, so his dick is against mine. "I feel how hard you make me. I feel how my heart skips a beat when I see you. You know what I feel from you?" I shake my head. "I feel like you want the physical without the emotional attachment." He slants his mouth over mine with a groan. My hands come up to grab his face to deepen the kiss, but he's already pulling away. "That's not all I want with you. So until you get on the same fucking page, we are. Just. Friends. I want to make you beg for it," he says hoarsely. "I want you to need me. I want you so fucked up that you don't know what to do with yourself. I want you to feel how I felt." He kisses my neck before standing up. "Mark my words, Micah; you will beg." He strides from the room and is gone before I can stop him, shutting the door behind him.

Fuck.

I want to be pissed at him for playing with me, but I deserve it. Hell, I don't even deserve his friendship. I took what he felt for me and threw it back in his face, making him feel wrong for his feelings, all because I didn't know how to handle my own.

The conversation at Marcella's the night we got Nina out of Viktor's house plays on repeat in my head every goddamn day. Evander had already given me the ultimatum to tell Les and everyone about us, or he was done. Like a dick, instead of telling him I wasn't ready, I led him on, making him believe I was going to. It didn't take him long to figure out I was full of shit. I wanted more with Van. I wanted everything he offered me.

But I was a fucking coward.

CHAPTER 1

MICAH

NOW

W hat do you do when the person you love the most gets their happily ever after, but you're still a miserable bastard?

That's how I feel watching my niece, Alessa, get married to the loves of her life. I'm happy for her, damn happy; she deserves this. She went through hell to get here, and watching her dancing and laughing with the guys makes my heart full. But my eyes keep tracking to the bar where the reason I'm a miserable bastard is currently standing.

Evander Perez.

The one I never saw coming. He was the first real love of my life, and I fucked it up because I couldn't wrap my head around being in love with a man.

Six months ago, he told me he wanted to be friends, and I've tried. But even then, he keeps himself at a distance and closed off. Not that I blame him.

"Why do you look like someone kicked your puppy?" Mateo, Evander's brother, asks, sitting at the table I've been at all night.

"I don't," I reply, taking a sip of my scotch.

Mateo snorts. "Yes, you do." I look over at him and see the

5

moment he sees where I'm staring. He rolls his eyes. "When are you two going to stop playing fucking games?"

"I'm not playing a goddamn game," I reply with a glare.

"Come on. I've never seen two people so miserable."

"I've tried, Tay. I've told him how I feel and what I want. That's not what he wants anymore."

I've told him repeatedly, and he shuts me down every time. He doesn't want to hear it; the more I tell him, the more I feel him slipping away from me.

"Have you done anything to prove it?" He runs his fingers through his hair. "Look, man, you're one of my closest friends, and I don't mean anything by this, but you fucked up. *Big* time. It's going to take more than some words to fix that."

I lean my head back on my chair, staring at the ceiling. "I don't know what he wants from me. He wanted to be friends; that's what I'm doing. Anything else, he shuts down."

"Maybe try harder," Mateo says, making me sit up with a glare. "You aren't stupid, Micah. This isn't one of your little conquests that you hit it and quit it with. You need to put in more effort."

I haven't had any conquests, not that I'm going to tell him that. "Why are you even talking to me about this?"

"Because it sucks watching what you guys are going through," Mateo chuckles. "Plus, you don't have anyone else to talk to."

"Why does everyone think I don't have any damn friends?"

He gives me a dry look. "Because you don't, besides Les and us."

"Fuck off," I mutter. He's right; I don't have anyone but them. Les doesn't even know half the shit going on because I don't want to bother her with my damn problems.

Mateo grins. "Tell me I'm wrong."

"Go away."

He laughs. "Truth hurts, Micah."

"My fist will hurt when I punch you in the face," I threaten, and he laughs harder. "Sometimes I don't fucking like you."

"You love me. I make your life less boring."

"My life isn't boring, asshole."

6

He stands with a grin. "That's because you have me." He points at me. "Fix things with Van."

With that parting shot, he walks over to his brother. Mateo says something to him, and Van slides those brown eyes over me. I meet his stare head-on, not even blinking, letting what I'm thinking broadcast all over my face. Just like I always do. I don't hide from him anymore. I let him know everything I'm thinking, which usually makes him avoid me for weeks.

I don't know how else to prove I want everything with him. I haven't been with anyone since Van and I started messing around; all I want is *him*. Even then, I knew that and was too fucking stubborn to admit it.

I let my eyes roam around the room. Everyone is dancing and having fun. Alexey and Dmitri have Les' stylist, Bridget, sandwiched between them on the dance floor. I shake my head. That girl doesn't know what she's getting herself into there. Ghost and Caden, two guys that work for Les, are off to the side, flirting with one of the servers for the reception. Lucas, Landon, and Noah, the boys we took off the street, are sneaking booze behind Gerald and Boone's back. Gerald and Boone used to be guards for my brother Luca before he passed away, and they'll kick their asses when they catch them.

Thoughts of my brother always come with a wave of sadness. Although he was my half-brother and was twelve when I was born, he never treated me differently. He died young at forty-five of cancer, leaving Les and me to lead the Italian Mafia. Luca would be so fucking happy for Les. Not just for finding the guys she wanted to spend the rest of her life with, but for stepping up to lead this family.

I look around again at everyone and take a breath. Months ago, I didn't think we would ever get to a point where we could relax. Since we took out Viktor, the leader of the Russian Mafia, it's been quiet. Too many people are afraid to step up against us now that we have taken him down. Alexey and Dmitri, Viktor's sons, weren't ready to step up to the plate, so they put someone else in charge until they're ready. They seem content, for now, to run around with Ghost and Caden.

Like a magnet, my eyes pull back to Van, moving through the

crowd toward Les and Leo, his other brother. He hugs them and walks to the elevators that take you to the rooms. Les got rooms for everyone, so no one had to go home, and the party could continue after they left for their honeymoon. They're going to Lake Como, Italy, for three weeks, leaving me to run everything while she's gone.

I throw back the rest of my scotch, stand up, and go to say my goodbyes. Van and I have a score to settle, and it's happening. Tonight.

"Hey, shithead," I say, wrapping her in a hug.

"Hey," she replies with a smile.

"You guys getting ready to take off?" I ask.

"Yeah. Are you okay?" she asks, looking at me closely.

"I will be," I assure her, depending on how this talk goes with Van. I kiss her forehead. "Have fun on your honeymoon. Love you."

"Love you too," Les replies. I give her one last hug, nod to her guys, and disappear to the elevators.

I punch the button for the top floor where mine and Van's rooms are. Strolling to his room, I knock and lean against the door frame to wait. He jerks the door open, and his eyes narrow slightly when he sees me standing here.

"What do you want, Micah?"

Without giving him time to react, I push him back into the room, step inside, and shut the door behind me.

"It's time we talked," I say, tilting my head.

"And this talk couldn't wait until the morning?" Van asks, crossing his arms over his chest.

Something about that defensive move snaps me into action. I grab him by the front of his shirt and spin us so his back is pressed against the door. Pushing my body against his, I run my lips down his neck.

"No, it couldn't wait," I say. "Damn, you look good enough to eat, *Amore mio*," I groan. We had to wear the same classic tux, but Van lost his jacket and bow tie, leaving him with his shirt half unbuttoned.

"Micah," Van warns, putting his hands between us to push me away.

I slap my hands on either side of his head on the door, my lips hovering right in front of his. "I'm done playing this game. I don't want to be fucking friends. I want to let this entire world know. You. Are. Mine."

"What does that even mean?" Van asks breathlessly.

"It means I'm done hiding." I bend my head, letting my lips rub up his neck. A shiver rolls through him. "I don't mean just sex. I want everything with you."

"Micah," he says again, pushing against my chest. I finally lean back so I can see his eyes. "Don't fuck with me."

"I'm not fucking with you, *Amore mio*," I say adamantly. "Give me the chance to prove it to you. This time without you," I stop and swallow, "I never want to do that again. I will spend however long it takes to prove to you that I'm ready. Please, Van. I listened. I *heard* you. I need you in my life." He told me I would beg for it, and he was fucking right. I'm not ashamed to admit anymore how much I need him.

He searches my eyes, and the truth is staring right back at him. I'm giving him the one thing he wanted since he told me he was falling in love with me, and I shut the door in his face. He crushes his lips against mine, accepting what I'm saying.

I groan when I sink my tongue into his mouth. My hands come down to his face, tilting it to control the kiss. His hands slide to my hips, jerking me closer.

We stagger to the bed, lips still connected, falling onto it with me on top of him. I grind my hard cock against his, and he moans, hot and needy.

"Fuck," I breathe, pulling my mouth from his. "I want you so fucking bad." I kiss down his neck and chest, where his buttons are undone.

He pushes his hips up. "I want you. Now."

My head snaps up, my eyes zeroing in on his face. "I don't have anything with me. We can go back to my house," I suggest. I didn't plan on this happening, but I would love nothing more than to wake up to Evander in *my* bed in the morning.

He shakes his head. "My wallet." I raise a brow. "You know I keep some in there from before, you know, just in case," he explains and finally smiles.

"Are you sure?" I don't want him to think I'm pressuring him. I want to do this right this time.

He nods, so I jump from the bed. I roughly jerk my shirt from my slacks, my fingers going to the buttons on my shirt. He stands up and starts doing the same, never taking his eyes off me. The shirt falls from his shoulders, and I have to remember to breathe. Evander isn't as broad in the shoulders as me; he's leaner but has cut pecs with a light smattering of dark hair, carved abs, and a v-line that I love to run my tongue on.

"You look like you want to eat me alive, *Amore mio*," I joke, stalking toward him again, my hand going to my belt.

"I kind of do," he admits honestly.

I step into his space. "Good," I growl.

We make quick work of the rest of our clothes and fall back onto the bed, my naked body finally sliding over his. "Shit," he grunts when I slide down, taking his cock into my mouth. "Micah," he groans when it bumps the back of my throat. My eyes flash to his face, and I almost come on the damn spot. "Please," he begs.

My mouth pops off, my hand still swirling. "Are you sure?" I ask again.

"Yes, Micah," he answers, lifting his hips to fuck my fist.

I lean over and grab his pants, pulling his wallet free. Handing it to him, he pulls the lube packet out and tosses his wallet back on the floor. Taking the packet from his hands, I rip it open and squirt some onto my fingers.

"I haven't been with anyone since you," I admit. I need him to know I haven't been fucking around while we were apart. All the time we weren't together, I treated it like we were.

"I haven't either," he answers. Goddamn, if that doesn't make me happy.

I slide my fingers between his ass cheeks, circling his back hole. When his eyes latch onto mine, I slide a finger inside him, working it a few times before adding a second. "Fuck," he moans.

"That's it, *Amore mio*," I say gruffly. "Tell me how good it feels." I work my fingers until he's pushing down on them, begging for more. "You want my cock?"

"Yes."

I search his eyes this time, and the truth is right there. He wants me as much as I want him. I slick my dick up and line up. I push forward, my eyes never leaving his.

Once past the resistance, I groan as I slowly slide the rest of the way in. "Fuck," I choke out when my thighs settle against his. "I've missed this ass." I lay my chest against his. "I've missed you."

Van nods, working his hips down to get me to move.

Anchoring one hand on his hip, I start to move slowly. His hands slide up my back, feeling the muscles shift under his fingers. *I forgot how good he feels.* Both our breaths are coming in pants, eyes locked together. No matter how often we had sex before, I've never looked him in the eye like this. I drag my cock across his prostate, and his back bows, his cock throbbing between us. He slams his lips against mine, kissing me almost brutally. I kiss him back with the same intensity, my thrusts speeding up.

I jerk my mouth away, laying my forehead against his. "I was serious earlier. I want everything with you."

Do we even know what that means? I've never been in a relationship; I've openly admitted that. He's been in one that was years ago. Could either of us do this without fucking it up?

I shift my hips, dragging slowly out of him, making him gasp. Fuck, I've missed the sounds he makes and how he makes me feel.

Laying my forehead back on his, I start moving in short, shallow thrusts, the head of my cock rubbing his prostate repeatedly, my eyes never leaving his. He reaches between us and wraps a hand around his cock, stroking.

I slam my hips forward, burying myself completely. "Fuck. Yes," Van grunts, stroking harder.

I sit back on my heels, wrap my hands on his hips, and slam forward again, watching his face. I pull down at the same time as I thrust into him, making him stroke his cock faster. "You going to come for me, *Amore mio?*" I ask gruffly.

"Yes," Van moans. "Fuck me, Micah."

I start hammering my hips forward so hard that I grunt at the impact when my thighs slap his. "Goddamn, you feel good," I groan.

That's his undoing. His abs bunch, and his hand tightens on his cock. "Micah," he half moans, coming all over his chest.

"Shit," I hiss, moving faster. Jerking him down on my cock, I feel myself swell inside him, and the first splash of my cum inside him has more pouring out of his cock. I collapse forward, not caring about the mess on his chest. Both our chests are heaving, trying to suck in air. I groan and pull out of him, collapsing back on his chest.

"I love you," I say against his neck, and he freezes. I pull back so I can see his face. "I should have told you that months ago, Van. But I was a stubborn asshole."

He stares at me for so long that I wonder if he even heard me. He frantically shoves at my chest until I roll off of him.

"What the fuck is wrong with you?" Van demands when he gets to his feet at the foot of the bed. *What the fuck?*

I sit up on the bed. "What do you mean?"

"You can't just say that!" Van yells, raking his fingers through his hair. "Goddamnit, Micah."

"Isn't that what you wanted?" I ask, confused as hell.

"Do you even know what love is? I poured my fucking heart out to you, and you didn't even care."

"I did fucking care," I grind out, sliding to my feet in front of him. "I've been trying to tell you, but you wouldn't listen to me."

"Do you blame me?" He throws his hands in the air. "You can't just come in here, fuck me, tell me you love me and expect me to say it back. Too much time has passed. I can't do this with you."

My heart sinks to my feet. "What are you saying?"

"I won't set myself up to be hurt again," he says, not looking me in the eye. "It's too late." He walks off, slamming the bathroom door behind him.

I slam my legs into my pants, not bothering with a shirt. Gathering the rest of my clothes, I make it to my room, flopping down on the bed.

Why the hell did he let me in if he didn't want this? I told him how I felt before we had sex; I thought we were on the same page.

I rub my chest, my heart twisting painfully. I've never felt like this before. I know the pain of losing my brother and thinking I had lost Les. But this is different. I don't know how to deal with this.

Taking a quick shower to get his smell off me, I send a message to my bodyguard Gray that we're leaving. I need to go home; I can't stay here knowing I could run into Van again.

I'm so fucking confused that I don't know what to do with myself. Is this what he felt? No wonder he hated me.

Gray knocks on the door minutes later. "Everything good, Boss?" he asks when he steps inside.

I hired Gray six months ago after all the shit Les went through with her having a mole among her guards. He came highly recommended, so I gave him the job on the spot.

He's every bit of six-foot-five, two-hundred-thirty pounds of solid muscle. I can take care of myself, but I need the extra backup. You never know when someone is going to try to fuck you over.

"Yeah," I answer shortly. "And stop calling me boss." I've told him that a thousand times, and he never listens. He raises a brow but doesn't comment. I grab the small bag I had for tonight. "Let's go."

I pull open the door and come face to face with a drunk Mateo.

"You leaving?" he asks when he spots my bag.

"Yep. See you around." I start to walk away, and he grabs my arm.

"What's wrong?" Mateo asks. This asshole can always read me like a book.

"Ask your brother," I answer before I can stop myself.

He drops my arm and frowns. "What does that mean?"

"Nothing," I say with a shake of my head. "I'll talk to you later."

I walk away before I spill everything to Mateo. Mateo is my best friend, but Van is his brother. No way will I put that on him. I stab the button for the elevator, and he gives me one last look before letting himself into his room, but not before he checks out Gray. I roll my eyes at that.

When we get to the bottom floor, I'm more pissed than hurt.

If Evander thinks I'm giving up that easily, he has another thing coming.

CHAPTER 2

EVIE

I t's just after one in the morning, and the party I am serving is still in full swing. Not that I care. They all look like they are having a blast. This is the most high-profile party I've served at, and everyone is genuinely nice.

I have to admit I am a little jealous. I haven't been able to have fun in a long time, not working three jobs to keep my head above water.

Sweeping my brown hair off my neck and smoothing down the pants of my uniform, I take the tray with drinks and start making my rounds. The uniform is form-fitting and too tight for my bigger body, but it's what we have to wear, and this job pays the best. So, I suck it up and smile when someone smiles at me, even though all I want to do is go home and pass out.

I've never seen so many beautiful people in my life. Everyone is dressed to the max for the fancy wedding reception. I still couldn't wrap my head around the fact that the bride married six guys or committed, since that's all she could do legally. But she looked radiant, and the guys looked head over heels for her. And each other. I don't judge them, however. Love is love, no matter what.

"Thank you," a guy says with a smile when he takes a glass. I'm not going to lie and say my eyes haven't stayed almost glued to him all night long. He is tall, the tux he wore is molded to him, thick brown hair, and green eyes that are so bright they almost look feline. He is gorgeous. I might be jaded thanks to an asshole of an ex, but I can still appreciate what is right in front of me. He lost his jacket and bow tie a long time ago. His crisp white shirt has a couple of buttons at his neck undone, and his sleeves are rolled up, showing off toned, tan forearms.

"You're welcome," I reply with a smile. He has smiled and flirted all night, but I blame all the alcohol he's been consuming. No way a guy like that would take a second look at a girl like me. He would go for girls like supermodels. Tall and long legs. Not a short, chubby girl with dull brown hair and enough baggage to last a lifetime.

"Mateo!" the one I noticed earlier with bright blue hair yells. "Come do shots with us!"

Mateo. I like that name.

Mateo turns back to me with a grin. "You want to hang with us?" he asks.

"I'm kind of working," I say with a laugh.

"After?" he asks, leaning close enough that I get a whiff of his expensive cologne. Is he really flirting with me? I shake those thoughts from my head. Even if I wanted to, I couldn't. Not with the threat of my ex still breathing down my neck.

"I can't," I tell him regretfully.

"You have a pen?" Mateo asks, making me frown. I reach into my pocket and pull one out I was using earlier to write the stock down. These guys went through so much alcohol that I couldn't keep up when I needed to restock. I hand it to him, and he grabs my hand. Little shocks run up my arm from his touch. *What the hell is that?*

"In case you change your mind," he says, writing something on the back of my hand. He slides the pen into the breast pocket of the vest of the uniform with a smile. "What's your name?"

A lie is at the tip of my tongue, but I know I'll never see this guy again. "Evie," I answer honestly.

"Hm," he hums. "Beautiful name for a beautiful woman," he compliments, and my heart rate spikes. "Find me," he says, walking backward toward his friends.

I have to physically remove my eyes from his broad back to get my feet moving. I look down at my hand to see what he wrote. It looks like a phone number and a room number. He must be staying at the hotel.

Too bad I couldn't take him up on his offer. Not just because of Aaron, my ex, but because I was never that type of girl. I didn't have that kind of attention growing up until Aaron, which is why I fell for his bullshit.

"Who was that guy?" Jenn asks me. I met her when I started working for the catering company, and she is my only friend here besides one other. However, I don't know if I would classify him as a friend. We grew up together, and he's the first person I called when I found myself in Abbs Valley on the run.

"Someone from the party," I answer.

"He's smoking fucking hot," she says with a laugh.

I nod my head in agreement. "I'm going to take this trash out," I tell her.

I gather up the two bags and make my way to the backdoor for the dumpsters. I push the door open and breathe in the night air. I toss the bags in and lean against the wall, giving my poor feet a break.

I'm from California, but Abbs Valley is very different from Fairview, the small town I'm from. It's about four hours from here, and where I got myself into the mess I am currently in.

"Hey, baby," That voice has every muscle in my body locking up. I turn to the voice, and my lungs seize. He finally found me. "Did you really think you could run from me, Evie?"

I lock eyes with Aaron, the asshole monster ex that has put me on the run for almost eight months. Words are locked in my throat; I can't think or take a full breath. My eyes dart to the hotel's back door, and he laughs cruelly.

"Don't even think about it," he threatens, stepping forward. "Do you know what I've been through trying to find you?"

I step away from the wall and start walking backward, away from him. "Why are you here?" I whisper.

"I came for you, baby," Aaron says softly. I know better than to think he is being genuine. I fear him more when he's talking to me like that than when he is yelling at me. "It's time to come home."

"No," I say, walking around him in a circle toward the door. If I could get in, I could yell for help. "I'm not going anywhere with you."

Aaron's brown eyes take on that scary gleam, and I regret opening my mouth. He moves fast, snatching my arm in a painful grip. "That mouth always got you in fucking trouble. I'll just have to teach you how to speak to me again. Come on," he threatens, jerking my arm.

"Stop! Let me go!" I yell, struggling to get away. "You're hurting me!"

He tightens his grip. "You haven't seen hurt yet, you stupid bitch," he growls in my face. He starts dragging me toward the end of the alley, where I see a car parked. I don't even have to see through the dark tint to know who else is sitting in that car. Wraith, Aaron's second in command, is almost worse than Aaron. No way Aaron would come all the way here without him.

"I think she said to let her go." That deep voice comes from behind us. I double my struggle, hoping like hell I could get away.

"Fuck off," Aaron says without even turning around.

I finally break his hold and spin on my heel, coming face to chest with the mysterious voice. He gently grabs my arm and pulls me behind him before I can see his face. *Who the hell is this guy?*

"Who the fuck are you?" Aaron demands.

"A friend," the guy answers, making my eyebrows shoot up. I've never seen this guy before in my life.

"A friend?" Aaron laughs. "Get the fuck out of the way. That's my girl."

"You drag your girl around like that?" The guy asks, taking a step forward. I clutch the back of his shirt in a warning. He doesn't know what he is getting into with Aaron.

"What I do with her is none of your fucking business," Aaron grinds out. "Now fucking move."

"I don't think I will," my savior says, rolling his shoulders back. "You have two seconds to get out of here."

"Or what?" Aaron sneers.

"Or I'll let him go on your friend." I look around his arm, and my eyes widen. A huge guy is standing with Wraith's shirt clutched in his fist.

Aaron laughs loudly. "You think I'm scared of you? Fuck off."

Before I can grab him again, the guy is moving. He hits Aaron so hard in the face that Aaron smacks into the side of the building. He doesn't let up, even when Aaron stops fighting back. I clap my hand over my mouth, trying to keep the noises inside.

"Boss," the big guy says, walking up. "Boss," he says louder, grabbing the guy's arm. The guy jerks away, going back to Aaron. "Boss!" he yells, and that gets his attention.

Boss straightens up, chest heaving. "Get in your car and go back to wherever you came from. If I see you around her again, I'll fucking end you," he threatens with a kick to Aaron's kidney.

Aaron scrambles to his feet, blood pouring from his face. He jerks the passenger side door open and turns his eyes back to me. "This isn't over." He slams the door, and Wraith steps on the gas.

My savior turns around, and I'm struck dumb for a second. His eyes are the first thing I notice. Ice-blue eyes that stand out even more because of his jet-black hair. I remember seeing him inside at the party when I served him a drink. You noticed someone who looked like him.

Everything hits me about what happened, and I take a step back.

"No, no, no," I repeat. This just made it worse. Aaron is going to kill me for sure, and now I have involved two other guys just for protecting me. "What did you just do?"

My savior frowns. "Did you want to go with him?"

"No," I say miserably. "You don't know what you just did."

"What did we just do?" the big guy asks, crossing his arms over his chest. His hazel eyes are narrowed suspiciously.

"I have to go." I spin on my heel, and a hand grabs my arm before I can reach the door.

"Wait a minute," my savior says, turning me gently to face him. "You aren't going anywhere alone."

"I have to get back to work," I lie. I am hightailing it from Abbs

Valley as soon as he lets my arm go. I thought I was safe here. I hadn't heard from Aaron, but he was just biding his time.

"Not happening," my savior says.

"What does that mean?" I demand before I could stop myself. I don't know this guy; he just beat the shit out of Aaron without a care, and what do I do? Backtalk him like an idiot.

The big guy runs his hand over his buzz-cut black hair. "It means it's not safe to be anywhere alone right now."

"I'll be fine. I know someone that's staying here," I lie again. Technically, I do. His number is written on the back of my hand, but it isn't like I am actually going to call him.

My savior lifts a black brow and tilts his head to the side. "Do you now?" Shit. I forgot he was at the wedding party and the hotel was booked just for them. "Look, you don't know me, and I get it. But you don't need to be alone. Do you have a car?" he asks, and I shake my head. "I'm not leaving you until you call someone to come get you, or we'll take you home. The party is wrapping up now, so you don't have to worry about that."

No way they are seeing my run-down apartment building. I sigh and pull my phone from my pocket and dial the only other person I know here.

"Hello?" he answers on the second ring.

"I need you to come pick me up. I'm at Abbs Valley Elite hotel for an event. I'll explain when you get here. I'll be in the back alley," I tell him. He gets so quiet that I think he hung up. "Are you there?"

"Yeah," he grunts. "I'm on my way." The line goes dead, and I'm stuck with two guys I don't know.

"Thank you," I say, finally remembering my manners. They didn't have to get involved. They could have kept going and pretending they didn't hear anything.

"You're welcome," my savior says with a smile. *Does everyone here have to be so damn attractive?* "What's your name?"

"Evie," I answer automatically and want to kick my own ass. That's the second time I've given someone I don't know my name tonight. "Is your hand okay?" I ask, nodding my head toward it.

He lifts his hand to look at it, flexing his fingers. "It will be. Who was that?"

"My ex. You guys need to be careful. He's not a good guy," I warn.

Blue eyes barks a laugh. "I'm more worried about you, Evie." The way he says my name in that deep voice makes my palms sweat. What the fuck is wrong with me? "Do you need to tell someone you're leaving?"

"No," I sigh.

It doesn't matter since I will be on my way somewhere else when my ride shows up.

"Take this," my savior says, digging his wallet from his back pocket. He flips it open, pulls out a card, and hands it to me. "If you need me for anything, call," he says.

I look at it. It's just a phone number. "Okay," I reply. I won't, but he doesn't seem like someone you argue with.

A few minutes later, I see a familiar truck pull into the alley. "That's my ride," I say, pointing toward it.

Mr. Tall, dark, and blue eyes turns around, and his body goes rigid when the driver steps out. "Hartley fucking Cruz is your ride?" he growls.

"Uh, yeah," I answer, confused.

Hartley steps up, a muscle ticking in his jaw. "You ready, Evie?"

"I need to grab my purse," I reply, looking between them. They definitely know each other, and it isn't on good terms. That much is obvious.

Mr. Muscles pulls the door open for me and waves me forward. I step through, leaving the other two in an intense standoff. I go to the room where we kept our stuff and get my purse. I turn around and walk into muscles. I didn't even know he followed me in.

"Sorry," I mutter. He towers over my five-six frame, but surprisingly, he doesn't scare me.

"All good," he replies with a slight lift to his lips that is almost a smile. "You got everything?" I nod, and he leads me back outside, where they're still glaring at each other.

I walk around them, and Blue Eye's hand shoots out, grabbing my arm. He locks me in his blue-eyed stare. "If you need anything, call," he repeats.

"I will. Thank you again," I tell them both. I don't know what would have happened if they hadn't shown up when they did.

I shiver at the thought.

"WHAT HAPPENED BACK THERE, EVIE?" Hartley asks once we're in the truck.

"Aaron showed up," I tell him. I called Hartley when I got to Abbs Valley a month ago. He moved here to pursue law enforcement when he was eighteen. We stayed in contact for a while but lost touch when I started dating Aaron.

"Goddamnit. Are you okay?" Hartley asks, pulling onto the main road.

"Yeah," I answer. "How do you know those guys?" I ask.

Hartley grunts. "Let's just say that we've had run-ins with each other in my past line of work." Hartley told me he was the chief of police, but he turned in his resignation. He wouldn't tell me why, and I didn't push. It seemed like a sore subject.

"Oh," I say lamely. I don't know what to say back to that. "They stepped in and ran Aaron off."

"Good," Hartley growls. "You can't go home alone. I'll take you to get some stuff, and you can stay with me."

No way in hell. I can't run if I'm under his thumb. "I'll be fine."

"I know what you're thinking," Hartley says, glancing at me, then back to the road. "You aren't running again. I can keep you safe. I wish you would have come to me sooner."

"I didn't even know if you would answer the phone," I tell him, ignoring him calling me out.

He stops at a red light and turns to face me. "Why the hell would you think that? We were best friends growing up. That didn't change just because we went a couple of years without talking."

Hartley moved in next door when he was seven, and I was five; we became instant friends. It sucked when he left, but there was nothing in Fairview for him, and I still had two years of high school left.

He pulls in front of my apartment building and slides from the truck. He pops my door open. "Make it quick. Get something for tonight, and I'll bring you back tomorrow," he says.

"Seriously, Hart. I'll be fine," I argue, pushing the main lobby door open.

"Really? That door doesn't even have a fucking lock," he says, sliding his hand onto the small of my back, blocking me from two guys standing in the hallway.

I lead him up to the third floor and unlock my door. I shove it open and step inside before I answer. "It's all I can afford right now," I reply, embarrassment flooding me. My apartment is all one room with a small bathroom. It has a threadbare couch, a single bed, and a dresser. Everything else came with the apartment.

"You could have stayed with me," Hartley says, looking around. "Jesus, Evie, you shouldn't be here. I could kick that door in with no effort."

That's because you're huge now, I think, but don't dare say out loud. When Hartley moved, he was tall and skinny. But the years have been good to him. His hair is still the mass of dark blonde waves, and his forest green eyes are still kind, but that's where the similarities end. His black shirt is stretched across his shoulders and chest. His biceps look like they are about to rip the sleeves. Hartley was always attractive, but he got hot over the years. I giggle at that thought and make my way to get my clothes together.

"Like I said, I couldn't afford anything else, and I didn't know if you would be receptive of me in Abbs Valley," I say, shoving things into a bag. I move to the bathroom for my toothbrush and hairbrush.

"It kind of hurts that you would think I'd turn you away," Hartley replies, leaning against the bathroom door frame.

Honestly, I don't know what to think anymore. I never thought I would be mixed up with someone like Aaron. He warped my mind the whole time we were together, making me believe I had no one but him.

"I'm sorry," I tell him quietly.

"It doesn't matter now," Hartley smiles. "You can stay with me until you find something better."

I nod like I agree, but I'm just trying to figure out how I will get away now.

CHAPTER 3

EVANDER

"You did fucking what?" Mateo asks the following morning. We just left the hotel and are on our way home.

"I'm not repeating myself," I snap. Mateo shakes his head and looks out his window.

I still can't get over what happened last night. I had all intentions of kicking Micah out of my room, and then he said what he said, and I couldn't.

I've spent the last six months trying to get over him, but he's relentless. He's always around, flirting and making me remember what it feels like to be with him. But never once has he told me he wants to be with me or loves me.

Micah is my first real love and my first heartbreak. I can't do that with him again.

I feel like shit for kicking him out of my room after he told me he loved me, but I panicked. I could feel those words grabbing hold of me and pulling me back under his spell. The truth is, I don't believe him. I don't think he would lie to me just to sleep with me again, but monogamous isn't in Micah's vocabulary. Especially with me.

Micah was always at New Vision, the sex club Mateo and I own. Even before he knew we were the owners. He had a woman every night, sometimes multiple, so his admission that he hasn't been with anyone shocked me.

I can't wrap my head around the guy who shut a door in my face when I told him I loved him to the guy who told me he loves me and is done hiding.

"I'm going to say something, and then I'm done with this shit," Mateo says, turning to face me. "He finally said those words you've been wanting, and you do the same thing to him as he did to you. You need to figure out what the fuck you want, Van."

"I don't trust him."

"You're an idiot," Mateo laughs. "You really think he would say that shit if he weren't serious? This is *Micah*. It might have taken him longer to come to terms with being in love with you, but he still did. Get your head out of your ass before you lose him for good."

"Why are you defending him?" I ask, getting pissed off.

"Because he's done exactly what you've wanted for six goddamn months. You wanted to be friends, so that's what he's done, even if he didn't want to be. You wanted space; he gave you that. Then he gave you what you wanted when he was finally done with the bullshit. I love you, Van, but you're wrong about this."

The SUV pulls to a stop in front of our house, and Mateo is out before I can reply. Making my way inside, I go straight to my office and shut the door. I sit down behind my desk and let my thoughts run.

I knew Micah growing up; it was hard not to. He was ruthless and mean for much of his teenage years until his brother Luca stepped up.

When Micah and I started messing around, it was to see why we were attracted to each other. Before long, he had me wrapped around his fucking finger. We didn't have sex for the first time until we were stuck in the pool house at Les' house. It was always dirty texts, touching, and kissing before that. So when we were in close proximity, it exploded after weeks of foreplay. He snuck into my room that night, and the rest was history. I was already half in love with him and thought he felt the same. I was wrong, and I can't afford to be wrong again.

26

Mateo is right, however. I need to either accept what Micah said or let him go.

Watching Leo commit himself to Les last night made me so damn proud, happy, and sad all at the same time. It's a fucked up mix of emotions. They deserve every bit of happiness after what they all went through together. I'll miss them while they're on their honeymoon for three weeks. Leo felt terrible for missing our third anniversary of opening New Vision, but I told him not to worry about it. I planned on having many more.

My phone dings with a text message, and I almost ignore it when I see the name on the screen. I sigh and swipe it open.

MICAH

I meant every word, Van. I know I fucked up, and I'll spend the rest of my life proving how sorry I am. I've missed you, and last night was the first night I felt true happiness since I lost you. Can we please talk?

I stare at the message for a long time, my heart beating out of my chest. I just knew when he left my room last night that was it. That there is no way that Micah will still fight for us. Can he be serious? Could we really have what I wanted? Micah isn't the type to pour his heart out, and he's done it twice in twenty-four hours. For me. My fingers hover over the screen to close out the chat when another message pops up.

MICAH

I can see that you've seen this. Please, Amore mio. Just come talk.

There's that damn nickname again. He called me that the first night we had sex, and that's why I thought he was all in. *Fuck.* I need time to think about everything, and I can't do that with Micah hovering.

I need time.

MICAH

I gave you time. Please don't do this.

I'm sorry. I can't right now.

I close the chat screen before he can reply and flip my phone upside down.

I need to get ready for our anniversary party at New Vision.

This thing with Micah will have to wait.

"You've officially lost your damn mind," Mateo declares.

We've been at this anniversary party for two hours, and I already want to throttle him. I should have kept my mouth shut.

"I just said that I needed to give this time," I say evenly, trying to keep my temper in check.

"Why?" Mateo demands. "So you can talk yourself out of it?"

"I'm not going to talk myself out of it."

"Yes. You are," Mateo insists. "I know you, Van. If it isn't tied together in a nice little package, you don't want anything to do with it. Eventually, brother, you'll have to let go of that rigid control. And you should start with this mess with Micah."

I can't let go of my control. That's what got me in this place with Micah to begin with. I can't be like Mateo and throw caution to the wind. I learned my lesson growing up with a tyrant for a father like Frankie. I protected Mateo from everything I could so he could live the life he wanted, so I took the brunt of Frankie's wrath. It wouldn't change a damn thing, but sometimes I wish I could let go.

"Look who's here," Mateo says with a grin, jerking his head toward the crowd.

Micah is striding toward the bar where we're standing. Like a magnet, his eyes slide to mine, and the look in them makes me want to run the other way. He looks determined, and I've seen that look before.

"Hello, Micah," Mateo greets.

"Hey, asshole," Micah greets back, then looks at me. "Hey, Van."

"Hey."

Why did he have to come tonight when everything was so fresh and raw? I invited him weeks ago, but I figured he wouldn't show up after last night. I was wrong. He turns to the bar to order a drink, and I let my eyes slide over him.

His black hair is fixed in a deliberately messy way, and he's dressed in all black. His button-up is stretched across his broad shoulders and tucked into a pair of black slacks that are molded to his ass.

"You're drooling," Mateo whispers.

"Fuck off," I grumble, looking over the crowd.

When Mateo and I took over for Frankie when he died, we shut every one of his businesses down except a nightclub and two restaurants. After we built some capital, we opened our own places, including New Vision.

New Vision is an upper-class sex club. Before you step through the doors, you need a background check and a complete physical, including an STD panel that you have to repeat twice a month or lose your membership, and you have to undergo an interview process. It sounds like a lot, but we want to ensure people can come here and feel comfortable giving into their basic desires. Mateo and I worked hard on this place and are damn proud of it.

"Hi, Micah," a feminine voice purrs, and my head moves that way automatically. Vivian, one of our regulars, is plastered to Micah's side.

"Hey, V," Micah says politely.

"Did you come to play? I've missed seeing you around."

Micah holds up his wrist, indicating his red bracelet. "Sorry, V. I didn't come here for that tonight."

She pouts her red lips, making me grind my teeth. "Pity. It's been so long," she says seductively. "You were always my favorite."

"Red means no, V," Mateo reminds her. She pouts again, runs a fingernail down Micah's chest, and strides back to her group. "Red?" Mateo asks Micah in surprise. It's a surprise to me too.

We have a system with the glowing bracelets. You wear red for observing, yellow for participating but need to discuss limits, and green means you're down for anything. I've never seen Micah with the red one.

"Like I said, I'm not here for that," Micah replies, and I can feel his eyes burning into the side of my head.

"I need to go check on something," I say and start moving through the crowd, smiling at the greetings from everyone. I know I'm running away like a coward, but I can't keep my resolve that I need to think with him looking at me like that. Micah is my weak spot, and time hasn't changed that.

I get to my office, and before I can sigh in relief, Micah pushes in behind me. He shuts the door and turns slowly to face me. I expect him to crowd me like he did in the hotel, but he leans against the door and crosses his arms over his chest.

"I just want to talk," Micah says softly. He rubs his finger across his bottom lip, the only nervous gesture he has, and that's when I see his swollen, bruised, cracked knuckles.

"What happened to your hand?" I ask.

"Interesting turn of events last night," he replies, making me frown harder. "I was leaving and heard a girl yelling. Gray and I ran toward the noise, and a guy was dragging the girl to his car." He shrugs. "I intervened."

Of course he did. Micah wouldn't let that fly, and he handled it by the looks of his hand. "Is she okay?"

Micah barks a laugh. "Yep. You'll never guess who picked her up." I lift an eyebrow. "Hartley Cruz."

"As in former police chief?" I ask in disbelief.

"The same one. He's still a giant fucking prick," Micah says, making me chuckle.

After Hartley's giant fuck up with Les' stalker case, no love was lost between him and Micah. He tried to make it right in the end, but that didn't change the fact that he all but called Les and Zane liars.

"Who was the girl?" I ask.

Micah shrugs. "One of the staff from the party. She didn't look familiar, but her boyfriend did. I've seen him before, but I don't know where."

We lapse into silence, neither of us knowing what to say. Micah finally sighs after a minute.

"I'm sorry about last night. That wasn't my intention when I came to your room." He finally looks at me. "I won't take it back, Van. I meant it. I know I have to prove that I love you, and I'm willing to do that if you give me a chance."

"Do you even know what love is, Micah?" I ask again.

He shoves his hands in his pockets, looking more unsure than I've ever seen him. "I know I love you, or it wouldn't hurt this bad. You're in my dreams, my every waking thought. All I can think about is you, *Amore mio*. Please give me a chance to prove I can be the man you deserve."

Every vision I've ever had for us opens back up in front of me. Micah is handing me his heart; all I have to do is reach out and take it. I can't lead Micah on anymore, or I'm no better than he is when he broke me the first time.

"I love you too," I say gruffly. Micah's face blooms with hope, and he takes a step forward. "We have a lot to work through, but I'm done fighting this."

"What are you saying?"

"It means I'm willing to give you another chance. But if you hurt me again, I will kill you this time."

Micah reaches out and tugs me to his chest. He wraps his arms around my neck, and I slide mine around his waist. "I'll never hurt you again, *Amore mio*. I don't deserve this, but I won't fuck it up."

Something in my heart settles, and I can feel how right this is.

"You have to start opening up to me," I say, pulling back to see his eyes. "And stop hiding shit."

"I know," Micah nods. "You have to be patient with me, though, Van. I've never done this before."

"I can do that." I've had one relationship in my twenty-five years with a girl my father made me date. We both knew what we were doing going into it, so no one was hurt in the process. Micah and I will be starting on even ground.

"Fuck, I've missed you," Micah says gruffly, jerking me into a hug. I hug him back just as tight, relieved that we're giving this a shot.

"I missed you too."

He squeezes me tight one more time before jerking my lips to his. There is no hesitation from me like last night. This is my chance to let go and do something for myself, finally. And that something is Micah.

Before I know it, he has me laid on my couch in my office; his lips sealed over mine.

He pulls back and lays his forehead against mine. "Come home with me."

I raise a brow. "I kind of have a party going on out there."

"I meant after," Micah chuckles. "I plan on being your arm candy first," he says, waggling his brows.

"Are you ready for that? If you aren't, we can work up to that."

"I'm ready," Micah says, pecking my lips. "I wasn't joking when I said I want to tell the world you're mine. That starts tonight. Are you ready for that?"

"I'm ready."

"Good," Micah breathes like he was expecting a different answer. He rubs his body against mine, and I can't stop the groan. "Let me make love to you, and then we can go out there to enjoy the rest of your party."

I nod. "There's lube in my desk."

"Thank god for sex clubs," Micah grins. He slants his mouth over mine in a quick kiss. "I want you to smell like me for the rest of the night. That way, no one can mistake who you belong to."

My breath hitches at the promise in his words. "You belong to me too."

"Yes, I do, *Amore mio*, heart, and soul."

Same here, *Mi rey*, same here.

CHAPTER 4
MATEO

I knew my brother wouldn't be able to resist Micah for long. It was just a matter of time before they ended up back together. I just gave them a push now and then.

Watching them walk back to the bar right now, I could fucking weep with relief. Those are the two most hard-headed assholes I've ever met. Van says something to Micah, they split in different directions, and Micah heads my way.

I grin when he approaches. "Where have you been?"

"None of your fucking business," Micah replies, signaling for the bartender.

"Where'd Van go?"

"He's talking to Cian Moren."

My eyebrows shoot up. "Irish Mafia Cian Moren?"

"How many people do you know with that name? Yes, the same one."

"If he's here, that's a good sign, right?"

Micah takes a sip of the scotch and turns to face me. "It is. He was the last holdout, wasn't he?"

"Yep."

Van and I have been busting our asses for months, trying to lock down alliances. Frankie died, and we got to be leaders of the Mexican

Mafia and had fuck all to show for it. He didn't leave a single ally for us. But after the disaster of trying to ally with Micah's niece, Les, the Italian Mafia's leader, by setting her up, we did it Micah's way after that. Van and I still feel like shit about how we went about that, but it turned out for the better. My brother, Leo, found love with her and her guys, and I couldn't be happier. Plus, I gained an awesome sister-in-law, Micah became one of my best friends, and Micah and Evander found love.

Cian Moren is the newly appointed leader of the Irish Mafia after his dad had a stroke and the last one we had to lock down. I see him and Van shake hands, hoping we finally did.

"Is it done?" I ask when Van walks up.

"Yeah. He said he wants to branch out and likes how we're doing things," Van answers with a smile.

"Finally." *It's about damn time.*

"I'm proud of you, *Amore mio*," Micah replies.

"Wait a damn minute," I demand. "Where's asshole Micah, and who the hell are you?"

"What?" Micah laughs.

"The Micah I know doesn't say shit like *Amore mio*," I say, exaggerating Micah's deep tone. Then it hits me. "Holy shit! You guys finally stopped fucking around!"

"Yes," Van says, rolling his eyes. "Now shut up."

He knows me better than that. "So, is that where you guys were?" I lean closer and sniff Van. "You guys were totally fucking."

"Jesus Christ, Mateo," Micah sighs. "I already said it was none of your business."

I shrug. "You don't have to tell me. I can figure it out because Van smells like your cologne, and you have a shit-eating grin on your face."

Micah's grin widens. "I wanted everyone to know he's mine." Micah kisses Van, and my mouth pops open. "I'll be back," he says and walks through the crowd, where I see Alexey and Dmitri.

I turn to Van, and he has a smile playing on his lips. "So," I prompt, dragging the word out.

"He said he was done hiding." Van shrugs. "He was serious."

"What about you?"

"I'd already come to terms with it," Van answers, looking over to where Micah is standing. "This is what I wanted, Tay."

"I'm happy for you guys," I say genuinely. Van turns to me with a smile. I let out an almost girlish squeal and jerk him into a hug.

"Damn it, Mateo." Van laughs but hugs me back. "I'm happy too."

I pull back and wipe a fake tear from my cheek. "My boys are all grown up."

"You're an idiot," Van says, eyes catching on Micah again.

"And you're obsessed," I laugh. Not that I blame him.

Van shrugs. "Probably."

Micah starts walking back, and his eyes don't leave Van. That makes two of them. Micah leans against the bar and puts one arm around Van's waist, his fingers on his hip. I see Van relax in his hold but know my brother is still worried Micah will change his mind. People are staring, but Micah seems oblivious to their attention; his sole focus is on Van, which is a good sign.

I know it was hard on both of them when this started because they were both straight until that point. I knew I was bisexual at a young age, but with a father like Frankie, I couldn't even begin to examine what that meant. When I was sixteen, I told Van, and he didn't seem the least bit surprised but supported me no matter what I did. Since Frankie's death, thanks to Les, I've been free to be who I want. Now, Micah and Van have that too.

My eyes catch sight of my current enjoyment walking up behind Micah.

"Hello, Gray," I purr, making the big guy's face bloom with color. "You're looking good." And he sure as fuck does. A dark green button-up with just enough buttons undone at the top to tease a tattoo on his chest. Black slacks stretched across his massive thighs.

"Hello, Mateo," he answers in that deliciously deep voice of his.

I nod to the crowd. "See something you like?"

Gray frowns. "I'm working."

"You're officially off the clock. Go have fun," Micah says, taking Van's hand and leading him away.

Gray leans back against the bar, and I scoot closer. "You need to loosen up," I tell him. I can think of a few ways to loosen him up. I started flirting with him weeks after Micah hired him, and he hasn't taken the bait yet. "What about her?" I ask, pointing to a leggy blonde. Gray shakes his head. "What about her?" I ask, pointing to a brunette. Gray shakes his head again.

I look around a few times and decide to test something. "What about him?" I ask.

Gray looks at me with a raised brow. "No."

"Come on, give me something to work with here," I laugh. "What's your type?"

"I don't have a type."

"Everyone has a type," I argue.

"Honest and loyal are my type."

"What's your preference?" I ask, hinting at what I've been dying to know.

"Are you asking me if I'm gay, Mateo?" Gray asks, and I bark a laugh.

"If I would have known I didn't have to tiptoe around it, I would have asked."

Gray frowns. "Why would you have to tiptoe around?"

Because I've all but thrown myself at you, and you haven't returned the interest. I decide to ignore his comment. "So, are you gay?"

"No," Gray says, and my heart sinks. He turns his body toward me, letting his eyes travel from my head to my shoes—something he's never done before. It feels like it's his hands running over me. "But I'm open to trying new things."

My mouth drops open, causing Gray to grin, turn on his heel, and walk away.

Did he just suggest what I think he did? I don't know if he realizes he just gave me the okay to push harder.

This should be fun.

CHAPTER 5
EVIE

"Hartley," I sigh. "I have to go to work to support myself and pay bills." We've been having this same argument for twenty minutes, and he isn't budging.

"He found you, Evie. You don't think he knows everywhere you work?" I have thought about that, but it doesn't change the fact that I need these jobs, especially since I probably lost the catering job last night because I was supposed to be on the road by now. "I'll pay..."

I hold up my hand before he can finish that sentence. "Not happening. You can either take me to work, or I'm calling an Uber. Either way, I'm going." Today is my eight-hour shift at the coffee shop. I'll be in public, and the shop is always busy. Aaron is insane, but I don't think he'll come after me in broad daylight surrounded by witnesses.

"Fine, I'll drive you." I breathe a sigh of relief. "But I'm staying until your shift is done." He marches out of the room, and I do the mature thing and flip him off behind his back. It's like nothing has changed between us in our years apart.

I appreciate Hartley for giving me a place to stay last night, but I can't stay with him forever. I need to pull whatever money I have saved, get paid Friday, and then I need to run. It's the only thing I know to do without putting Hartley in danger.

I pull on the black slacks and polo shirt for my uniform, grab my purse, and meet Hartley in the living room. He turns around when he hears me walk in, and I can't get over how much he's changed. Hartley used to be full of smiles, and since last night, I don't think I've seen him smile once.

"You don't need to babysit me. You'll get bored," I try to reason.

"I used to sit on stakeouts for hours, Evie. I'll be fine."

"Still just as bossy as ever," I quip.

"Still just as hard headed as ever," he jokes, and I see a slight tilt to his lips. So, his smile muscles still work; good to know.

We walk to Hartley's truck, and he opens the door for me, waiting for me to get in before he shuts it and moves to the driver's side. Hartley backs out of the driveway, and I look at his modest house. It's a simple three-bedroom, two-bathroom home that sits on a few acres but is comfortable inside. He told me last night that his mom came and decorated it for him, which made me smile.

On our way to the coffee shop, Hartley drives past the Abbs Valley Elite hotel, and my mind wanders to my gorgeous blue-eyed savior and his hot, hazel-eyed friend. In my frazzled state, I didn't even think to get their names, and Blue Eyes' card is burning a hole in my purse.

And then there was Mateo from the party, which I'm sure has forgotten all about me by now. I'm not even sure why I wrote his number on the card.

I turn to Hartley. "How did you know those guys from last night?" I noticed the immediate tension between them but didn't ask last night.

A muscle in Hartley's jaw ticks. "Let's just say I've had run-ins with them before."

"When you were a cop?"

"Yes."

"Are they bad guys?" I couldn't see that. They jumped in and saved a girl they didn't even know without hesitation. I didn't get any bad vibes from them. Looking back, I did about Aaron, but I ignored it like an idiot.

"Why are you asking?"

"Just curious. They saved my ass." I want to ask their names, but Hartley seems less inclined to divulge that information. Maybe I can message the number and tell him thank you. *Nope. Shut that shit down right now, Evie.*

Hartley grunts and pulls in front of the coffee shop. "Don't leave here without me and don't go outside without me."

"Sir, yes, sir." I salute and push my door open.

"I'm serious, Evie," Hartley says in a softer tone. "You have my number, and I'll be right out here."

I nod. "For the record, I still think this is overkill." I smile sweetly and shut the door.

Escaping is going to be more complicated than I thought.

THE COFFEE SHOP is busier than usual for a Sunday, and the first four hours pass in a blur.

"Who is that?" My coworker Amber asks, walking up beside me.

"Who?" I smile at the guy in front of me and hand his order over.

"The two that just walked in. Damn. I got them." She fluffs her blonde hair and pulls her polo down a little. I suppress an eye roll. Amber flirts with every guy who comes here, so it shouldn't surprise me.

I'm in the middle of filling a smoothie order when she flounces back over. "They want you," Amber huffs, and my heart skips a beat. Is Aaron here?

I shove down the panic before I run from here screaming. "Where?" I ask, and she points.

I follow her finger, and my heart beats faster for an entirely different reason when I lock eyes with Mateo from the party the other night. He smiles, and I almost wilt on the floor.

"I'm not waitressing today," I say, trying to get out of going over there. What the hell is he doing here?

"Well, he asked for you, so go."

I check my apron pocket and make sure I have my notepad and pen, trying to calm my beating heart as I walk to the table.

"What can I get for you?" I ask, surprised my voice came out steady. *Does he have to be so hot?*

"I'll get a black coffee and a bagel," the other one answers, and I finally look at him. Dark brown hair and eyes. Definitely brothers, and he's just as hot. *Am I drooling?* I have to fight myself to stop from making sure I'm not.

What is wrong with me? I haven't so much as looked at a guy in the eight months I've been on the run, and within the past forty-eight hours, I've eyeballed everything in my path.

"You never called, Evie," Mateo says, pulling my attention back to him. He remembers me? "I have to say; I was a little hurt."

I snort before I can stop myself. "I'm sure you were. What can I get you?"

"Same as my brother," he answers. "And a date." I hear his brother chuckle and try not to look at him because I know my face is flaming red by now.

"I'll be back with your order." I turn on my heel and try not to run back to the counter. Flustered doesn't even cover what I am right now.

Pouring their coffee, I take several deep breaths. I blamed his flirting on the alcohol last time, but he's sober right now. No way he's interested. You can tell by his expensive clothes and that high-profile reception Friday night that these people bleed money. Maybe he's bored with his high-rise office job and wants to slum it a little with the help. *Bitchy much?* I don't usually judge that harshly, but I can't wrap my head around that he might want me.

Piling their order on a tray, I walk back to the table, trying not to trip over my feet. When I get there, Mateo is alone.

"Here you go," I smile, setting everything on the table. "Is there anything else I can get you?"

"Yeah. That date."

Walked right into that one, didn't ya? "I can't date customers." *That's the best you can do?*

"Good thing I'm not a regular then," Mateo says, opening the full force of that blinding smile on me. *Is it hot in here? Nope, just me.*

"Why are you here?" I blurt out. Is he following me? I'm even more than paranoid at this point.

His eyebrows shot up. "We were looking at a few places to buy on this strip and stopped for coffee."

The coffee shop, lamely named The Coffee Shop, is in the nicer part of Abbs Valley, so buildings down here aren't cheap. So, maybe he's a realtor? *Why do you care, Nosey Nelly?*

"Oh," I mutter, embarrassed.

"So, how about that date now?" Damn, he is persistent.

"I can't. I'm sorry." I really am sorry. I would love nothing more than to go on a date and enjoy myself, but I can't do that right now, which makes me sad and pissed me off at the same time. I'm twenty-three. This is when I should have been having fun, and Aaron took something else from me once again. "Enjoy your coffee."

I take over Amber's orders at the counter and try to get my mind back to where it needs to be. If I wipe out what I have hidden at my apartment, I have a little over three hundred dollars. Tips are pretty good here so far today, I have a hundred dollars at Hartley's, and if I hold out until Friday, I'll have my paycheck from here and the diner by my house. It won't get me far, and I'll have to stay at a shelter for a while again, but I can do it. I need to get as far away from Abbs Valley as I can.

"Did you really turn him down?" Amber demands. I try to like her, but she doesn't make it easy. She's like every girl who bullied me for being fat in high school, but she never grew out of the high school stage. "It's not like guys throw themselves at you, Evie. Maybe if you lost some weight, but even then, you aren't his type. Why did he want you, anyway? I would have taken him up on that offer like that." She snaps her fingers. I can feel those insecurities creeping to the surface. All the insults Aaron threw at me because of my weight flash through my mind.

"Good thing I didn't ask you then." I don't even have to look to know that voice. That voice has been in my head for two days. "I came to shoot my shot one last time, Buttercup." *Buttercup?* "Go to dinner with me tomorrow night." I look up into his bright green eyes and get lost. They are so pretty, with their odd color and darker green swirling around the pupil. "Please," he says with a smile.

Amber huffs and stomps away; Mateo doesn't even spare her a glance.

"Why?" I whisper.

"Why not? You're beautiful and I'd love nothing more than to show you off on my arm. So, what do you say?"

I feel like I'm zapped back to high school when Marcus White asked me on a date in the eleventh grade. He was the star quarterback and ridiculously good-looking. I couldn't believe it and said yes. My mom was so happy she went out and bought me a brand new dress just for him to stand me up. It turned out it was a joke, and I was the punchline. Mateo doesn't seem anything like Marcus. *Aaron didn't seem like a sadistic monster, either.*

I open my mouth to tell him I can't again.

"Okay," I breathe.

Son of a bitch.

I THOUGHT Hartley's head would explode when I told him I was going on a date. But I can't figure out if it's the date part or who I'm going with that's the problem. It dissolved into a mini argument where he told me to do what I want, and he hasn't spoken to me since.

Now that the date is a few hours away, I realize I don't know what to wear. All I have is my catering uniform, The Coffee Shop uniform, and a pair of jeans. Mateo said he wanted to take me to dinner but didn't tell me where. He added his number to my phone and told me to text him my number. I pulled up his contact forty times, only to chicken out each time. I'm seconds away from calling off the date altogether. Why the fuck did I agree in the first place?

Because you got one look at those green eyes and pretty smile then turned into a wanton hussy. I giggle at myself and pull up his contact again. Chewing my bottom lip, I type out a message.

> This is Evie.

Before I can overthink, I hit send and stare at the screen. After five minutes, I toss the phone on the bed and start pacing. What if this was some sick joke? Do adults still do shit like that? My phone pings, and I pounce on it. *Down, girl.*

MATEO
I thought you were going to stand me up, Buttercup.

Me stand him up?

> Um, no. I don't know what to wear.

MATEO
Casual's fine.

Does that mean jeans? I'm such a mess. It won't take him long to figure that out and run the other way.

MATEO
Wear jeans and that gorgeous smile.

> Smooth. Haha. What time?

MATEO
Meet me at The Coffee Shop at 7. I can't wait to see you.

I can't wait to see him either, but I refuse to put myself that far out there.

Yet.

CHAPTER 6
MATEO

"You have a date?" Gray asks.

"Yes. A date. I do that sometimes. Why? Are you jealous?" I tease with a grin.

"No. But why are you telling me?"

Because I need to know if I go on this date, you would still be interested in me. I still don't know if he is or not. I shrug. "I don't know. I was just making small talk."

I've been sitting on the desk in the guardhouse where Gray usually is, staring at a wall of cameras surrounding the property. I just got the text from Evie and almost fell off the damn thing. I've thought about her nonstop since Friday and was half tempted to call the catering company to track her down when I walked into The Coffee Shop yesterday. I clocked her as soon as I walked in and stopped dead in my tracks. She didn't even notice me until the blonde pointed me out. I didn't like what that girl said to Evie or how Evie's face fell.

She seemed interested but hesitated, like she couldn't figure out which angle I was working. I could have whooped with joy when I got that little breathy okay.

"Where are you taking her?"

"Probably Les' Place." Les' Place is a diner Les bought out, and I

45

loved the food. Evie didn't strike me as the fancy restaurant type, so I thought it would be perfect.

"Where'd you meet her?"

I laugh. "The wedding reception. She was one of the servers."

I saw her almost as soon as we walked in and knew I needed to talk to her. She warmed up to me, but I could tell she wasn't used to the attention. Why I wouldn't know. Evie is gorgeous. Long brown hair with a buttercup behind her ear, big brown eyes, and one of those thick bodies with curves in all the right places.

"Really?" Gray raises a brow. "The girl from outside was a server."

Ah, the girl Micah went all knight in shining armor for and pummeled some dick in the alley. That was a funny story and way out of the ordinary for Micah. But that was the night Van kicked him out of his hotel room, so Micah had some aggression to work out.

"I wish I could have seen Micah knock him on his ass."

Gray chuckles. "It surprised the shit out of me."

Gray goes back to click through the video footage, and I take a second to study his profile. He keeps his hair buzzed short. He has a square jaw and a nose that has been broken too many times and never healed right. But he has these hazel eyes and full lips that draw your attention to him. Even when he preferred to stay in the background. I was instantly attracted to him, even though he isn't my usual type. He is about four inches taller than my six-foot-one and has more muscle. I don't generally like guys bigger than me, but I sure as fuck liked Gray. Hence, flirting with him for six months.

"So, about Saturday night." I say.

"I was wondering when you were going to bring that up. What about it?"

I hop off the desk and step closer to him, testing a theory. Any time I flirted, I never stepped over the line to make him uncomfortable except by saying stuff to make him blush. But let's face it, that was just fun. I move in front of him and step between his spread thighs, leaning down to brace my hands on the arm of the chair. His face blooms with color, but he doesn't move.

"Have I finally worn you down, Gray?"

"You have a date, Mateo. Why are you still flirting with me?"

"I have a date, not a marriage proposal. If you want to make things official, I'll call off the date." I waggle my eyebrows at him. I am so close I could watch his pupils expand and feel the heat rolling off him.

He reacts before I blink and wraps a big hand around my throat. At first, I thought I'd finally gone too far, and Gray would kill me. Then he stands up, using his hand on me to push me backward until my ass hits the desk. He steps in close and squeezes harder to test my reaction. Usually, I would have shut this shit down; it wasn't my thing. But with Gray, I know something is lurking in there, and I am going to coax it out. Apparently, I found the hot button.

"Six months, Mateo. For six months, I've tried to ignore my body's reaction to you," Gray rasps, making my eyes widen in surprise. "I want you to go on this date and then come back and tell me about it."

I lift a brow. "You want to know if I fucked her?" I force out past his hold. It isn't threatening, but enough to steal my breath for a second. And my body loves it. *Who fucking knew I liked getting choked?* I don't plan on fucking Evie tonight. That isn't my style, but I wanted to see Gray's reaction.

"I want to know everything," Gray says, and his face softens. His thumb starts rubbing on my neck in an almost loving gesture. "I don't know what it is about you, but I'm...interested."

Before I can reply to that cryptic remark, he seals his lips over mine with a groan. Almost like he's been dying to do it. I know I have. I slide my hands around him and up his back, feeling the thick muscle shift beneath my fingers. I finally got past whatever mental wall Gray had up when it came to me. *Fuck yeah.*

He strokes my tongue with his a few times before pulling back, laying his forehead against mine. "You'll come back?" There is so much hope on his face that there's no way I could say no. It's like I am seeing a new side to him since he finally let himself have what he wanted.

"I'll come back," I promise.

"Good." He pecks my lips and steps back.

Van had been here at Micah's since the night of the anniversary party, and I usually went home after bugging Gray. He's never asked me to stay or come back before. I don't know what it means, but I am willing to explore it.

I WAS LEANING against the side of my black Porsche, about to call it a night, thinking Evie stood me up when she pulls up in an Uber. Thirty-five minutes late.

"I'm so sorry," she says in a rush when she steps out. "The Uber got lost on the way to.... the house, and I forgot my phone."

"It's okay," I reply with a smile. Any annoyance about her being late disappeared when she stepped out of that Uber in a pair of stoned, washed skinny jeans, yellow shirt, and knee-high boots. Her hair is down, and her face is void of all makeup. She never looked more beautiful.

I walk around to the passenger side and pop the door open. "This is your car?" she asks, mouth hanging open.

"No, I stole it." I keep a perfectly straight face and watch her try to make out if I'm serious.

"You could have stolen a better one." She slides into the passenger seat with a smile.

I'm still laughing when I get into the driver's seat and start the car. "Go easy on my ego, buttercup."

"I don't think you have any issues with your ego," Evie says dryly.

I pull away from the curb and glance at her. "I could have picked you up instead of you taking an Uber." I told her that when we set up this date, but she was adamant she meet me somewhere. I think it's because she tried to talk herself out of it. Even though she is joking with me, I can see how nervous she is. She's almost pressed to the passenger side door, and her hands are clasped together in her lap, so tight her knuckles are white.

"I know. I just...felt better this way."

I nod because what else could I say? She doesn't know me.

I drive further into downtown Abbs Valley where it used to be run down, but slowly between Van and me, along with Les and Micah, we've been buying up the properties, trying to bring life back to it. We have big plans for it, and I'm excited about getting started.

"Where are we going?" Evie asks.

"A diner called Les' Place." The proceeds from this diner go to charities and homeless shelters after the employees wages are paid. Les even let the original owners have full reign over the place.

"A diner?" I pull the car in front and turn to face her. She's frowning.

Is she not happy with a diner? Did I get her all wrong?

"Yeah. My sister-in-law owns it, and they have the best burgers." Before I rethink bringing her here, I push my door open and stride to Evie's side. Her door is half open before I get there, so I put my hand on it to stop her progress. "Shut the door. That's my job."

Evie rolls her eyes. "I can open my own door."

"We're not moving until you shut it." I cross my arms and lean my hip against it. She giggles but lets me shut it just to open it right back up. I stick my hand in to help her out, and she hesitates before her hand slides into mine. Once she's out, I shut the door and tuck her hand onto my arm.

"That was an impressive display."

"A woman should never have to open her own door." What kind of assholes has she been with? She gives me a curious look, and that frown comes back to her face. I am going to chase that frown away tonight.

Opening the main door to the diner, I'm met with the smell of grease, fried foods, and Greta, the shop's owner.

"Mateo!" she crows, wrapping me in a hug. Greta and her husband, Paul, are in their seventies but work their asses off. They were barely keeping this place open when Les bought it. She updated all their appliances, redecorated it, and had a grand re-opening. The place has been booming since.

"Hello, Greta," I say, placing a sloppy kiss on her cheek.

She swats my shoulder. "Paul's going to get you."

"Tell him to come out here, and I'll give him one, too."

Greta gives me one of her full belly laughs that I've grown to love. "Your trouble. Who's this?"

"This is Evie, my date for the evening."

"Nice to meet you," Evie says with a genuine smile. It's impossible not to like Greta.

"Aren't you a pretty thing! Come with me. I'll show you to our special table." Greta gestures over her shoulder and leads us back to the booth in the back corner. The only private booth they have.

I help Evie into the booth, half tempted to sit beside her but slide into the other side instead. I don't want to overwhelm her. Greta gets our drinks and leaves us to look at the menu.

"I love her," Evie laughs.

"Greta's awesome," I agree.

"So, your brother's wife owns this?" I nod. "The one from The Coffee shop?"

"No, my other brother."

"How many brothers do you have?" Evie asks. She seems less nervous here, and that's what I was hoping.

"Just Evander and Leo. You were at Leo's wedding reception." I watch her eyes widen when it dawns on her.

"That was your sister-in-law? So that means...."

"She has six husbands? Yep," I laugh.

"They all looked so happy," she says with a wistful smile.

"They are." The guys didn't hide their affection that day. They openly hugged, danced, and kissed. I doubt she missed it. I'm surprised she didn't ask about it.

It's something I wish for myself one day.

"So, what's it going to be?" Greta asks.

"Someone said you had the best burgers," Evie smiles. "I'll take that and some fries."

"I'll have the same. And two chocolate shakes."

"You got it." Greta bustles away.

"Two shakes?" Evie asks with a raised brow.

"One's for you. You have to dip your fries in it." Evie wrinkles her nose in disgust, making me laugh. "Don't knock it until you try it." Evie lapses back in silence, swirling her straw in her drink. "Tell me about yourself." That seems to startle her. She looks up with wide eyes, almost like panic.

"There isn't much to tell."

"Are you new here? Because I would have definitely noticed you before." That makes her blush and look away.

"Yeah. I'm from Fairview."

"That's like what? Four hours from here? What brought you to Abbs Valley?" I watch her face completely shutter. *Evie's hiding something.*

"I wanted to get away from my small town." Her answer is almost defensive, and it's confusing. One minute she's open, and the next, it's almost like she'd rather be anywhere but here. "What about you?"

"I was born and raised in Abbs Valley."

"What do you do for a living?"

"I'm a business owner." Partially true. It's not like you could tell a girl on the first date that you are the leader of the Mexican Mafia and have just recently started running the Mexican cartel.

"How old are you?" she asks.

"Twenty-three." Her eyebrows shoot up.

"I am too."

"See. We already have something in common." I smile, trying to loosen the tension in her shoulders. She was fine until I asked her about herself.

"Why did you ask me out?" Evie blurts out. She's asked me that before, and I couldn't understand why she didn't believe me.

"I'm interested in you, Evie."

"Why, though? I'm sure plenty of girls are throwing themselves at your feet."

"Why don't you believe me?" I throw back at her.

She frowns again. "Guys like you don't like girls like me."

"Guys like me?" I ask, trying to keep the defensiveness out of my voice.

"Never mind," Evie mutters.

"Did I do something wrong?"

"No," Evie sighs. "I'm sorry. I never got the attraction, and now you brought me here. I just..."

"Just what?" I prompt gently. Someone has torn this girl down, and that thought pisses me off. She has this light to her when she's not being secretive or defensive. Like she had the night of the reception.

"I thought you were ashamed to take me anywhere else," she says quietly. *Holy shit.*

On instinct, I reach over and take her hand lying on the table. She almost jerks it out of my hand, but I hold on. "I brought you here because I figured you would feel more comfortable, and I really like the food."

"I ruined the date, didn't I?"

"Not at all," I assure her.

Greta sits the food down with a smile, and I reluctantly move my hand.

We start eating, and Evie makes a noise that makes my ears perk up when she takes a bite of her burger. Almost like a moan.

"Holy shit, this is good."

I laugh. "I told you. Now, try this." I dip a fry in my shake and hold it to her plump lips. She wrinkles her nose again, and I lift a brow, waiting. With a roll of her eyes, she takes it from my fingers. Her lips barely graze the tips, and it shoots straight to my cock. *I need to get laid if something that simple turns me on.*

"Oh, my god." There's that damn noise again. "That's amazing."

"Ha! Doubt me again," I say with a smug grin, taking a bite of my burger. I meant more than just the food. I don't want her to doubt why I asked her out. I might not do relationships, but I know how to make sure everyone has a good time. I'm not against relationships; I just haven't found anyone I really wanted to start one with.

We eat in silence, but it's not uncomfortable. Both of us just enjoying the food.

"That was good. Thank you for bringing me," Evie says, and it's the first time she's looked happy to be here.

"We aren't finished yet, buttercup," I assure her and signal Greta for the bill.

After I pay, I kiss Greta on the cheek and slide a hundred-dollar bill into her apron. The same thing I do every time. She stopped arguing with me after the fifth time. "Tell Paul I said hi," I say, holding my hand out for Evie. She slides it into mine, this time without hesitation.

"Will do. Come back and see us," Greta tells Evie with a little wave.

This date isn't going as planned, but I refuse to let that deter me. Something tells me Evie hasn't had someone to treat her right. And even if it is just for a few dates, I could give her something to look forward to.

I just hope she likes what I planned next.

CHAPTER 7
MICAH

I haven't been this happy in a long damn time. For the past week, Van has woken up in my arms. We've spent every minute we could together. We've talked about everything that happened between us, and I've been working on being more open with him. It's been hard, but I would do anything for Van.

Pulling Evander closer by my arm over his waist, I take a moment to appreciate that he even forgave my dumbass.

"Morning," Evander says gruffly.

"Hm," I hum, running my lips over the back of his neck. "Morning."

I took him on a date last night, and we couldn't keep our hands off each other and ended up leaving early. We were naked as soon as we were back at my house, and I was balls deep in his ass. I've never given up control enough for him to do it to me; one of these days, I would have to.

"Don't get any ideas," Evander mumbles, still half asleep.

"What ideas would that be, *amore mio*?"

"The idea that your dick is coming anywhere near my ass again."

I breathe a laugh. "But it's such a nice ass." I slide my hand from his waist to his neck, turning his face to mine to seal my lips over his.

He opens immediately, letting me stroke my tongue with his. I pull back and peck his lips once. "I'm going to make breakfast."

Showering quickly, I make my way downstairs and shoot a message to Les to check in like I do every morning. It's weird not seeing her every day, but I'm sure she is having a great time on her honeymoon. I throw the pre-made breakfast casserole in the oven and set the timer when my phone pings.

LES
Is there something you want to tell me?

I love you?

I say, playing dumb. I haven't told her about Van and me yet, so that meant Leo spilled the beans. Mateo and his big ass mouth.

My phone rings with an incoming video call, and Les' face fills the screen.

"Don't look at me like that," I laugh. She is glaring daggers through the screen.

"Why did I have to find out through Leo that you and Van were back together?"

"I just hadn't told you yet."

Les huffs. "So, are things good?"

"Things are great, shithead."

"Oh my god!" Les squeals, and I hear several chuckles behind her. "I'm so happy for you guys! I really wanted an auntie, but I will take another uncle." She starts cracking up laughing. "Van is my brother-in-law and my uncle."

"Can't be any worse than your husbands almost being step-brothers."

Les barks a laugh. "Don't remind me. We got the wedding invitation before we left."

Ryder's dad and Leo's mom were stuck together during the mess with Viktor and fell in love. They recently decided to get married, which made for many jokes between all of us.

"Seriously, Micah, I'm really happy for you. You guys deserve this."

"I'm so fucking happy, shithead," I say honestly. Les' eyes fill with happy tears. "I'm going to go before you get weepy on me."

"Fuck you," she laughs. "I'll talk to you later. Love you."

"Love you, too.

I disconnect the call as Van comes around the corner in nothing but boxer briefs. "Mateo's on his way with clothes."

"I'm fine with you walking around like that," I say, pulling him against me. "Why don't you bring some stuff here?"

We did this every morning, and I couldn't understand why he wouldn't just plan to stay because we both knew he would.

"I will next time."

Van backs me up against the counter until his body is pressed against mine. "Van," I warn. "I'll bend you over this fucking counter."

"Is that supposed to stop me?" he chuckles, but it comes out husky. He kisses my neck, rubbing his hard cock against mine in my thin ball shorts.

"Is that what you want, *amore mio*?" I ask, running my hands down to his ass. "You want me to take you right here in the kitchen?"

"I can't get enough," he groans, and my cock jerks against his. I feel it, too; that constant pull to touch him. His lips latch onto mine, and I let him control the kiss for once. I slide my hands inside his boxers, directly on that tight ass, and love the shiver that rolls through him.

"Don't mind me," Mateo says dryly, causing Van to take a step back. I don't even try to hide from Mateo what his brother does to me.

"Impeccable timing, brother," Van says, snatching the bag Mateo is holding out with his clothes. Van gives me one last heated look before disappearing back upstairs.

"What you cooking?" Mateo asks, sliding onto the stool at the kitchen island.

"Nothing for you, asshole," I mutter, adjusting my cock.

Mateo grins. "It's not my fault you guys were about to get freaky in the kitchen."

"It's my fault for giving you the damn code to get into my house," I grumble.

About the time the timer goes off on the stove, Van comes back around the corner. His dark brown hair is still wet from his shower, not in his usual perfectly styled way. His brown eyes latch onto me again, and I'm seconds away from dragging him upstairs when Mateo bumps me out of the way with his hip.

"I'll get this," Mateo laughs.

I completely blocked out the timer when I laid eyes on Evander.

"You're taking her out again?" Van asks Mateo after breakfast.

Mateo shrugs. "Yeah. I like hanging out with her."

"Haven't you taken her out every night this week?" I ask. Mateo usually had a three-date minimum. "And what about Gray?"

"I have. What does Gray have to do with anything?"

"Mateo, you sneak into my house every night and leave before we get up," I say dryly. I have Gray staying at the house just in case I need him in a hurry. Or, at this rate, to make it easier for him and Mateo to sneak around.

"We just hang out," Mateo insists. "But back to Evie. I might need to do some digging on her." Evie? Why does that name sound familiar?

"Why?" Van sighs.

"She's hiding something."

"You're hanging out with a girl you think is hiding something? Don't you think that's a little suspicious, given who we are?" I point out.

"No, because I'm not a suspicious bastard like you. I don't think it has something to do with us. It has something to do with her past."

"Why do you even care, Tay?" Van leans forward on the couch and looks hard at his brother on the love seat. "It's more than you just like hanging out with her, isn't it?"

Mateo rolls his eyes. "I just met the girl a week ago."

"Then why do you want to know what happened in her past?" I ask, curious.

"I don't know." Mateo runs his fingers through his hair. "She's constantly looking over her shoulder, won't let me pick her up at her house, questions why I keep taking her out, and has this look that says something fucking bad happened to her."

"What kind of bad?" Van asks. If Mateo thought something had happened, it probably has. "Do you think she's in danger?"

"Possibly."

"You need to find out," Van insists. "If you like this girl, maybe we can help." That's the thing about us. People see us in a bad light, in a way they probably should. But one thing we aren't going to stand by and let happen is someone harming this girl.

"We?" Mateo asks with a grin. "When did this become we?"

"Don't start your shit, Mateo. I'm being serious. You don't need to do this alone."

"I'll see what I can find out." Mateo stands from the love seat. "I'm going to go fuck with Gray."

As soon as the front door shuts, Van turns to me. "What do you think about this?"

I shrug. "Mateo's a grown man, and he can handle himself."

"I've never seen him like this before."

"He only said he liked hanging out with her, *amore mio*. I don't think it means any more than that."

"I don't like that she's secretive. That shit can be dangerous, and you know it."

I pull him to my side. "Let's see what he finds out and go from there. You know I won't let anything happen to Mateo."

"I know that." Van pecks my lips. "What do you think about him and Gray?"

"I'm fine with it, but I don't understand why Mateo thinks he has to sneak in and out of the house when he comes to see him." I chuckle.

"I think he does that for Gray."

That's probably true. I've watched Mateo around Gray for the past six months, and at first, it was just Mateo being Mateo. He would flirt with Gray to get him to blush; then, it turned into them spending hours in the guard house, and Mateo was adamant that they were only talking. And I believed him. I hired Gray on the spot, not knowing much about his past because that's how things worked. I just hoped he would let his guard down around Mateo.

I kept thinking about the name Evie and why it sounded familiar and couldn't place it. It was like it was beating at the back of my skull.

"I have a few things to do at Skyline and New Vision. Are we still on for later?" Van says, interrupting my thoughts.

"You don't have to ask me that, Van."

"I was thinking maybe I should stay at my house tonight." That thought makes me frown. Why wouldn't he want to stay here with me? "Don't make that face. I've been here every night this week."

"So? I like having you here." I'd tell him to move in right now if he wouldn't flip his shit.

"And I like being here but..."

"But what?" I insist when he trails off.

"I just think I need to go home."

"You are home." The words leave my mouth before I can stop, and just like I suspected, Van's eyes widen, and he's looking at me like I grew another fucking head.

"This isn't my home. We aren't there yet, Micah." Van goes to stand from the couch, and I pull him back down.

"Where are we then, Van?"

"We just started a relationship."

"We started a relationship six goddamn months ago."

"No, we started fucking six months ago. We just started dating a week ago." He is starting to get just as pissed off as me. I couldn't help but feel hurt by his statement even though I'm the one who originally lessened what we had to fucking. I can't help but think about that night. Van gave me an ultimatum when we were still staying under Les' protection in her pool house. He told me I needed to tell Les about us, or he was done. I told him that once everything with Les calmed down, I would. He saw right through that not long after that. And then the fateful night at Marcella's after we raided Viktor Orlov's house to save his wife, Nina.

I jerk the door open when someone knocks, expecting Les. I felt like shit for yelling at her, but I was a fucking mess anytime someone mentioned Evander and me.

I didn't expect Evander on the other side of the door, head down and hands shoved into his pockets. "Can I come in?" *Van asks.*

I wave him inside, shutting the door behind him. I lean against it to keep from reaching out to him like I wanted to, but I know what I would have to do if I did. I would have to admit how I felt about him, and I wasn't ready for that.

"*I am leaving for Cabo,*" *Van announces, finally turning to face me.*

I raise a brow. "*Okay?*"

Van sighs. "*Why do you have to be like that?*"

"*Like what?*"

"*So goddamn dismissive.*"

"*I just said okay, Van. What do you want me to say?*"

"*Maybe ask why.*"

"*All right, why?*" *I knew I had walked into a trap the minute I said it. Van stands straighter, and his dark brown eyes never leave mine.*

"*I need a break. From Abbs Valley, from everything going on.*" *He swallows.* "*You.*"

"*Why from me?*" *As far as I knew, we were no longer a thing. Van couldn't take it for what it was—always trying to get me to admit my feelings. I wasn't that person. Did I lead him on to make him think I was? Yes. I couldn't stay away from him.*

Van laughs, but it's humorless. "*You don't get it, do you? I love you. I'm in love with you. I have been since the beginning, but you didn't want to hear me the first time I said it. You were content to lead me around like a puppet on a goddamn string. I'm not that guy anymore, Micah. If you let me walk out of that door and go to Cabo, that's it; I'm done.*"

My lungs seize in my chest, which was already killing me from getting fucking shot. Yes, it hit my vest, but it still hurt like a bitch. Van is telling me that this is my last chance, and I couldn't get the words to leave my mouth. I've been confused from the beginning about how I felt about him, and he seemed to be more at ease with it. I couldn't wrap my head around falling in love for the first time, and it was with a guy.

"I can't give you what you want, Van." I open the door. "You need to go to Cabo if that's what you need to do. But I'm not begging you to stay. What we had was just fun and fucking. I don't know where you forgot that."

"Probably about the time you started calling me amore mio," Van says through clenched teeth. *The first time I called him that was the first time we slept together. I was in the moment, and it slipped out. I couldn't take it back, but I could have stopped calling him that after.*

I shrug, feigning indifference. "It was just a pet name, Evander."

He pushes by me and spins on his heel when he's on the other side of the door. "Why can't you see how much I love you? Why can't you see past all your macho bullshit about me being a guy and see me?"

"I don't see you as anything more than a fuck." *I shut the door on his hurt expression and know I have just made the biggest mistake of my life.*

Even then, I still can't get my body to move to open the door and tell him I love him too.

We had no idea Les would get kidnapped twenty-four hours later, but Van still left. After two weeks of working side by side with me looking for her and Zane, he couldn't take it anymore. He left for Cabo, and I heard from him twice the whole two months he was gone. I messaged him non-stop, realizing how stupid it was to fight my feelings after seeing how fast you could lose someone when I thought we had lost Les. When he came back, it was no different; he still wanted nothing to do with me. Not that I blamed him. My words were harsh and callous. And a bunch of fucking lies.

"What we had was more than that," I say softly, knowing this is just as fresh for him as it is for me. And it sucked to realize he still didn't fully trust me. "I loved you then, *amore mio*. And I will spend however long it takes to prove it. So, you stay where you feel comfortable. I'll always be here when you're ready to come home." I kiss his lips and leave the room, letting him make up his mind.

Van is mine, no matter where he chooses to sleep.

CHAPTER 8
EVIE

Seven days.

That's how many days in a row Mateo has taken me on dates.

I find it impossible to say no to him, even though I know I shouldn't be entertaining the idea of dating him.

But I was having fun for the first time in a very long time. He's taken me to do everything. Dinner, movies, walks on the beach and bowling. He even took me to play laser tag because I told him I'd never been before.

Mateo is perfect, and that's the scariest part. I found myself waiting every day for his texts or phone calls. And he still hasn't even tried to kiss me yet. I wanted to believe he was interested in me because he's shown interest; he's just never acted on it.

Things with Hartley are tense, however. He barely speaks to me and won't answer my questions about Mateo, no matter how much I pester him.

"You're going out with him again?" I look up from putting on mascara to Hartley leaning against the doorway of my room.

"Yes." I sigh. "If it's a problem with me going out with him and staying here, I'll go back to my apartment." I would if it would make Hartley more comfortable, even if it sent fear racing down my spine.

At Hartley's, I could sleep without waiting for someone to come busting through my front door. I went there to get more of my stuff when I left my date with Mateo, and it felt like someone was watching me the whole time.

"I wouldn't send you back there alone, Evie." Hartley rakes his fingers through his hair. "You don't know what type of person he is."

"How am I supposed to know if you won't tell me?" We have this same conversation every time he realizes I am going out again.

"It's not my place to tell you." And that's always the same answer.

Hartley hinted that Mateo wasn't a good guy, but I couldn't see him being evil. He is always polite and funny and always ensures I'm having fun.

"I don't know what you want me to say."

"How about you won't fucking go?" Hartley steps into the room. "If you want to go do stuff, I can take you. It could be like old times." There is so much hope in Hartley's face that I almost agree.

As much as I wanted that, it wouldn't be like old times. We are different people now. Hartley is almost emotionless now, and I am trying to find who I was before Aaron. Mateo is helping with that, even if I don't want to admit it. I could laugh and joke with him without worrying he would backhand me across the face. I know Hartley wouldn't either, but there is just something about Mateo. *He makes you feel beautiful.*

"I want to go," I tell Hartley honestly. I watch his hopeful expression turn completely blank.

"Okay." Hartley turns around and leaves the room.

The only thing that makes me nervous about Mateo are his questions. I couldn't tell him anything without spilling the whole story about Aaron. I wanted Mateo to like me, not run him off. Nobody wants a girl that is hiding from her ex. I haven't heard anything else from Aaron, but I know it isn't over. Hartley would park outside The Coffee Shop or the diner while I was working, and I was with Mateo every night. But that isn't going to stop him.

My phone pings with a message, and I look at it with a smile.

MATEO

I can't wait for you to see what I have planned.

Now I'm intrigued. Give me a hint?

MATEO

No damn way. I worked hard on this. Besides, I want to see you do the clapping giddy thing again.

I shake my head at that. I got a little excited when Mateo took me to play laser tag. Mateo laughed and said it was the cutest thing he'd ever seen.

I did no such thing.

MATEO

Bullshit. See you in an hour, Buttercup.

I still haven't asked why he calls me buttercup. All I know is it makes my heart do a flip and butterflies attack my stomach.

It's getting expensive taking Ubers to the dates, but I don't know how it would go over with Hartley if Mateo picked me up here. Even if I wasn't staying at my apartment right now, I still needed to pay the bills, and I'm on a fixed income. Gnawing my bottom lip, I shoot off a message before I can rethink it.

Can you pick me up?

MATEO

Of course. What's the address?

Mateo has repeatedly told me he would pick me up, and I felt I could trust him. Hoping I'm not making a huge mistake, I send him the address and go in search of Hartley to warn him. I look all over and find him on the back porch, sipping a beer. I slide the door open, and he doesn't even turn around.

"Mateo is picking me up here." I wince and wait for his reaction.

"Okay." Okay?

"I don't want you to be mad at me." I sit in the chair beside him.

"I'm not mad, Evie."

65

"Tell that to your constipated-looking face."

He turns slowly to face me with a raised brow. "Constipated looking face?"

"Yeah. You always look constipated when you're pissed off."

"No, I don't," he scoffs.

"Uh. You do. I could never tell if you wanted to cuss me out or you needed to take a shit."

I wish I could take a picture of Hartley's face. I can't tell if he wanted to be mad or laugh. Finally, he laughs, and it's music to my ears. His laugh is deeper than it used to be, but it's still so full of joy that I want to bottle it up.

"If you weren't always such a pain in the ass, I wouldn't have that problem."

My mouth pops open. "I wasn't the pain in the ass; you were."

He snorts. "Tell that to my broken bedroom window."

"That was your fault, Hartley James Cruz!"

"Bullshit. You were the one who didn't catch the ball."

"You were the one who threw it!"

One day, we were joking around in his room, and he tossed a baseball at me. I wasn't a sports person, so I missed it, and it busted right through his bedroom window. Hartley's dad, Carlos, made us do chores around the house to pay for a new one. Carlos wasn't Hartley's real dad, but he raised him like he was, which is why Hartley chose to be a police officer just like him. I still wanted to know why Hartley quit the force, but I didn't want to ruin the moment.

"It's not my fault you have butter fingers."

"Whatever," I huff, making him chuckle. "I still have callouses from digging up that garden."

"At least he didn't make you clean out the damn gutters."

I laugh. "Touché. How are Linda and Carlos?"

"Mom and Dad are good. They were here visiting not too long ago. How's Claudia?"

I shake my head. "I don't know. We haven't talked in a while." So much for fun times.

"Why not? Is she still upset that you left?" Hartley angles his body so he can see me better. "I'm sure she would be happy to hear from you."

"I've tried to call her." The only reason I know she's okay is because I still talk to my cousin. "She's had a hard time ever since Dad died." My dad was sick for years and passed away three years ago, and he was no longer there to be the buffer between my mom and me. We never saw eye to eye unless I did exactly what she wanted. All the alcohol she drank didn't help, either.

"I'm sorry, Evie." Hartley squeezes my arm.

"It's okay." I smile. I wanted nothing more than to have a relationship with my mom like Hartley does with his parents.

I hear the familiar rev of an engine pull into the driveway and watch Hartley's whole body tense. His face shuts down, and he turns to stare off the porch.

And just like that, the magic moment is gone.

"This is the second best date I've been on," I declare. Mateo brought me to a place called Lookout Point, where you could see Abbs Valley lit up below. He picked up food from Les' place and set up a picnic. I, in fact, did do a happy dance.

"Second best? What was the first?" We just finished eating and sat on a blanket, enjoying the view.

"Honestly, laser tag," I laugh.

"If you liked it that much, I'll take you again." Mateo turns to me with a smile, and I can't get over how gorgeous he is.

"I'd like that."

We lapse into silence, just enjoying each other's company. Over the course of this week, I've found out a lot about him. But I felt terrible because I wouldn't tell him anything about myself, and he never pushed, which felt odd. My mind kept trying to pick apart everything between us, dredging up Aaron telling me I wasn't good enough for anyone else. I was getting better at accepting Mateo's compliments, but it was hard won.

"Buttercup." I turn with a smile at the nickname and suck in a breath at how close Mateo is to my face. He slides his hand up my face and cradles the side of my head. "I really want to kiss you."

My heart starts thumping in my chest, and my palms get sweaty. What if he doesn't like it? What if he realizes he doesn't want me after kissing me? I'm not a virgin, but Aaron was my first, and he didn't leave me a lot to go on. It was always about him. *Pucker up, dumbass; this is what you've been wanting.*

I nod, and Mateo seals his lips over mine. His tongue licks across my lips, and I open for him. With the first stroke of his tongue against mine, I clutch the front of his shirt, feeling the hard muscles underneath. *Holy shit, I am going to self-combust.* His lips and tongue move confidently against mine, making me forget everything I was thinking before.

Mateo pulls back with a groan, laying his forehead against mine. "I've been wanting to do that since the wedding reception."

"Why haven't you?" I whisper.

"I wanted to make sure you were ready." Tears spring to my eyes before I can stop them. Mateo is good at reading me, even when I don't want him to. He can tell when I don't want to talk about something and when I feel uncomfortable. He listened to everything I said, which is why we've had a series of dates in a week. Each of them was carefully planned for me. I've never had that before. I never dated in school because I wasn't what guys usually went for. And now I have a guy as special as Mateo looking at me like he is right now.

"I'm ready," I tell him.

When Mateo kisses me this time, I can tell he was holding back the first time. He slides his hand to the nape of my neck to hold me tighter against his lips. It's not like I was going to move, anyway. This kiss is all-consuming, and I can feel it everywhere. Mateo pushes forward, and the next thing I know, I'm flat on my back, and his hard body is sliding against me. I try to shut down my mind so I can enjoy this instead of pointing out the glaring differences between his hard body and my soft one.

Mateo pulls back with a frown. "Where did you go just now?"

"What?" I ask breathlessly.

"You were into it; then I lost you."

"I'm sorry," I say miserably.

He plants his hands on either side of my head but doesn't move. "Talk to me."

Could I really tell him where my mind went without him thinking I was forty shades of fucked up? I search his eyes and decide that if I am ever going to move on with my life, I need to start with being honest.

Before I can open my mouth, my phone starts ringing. Only a handful of people have this number, and one is lying on top of me. "I have to get that."

Mateo gives me a look but sits back, pulling me to sit up with him. I fish my phone out of my pocket. An unknown number flashes across the screen, and I almost don't answer it. Hoping it might be my mom, I slide to answer.

"Hello?"

"Baby." All color drains from my face, and Mateo doesn't miss it.

"How did you get this number?" I whisper. I didn't have a regular phone plan, so he couldn't have found it by my name. I always bought burners, and I never kept them long.

"I have my ways, baby. It's time for you to come home." I don't miss the growl in his voice, making me want to throw up.

Mateo mouths, *who is it*, and I shake my head. He takes my phone and flips it to speakerphone with a look, daring me to argue with him.

"That's not my home. Please leave me alone."

"You've had your fun. I'm getting tired of the games, you stupid bitch." I watch Mateo's face darken to a look I haven't seen on him. "Who are you with?"

"What?" I squeak. How does he know I am with someone?

"Don't play dumb. You're mine. Did you really think I was going to let you go? You might be fat and lazy, but you had your uses. Meet me at your apartment."

Why does he even want me back if he thought those things about me? It's like some sick game I don't know how to play. The shame hits me like a freight train that Mateo had to hear that. Now he is going to know exactly why I couldn't hold a decent fucking conversation without feeling like something terrible was going to happen.

"Hang up," Mateo grits out.

Aaron laughs through the line. "Tell that motherfucker to shut up, or I'll gut him like a goddamn fish. Ten minutes, Evie." The line goes dead, and I can't even look Mateo in the eye.

"Buttercup," Mateo says softly. He puts his fingers under my chin to raise my head when I don't move. "Who was that?"

"My ex." The tears start flowing, and Mateo jerks me to his chest.

"Let's go back to my place, watch a movie, and talk."

I know I should say no, but it feels too good to be in his arms.

"Okay."

CHAPTER 9
MATEO

I will kill the motherfucker when I get my hands on him. Evie no longer needs to tell me why she acts the way she does. The phone call just answered everything.

I look over at her in the passenger seat, and the girl I was kissing is replaced by the girl I took out that first time that questioned my motives.

Who the hell talked to a woman like that?

I reach over and take her hand in mine, surprised when she lets me. I'm still amazed that she even agreed to go to my house. We've kept everything strictly public, so when she said yes, I was relieved. I wanted to give her a safe space to talk to me if she wanted to. I won't push her and will be there when she is ready.

Swinging back on the highway to take us back to my place, I rub circles on her hand with my thumb until I feel her start to relax.

"Asshole," I mutter when a car comes up behind me with its high beams on. I slow down, hoping it will pass, and when it doesn't, I get a sinking feeling in my gut. "Buttercup, do you have your seatbelt on?"

I see her glance at me. "Yeah."

"Okay. Hold on for a second." I put her hand on my lap so I can

71

switch gears and stomp on the gas. The car speeds up behind me, confirming my suspicions that we are being followed.

"What's going on?" Evie asks, and I don't miss the quiver in her voice.

"Don't panic, but I think we're being followed." I don't want to scare her, but I need her ready for anything. Evie doesn't say anything, but I can hear her sniffle and know she's crying again.

I hit the button on the steering wheel, telling it to dial Gray.

"Hello?"

"Gray, I have a tail."

"Where?"

"Eighty-one. I'm on my way home." I sneak a glance at Evie. "With Evie."

"I'm headed your way. Can you lose it?"

"I could if I was alone." I could drive like a psycho, but I wasn't risking her more than I had to.

"Shit," Gray mutters. "Keep the line open."

I had plans to tell Evie about Gray tonight, but things went sideways when I kissed her. I want to see her in a more serious way, and she deserves to know that I am seeing Gray, as well. Honestly, I have no idea what Gray and I are doing. After he kissed me, it hasn't happened again. But he does ask me to come to see him every night, and I do without fail. We sit up and talk about everything, including Evie. Gray is cool with me seeing her, and I know he wants to take things slow. I just hope Evie is as understanding.

The car speeds up behind us, straight into the back of the car, causing me to fishtail. I correct with a slide of the wheel, switch lanes, and open the car up. "Goddamnit." These assholes are pissing me off.

"Take exit forty-seven. I'll be waiting," Gray says.

Shit. I would have to cross four lanes of traffic to get to that exit. "Hold on tight, buttercup."

Without letting my foot off the gas, I cross the lanes, nearly taking out a truck in the process. Evie lets out a little squeak, and her hand tightens on my thigh. I see Gray's jacked-up blue Dodge Ram sitting in a wide spot and slide to a stop beside him.

"Stay in the car," I tell Evie and step out. I'm pretty sure we lost them with my stunt, but I need to be sure.

"You good?" Gray asks, walking towards me.

"Yeah." I walk to the back of my car. "Fucking hell." The bumper is bent and cracked, and my driver's side tail light is busted. It hurt to look at, but it could be fixed.

I see Gray holster his Glock. "What's going on?" I give him the rundown of Evie's conversation with the ex and watch Gray's face darken. "What kind of asshole talks to a female like that?"

That was my exact thought. "I don't know. I'll take her to the house and see if she'll talk to me." I rake my fingers through my hair. "I knew something was going on, but I never thought it was like this." This was more than a phone call. Evie was scared out of her mind when she heard his voice. I needed to get to the bottom of it. "You coming?"

Gray raises a brow. "You want me to come on your date?"

"The date is kind of over, Gray," I say dryly. "It would make me feel better if someone else was there. It probably would her too."

"All right."

"Do Van and Micah know where you went?" The last thing I need is those two assholes coming to the rescue. I have a feeling Evie is going to have a hard enough time with Gray.

"They weren't home when I left. Micah gave me the night off and took one of Evander's guards."

"Good. We can take the long way to the house. See you there."

I slide back into the car. "Are you okay?" I ask Evie.

She turns her tear-stained face back to me, and I feel murderous all over again. "Take me home. You shouldn't get involved in this. I don't want to see you get hurt." I almost snort at that. She doesn't know I am a trained killer, and her douchebag ex doesn't scare me.

"No can do, buttercup. I'm already involved." Shoving the car into first gear, I pull out behind Gray.

"Mateo, please," Evie says miserably. "He's going to kill you."

I take her hand in mine and kiss her knuckles. "Don't worry about me. Why don't you tell me what all that was about?" She is already shaking her head before I finish that sentence. "Evie, please talk to me."

"No," she cries. "The more you know, the more dangerous it is. Take me home. I have to go. I can't stay here anymore."

"What do you mean, you can't stay here?"

She jerks her hand away. "In Abbs Valley. He found me, and now he knows about you. I should have never agreed to see you because it will be my fault if something happens to you. Please, take me home." Evie is nearly hysterical, and she needs my undivided attention. I flash my high beams to get Gray's attention and pull to the side of the road. He pulls over seconds later.

I turn to face her and pull her hand back into mine. "Evie, nothing is going to happen to me. I can help you if you tell me who that was. I know we just met, but you can trust me, buttercup."

"No, no. It's not that easy! He always told me he would kill me if I told anyone! And he will! Take me home." The cute little house I picked her up at wasn't secure like mine, but I don't want to kidnap the girl. I saw the black truck in the driveway and knew she didn't live alone, but could they protect her like I could? I send a message to Gray and nod my head at Evie. I pull out, and he pulls out behind me. "What are you doing?"

"Taking you home." I hear her sigh in relief, but it will be short-lived.

I'm not leaving her there alone.

"You can't go in there! You said you were taking me home!"

"Yes. I said I was taking you home, but I never said I was leaving you here." I get out of the car before she can argue anymore, and she scrambles out behind me.

"Mateo! You can't stay here!"

I eye the black truck and then look back at her. "Why? Is that your boyfriend's truck?" I knew it wasn't, but I needed to confirm.

"What?! No!"

I shrug. "Okay then. Let's go." Gray's truck door shuts behind me, and I watch Evie's eyes widen, but it isn't out of fear.

She gasps, and I turn to Gray in confusion. "What is this? Is this some kind of setup? Oh god, I think I'm going to puke." Talking about one extreme to the next. I hated that she was so damn paranoid, but I have no idea what she means.

"Buttercup, calm down. What are you talking about?"

"This is the girl from the wedding reception," Gray explains when Evie doesn't. She's seconds from bolting inside the house.

Hearing the front door open, I look up to see who's standing there, and it all slots into place. This was the girl that was being dragged across the alley. The one Micah beat the shit out of her ex for. The one that knew Hartley fucking Cruz. And she was fucking living with him.

"It looks like we have a lot to talk about, buttercup." I try to keep the bitterness out of my voice but fail miserably. I've never been jealous in my life until right now.

"No. You need to go. Now." Evie goes to turn on her heel, and I grab her arm to stop her.

"I'm not leaving until you tell me what's happening."

"Why do you care?! You don't know me!"

"I want to know you," I say quietly. More tears splash down Evie's face when she closes her eyes.

"What the fuck is going on?" Hartley demands, walking down the steps.

I grind my teeth at the sound of his voice. He might have made up for fucking up Les' investigation into her kidnapping, but he was still the sack of shit who's been investigating all of us. He quit the force, but did that mean he wasn't doing his own investigation? I look back at Evie. Is she helping him? Jesus Christ. I am starting to sound like Micah. None of that added up. You can't fake that kind of fear.

"She got a call from the ex," I say, finally turning to face him. Hartley's jaw is locked tight, and his hands are balled into fists. "We were followed, and I didn't want to leave her alone."

"As you can see, she's not alone. And I heard her tell you to leave. Maybe you should fucking do that."

I wasn't usually a violent person, but right now, I wanted to punch that judgmental look right off his goddamn face. Did he know she was seeing me? If so, why didn't he tell her who I was?

"I'm not leaving." I cross my arms over my chest. I wanted to rip her away, stuff her back in my car, and take her home with me. *Geez, Mateo, crazy much?* "I can help."

"I don't need your kind of help," Hartley growls, taking a step toward me. Gray steps in between us, and I have to hide a grin.

"Mateo, thank you for this week," Evie says, grabbing my hand. "I appreciate your offer to help, but Aaron isn't *good*. You need to go. I can handle this."

I'm working up for an argument when I hear the roaring of a car engine. I spin around when headlights flash across us, speeding our way. The SUV fishtails when it slams on the brakes, and a guy jumps out of the passenger side with a semi-automatic. *Shit.*

"Get down!" I yell, grabbing Evie. I get her on the passenger side of my car right when they open fire.

"Get her out of here!" Hartley yells.

I jerk open the passenger side door, ducking when I can hear bullets pinging off the top of the door. "Get in." She doesn't hesitate to my relief.

I run to the driver's side while Gray covers me. I'm in the car and tearing through Hartley's lawn before you can count to five. They fire at the vehicle, but it's just a warning. They aren't looking to kill her, just us. I hit the main road with a bark of tires, the car sliding sideways. Correcting right before we careen into a ditch, I hit the gas.

"Give me your phone," I tell Evie. She hands it to me; I stab the button for the window and toss it out. There is no other way they knew where we were besides tracking her phone. "I need you to tell me who I'm dealing with now." I risk a glance at Evie, and her face is deathly pale. I know I needed to be gentle with her, but I need to know what I just got mixed up in. "Now, Evie."

"Aaron Rockford," Evie whispers.

"Fuck." I slam my hand on the steering wheel. This isn't just some asshole ex. This is the leader of the fucking Bulls. One of the most violent gangs just north of us. Aaron is sadistic and certifiably insane. "How the hell did you get mixed up with him?" I glance into the rearview mirror and don't see anyone, so I slow down a tad past death-defying speeds on a curvy road. I could handle it and drive this car with my eyes closed. But Evie looks seconds away from passing out.

"I didn't know when I met him, and when I did, it was too late." Evie's no longer crying; there's no emotion in her voice. That is worse than the tears. "Where are we going?"

"My house." I grab her hand, and it's cold and clammy. She nods without argument and slides further down into the seat.

My phone rings through the car's speakers, and I stab the button to answer when I see Gray's name.

"You good?" he asks as soon as the call connects.

"I'm fine. Did you get out?"

"Yeah. They left when you did. You don't have a tail?"

I glance in the mirror again. "No, I lost them. Come to the house."

Gray sighs. "We have another issue. Hartley's behind me." I don't give a shit at this point. It would probably make Evie feel better, which is the main goal.

"It doesn't matter. See you in a bit."

I disconnect the call, and Evie starts giggling. It's watery and nearly hysterical, but the sound still makes me smile.

"What's so funny, buttercup?"

"I don't know. Nothing about this is funny." That doesn't stop the giggles, however.

Evie is about to lose her shit now that the adrenaline is wearing off.

I need to get her safe at my house. Now.

CHAPTER 10
HARTLEY

What the fuck am I doing?

I've asked myself that a thousand times since Evie walked back into my life.

Now I am following two guys who hated my existence to ensure she is safe.

I know very little about what happened when Evie was with Aaron; all she told me was that she was on the run from him for eight goddamn months instead of calling me. I could have told her who Mateo was, but she looked so happy, I didn't have the heart to say anything. Plus, I knew he would keep her safe, no matter who he was. I thought Aaron was just another excuse for an abusive man, but after the display tonight, I was wrong.

We pull up to the gate of the Perez mansion, and I'm surprised when the guard doesn't stop me from going through. I put my truck in park and take a deep breath before stepping out.

"I'm doing this for her," Mateo says, walking around to the passenger side to help her out. When she gets out, my heart sinks. All the color is gone from her face, and her usual bright brown eyes are dull.

Mateo jerks his head for me to follow, and I half expected someone to shoot me when I stepped through the front door.

Mateo leads Evie into a massive living room, whispers something to her, and motions for me to follow him. As soon as we reach the kitchen, he whirls around.

"Did you know her fucking ex is Aaron Rockford?" Mateo hisses.

I cross my arms over my chest. "No. I didn't. I can take her and leave if it's a problem."

Mateo's eyes narrow. "I don't know if you suddenly forgot who the fuck I am, but I won't hesitate to shoot you if you try to take one step out of that goddamn door with her. I only allowed you in *my* house because I thought it might be good for her. Don't make me regret that decision."

I swallow my argument because he is right. He didn't even have to let me through the damn gate. "What's your plan?"

Mateo snorts. "You really think I'm going to tell you that? My only plan for tonight is to find out what the hell is going on and keep her safe. Tell me what you know."

"I don't know much," I admit reluctantly.

"You didn't think to ask questions? You're a fucking cop, for Christ's sake."

"*Was* a cop. And Evie's not a suspect; she's a friend. She didn't need me grilling her for information." And I knew the minute I tried, Evie would take off. I figured the best plan was to give her a safe place to stay until she would open up to me. It looks like she didn't open up to him either, which gives me some sick satisfaction.

Mateo rakes his fingers through his hair, and he actually looks worried. Not about getting shot at or what we're up against, but about her. Given how I feel about her, I hate it.

He leaves the kitchen without a word, leaving me to follow behind him. We find Evie in the same spot, legs curled under her, staring at her lap. Gray looks up from his place, leaning against the wall without a word, glaring a hole through my head.

I have to remember I am doing this for Evie because, with one wrong word, I am going to die tonight.

Mateo sits beside her, and I sit on the love seat to face them. "Talk to me," he says gently. I sit back and let Mateo do the talking.

"I met Aaron at a diner I worked at," Evie says dully, resigned to the fact she couldn't hide anything now. "I moved in with him a month later."

"How long were you together?"

"A year."

"How long have you been running from him?"

"Eight months," Evie whispers, and I watch Mateo close his eyes. When he opens them, they're burning with anger.

"Fuck, buttercup." Mateo pulls her into his arms, and I grind my teeth when she goes willingly. If I wasn't such a coward, that could have been me. But I couldn't give her the comfort she needed when I hated myself for how I treated Alessa Poletti. I'm no good for Evie in that way, but I could be a friend. Just like I've always been until she started dating Aaron. If I had pushed harder to keep in contact with her, none of this would have ever happened. I would have known the name and got her as far away from him as possible.

Mateo rubs circles gently on Evie's back until she relaxes against him. "Why don't you get some rest, and we can talk more in the morning?"

"I can't stay here. I have to lea..."

"None of that," I interrupt. "You aren't leaving. It's time you accept some help. You don't have to do it on your own."

"He's right," Mateo agrees. "We can protect you."

"No, you can't." Mateo puts his finger gently against her lips.

"Yes, we can. Now stop arguing and come on." Mateo stands from the couch and pulls her to her feet.

"You're bossy," Evie mutters, making him laugh.

"You have no idea how bossy I'm about to get, buttercup." Mateo leads her from the room, leaving me with Gray, who's still glaring. The hostile silence is worse than if he was yelling at me.

I knew of Gray but didn't know him like the others. Everything surrounding Gray is just rumors. Those rumors pointed to him as one of the most lethal assassins on the west coast, but we could never prove it. Then the killings stopped right about when he started working for Micah Poletti. Just because I'm not on the force anymore doesn't mean I don't pay attention. I was already public enemy number one in a city overrun with gangs and the Mafia, but now I don't have a badge, which puts an even bigger target on my back.

Fifteen minutes later, Mateo comes back to the living room with his phone to his ear.

"Hey Les," he greets. *Fuck.* "I hate to bother you, but I need to borrow some of Holden's shit, and Holden for a minute." Holden is one of Les' six husbands. The genius hacker. It was smart to call him, but hearing him say Les' name makes me feel guilty as hell, no matter what I did to fix it.

"What did you get yourself into, Tay?" Les asks. Her voice filters through the room when he switches it to speakerphone.

"What I just got myself into is a long ass story," Mateo sighs. "What do you know about Aaron Rockford?"

"The Bulls Aaron Rockford? He's a crazy son of a bitch with no moral compass. Why?"

"That's what I got myself into. I need all I can on him. The less public information," Mateo explains.

"Shit, Tay. How in the hell?"

"I can't explain right now, but I promise I will. Can I talk to Holden?"

Les sighs. "Yeah, hold on, he's with Ryder and Zane." Zane is another source of guilt for me.

Mateo winces. "Damn, Les, never mind. I'll figure it out. I don't want to interrupt them."

"It's eight in the morning here, Mateo; they aren't fucking," Les says dryly. "I just meant he's outside with them."

"Please don't tell Leo anything yet. Not until I know what we're doing."

"I don't like lying to them, Tay. Do we need to come home?"

"No! I promise I'll tell him; I don't want him to worry while you're on your honeymoon."

"I'll do what I can, but if he asks me straight out, I'll tell him." With that, I hear her yell for Holden.

"Hello?" Holden answers.

"Hey, man. Look, I need some of your spy gear shit."

"Of what kind?"

"Anything you can loan me. Mostly I need your," Mateo cuts his eyes to me. "database." I almost roll my eyes. I know exactly what they are talking about.

"There's a black laptop with a green star sticker in my office that should have what you need. Take anything else you want. Do you need my help?"

"Not yet. Get back to your wife. Thanks, bro."

Holden chuckles. "If you need me, call."

Mateo hangs up and looks at me. "How do you know Evie?"

"Why are you doing this?" Instead of answering a question that is none of his damn business, I start asking my own.

"Because no matter what you think about me, Hartley, I care about her."

"So do I. What's your angle here?" I watch his jaw clench at that question.

"I don't have an angle, jackass."

"We grew up together," I say through clenched teeth. Our arguing won't help Evie, and they would try to ice me out if I pushed. That would happen over my dead body. *If you keep talking shit, that's exactly what you'll be. Dead.*

"So, you let your childhood friend run for eight fucking months without help? I knew you were a piece of shit, Hartley, but that takes the cake."

"I didn't know," I hiss. "I moved when I was eighteen, and we lost contact when she started dating him." I thought I was doing the right thing and giving her space. At first, she sounded so happy with him, so I had no idea what was happening. I didn't want to stand in her way, and we eventually stopped talking. Now I know why.

"If you guys were so close, why didn't she call you?" I've asked myself that question, and her answer broke my damn heart. Never in a million years would I have ignored a call from Evie. Even if she was on the run while I was looking for Zane to arrest him.

"She didn't want me to get involved," I lie.

I hear the front door open, and Mateo frowns. I look up and watch Evander Perez walk into the living room.

With Micah fucking Poletti behind him.

y resolve to go home turned into asking Micah to come home with me tonight. I lived and breathed Micah before and couldn't do that to myself again. Not yet, anyway. But the words left my mouth before I could stop them because I needed to be with him. Inviting him here made me feel like I had some semblance of control instead of staying with him all the time. Even though he didn't come right out and ask, I heard the undertone of me moving in with him. I couldn't give up my freedom entirely to him. I would have in a heartbeat before, but that was before he ripped my heart out.

I forgave him, and I am all in our relationship, but those words and how he looked at me were still burned into my brain.

"Are you sure you want me to stay, *amore mio*?"

I thought we would have one hell of a fight earlier, but he surprised me when he left the decision in my hands. Micah is bossy and overpowering on the best of days, so the fact that he is listening to me shows me how much he wants this. *So why can't I move past what happened between us?* He's done everything I've asked of him and then some.

"I'm sure." I key in the code to the house, eyeing the two trucks in the driveway behind Mateo's car. What the hell?

Rounding the corner into the living room, I stop dead in my tracks, making Micah run right into me. Before I can open my mouth, Micah is already moving forward.

"What the fuck are you doing here?" Micah growls, lunging toward Hartley Cruz. I grab his arm before he can get closer. Hartley jumps off the love seat, hands balled into fists.

"So, there's been a development. Have a seat, and I'll explain. But keep your voices down," Mateo says, and I cut my eyes to him. Is he fucking serious? "Please."

I pull Micah down into the chair beside me, and Hartley sits on the far end of the love seat. "Start explaining." He better have a damn good reason for this asshole sitting in my house.

"You know the girl you saved from the wedding reception?" Mateo asks Micah, and he nods. "That girl is Evie." Micah looks at Gray, and Gray confirms what Mateo is saying with a nod.

"I knew that name sounded familiar," Micah mutters.

"And the guy you beat the shit out of?" Mateo continues. "Is Aaron Rockford."

"What the fuck?" Micah and I say at the same time.

"Oh, it gets better. He followed her tonight, fucked up the ass end of my car, and then took a shot at all of us at Hartley's house."

"Start from the beginning." I need to know the full details. We get into trouble all the time, but I don't like that Mateo was alone when all this happened. He could take care of himself, but he is still my little brother.

Micah and I listen as Mateo explains everything he's learned from Evie, which isn't much. But it's enough to piss me off. I can't stand a man who lays a hand on a woman. Mateo didn't know if that's what happened, but as soon as he said she was jumpy if you moved too fast, that answered the question.

"That doesn't explain why he's here," Micah says, jabbing a finger at Hartley.

"He's here because Evie knows him, and I wanted to make sure she was comfortable."

"Where's Evie now?" I ask.

"Upstairs in my room."

"What's your plan?" I knew he had one. After only a week, Mateo was hooked. Something that's never happened before.

"I need to get some stuff from Les' that Holden said I could use. I need to do some digging. And I need to find out how the fuck he found her tonight."

"You need to find out how he found her at all," Gray adds, eyes never leaving Hartley.

"I'll talk to her in the morning; she needs sleep tonight," Mateo sighs. "This is bigger than what I imagined."

Mateo already knew something was up, but none of us would have guessed we would be going against the Bulls.

"You aren't alone, Tay," I assure him. "We'll do what we can. But he needs to go." I could feel Micah seething beside me. It's going to take one wrong move, and Micah will kill Hartley.

"I'm not leaving her," Hartley says evenly. "She can go back home with me."

"They know where you live, Cruz," Micah grits out.

Hartley shrugs. "I'll take her to a safe house."

"She's not leaving my sight," Mateo says. Then he looks at me, and I know what he will say before it comes out of his mouth. "He needs to stay. Evie needs everyone she can get, so she knows she's not doing this alone. I ditched her phone just in case he was using that to track her, and she's safer here." He looks back at Hartley. "You know I'm right."

I glare at my brother, and he grins. "He can stay in the guest room." I answer.

"What the hell..." I hold my hand up to Micah to cut him off.

"We can figure it out tomorrow."

"I'll watch him," Gray says in a deadly voice.

Hartley's fists are clenched so tight his knuckles are white, but I can tell he's not going to leave her or argue.

I pull Micah to his feet, practically dragging him from the room. I shut the door and watch him pace when we get to my room.

"Micah."

"Hartley fucking Cruz. You're going to let him stay in your

house?" Micah whirls around, and his blue eyes are blazing with anger. "You know what he did to Les."

"I know," I say slowly. "But Mateo is right. If this girl went through anything like I'm suspecting, she needs familiar faces."

"Fuck." Micah rakes his hands through his hair. "I can't be around him, Van."

"We'll get rid of him in the morning. But for tonight, he stays."

"Mateo sure knows how to go all out for the first girl he likes."

"You caught that, too?" I ask.

"How could you not? I watched the way he talked about her. Mateo has his first girl crush." Micah laughs at that, and some tension drains from his body.

"Gray's the first guy crush. Leave it to Mateo to do it all at the same time."

Micah sighs. "What are we going to do to help?"

That makes me smile. I knew there was no way Micah would step back and not help. "I don't know yet. We can figure it out." I walk until I'm right in front of him, my fingers going to the buttons on his shirt. "Until then, I have another idea."

Micah raises a brow but doesn't stop me. "What's your idea, *amore mio*?"

"Let me make you feel good." I pull his shirt from his slacks, pushing it off his shoulders. Micah steps forward, and I put a hand on the center of his chest. "You aren't in control tonight." Any other time, he is. But tonight, I need to be.

Micah raises an eyebrow but steps back. I undo his pants and push them off his hips. He steps out of them, and my eyes land on the scar on his left thigh. I thought for sure that when Viktor took him, he was dead. Micah was shot in the leg in the scuffle, trying to escape that day. It tore through the muscle and left him with a slight limp when he walked, but he survived. That's when I knew I needed Micah in my life, but I didn't know if I could be with him again.

"Lay on the bed," I demand and watch Micah give me that grin that makes me want to drop to my knees in front of him. *Not tonight.* He does what I say as I undress down to my boxer briefs. I get the lube from my bedside table, toss it on the bed, lie beside him, and run my hand over his abs. Kissing his neck, I can feel how badly he wants to take control of the situation. I slide my hands into his boxers and wrap my hand around his hard cock, stroking.

"Fuck," Micah grunts, his cock jumping.

"Take them off." He doesn't hesitate at that command. Stroking his cock hard a few times, I let go and run my hand down his thigh and over his tight ass.

"What are you doing?" Micah asks breathlessly.

"Let me show you what it feels like." Micah never lets me do anything to him. It's time he trusted me enough. "Bend your knees."

I watch the emotions pass over his face, and just when I think he's going to say no, he plants both feet on the bed.

"Do you trust me?" I ask.

"Of course," he answers without hesitation.

I grab the lube, and he watches every move I make. I squirt some on his cock, then on my fingers. "Spread your legs." Micah lets out a shuddering breath, and his knees fall apart. "Relax, *mi rey.*" He groans at the nickname that slipped from my mouth one night when he had me bent over the desk in my office.

Sliding my fingers between his ass cheeks, I wait until his body is relaxed before I tease his asshole with the tip of my finger—his body tenses. "Relax," I say again, kissing his neck.

"Van...." I can hear the argument in his voice and brace myself. He takes a giant breath, releases it in a whoosh, and goes slack on the bed.

Using my middle finger, I slide it inside him. "Stroke your cock."

Micah wraps his fist around it and slides it up, swirling his hand around the head. I tease him with one finger until he starts jerking his cock faster, then add a second.

"Oh, fuck," Micah chokes out.

"I want to fuck you. I want to feel my cock sliding in and out of you," I say against his neck, making him shiver and stroke his cock faster. "I want to make you feel the way you make me feel."

I move my fingers, so they rub across his prostate, and Micah lets go of one of those sexy deep groans, making me grind my cock on the side of his thigh.

Moving my fingers faster, I seal my lips over his, dominating his mouth like he usually does mine. Micah's hips start moving to fuck himself onto my fingers. "That's it, *mi rey*," I encourage against his lips. "It feels good, doesn't it?"

"Yes," Micah groans. "Fuck." There is something sexy as hell watching him chase his pleasure with his hand wrapped around his cock. But I don't want him to come yet.

I slide my fingers free. "Fuck me," I say hoarsely.

Micah moves so fast that he hits my chest with an oof. He has my boxers off and lubing up his cock in record time. Putting his hands behind my knees, he pushes until I'm wide open for him. With a warning tap on my leg not to drop them, he moves one hand to line himself up. "Fuck, *amore mio*, you got me fucked up right now." That's exactly how I wanted him. I wanted him to feel what I felt when he took me like this. He snaps his hips forward, burying himself to the hilt in one firm push. I breathe through the burn, and my back bows when the pleasure hits.

"Is that what you wanted?" Micah asks, slamming his hips forward.

"Yes. Fuck."

He lays down, so his chest rubs against mine, never stopping his fast strokes. "I love this ass," Micah groans in my ear. He runs his hands under my shoulders and curves his fingers to pull me down with each thrust. "Is this what you want to do to me?"

"Yes," I breathe. He's fucking me so hard that my back is scooting up the bed. I push one hand against the headboard, keeping myself locked in place for him.

"I want you too." Micah licks across my top lip but pulls away before I can kiss him. I love him like this. So lost in lust because of me. "You going to fuck my ass good, Van? Make me beg for your cock? Like you beg for mine?"

"Shit, Micah," I groan, trying to grab my cock. He knocks my hand away.

"No. You're going to come just from me fucking this tight ass. Answer my question."

"Yes. Goddamnit, yes."

"You like begging for my cock?"

I wasn't ashamed to admit I had begged for his cock before. "Yes."

"Beg me. Beg me to fuck you until you come all over both of us."

"Fuck me, *mi rey*, please."

"You can do better than that. Now. Fucking. Beg." This is the side of Micah I missed. The unhinged side. Don't get me wrong, I liked when Micah was sweet, but goddamn, this side makes me crazy.

"Fuck me harder. Please. Please!"

He slams into me harder, my cock already twitching between us. "That's it," he grunts. "Come for me."

That's all it took. I groan out my release and feel him swell inside of me. He buries himself inside of me and comes deep inside me.

I look into his blue eyes, and they are still slightly unfocused. He looks at my chest, leans down, and licks up my come. He seals his mouth over mine, making me taste myself.

We pull back, both of us breathless. "I love you," Micah says, his eyes returning to normal.

"I love you too, *mi rey*."

"Fuck," Micah groans. "You know what that name does to me."

I grin. "I do."

"If you wanted me to fuck your brains out, all you had to do was ask."

"It was more fun this way."

"That it was, *amore mio*, that it was," Micah laughs. "Now let me clean you up in the shower."

CHAPTER 12
GRAY

I had no idea that when I took this job six months ago, it would turn into this.

I never expected to feel at home for the first time, and I never expected to meet Mateo. Or feel anything for him.

I started working for Micah because I was getting swallowed by the life I was living and needed out. Mateo saved me, whether he realizes it or not. I was restless and angry until the first time he made me laugh. I know it took me six months to act on my feelings for Mateo, but I wanted to be sure I could handle whatever he offered. I never classified myself as gay or straight; I just existed. Everybody was attractive to me; I didn't feel the importance of putting a label on it. Messing around with a guy just never presented itself until Mateo. Not that I had much of a chance to mess around with anyone. Growing up the way I did, I didn't have time for that, and when I was older, I felt better just being alone. People often found me intimidating or overbearing. So, I just floated through life to cover that part of myself. The only person who seemed to be able to deal with that is Mateo, and we've only scratched the surface of who I am.

Watching him with Evie right now, I know I should feel jealousy because we are starting on whatever path, but I'm not. After every date, he would come to my room at Micah's and tell me about it. I watched him get more excited each day about taking her out. But at the end of the night, he still came to me.

Evie, being in danger, changes everything, and I will stop at nothing to protect her for him.

I could see what he saw in her. She has shiny, long, brown hair and big, brown eyes. Her cheeks are full, and her lips are plump. She is quite possibly the most beautiful woman I've ever seen.

The only problem I could see right now is Hartley Cruz. I've never encountered him face to face; I was too good at hiding who I was. Hartley isn't stupid, so I'm sure he suspected me, but he couldn't pin me down.

"You aren't leaving, buttercup. End of story."

When Evie woke up, Mateo fed her breakfast, and this current argument happened.

"I can't stay here! Mateo, you don't even know me, and you don't know what you're getting yourself into."

"I'm not letting you go out there alone. You can fucking forget it." I give Mateo a warning look that says he needs to dial it back.

"I've been doing it just fine. He only caught me because I stayed here too long."

"I don't think that's true," I interrupt. I uncross my arms and lean on the island in front of them, trying and probably failing to make myself less intimidating. "I think he's been waiting for you to get complacent before he made a move."

"What do you mean?" Mateo asks.

"I thought about it last night." While I was on guard duty, making sure Hartley didn't leave his room downstairs. "I think he's been following her this whole time."

"Why do you think that?" Evie says quietly.

I shrug. "I don't know for sure; it's just a theory."

"It makes sense," Mateo muses. "How did he get the number, though?"

Evie informed us she was using burner phones so that a phone plan wouldn't lead him to her. It was damn smart. "Where have you been besides Hartley's and with Mateo?"

"Work." I watch her face pale. "And my apartment."

"When?"

"Two nights ago. Oh god, was he there?"

I shake my head. "He wouldn't have to be there."

"I don't know how any of this works!"

"It's okay, buttercup. We can check the apartment and see what we can find."

Micah and Evander walk around the corner, Micah's eyes scanning for Hartley. When he doesn't see him, his shoulders relax.

"Morning, Boss."

"Stop calling me boss, Gray," Micah grouches. He tells me that all the time, but it feels disrespectful to call him anything else.

Evie turns around slowly on her stool and lets out a little gasp when she recognizes him. "You!" This morning, it took us ten minutes to convince her we didn't set her up. I have to admit; that it does look weird.

"In the flesh," Micah says dryly. "I'm Micah, by the way."

"How...why... I don't..." Evie stutters. "How is this happening?"

"Take a breath," Mateo chuckles. He gestures to Evander. "That's my brother you met at The Coffee Shop, and that's his boyfriend, Micah. My sister-in-law, Les, is his niece."

"I feel like my head is going to explode," Evie says, laying her head on the island.

Mateo rubs her back. "Look, I know this is a lot, but I need you to know you have a team behind you now. We're a family, and we want to help."

"Why? I'm not worth all this trouble," Evie mutters, and I have to give Mateo another warning look when his face turns thunderous.

"Evie, look at me," I say gently. When her head lifts, she has tears in her eyes. "Mateo thinks you're worth the trouble, so quit second guessing everything and accept the help that's being handed to you."

I couldn't think of a better place where she would be safe than with us. People saw us as the bad guys, and we are. But we also know when we could be good.

Evie's bottom lip trembles, but she nods. "What about Hartley?"

Micah growls under his breath, and Evander elbows him. "What do you want to do about Hartley?" Evander asks.

"He's my friend," Evie whispers, wiping tears from her cheeks. "He's kept me safe until now. They know where he lives. It was my fault for going to my fucking apartment."

Mateo explains our theory to Micah, and he nods. "He could have put something there to sniff out her phone. It would be easy as hell after that to hack it." Micah shrugs. "I also agree he's been following her this whole time. What can you tell us about him?"

"He's a narcissistic piece of shit," Evie says hotly. "But he's also grade-a fucking nuts."

"Why would you be with someone like that?" Mateo asks. I am curious myself.

"I didn't know any of that. He was charming when we first met, and it was too late when I realized it was all a lie."

"How did you finally get away?" I ask, changing the subject. I watched her body language; if we pushed for information about their relationship, she would have clammed up.

"Aaron and his second in command, Wraith, got called away at the same time, which never happened. I already packed a bag just in case I ever got the chance, so I grabbed it and took off."

"Good girl," Mateo says, kissing the side of her head. Her cheeks darken, and she gives him a small smile. "Does he have ties here?"

Evie shakes her head. "I don't know. He never involved me in his business unless he tried to scare me."

"We need to go to Les' and get Holden's computer," Micah says. "We need everything we can on him." Micah holds up a hand when Evie opens her mouth. "We're helping you. Might as well get on board."

Her lips snap closed, but I don't miss the twitch in her eye. She has a fire down deep in there and wants to argue. I was hoping she would. Evie doesn't seem like she's always been this scared woman sitting here.

Mateo laughs. "You think I'm bossy? You haven't seen anything yet."

"I'm not fucking bossy," Micah snaps, making Mateo and Evander laugh.

"I seem to remember differently," Evander says with a raised eyebrow.

Micah's eyes heat, and I feel like I'm invading a private moment. "That's different, and you like it."

"Wow," Evie breathes, and Micah's head snaps to her like he forgot she was there. Evie clears her throat. "Sorry. I was lost in the moment."

Micah rubs the back of his neck, looking uncomfortable as hell. Mateo starts laughing uncontrollably, making me chuckle along with him.

"You will do just fine here, buttercup."

"WHAT ARE we expecting to find here?" Hartley asks. I got roped into bringing him to Evie's apartment while Evander and Micah went to get the computer, and Mateo stayed with Evie.

"Anything that looks out of place." I hand him the device that detects listening devices, a camera, or, in this case, something that would clone her phone. "I assume you know how to use that."

I could hear Hartley's teeth grind from behind me. "Yes. I know how to use it."

I get to Evie's apartment door and shake my head. She had no business staying here, even without a psycho ex. Sliding the key into the lock, I can feel it give before I even turn the key all the way. "Jesus Christ," I mutter, shoving the door open.

This place is a security nightmare. The main door doesn't lock, her locks are useless, and the only means of escape is down the stairs.

Silently, Hartley and I sweep the room, finding several bugs and what we are after. We start packing her stuff in any random bags we can find, both knowing she isn't coming back here. I would pay to get her out of her lease if she has one.

We don't talk again until we're back in my truck. "He's watching right now. I can fucking feel it," Hartley says.

I nod, shifting the truck into drive and pulling away from the curb. "Me too."

Before we left the house, we had a long talk about Hartley. None of us wanted him around, but we all saw how important he is to Evie, and she is important to Mateo. We would take care of this problem, and he would be out of our way—no big deal.

"Do you think he planted any on her?"

I thought about that earlier, which is why Mateo swept her at his house, and I let the device run while we were packing. "If he did, we'll find it."

We quickly stopped at Hartley's and grabbed what he needed from there. So far, we didn't have a tail. Aaron is too big of a pussy to come after us without Evie with us.

"Why are you doing this?" Hartley asks.

"Doing what?" I would much rather he didn't talk at all.

"You don't know her. None of you do. But you're going to drop everything for her? I don't fucking buy it. It doesn't make up for who you are."

I slam on the brakes and jerk to the side of the road. "You don't know the first thing about me," I say in a deadly tone. "If you have a goddamn problem with us, you can get the fuck out now. The *only* reason you're still breathing is because of Evie and Mateo, so I suggest you shut your mouth."

I can tell he wants to argue, but he turns to look out the window instead. Good choice. I haven't shot anyone in a while, and my finger is getting twitchy.

CHAPTER 13

MATEO

"You're lying," Evie laughs. We've been talking on the back patio by the pool for hours. I truly enjoy her company. She is easy to talk to, and her sense of humor is the same as mine. As scary as that is.

"No. I swear," I say, crossing my heart. I told her a story about when Van and I stole the principal's car in high school, parked it at a strip club, and then sent pictures to his wife. Frankie was so pissed that he beat us for days. I wasn't telling her that part. Even though Van and I knew the consequences, we had a blast that day.

"You, I could see. Evander? He seems so...serious," Evie says. Funny how she's already picked that up.

"He didn't used to be," I tell her. "Van just had to grow up way before his time." Primarily because of Frankie. The minute Van graduated high school, Frankie started making him go on missions with the rest of his men. That made you grow up fast. He did the same to me.

"Why do you guys hate Hartley?"

"Not my story to tell. Let's say there is some tension between him and us." If Hartley wants to tell her what happened, that is on him. Do I agree with what he did? Fuck no. But I could try for her if Evie saw the good in him.

"I could sense the tension," Evie says dryly. "Okay. I have a question," she states, turning to face me, sitting criss-cross on the lounger.

"Hit me."

"Are any of you married or in a relationship? Because I don't want to get my ass kicked by some woman thinking I'm sleeping with her man," Evie states, making me laugh.

"Don't you think you should have asked me that by now? Van and Micah are the only ones in a relationship." I saw how she looked at them when they gave each other fuck me eyes; she wasn't repulsed by it. Which gives me hope for when I tell her about Gray.

"Why?" Evie asks suspiciously. "A bunch of hot dudes and no ladies that claim them. What gives?"

"You think we're hot?" I ask, waggling my eyebrows.

Evie giggles. "You know you're hot, and you didn't answer my question."

"I guess we just haven't found the right person yet," I answer honestly.

"That makes sense; I guess," Evie says, sitting back on the lounger.

I wanted to ask her about Aaron, but she gets this look in her eyes that I don't like.

"What's your favorite flower?" I ask instead.

"Roses," she answers. "You?"

"Buttercups. When's your birthday?" I didn't even have a favorite flower until I saw Evie with one stuck behind her ear the night I met her.

"Last month," she laughs. "What are you doing?"

"You've never played twenty questions before?" I inquire. She shakes her head. I grab my chest and gasp. "Never? That changes now."

"Fine," she says. "When's your birthday?"

"December. What was your high school mascot?" I ask.

"Tigers. What's your middle name?"

I wrinkle my nose. "Why did you have to go there already? Antonio. What's yours?"

"Damn it, I didn't think that through," she giggles. "Louisa. What's your favorite color?"

"Brown." Just like her eyes. "Is Evie your real name or a nickname?"

"My real name is Evelyn. Do you have any pets?"

"Evelyn Louisa. I like that. No time for pets. What's your favorite color?"

"Blue. How bad was the damage to your car?"

"Not bad at all." Nothing a couple of thousand dollars won't fix. "What is your favorite memory growing up?"

She laughs. "Oh, that's easy. This boy used to bully me during my senior year of high school for being overweight. Anyway, Hartley was captain of the baseball team, so he asked this kid to hang out with him and some buddies. I was so pissed until the next morning." She's giggling, so I know it must be good. "They tied him to the flagpole in his underwear right before school as a lesson."

My mouth drops open. "Hartley? Everything has to be by the book Hartley?"

"Yes," Evie laughs. "Hartley wasn't always so straight-laced. He was fun."

"You guys were close growing up?"

She nods. "We were best friends," she says, then points at me. "That was three questions in a row. It's my turn."

"Hit me with them," I declare and put my arms behind my head.

"What's your favorite childhood memory besides stealing a car?"

Sadly, I don't have many, and the ones I do include Van. We weren't allowed to be regular kids. Hell, I learned how to build and diffuse explosives at twelve. We didn't have toys growing up, and the ones we did were few and far between. We didn't get play time; we didn't ride bikes, and we didn't go to carnivals or amusement parks. Nothing we ever did was as a family.

"Van and I built a fort in the backyard of old lumber and stuff we found lying around. We spent hours in that thing telling ghost stories, and we even slept in it a few times." I smile at that. She doesn't need to know Frankie made us tear it down when he found it.

"That sounds awesome," Evie says. "Are you close to your parents?"

I shake my head. "Both my parents are dead."

"I'm sorry to hear that." Evie reaches over and squeezes my bicep before dropping her hand. I wanted to grab it and put it back.

"It's okay," I say with a smile. It's much better that way. "You have one more."

"Are you sure you don't mind me staying here?"

"Not at all. The more time with you, the better, buttercup."

She looks over at me, and I can see her struggling to accept what I just said. "I don't deserve you."

"It's the other way around." I'm not good enough for her, and I know I shouldn't get involved, but she is fast becoming an important part of my life. "I need to tell you something."

She lifts an eyebrow. "That sounds ominous."

"It's not bad. Well, I guess that depends on how you take it." I sigh. "I'm bisexual."

"Okay," Evie says slowly.

"And Gray is more than a friend. I think."

"You think?" That's what she picked up from that?

"It's new. But I wanted you to know."

"Am I coming in between you two? Because I won't be that person."

Bless her cute little heart. "No. Gray and I talk about you. He's okay with me seeing you. Is it a problem?"

Evie doesn't answer for a minute, like she's trying to think of her words carefully, making me nervous as hell.

"I don't want to come between you guys."

"You won't," I assure her.

"Then no." She shrugs. "I think it's awesome. Is it a little weird seeing a guy who already might have a boyfriend? Yes, but not because you're seeing a guy. Is your relationship open?" Just like that. I knew she was perfect.

"Like I said, it's new, and you're the only other person I'm seeing."

"So, it's kind of like me, you, and Gray are together." Evie giggles, and I finally relax. Then I think about what she said. Not a bad idea, but Evie isn't ready for that conversation.

"If you want to look at it that way, then yes. Are we together?" I have no idea how to do this. We've been seeing each other for a week, and it's been the best week of my life.

"Oh, I didn't mean to assume! I was just...." Evie's face turns blood red, and she covers it with her hands; I tug them away.

"Is that what you want? I'm going to be honest. You and Gray are my first."

"Aaron was mine," Evie says quietly. "I just... I like you, and that scares me."

"I feel the same, buttercup. But if you want to give it a shot, I do too."

"I do," Evie whispers.

I drag her lounger closer to mine, making her laugh. "Good."

Pushing my hand into her hair, I pull her lips closer to mine. Her eyelashes flutter, and her hands land on my chest. I rub my lips against hers so she knows what I'm about to do, but she doesn't wait for me to make a move this time. Evie seals her mouth over mine, opening immediately for me to slide my tongue into her mouth. *Hell yeah.* I've been dying to kiss her again since last night. Sleeping next to her last night was torture with that delicious ass pressed against me. It didn't help that I could hear Van and Micah fucking in the next room. Hearing your brother beg for cock should be a turn off, but it wasn't for me. I still don't know how she didn't wake up.

Evie makes a little sound in the back of her throat, making me groan in response. If she is this responsive just by kissing, I wonder how responsive she will be when I get her under me. *Down, Mateo. Now is not the time.*

"I like kissing you," she whispers against my lips before sinking back into it. Her hand starts roaming over my chest and abs, and I know I need to stop it before it gets too far.

I pull back and peck her lips. "I like kissing you, too." I move my head when she tries to kiss me again and watch her face fall. "None of that. I love kissing you, but your wandering hand was doing things to me."

She frowns and then busts out laughing. "Oh. My bad."

"Your bad?" My mouth pops open. My dick is hard as a rock, and all she says is my bad?

"It's not my fault you can't control yourself."

I roll over so I'm on top of her, making her laugh. I look into her eyes, and it takes my breath away. *Holy shit, I'm fucked when it comes to this girl.* "Beautiful," I whisper, pushing her hair behind her ear.

"When you say it like that, I believe you."

"I'll tell you how beautiful you are every day, buttercup," I promise.

That's one promise I knew I could keep.

"Did you find anything?" I ask Gray, flopping down in the chair next to him at the dining room table. Micah and Van got back with Holden's computer, and Hartley and Gray have been digging into Aaron since. They also found the device that cloned Evie's phone to hack into her location and several bugs. It pisses me off to know that this fucker has been stalking her the whole time she thought she was safe.

"Not yet," Gray answers, gesturing to Hartley. "He's doing the digging."

I raise my eyebrows. "You gave him access to that database?"

"I'm right here," Hartley mutters. "And all I'm looking for is Aaron. I don't give a fuck about you guys."

"Wow, Hart, that's harsh." I clutch my chest like my heart is breaking.

"The truth is the truth. And don't call me Hart."

"You know that's all I'm going to call you now, right?"

Hartley shakes his head but doesn't answer. I know he felt

terribly out of place here, and I actually feel bad for him. But he is being the bigger person and sucking it up for Evie. So I could return the favor by not treating him like shit. He gets enough of that from Micah.

"Where's Evie?" Gray asks, kicking back in his chair.

"By the pool."

"Is she okay?"

"Yeah. She will be. Evie's strong; she just has to find that again."

I am dying to know how Evie was growing up, but I don't think Hartley would answer me if I asked. If anyone has any insider information, it's him.

"She seems to be. She wanted to argue with Micah really fucking bad this morning," Gray chuckles.

"How could you tell?"

"Body language." Gray shrugs. "She didn't like him telling her what to do."

"You studying my girl, Gray?"

He turns his head to look at me. "If I was?"

I think about what Evie said about me, her, and Gray being in a relationship, and I search for that jealousy about Gray and Evie. It doesn't come. I know she was joking, but the thought has been on my mind since she said it. She didn't have a good example of how a woman should be treated. Would it do any harm to have someone else besides me show her? I shrug. "I don't care. Study away."

Hartley stands up from his chair so fast that it almost falls over. "Evie's not that kind of girl," he growls.

"And what kind of girl is that?" I ask.

"The kind of girl who would want to be passed around between you assholes. I knew you had a fucking motive. Evie and I are leaving. Now."

He goes to leave the room, and I step into his face before he can even think about taking her from me. "Let me tell you something, Hartley. I'm the only goddamn ally you have here, so I suggest you sit down and shut the fuck up. If you *ever* threaten to take her from me again, I'll pull your spine through your asshole."

"What's going on?" Evie says from behind me.

I give Hartley a look promising pain if he opens his mouth, but I won't back down. Hartley clenches his jaw so tight I'm surprised his teeth haven't fucking cracked.

"Yeah, Cruz. Why don't you tell her what's going on?" That comes from Micah, and I know where this is about to go. I step back.

"Nothing's going on, just a misunderstanding. Right, Hart?" I say between clenched teeth.

"No," Micah says. "I think she should know why we don't want him here."

I know what Micah is trying to do. He's hoping that if we tell Evie what Hartley did with Les' investigation, Evie will want him to leave. I don't know if she would or not, but it would hurt her to have to tell him to go. I don't want that for her.

"I don't think this is the time." I turn to Micah and beg him with my eyes to shut up.

"It's the perfect time. She needs to know how he treats vict...."

"That's enough," Van barks, causing Evie to jump. "You're out of line, Micah." Micah's eyes narrow on my brother, and he looks seconds away from blowing a gasket. Van holds up a hand to cut him off before he can talk. "I know this is hard. I do. But there are more important things at play here."

"More important?" Micah hisses. "He'll just fuck this up, too. That's what he's good at." Micah turns to Gray. "Let's go."

Micah storms from the room, and the front door slams seconds later. Gray gets to his feet. He squeezes my shoulder on the way by. "I'll talk to you later." As much as I don't want him to leave, Micah is his boss, and he doesn't have a choice.

"I didn't mean to cause a fight," Evie says softly. Before I can comfort her, Van steps beside her.

"It's not your fault." Van smiles. "Micah is just passionate about this cause."

That's an understatement. I see it from Micah's point of view and understand his anger. But Micah is also good at holding grudges. Hell, his niece married his one-time enemy, Zane, and he still doesn't like him.

I just hope he could work it out, so it doesn't cause a rift between him and Van.

Again.

CHAPTER 14
MICAH

"Where are we going, Boss?" Gray asks when we get in his truck.

"Home." I don't even have it in me to tell him not to call me boss. Gray grunts and shifts the truck into drive.

I know I overreacted, but fuck, Hartley gets under my skin. What happened to Les is still very raw in my mind, and the way that jackass handled the situation was worse than fucked up.

I don't allow many people to talk to me the way Van did; the only reason he's still standing is because it is Van. He's one of the few that can put me in my place without fear of repercussions.

My phone rings, and I look at it with a sigh expecting to get my ass handed to me again, when I see Les' name flash across the screen.

"Hey, shithead," I answer.

"So, are you going to tell me what's going on?" I've been waiting on this call.

"How much time do you have?"

"Plenty for you. What's up?"

I rub my forehead, trying to get my thoughts in order, then I explain the whole thing starting from the night of her reception. I finish with what just happened, and she's silent for a minute.

"Okay," Les says slowly. "Before I break this down for you, are you guys willing to go to bat for this girl? Aaron is no joke. He might not be as strong as us, but he gives zero fucks about who he hurts in the process."

Are we willing to do that? I know Mateo is all the way in. That's a given. Van would do anything for his brother, and I suspect Gray would do anything for Mateo. But am I? I hate what she is going through, but there is already tension between Van and I, and she's been there less than a day.

I sigh. "Yes. And I get it."

"All right. Then you need to know something, and I know you aren't going to want to hear it, but I think it will help."

"Okay."

"After we got rid of Jay, I reached out to Hartley. Zane was facing serious prison time for the case opened against him for murder because his service weapon was found at the scene. Hartley pulled in every favor he had left to get those charges dropped against Zane, and I suspect he made the murder weapon disappear. In my book, what he did more than made up for him botching my investigation."

"How can you say that, Les? He refused to fucking investigate because of who you were. Maybe if he had pulled his head out of his ass, we could have found you faster."

"No, you wouldn't have," Les says softly. "The best guys were already on the case. My guys. Hartley couldn't have offered anything more than what they were already doing. We were raised to hate cops. He was raised to hate criminals. He quit his job to turn over the mole in the department framing Zane. I honestly think he feels worse about what happened than I do. He made it right, Micah."

"What are you saying?"

"I'm saying you need to let it go. I have. You guys don't even know everything that girl has been through, and if you guys are going to protect her, you have to be a team. She doesn't need the arguing and fighting because she's automatically going to think it's her fault."

"How do you know that?"

"Because of the phone call you just told me about. Aaron conditioned her to always blame herself; from the sounds of it, that's not the first time he's put her down, either. She's scared, Micah; I've been there. Hartley has been in her life longer than any of you have, and he's willing to put the bullshit aside when I'm sure he'd much rather be anywhere than stuck with a bunch of guys who hate him. She needs him too."

"How did you get so smart, shithead?"

"I had some amazing men in my life who taught me everything I know, including you. If you need to take the day to cool down, do that but don't wallow in anger like I know you're going to do. And don't fuck things up with Van either."

"I love you, Les. Thank you."

"You're welcome, and I love you, too."

I disconnect the call and sit back in the seat with a sigh.

I am so damn proud of the woman Les has become. I've watched her grow into the leader her dad knew she could be. It took her some time, but she's turned into the best leader the Poletti's have ever seen. She is also the only one who saw through my bullshit.

I open up Van's text screen and take her advice.

> I'm sorry. I'm going to get some work done, and I'll come back later.
>
> If that's okay.

EVANDER

> It's always okay, and you have nothing to apologize for. But she needs to find out from him what he did. She doesn't need to hear it from you.

> I get it. I'll see you later. I love you.

EVANDER

> I love you too, mi rey.

I don't think he knows what that nickname does to me. And it has nothing to do with a godly complex. It turns me to mush every time. *Jesus Christ. I am turning into a fucking sap.*

Last night with him was more than I expected. He's never taken charge like that; he liked it more when I did it. But something about him telling me what to do had me hard as a fucking rock. There's no denying there is sexual chemistry between Van and me, but there was so much more.

I wanted to be a better man for him, but old habits die hard. Like my fucking temper.

Growing up, I would let it fly and fight anyone who got in my way. I got suspended from school more times than I can count, and the only reason I didn't get expelled was because of who my dad was. But I am a grown man now and don't have that outlet anymore, so I usually just let it fester like Les just accused me of doing. Van helps with that, though.

Walking into the house, I run over what Les told me about Hartley. It doesn't give him a sudden out in my book, but I would keep my mouth shut in front of Evie.

This would be over soon anyway, and things would return to how they were.

"What do you think about Evie?" I ask Gray. I just finished touring one of my new rental properties, and we are headed back to Van's so I could fix dinner. My way of an apology.

Gray shrugs. "She seems like a nice girl."

"You trust her?" I can't get the nagging suspicion out of my head that it's too coincidental that she is on the run from the Bulls *and* best friends with Hartley Cruz. The longer I sat at the house, the more I worked myself up to believe she's helping Hartley take us down. He isn't a cop anymore, but what better way to get your job back than to take down the Italian and Mexican Mafia? If it's true, using a beautiful girl like Evie as a cover-up is fucking brilliant. Her fear is either real, or she's a damn good actress. I've seen it play out both ways.

"Yeah. She hasn't given me a reason not to."

"We know nothing about this girl," I argue. What are the chances of me saving her and her captivating Mateo's attention all in the same night? She blows into our lives with an elaborate story about being on the run, but she's told us nothing else. Unless she's talked to Mateo, that could all be a lie.

"What are you saying?" If I explained any of this to him, he would probably call me a suspicious bastard like Mateo would. I might be, but I'm not willing to risk my friends or *family*.

"Just that we need to be careful," I lie.

Gray glances at me and then back to the road. "Mateo trusts her, and I trust his judgment."

"You don't think his judgment might be blinded by her pussy?"

"It's not like that."

"How is it not like that?"

"Because they haven't slept together yet."

That makes me pause. Mateo usually fucks the girl by the second date, if they get one. But he's been seeing this girl for a week, and is willing to give anything to protect her, and they haven't slept together yet? What kind of fucking spell does she have over him?

Pulling into Van's driveway, I already see Ghost's black Dodge Challenger sitting in the driveway. He and Caden step out of it when Gray pulls up. They are inseparable now that they've allied their gangs, the Vipers and the Disciples.

"You could have gone in," I tell Ghost dryly. I told them to meet me here so they could help.

"We just got here, dickhead," Ghost laughs.

I key in the code to the front door and push it open. I follow the sound of the voices in the living room. My eyes zero in on Evie on the couch between Van and Mateo and have to swallow the jealousy that flares up. *Get your shit together.* I trust Van. I don't trust her.

"Hey," Van greets me with a smile, and I relax a little.

"I called in reinforcements." I gesture to Ghost and Caden.

"Good," Mateo nods. "We might need it. Evie, this is Ghost and Caden." He introduces. She gives a shy wave.

Ghost and Caden get settled on the love seat while Gray and I take the chairs.

"Buttercup. I know this is hard, but we need more information. What can you tell us?"

"I really don't know much," Evie says softly. "I only met a few guys, and he never talked in front of me."

"Okay. What're some of their names?"

"Titan, Screwball, and Wraith." All street names, not real names. I don't miss how her voice quivers on the name Wraith. I'm catching myself scrutinizing everything she's doing. The way her voice shakes when she talks about it, how she folds herself more into Mateo, and how she looks you directly in the eyes when she talks. Could that be faked?

"Wraith?" Ghost asks, sitting up.

"Yeah, he's Aaron's second in command."

"What does he look like?"

A shudder runs through Evie. "Big, bald, and mean."

"Scar through his left eyelid?" Ghost asks. Evie nods. "Fuck. That has to be the same one. I was wondering where that asshole went."

"You know him?" I ask.

"Yeah. He used to be a Viper. He took off when Xander died." No big loss there. Xander was stabbing Les in the back while working for Viktor Orlov.

"Could he still have ties here?" Van asks.

"Yeah. His mom still lives in Concrete Row."

"Would she help them hide?"

"In a heartbeat."

"I want you guys on it," I order. "See what you can find out. They're here somewhere, and we need to find them."

"What do we do if we find them?" Caden asks.

"Call me."

Hartley slowly walks into the living room and silently hands me the laptop. I take it without a word, remembering everything Les said. If he called in favors to get Zane's charges dropped, he truly stuck his neck out to fix his mistake. I could even understand his suspicions that Zane just ran off with Les, but he *saw* how bad Zane looked when he got back. It took Zane and Les months to put the weight back on that they had lost in that place. How can you look at someone in that bad of shape and not do anything?

"What am I looking at?" I ask, scrolling through pages of reports.

"Everything I could find on Aaron so far. He has contacts everywhere. Maybe if we give them some incentives, they will start talking."

Mateo looks at me, and I subtly nod, giving him permission to tell him about Wraith. Hartley takes it all in.

"It's not a bad play, but we might get more out of his associates," Hartley replies. He looks tense as hell, and I don't blame him. Ghost and Caden are staring at him with complete hatred.

"Okay." I nod, coming up with a plan. "Ghost and Caden, you talk to Wraith's mom and start asking around. We need to make Aaron nervous. Take Alexey and Dmitri if you have to. We will talk to his contacts tomorrow."

"What about me?" Evie asks, looking around.

"You sit back and let us take care of it," Van says softly, and I have to keep from grinding my teeth. *You are being a jealous bastard, and this is temporary.*

Maybe if I keep lying to myself, I'll actually believe it.

CHAPTER 15
HARTLEY

I want to be anywhere but here, locked up in a house with a bunch of guys who hate me. But no way am I leaving Evie with them or risking taking her anywhere else right now.

I don't blame Micah for hating me. I fucked up royally when it came to Alessa's investigation.

"Hartley." I turn toward Evie's soft voice with a smile. "Can I talk to you?" I motion her in, and she sits on the edge of the bed. I'm hiding in the room that Mateo let me stay in after dinner and thought she went to take a nap.

"What's up?" I ask her, leaning back against the headboard.

"What's going on?" she asks, turning those beautiful brown eyes on me. Evie has always been gorgeous, even when we were growing up. Not that she would have given my skinny ass a chance.

"What do you mean?"

"I feel like I'm missing a huge piece of the puzzle with you and these guys," Evie says, turning and tucking her leg underneath her to face me. I don't know how much to tell her after what she had just got away from. I thought for sure Micah would tell her everything before Evander stepped in. "Why aren't you on the police force anymore?" I've been waiting for that question.

"I fucked up an investigation and turned my resignation in," I answer.

Evie's brow furrows. "You're human. People make mistakes all the time."

"Such an Evie thing to say," I joke. She always was a glass-half-full type of person. When she called and told me she was in Abbs Valley, I thought my heart would explode. After I found out why, I saw fucking red.

Evie rolls her eyes. "Seriously. What was so bad?"

I close my eyes and admit my biggest shame in my entire career. I don't want to see her face when I tell her this. "A guy on the force kidnaped Micah's niece and one of my detectives. I didn't believe it when they returned and refused to investigate." And I opened an investigation on Zane and had him arrested for murder with no proof.

"Why didn't you believe it?" Evie asks softly.

I sigh and open my eyes. "Some things didn't add up." And I was a judgmental asshole.

"What does that mean?" I could tell her, but I don't want to hurt her by telling her the truth about Mateo. He seems genuinely interested in her, and as much as that sucks, hurting her would suck even more.

"It doesn't matter. All that matters is that I fucked up. Hopefully, this will be over soon, and we can continue with our lives."

Evie's eyes fill with tears. "I can't do this forever."

"Come here," I tell her, opening my arm up. She hesitates before climbing up the bed, snuggling into my chest just like she used to. I wrap my arm around her and pull her closer. "We will get you out of this."

"I'm so fucking stupid, Hartley," Evie says miserably.

"Hey." I tip her chin up with my fingers to see her eyes. "You aren't stupid. You got in a bad situation."

"I should have got out sooner. The first time he..." Evie trails off, and I try to keep my rage from boiling over. She told me very little about her time with him, but I could piece the rest together. We've barely spoken since she's been back, and I was trying to give her space.

"Evie, you know this isn't your fault, right?" I ask.

"How is it not my fault? I moved in with a guy I barely knew. I should have known better at my age."

"You were twenty-two years old," I soothe. "That's not exactly the age to have all the fucking wisdom." I'm twenty-five and still don't have a clue what the hell I'm doing. I was the youngest chief of police in Abbs Valley and fucked it up. Evie giggles, and I soak in the sound.

Growing up, I had one goal: becoming a police officer. I worked hard for it. I moved from our small town Fairview, graduated top of my class at the police academy, and worked my way quickly to the top. Then I let my prejudice get in the way of what I always wanted to do. Save people. I don't know if we could have gotten to Alessa and Zane any faster than her guys, but I could have lent a few extra hands. And maybe they wouldn't have gone through what they did.

When Alessa left that file for me the night Zane was arrested, I could have thrown up when I opened it. She didn't even show me the worst of it. I didn't even hesitate when I turned Steve over to them when I found out he was the mole for Jay, even though I knew they were going to kill him.

As soon as you start on the police force in Abbs Valley, you're given a file on every gang and Mafia that's here. The Poletti's are at the top of the list to be taken down. No one has ever succeeded in even coming close. When Zane started on the force, and they discovered his history with the Poletti's, he was supposed to get close to Alessa again and feed information back to the department. That's why it seemed like such bullshit that they didn't just run off together.

Evie's soft sigh catches my attention, and I look down at her. She's fallen asleep, tucked into my side, her head resting on my chest. I slowly scoot us down on the bed and soak in the feeling that Evie is finally in my arms.

Where I always wanted her to be.

"You're going to stay here," Micah declares the following day. After breakfast, he pulled me to Evander's office with his huge-ass bodyguard, Gray.

I grit my teeth. "We don't have to stay here."

"You do," Micah barks. "You know she's safer here, so cut the shit." Why the fuck did it have to be him?

"Why the fuck do you even care?"

Micah's eyes narrow. "You might not think highly of me, but I won't stand for a man hitting a woman. If you take her out of my protection, you're signing her death warrant when Aaron finds you."

"I can protect her on my own. I can find us a safe house." I answer as calmly as I can. After sleeping with Evie in my arms last night, the last thing I wanted to do was let her get closer to Mateo. My head is all fucked up. One minute I'm okay with it because he makes her happy, and then I want to grab her and run.

"You have a safe house. And it's right here," Micah retorts. "If you don't want to be here, you know where the fucking door is. But she stays."

I count to ten in my head before I open my mouth again. "I'm not leaving her here alone."

"Then I suggest you shut up and take the help that's being handed to you. You're lucky I didn't shoot you on sight for what you did to Les."

I could sit here and argue this all day, but the truth is, I do need Micah's help. Aaron and the Bulls are violent and unpredictable. I couldn't put Evie at risk like that. I would have to suck it up and accept this for what it is. "Fine," I agree.

Micah smiles, but it's not friendly. "If I find out this is your way of gathering information on us, I'll scatter your body parts all over fucking Abbs Valley."

"Does Evie look like someone capable of being a goddamn part of that?"

Micah shrugs. "Maybe, maybe not. But you're an opportunist bastard that would use any excuse to bring us down."

"This isn't what this is about!" I yell, my patience finally running out. "I don't give a fuck what you do! All I care about is that woman out there."

Micah stands up and braces his fists on the desk when he leans forward. "I would think twice about raising your voice, Cruz." He nods his head at Gray. "He doesn't like it when people get loud." Gray is towering behind Micah, promising pain with his eyes. "Get the fuck out of my face."

I suck up everything I want to say and storm out of the office. I know I owe him, but goddamn, he pushes every button I have. I go straight for the back patio, the one Evie called paradise. She was right about that. It's built to where you could still see the view but tucked away like you are on your own private island. I sink into one of the lounge chairs, letting the tension bleed out.

Micah and I have gone round and round for years. I've seen some of the shit he's capable of but could never do anything about it.

"Can I give you some advice?" I look up at Mateo's voice; I hadn't even heard him walk out here. I gesture to the lounger beside me, and he sits down facing me. "Micah is only going to deal with so much shit. You need to get your head on straight and realize we aren't the enemies here."

"I've never been on this side," I tell him honestly. "I'm having a hard time separating who I was and who I am now."

Mateo sighs. "Look, man, I'm not going to excuse the bullshit you pulled with Les, but we all make fucking mistakes. That was yours. Yeah, we do bad shit." He shrugs. "But we do good shit, too. We had no control over the life we were raised in. Now's the time you need to realize that, or your time here will be harder than it needs to be."

I run my fingers through my hair. "I'll try. My main focus is Evie."

"Then quit fighting Micah every step of the way. She doesn't need the fighting all the goddamn time. That girl has been through some serious shit. The best way to help her through it is to make this as easy as possible." Mateo chuckles. "Now I have to have this conversation with Micah. Wish me luck."

He gets up and makes his way into the house, leaving me with what he said. I don't want to make this harder for her; it's hard enough as it is.

Laying with her in my arms last night was everything I've dreamed of for fucking years. I didn't want to leave her when I was eighteen, but she wasn't ready at sixteen for what I wanted. My goal was to start my career and return for her, but by then, she was with Aaron; I thought all hope was lost. She seemed so in love when I talked to her that I started distancing myself from her, too crushed to talk to her like everything was fine. Maybe if I had kept in contact more, I would have been able to pick up on when things changed. Or I could have realized who that asshole was and went to save her before shit got bad.

Either way, I'm not letting her go now. Evie is finally going to be mine.

CHAPTER 16
EVIE

M y life has taken a serious turn, and I don't know what
to do.

Being around Mateo all the time is amazing, but I
feel so out of place here.

Mateo and Evander's house is so huge that I am afraid to wander
anywhere by myself. The house I grew up in would fit in their living
room.

I knew Mateo had money just from the expensive clothes and
cars, but I didn't feel intimidated by it because he never gave me a
reason to be. All the dates he took me on were for me. He didn't do
anything to show off or shove it into my face. He always made sure I
was comfortable no matter what we were doing, and it's no different
now.

What I couldn't wrap my head around is him saying he wants to
be with me. We just met, and he doesn't know half of my past, but
none of that seems to bother him. He makes me feel things I haven't
felt in a long time. Happiness, confidence, desire, *lust*. I felt those
things initially with Aaron, but that ended quickly. I had to do what
Aaron wanted me to do; I have a choice with Mateo. I've never felt
pushed or rushed by him. Feeling his body sliding against mine twice
now stirred things in me that I didn't think I could feel anymore. But

things are still moving at lightning speed, just like they did with *him*. I don't want to compare the two because Mateo is *nothing* like Aaron, but I can't help but worry if I am getting into another mess.

Then there is his revelation about Gray. I was shocked at first. Not because Mateo was bisexual but because he was seeing Gray and me at the same time. I saw how Mateo's face lit up when he talked about him, which quickly turned my shock into curiosity. Gray doesn't seem upset with me being around, so I have to take Mateo's word that I'm not coming between them.

Gray is gorgeous in his own right. He is taller than Mateo and broader. His black cropped hair, watchful hazel eyes, and square jaw give him an intimidating appearance. But I'm not intimidated by him. I find his presence almost... peaceful. Like with him by my side, nothing could touch me.

Everyone made me feel at home here, including Evander. He is careful around me, like he's afraid I'd shatter if he were too loud. And it's almost eerie how much he and Mateo look alike.

The one I am intimidated by is Micah. I feel he doesn't want me here and would catch him watching me. It's like he is waiting for me to screw up. And I get the feeling he doesn't like me around Evander. Not that I would ever dream of doing anything. I saw how they looked at each other in the kitchen that day. All they saw was each other.

Micah is completely different now than the night he saved me. That night, he was sweet and caring. Now he's barely said two words to me since he ordered me to let them help me. I wanted to bite back, but so many black eyes made me seal my lips shut and nod.

"Buttercup." Mateo sticks his head through his bedroom door, and I'm slammed with guilt for falling asleep with Hartley last night. I only went in there to talk to him, and the next thing I knew, it was morning, and Mateo wasn't home. "What're you doing in here?" He doesn't look mad, but I know how fast that could change.

"I just took a shower and got dressed. Where did you go?"

"I had some things to take care of for work." He sits beside me on the bed and kisses my cheek. "Was Micah nice while I was gone?"

I shrug. "He doesn't talk to me much."

"You have to give him time. Micah is...well, Micah is Micah." Mateo laughs. "It takes him a while to warm up to new people."

"I don't think he trusts me," I say quietly. I don't know why that bothers me so badly.

"Micah doesn't trust many people."

We lapse into silence, and I can't stop the flutters that Mateo is mad about Hartley, and he hasn't said anything yet. "Are you mad at me?" I blurt.

He frowns. "Why would I be mad at you?"

"Because I slept in Hartley's room last night."

"Buttercup, he's your friend. Unless you guys were straight banging it out, I'm not mad."

I stare at him to see if he's serious when I see his lips twitch. I punch his arm. "Mateo! No! He's my best friend."

"Les married her best friend. Should I be worried?"

"Stop," I laugh.

"Seriously though, no, I'm not mad. Hartley needs a friend as much as you do."

"He told me what happened." I can understand why Micah is upset about it. I couldn't imagine the Hartley I grew up with doing something like that. But I don't know Hartley anymore. I can see the old him peeking through sometimes, but he is buried under whatever happened to him in the five years since we've seen each other.

Mateo sighs. "I love Les like a sister, and it fucking sucks what they went through. Could Hartley have done more? Sure, but it's in the past. Did he tell you what he did to make up for it?"

I shake my head. "No. He didn't even want to tell me the first part."

"Hartley's ashamed of what he did, and he *did* make up for it. But he needs to tell you that himself, too."

"You're kind of perfect; you know that?" He really is. He has such a big heart and a kind soul.

"You are the perfect one." He kisses the tip of my nose, making me laugh. "We're heading out in a bit to talk to some guys Hartley found."

"You're going?" That thought scares me. These are a bunch of businessmen going to talk to gangs. Ghost and Caden are the ones who seem to fit the bill to do that. They made me really uneasy at first, but the more they talked yesterday, the more at ease I felt.

"The sooner we find Aaron, the safer you'll be. Gray's going to stay here with you."

"Can't you stay with me?" I have nothing against Gray, but I would do anything to keep Mateo from going. I feel like they are getting way over their heads, but they won't listen to me when I try to tell them that.

"Buttercup, I can handle myself." He rubs his knuckles down my cheek. "But if you want me to stay, I will."

Just like that, my nerves settle until I think about the others going.

"Quit worrying." Mateo laughs, reading my mind.

I'm not used to having help, and I don't know how to act because of it.

I just hope they know what they are doing.

GRAY DIDN'T END up going with the others. Micah assured him they would be fine, so he, Evander, and Hartley left about an hour ago, and I've been a ball of nerves since.

"Will you stop fidgeting?" Mateo says. Me, him, and Gray are watching a movie in the living room, and I am tucked into Mateo's side. Gray is on the love seat, and I caught him watching us a few times. I couldn't tell if he was looking at Mateo or me, though.

"I can't help it," I huff.

"They're capable of taking care of themselves," Gray soothes.

"Will you call and check on them?" I ask, and both guys chuckle. "I'm serious." I have this feeling in the pit of my stomach that I can't get rid of. They walked into dangerous territory for me. I couldn't live with myself if something happens to them. They agreed to help me without hesitation. I still couldn't figure out why.

Mateo, I understand, even though I still feel like he should run the other way.

With a roll of his eyes, Mateo pulls out his phone and dials a number.

"Hello?" Evander's smooth voice answers. He and Mateo even sound the same, except Mateo's voice is just a bit raspier.

"Everything good, bro?"

Silence. "We're good. Why?"

"Evie said you were a bunch of pussies who couldn't handle yourselves, so she made me call."

"Mateo! I didn't say that!"

Evander chuckles. "Tell Evie we're fine."

"Will do. Anything?"

"Not yet. Maybe some potentials."

"Tell Micah to use his don't fuck with me voice."

"He has been. You know how this goes."

"I know. Someone will step forward, or we step harder."

My frown deepens the longer this conversation goes on. It's like they've done this before, but that's ridiculous.

"You know it," Evander replies. "I'm going to go, and Evie?"

My head snaps to the phone at the sound of my name. "Yeah?"

"Stop worrying." The line goes dead, and I'm still staring at the phone.

"Yeah, buttercup, stop worrying." Mateo laughs.

I huff and cross my arms, making him laugh harder. "It's not funny."

"I think it's cute how worried you are about them," Mateo says, kissing the side of my head. "If they get into trouble, they'll call the incredible hulk over there." If anyone could handle something, it would be Gray. Mateo said he was Micah's bodyguard, and I could see why. But if he is, why didn't he go with them?

I giggle at Mateo's name for Gray. Gray shakes his head, but I can see his cheeks start to darken. Is he blushing? That's incredibly cute.

"I'm not the hulk," Gray says, looking at Mateo with a glare.

"Yeah, you are. I'm just waiting for something to piss you off so you'll hulk out and rip your shirt off." I look up at Mateo, and he's grinning from ear to ear. This is the dynamic I wanted to see between them.

"That's not going to happen."

"That's a shame." Mateo shakes his head sadly, and I snort a laugh, causing Gray's hazel eyes to slide to me.

"Don't encourage him."

I grin at him, and Gray's brows furrow before he looks back at the TV. What the hell was that?

Mateo pulls me closer to his side, and I go willingly. Doubts still plague me about him and me, but it feels too good to pass up.

"I'm going to go check on the guards," Gray says, standing up from the love seat. Without another word, he leaves the room.

"Is he okay?" Is he mad about me cuddling with Mateo?

"Yeah. He doesn't sit still for long."

"Are you sure he's okay with us?"

Mateo tilts my face up to his. "He's more than okay with it, buttercup. Gray's not used to just sitting around."

"Then why did he stay?"

Mateo shrugs. "I wanted you to spend time with him, too. Get to know him, so maybe this whole thing wouldn't be weird."

"It's not weird to me, Mateo. I know it should be, but it's not," I tell him honestly. Most girls would have probably been pissed that he had someone else in his life, and maybe I should have been.

A look crosses Mateo's face before I can decipher it, and then his lips are on mine, and all thoughts fly from my head.

Mateo's kisses are almost like a drug. His lips are full but not overly so, and he could turn me into a puddle with one touch. They glide so effortlessly over mine, and when his tongue strokes mine, I couldn't stop the noise from escaping.

Without taking his lips from mine, Mateo turns and starts leaning into me until I'm lying on the couch, with his body over top of me. He lets the bottom half of his body rest between my thighs, kissing me harder. *Holy shit.*

Wrapping my arms around his neck, I run my fingers through the hair on the back of his head and feel his body shiver against mine. Do I have the same effect on him that he does on me? A moment later,

Mateo grinds his hips down, and I have my answer when I feel his hardness against me.

My hips raise on their own, trying to feel him again, and he answers by swiveling his hips and groaning into my mouth.

I feel his hand sliding down the outside of my thigh and wonder what it would feel like to feel him skin on skin. I could feel the hardness of his body against me and knew he was in great shape, but for the first time, I wanted to see it. His hand slides over my hip and under the hem of my shirt.

When I feel the warmth of his palm against my stomach, a flash of insecurity hits me so hard that my eyes fly open, and I reach down and grab his wrist to stop him.

He sits back on his knees immediately. I look up and expect anger in his eyes, but all I see is understanding.

"I'm sorry...."

"Don't you dare apologize, buttercup. I got carried away." He reaches down and hauls me into a sitting position. "Why don't we take a tour of the house?" He kisses me again, but it's soft and sweet this time.

I know he is trying to distract me and probably himself from what just happened, but I appreciate it nonetheless. I could feel the stirring of arousal with Mateo; how could you not? But I'm just not ready for that step yet.

But how long will he be this patient?

CHAPTER 17
GRAY

I feel like such an asshole.

When Evie smiled at me inside, it was like my world tilted on its axis, and all I saw was her. I know Mateo told me to study away, but I'm sure that didn't mean me checking out his girl.

So, I came to their guardhouse and told the guys to take a break and that I would watch the cameras. They didn't even question me.

I needed to feel useful and didn't while I was here. It took everything in me not to tell Mateo no when he asked me to stay here with him and Evie, but I wanted to get to know her for him. Then I ended up getting lost in those big brown eyes.

The door opens, and I expect one of the guards to step back through, but it's Mateo, and I'm hit with a sudden round of guilt.

He slides onto the desk beside the wall of monitors, just like he does at Micah's. "What're you doing here?"

"I just needed to do something."

Mateo tilts his head to the side, studying me. "Bullshit. What's wrong?" I don't even know why I tried to lie; Mateo could read me like a fucking book.

"Where's Evie?" I ask, ignoring his question.

"In the library. Apparently, she likes to read. She was like a kid in a candy store, so I left her alone. Now tell me what's wrong."

"What did you mean yesterday when you told me I could study her?"

"Is that what this is about?" I nod, and Mateo sighs. "This whole thing is fucking with me. I expected her to be mad about us, but she wasn't. Then she said something that I haven't stopped thinking about."

"What did she say?"

"She said it was kind of like me, you, and her were all together. And I didn't hate the idea." I know the shock shows all over my face because Mateo chuckles. "It would be the best of both worlds."

I shake my head. "I could never do that, Mateo. She's your girl."

"What if she was *our* girl? Evie's not ready for that yet. Hell, she's not even ready for me yet, but I think it's something that could happen down the road."

"What are you saying?"

"I'm saying I've seen how she looks at you, and I don't even think she notices it when she does." He hops down off the desk. "And I've seen the way you look at her." Heat starts creeping into my cheeks before I can stop it. He steps between my thighs, leaning down on the arms of the chair just like he did the first day I kissed him. "She's beautiful, isn't she, Gray?"

I nod because the words are locked in my throat. Mostly with being this close to him again. His lips brush against mine, and my control snaps. My hand shoots out, wrapping around his throat so I can take control of this. Mateo's pupils flare, waiting to see what I'm going to do next. "Are you teasing me?"

Nothing has happened since that first kiss, even though we've spent every night together. I wanted to give him time with Evie before I made a move, and I think he was giving himself time, too. But now we are both tired of waiting. He told me he and Evie had made it official, and now that I know she is okay with us, I am ready to take the next step. Whatever that is.

"No." Mateo pushes out past my hold. "I want you to want her as much as I do. As much as I want *you*."

I seal my lips over his with a groan and stand up. I walk him back until he's pressed against the desk, and I can feel my body against his. It felt so fucking good the first time, but I wanted more. We just need to get something out of the way first.

I pull back from the kiss and tilt his face up with my thumb under his chin. "This has to be about more than sex." I wanted to be honest with him. I don't do meaningless hookups; it isn't who I am. I don't fault anyone for them, but I can't do it. I refuse to be like my mother.

"Gray, I didn't spend the last six months flirting just to have sex with you." I feel him swallow against my hand. "I feel...different about you."

"What does that mean?" I move my hands beside his hips, caging him against the desk.

"It means I've had sex once since I met you and felt empty afterward. That's never happened to me before." I could tell he's uncomfortable with this conversation. We both are. But we needed to be honest with each other if I wanted what I thought I wanted. Mateo is the only one I've ever opened up to. He still doesn't know everything because shame keeps me from telling him.

"So, this isn't just about sex?" I clarify.

When he shakes his head, I search his eyes, and the truth is staring right back at me. Our lips crash together again, and it's different this time. I could feel the tension between us building until it eventually snaps. I slide my tongue into his mouth, and he groans deep in his throat. His hands go to my hips, jerking me closer. Pulling away from the kiss, I reach over and flip the lock on the door. My lips go to his neck, and I can't get enough of his body rubbing against me, trying to get even closer.

"Holy shit," Mateo whispers. Holy shit is fucking right. "I woke the beast."

I bark a laugh. He has no idea what he's just woken up. My hand goes to his throat. I tighten my grip and watch his eyelids flutter. "You wanted this," I remind him and slam my lips back against his.

I dominate his mouth, not giving him a chance to take over, and he lets me. He runs his hands under my shirt, up my back, and I can feel the skin bunch under his touch. I need more. I lean back, jerk my shirt over my head, and look at him. His pupils are blown, color is high on his cheekbones, and he isn't shy about checking me out. "Who knew you had all that ink?" Mateo says hoarsely. He takes a finger and traces the tribal art that works its way up my pec, and my whole body shudders. The tattoo runs up my ribs, my pec, over my shoulder, and turns into one big piece on my back.

"Off," I say and gesture to his shirt. I sounded like a caveman, but I couldn't string two words together to save my fucking life right now. He raises a brow but does what I say. My eyes zero in on the Perez tattoo on his pec. I trace my finger over it like he did mine, and he bites his bottom lip. Mateo is broad in the shoulders and lean in the waist. I never wanted to run my tongue over a guy's abs until right now.

"What do you want to do, Gray?" Mateo asks.

"Go slow."

Mateo nods, understanding. "I'm not that much of a fucking animal. I do have some self-control," he jokes, releasing some tension in my shoulders. His hands go to my jeans, and he pauses, asking that silent question. I nod.

He unfastens them and pulls until they pool around my boots, my cock springing free. He wraps his hand around it, and I can't stop the groan that rips from my chest. I haven't been with someone for a long damn time, too fucking long. Mateo and I have been dancing around this for months, and it's time we make it happen.

He strokes from base to tip in a tight grip. "I knew your cock would be huge," he comments. I breathe a laugh, and he smiles. "You want my hand or mouth?"

"Mouth," I push out past a dry throat. He sinks to his knees in front of me, eyes locked on mine, and his tongue circles the head of my cock. He tests my reaction a few times before sinking his mouth slowly down. He hollows his cheeks, sucking hard, and brings his mouth back up. "Shit," I grunt.

He takes my hand and places it on the back of his head, giving me permission to control it. I tighten my fist in his thick brown hair and fuck his mouth with shallow thrusts, watching his green eyes darken with lust. I push his limits, slide in, and feel him relax, taking me into his throat. Goddamn, he could suck a dick.

I feel him shift and look down past his face. He's pulled his cock out and is roughly stroking it in time with my thrusts into his mouth. His dick is long and veiny, and I wonder what he would taste like.

His other hand comes up to my ass, pulling me forward, encouraging me to fuck his mouth harder. I don't need any more encouragement than that. I place both hands on the side of his face and start fucking his mouth hard; he moans around the head.

"Fuck, your mouth feels good," I rasp, moving faster. I can feel the stubble on his jaw under my palms, which spurs me to go harder. I push in until his nose touches my pubic bone, and his throat bulges with my cock, stealing his breath. His eyes roll back in his head, and I can't take it anymore; I piston my hips forward. The wet slurping from his mouth stretched around my fat cock, and my harsh breathing echoes around the small room. I watch as he starts stroking his cock faster, just as turned on as me. I could feel sweat gathering at my temples and rolling down my back; I wouldn't last much longer.

"I'm going to come," I warn, giving him the chance to back away. He keeps his hand firmly planted on my ass to bury me in his throat. My balls draw up, and my release blazes down my spine. The first jet of come hits his throat, and he moans around my cock, ripping one out of me in response. He swallows greedily around the head, and I watch in fascination as he comes all over his hand.

He slides his mouth off my cock and gives me one of his signature grins. "Damn, you taste good," Mateo says breathlessly. I reach down and jerk him to his feet. I pull his hand, the one with come all over it, to my mouth. Then lick it. I wanted to taste him, too. "Oh, fuck," Mateo groans.

"You do too," I rasp when it's clean.

"That was fucking hot," Mateo says, running his hands up my chest. "How was your first trip to the wild side?"

I step against him until our bare cocks touch. "I want more," I tell him honestly.

"I can arrange that," Mateo says, sealing his mouth over mine. Fuck. I wanted to bend him over this desk, but I wanted to take my time with this.

Pounding on the door has us jerking apart. We get our clothes situated, and I peck his lips before opening the door. "To be continued."

"You bet your fine ass it will be, Gray."

MICAH CALLED RIGHT before dinner and said to meet him at his house. Mateo, Evie, and I pile into my truck to drive over, and the whole cab is filled with their scents. Mateo's is the cologne I've gotten used to, and Evie's is a subtle coconut. And it's driving me insane, even after my time with Mateo.

After we left the guard house, we made our way back to the house, where we barely made it in the front door before our lips were fused together again. I had him pressed against the door when I heard footsteps in the hallway and pulled away before Evie could see us. I wasn't ready to share this side of myself with her, no matter what Mateo said. It runs through my head repeatedly, and I catch myself looking at her in the rearview mirror. She's looking out her window and seems to be lost in thought. Would she be mad to know what happened between Mateo and me?

Mateo changes the song again, pulling my attention back to him. I push his hand away. "Will you stop?"

"Your music tastes are shit, Gray."

"I like his music," Evie says quietly.

"She likes my music," I say smugly, making Evie giggle. God, I could bottle that sound.

Mateo turns in the seat to face her. "How dare you? You're supposed to be on my side, buttercup."

"Not when you're wrong," she replies, giving him that smile she gave me earlier that made my heart beat a little too fast.

"Well." Mateo flops back in his seat. "I see how it's going to be. Just gang up on me; it's fine." Evie falls into laughter and leans up between the seats. That coconut smell that sticks to her skin gets even stronger.

"That's just a bit dramatic, don't ya think?" she teases. She seems less tense now that she knew the other guys were home safely. It was sweet that she worried so much about them, and I wish I could tell her why she didn't need to. Mateo eventually has to tell her who he is, but I left that up to him.

"Dramatic?" Mateo swings back to face her, and she laughs again. "I'm not dramatic."

I snort. "You're proving her point right now."

"You are," she agrees. She pecks his lips and pulls back just as fast. She sits back in the seat, and I catch her eyes in the mirror. I smile to let her know that was okay. I don't want them to hide from me. She takes a breath and returns my smile. I know none of this is easy for her.

"Fuck, I hope Micah is cooking." Mateo groans. "I'm so hungry."

"You're always hungry," I say dryly. I've never seen someone put away as much food as he did.

"Right?" Evie laughs. "It's like he's a bottomless pit."

"I'm not that bad," Mateo laughs. "Micah's food is the best, though. I could seriously eat my weight in whatever he cooks."

I nod because I could too.

I swing my truck in front of the house, and Mateo hops out, giving Evie the evil eye when she opens her door. With a sigh, she shuts it back. Mateo opens it with a grin and helps her out.

"I don't know why that's such a big deal," she says.

"Because you should never have to open your own door," I tell her.

"Ha! See." Mateo grins again, and she shakes her head with a smile.

"Wow," Evie breathes, looking up at Micah's house. "It's so pretty."

Micah's house is sleek and full of windows. The inside is all black marble and neutral colors. Thanks to Les, little feminine touches here and there, but it is one hundred percent a bachelor pad.

Mateo pushes the door open after keying in the code. "Honey, I'm home!" he yells.

"In here!" Micah yells back. We follow his voice into the kitchen.

"Oh, thank god," Mateo breathes when he sees Micah preparing steak.

"I'm going to put these on the grill," Micah says, picking up the tray. "We'll talk over dinner."

Without a backward glance, he disappears through the door. I didn't miss the tightening of his shoulders when his gaze slid over Evie. He asked me yesterday if I trusted her, and I do. Now I wonder if there is more to that question than what he was asking. Does he not trust her? I didn't pick up anything from her that would suggest she is untrustworthy, and my gut has gotten me this far.

I look at her, and she's frowning like she caught it, too. "Come on, buttercup," Mateo says, pulling on her hand. She was relaxed on the way over; now, her shoulders are tucked in like she is trying to hide. I don't like that. Her eyes find mine, and she seems to relax again when she sees me following behind them. I wasn't used to people looking at me that way.

Maybe Mateo is right.

CHAPTER 18

EVANDER

Micah pushes onto the back patio with a tray full of steaks and a scowl on his face. It took a while when we were out with Hartley, but eventually, Micah relaxed around him, and now he looks ready to spit nails.

"What's wrong?" I ask, walking to stand beside him.

He jerks the grill open. "Nothing."

"Micah," I warn. I knew he was lying to me, and he knows I want him to be open with me.

He loads the steaks on the grill, closes the lid, and turns to me. But his eyes slide past my shoulder, and they narrow. I turn around to see Evie step out onto the patio with Mateo and Gray and turn back to him. Is she his problem? He was all about helping her. Did he change his mind? That doesn't sound like him; he would do anything for a woman in trouble. "What's your deal?" I ask.

His eyes slide back to mine, and his expression evens out. "Nothing. I need to grab some stuff from inside." He steps around me, making a fast clip into the house. What the fuck?

"Hey, Evie," I smile. She turns to me from where she was watching Micah disappear into the house.

"Hi," she greets with a little wave.

Mateo leads her over to the table, pulling her chair out. I try to keep the shock off my face but know I failed when he glares at me over her head. It looks like I needed to talk with my brother. "What's his problem?" Mateo asks, sitting beside Evie.

I take my chair in front of them while Gray sits on her other side. "I'm sure it's nothing." Evie's chewing on her bottom lip, looking more than a little stressed out. "What did you guys do today?"

"We watched a movie, and then I lost Evie to the library," Mateo answers.

She smiles. "It's like my favorite place ever now."

"You like to read?" I ask.

"I do. It's a nice escape from reality."

I nod, agreeing. I used to hide to read growing up, getting lost in the books to pretend I was anywhere but with Frankie. He hated to see me reading, so when Mateo and I built our house, I made the biggest fucking library possible. "Did anything catch your eye?"

Evie giggles. "So much. I could live in there for days."

"If I don't have what you want, let me know, and I'll add some more."

"Evie likes dirty books," Mateo says with a grin, making her face bloom with color. Before I can fuss at him for embarrassing her, she smacks his arm.

"They're called romance. How do you know, anyway?"

"Same thing, and your stuff is in my room, remember? Hartley or Gray must have grabbed your smut stash."

I hide my smile with my hand when she turns her glare on Gray. He shrugs. "We grabbed what we thought you wanted. We didn't snoop."

"What were you doing going through my stuff?" she asks, turning back to Mateo.

"I didn't. I went to move the bag, which was heavier than shit, and I got curious."

She laughs. "That's going through my stuff, Mateo."

He shrugs, unapologetic. "That's the only thing I looked at, and your choices are...interesting." Now I am curious, but I won't embarrass her any more than he already has.

Even with her cheeks blood red, she meets his stare head-on. "I like what I like."

"Oh really?" Mateo grins again, and I know whatever is about to come out of his mouth will be bad. "Ménage à trois is what you like, buttercup?"

Her mouth pops open. "Did you read them?"

"No," Mateo laughs. "I looked up the titles online. But those weren't even the best ones."

"Mateo," she warns.

"Stop," I tell my brother when he opens his mouth again. I could tell she was uncomfortable with his teasing in front of us. I look back at her. "There is nothing wrong with what you read. Enjoy the library any time."

"Thank you," Evie says softly. "Where's Hartley?"

"With Ghost and Caden," I answer. Mateo's eyebrows hit his hairline. "He should be back soon, though."

"With Ghost and Caden?" Mateo asks slowly. "Why?" It was a shock to me when he went. He proved very useful today when we pressed those assholes for information on Aaron, which is why I think Micah relaxed around him.

"Ghost called and said they were headed to ask some more questions, and Hartley asked to go." Micah half told Ghost to take him because he could help, and the other half so he didn't have to be around Hartley.

"Good." Mateo slides his arm around Evie's shoulders, leaning back in his chair. "We need answers. People like that aren't loyal; someone will spill."

"Why do I feel like you guys are talking in code?" Evie asks, looking between us. I can't tell her we are because, to her, we are just a bunch of rich assholes.

"Because it's none of your concern," Micah says, walking up behind her.

"It is my concern. This is about me," Evie replies. I watch Micah's jaw clench.

"It is about you." Micah tilts his head to the side. "Maybe if you gave us more information, we wouldn't have to do all the leg work."

Evie frowns. "I told you he didn't tell me anything."

"How long were you with him again?" Micah retorts.

"A year."

"So, in that year, you didn't *accidentally* hear him talking about business?" Micah asks skeptically. I don't miss the emphasis on accidentally. Micah doesn't trust her; that much is clear now. Is he seeing something we don't?

"Micah," Mateo barks. "That's enough."

"No, it's okay," Evie says, laying her hand on Mateo's arm. "I tried not to because any time I did, it didn't end well for me." I see the fear flash across her face, and that's not something you can fake. Micah watches her like a hawk, trying to catch her up in a lie. I trusted his instincts, so I needed to make a point to ask him what the hell he was thinking.

Dinner was tense as hell. Ghost, Caden, and Hartley showed up right before, and I thought we could all enjoy a meal for Evie's sake, but I was wrong. Micah said very little, and he kept eyeing her suspiciously. After dinner was done, I found him in his office.

I sit in the chair in front of his desk, and he doesn't look up from his laptop. "Micah."

Before he can look up, the door busts open, and Mateo slams it behind him. "What the fuck is wrong with you?" Mateo growls. Mateo is seething; I can see it in the set of his jaw. That doesn't happen often, and when it does; it never ends well.

"Excuse me?" Micah says, looking up with a glare.

"She didn't deserve you treating her like that."

Micah waves his hand. "You don't even know her well enough to make that assessment. And this is my house."

"And that is *my* girl," Mateo grits, and my eyes widen in surprise. *When did that happen?* "I don't know what the fuck your problem is, but you won't talk to her like that."

"Come on, Mateo. You don't find this thing fucking suspicious?"

"What?" Mateo and I ask at the same time.

"It can't be a coincidence that she showed up at Les' reception, meets you, then me, and then shows up with fucking Hartley Cruz to be saved."

"Do you hear yourself?" Mateo asks with exasperation. "You know what Les told you about Hartley. I don't see him trying anything against us. It would be too easy to fucking kill him now."

"This isn't about Cruz. This is about her." Micah stands from his chair. "You've known her for a week."

"So what? You two knew each other for less time before you started messing around," Mateo argues.

"That was different," Micah retorts.

"It's not different." Mateo points at him. "You need to think about what you're saying. Has she given you any inclination that she was fucking us over? I know the answer to that. No. Evie isn't like that. I believe everything she's said, and if you don't want to fucking help, that's fine with me. I can handle it. I'm going to take her home before you can say any other crazy shit." Mateo jerks the door open and spears Micah with a look. "If you ever talk to or about her like that again, I won't hesitate to slit your goddamn throat." The door slams behind him, and I turn to Micah.

He flops down in his chair with a sigh. "I don't like this."

"Micah, I get that we've always had to watch our backs in these situations, but I don't think that's the case here."

"You're taking his side? You trust her?"

"He's my brother, and I trust him. If something is off about her, he will figure it out."

"So until then, you're just going to let her walk around your house waiting for the other shoe to drop?"

"Is this really just about trusting her, or is there something else?" Something else is lurking in Micah's eyes, something I've only seen once. Insecurity. Just as fast as I see it, it's gone.

"It's just about that. She's going to end up fucking Mateo over." He looks back down at his computer, blocking me out completely. I couldn't let him revert to old habits when shit got hard; he shut down. I stand up and walk over to his side of his desk, not giving him a chance to shut me out.

"Micah. Talk to me."

"I have nothing else to say. If you want to join them, you're welcome to leave."

Reigning my temper in, I shut his laptop softly instead of slamming it like I wanted to. "Are you jealous of her?"

Micah scoffs. "No." I tilt his face up to mine, and I see plain as day all over his face.

"You have no reason to be jealous, *mi rey*. Am I going to deny that she's a beautiful girl? No. But *you* are who I want."

His hands slide up the back of my thighs. "It's not that. I can't explain it. It's just this gnawing in my stomach that something is going to go very wrong, and I'm going to lose you."

"To her?" That's insane. She's with my brother, and I would never step over that line, no matter how many girls we've shared before. Evie seems different to him, and I am happy for him.

"In general, *amore mio*." Micah swallows, and I wait for him to gather his thoughts. It's never been his thing to talk about feelings, but with me, he tries. "I don't deserve you after what I did."

"Where is this coming from?" I thought we had moved past that.

"I feel like you're holding a part of yourself back from me." I frown. Am I? That wasn't my intention. I just wanted to go slower than the supersonic speed we were going before. I asked him to be honest with me, and I needed to give him the same respect.

I prop my hip on his desk. "I lost a part of myself when I was with you last time. You *consumed* me. When you ripped the rug from under my feet, I was so fucking lost, Micah. I have to protect my heart." I think back to our conversation before it started dissolving around us.

We were still staying in Les' pool house, and I had just realized that I was in love with him, and I couldn't do this with him anymore if he wasn't all in. So, I sucked up every bit of courage and approached him when Mateo went to the main house to talk to the others.

"Micah, we need to talk." I cross my arms over my chest and wait for

him to turn around. He is at the stove, shirtless and cooking. Why does he have to be so irresistible?

"About what?" He pops what he's making into the oven and turns around.

"I can't do this anymore."

He frowns. "Do what?"

I gesture between us. "This."

"Okay," he says slowly, leaning his palms on the island separating us. "Why not?"

"Because this isn't just some experiment for me anymore. I know what I want, and that's you. But I can't do this if you aren't in it with me."

"Are you giving me an ultimatum, Van?"

"No. I'm telling you that I'm done hiding what we're doing. I don't want to be some dirty little secret. If that's the path you choose, then I'm done."

"That's an ultimatum," Micah grits out.

"It's not a goddamn ultimatum. It's me telling you that I like you, and I want more."

"I told you from the beginning that I don't do relationships."

"Then that's all I need to know." With my heart cracking in two, I turn to leave the kitchen.

His hand snags my arm and spins me to face him. "I'm not saying never; I'm just saying I'm not ready yet. You're special to me, amore mio, but I'm just not there."

And just like that, I believed him. Until he accused me of being clingy when it was him sneaking into my room every night.

"I'll never hurt you again, *amore mio*. I can protect your heart if you let me." I see the sincerity in his blue eyes. Micah is finally where I wanted him to be, so why am I holding back?

"You have to give me time."

I see the disappointment all over his face, and I want to take it back. He nods, pushes back from the desk, and stands up. "Take all the time you need."

He leaves the room, leaving me staring at the door.

If I don't get my shit together, I will end up pushing him away, and that's not what I want.

CHAPTER 19
MATEO

When we got back to the house after that disastrous dinner with Micah, Evie disappeared upstairs. I gave her some time and gave myself some to get my temper in check.

Micah has always been an asshole; I've gotten used to the fact that it's just his personality, but he's never been outwardly rude like he was to Evie, and it made my blood boil. I wanted to punch my best friend for how he treated her, but something in his eyes made me pause. Micah was fighting something inside himself, so I just left him with a threat of death and took my girl home with Gray.

I floated on goddamn cloud nine after spending the day with Evie and everything that went down between Gray and me. We finally stepped over that line, and there is no turning back now. I finally got it out in the open to Gray that I wanted him to pursue Evie, so maybe we could have what she suggested. I know it was a joke, but like I told Gray, I saw how she watched him. Then Micah had to be a super douche and ruin it all.

Taking the stairs two at a time, ready to talk to Evie, I push my bedroom door open. She spins around in nothing but bra and panties, and I'm struck fucking speechless. Then I remember my manners. "Shit, buttercup, I'm sorry." I close the door but can't get the vision out of my head. She is thicker than I first thought, and goddamn, if that doesn't make my dick pay attention. *Settle down, asshole.* I need to remember I have a roommate and not just bust into a room.

"You can come in now."

I push the door back open, and Evie's sitting on the side of the bed, fully dressed, with her shoulders slumped. *Shit.* I know how she reacted when I tried to touch her downstairs. "Hey, buttercup. I just came to check on you."

"I'm fine." She sniffs, and I see red. Is she crying over what Micah said? I take it back; I still want to punch my best friend in the face.

"What's wrong?"

"Nothing."

"Buttercup," I plead. "Talk to me."

"I saw your face, Mateo; you don't have to pretend anymore." Wait, what?

"I don't follow."

"Just now. I know I'm not built like other girls." Her voice is so small, unlike the Evie I've gotten used to. "It's okay if you don't like it."

"Buttercup, I fucking love it." I step into the room and shut the door. Is this coming from her ex or her? I could only imagine the poisonous shit he filled her head with.

"You don't have to lie." She jumps from the bed, whirling to face me, swiping tears from her cheeks. "I get you're just trying to protect my feelings, but you don't have to. I get it; I do. I'm built like this, and you're built like that. I'm big and not the usual girl you go after. Now you're stuck babysitting an emotional train wreck." She cuts off her rambling by tucking her lips in. I love when she gets nervous and word vomits everything; it's cute.

"Are you done?" I ask, humor lacing my voice. Her face blooms with color, but she nods, letting her eyes drop to the floor. I tuck her hair behind her ear, tracing my fingers down her cheek until I reach her chin, tipping her eyes back to mine.

"My face just now? You saw every filthy thing I wanted to do to you. And I don't think you're an emotional train wreck. I think you're someone who went through some heavy shit, and you haven't realized how fucking strong you are." I let that sink in and move my hand to cup the side of her face, my thumb rubbing the tear rolling down her cheek away.

"You're built to perfection, buttercup," I declare. "I never want to hear another negative thing come out of your mouth talking about that gorgeous body like that." She doesn't push me away, so I move in closer. "*You* are fucking gorgeous."

"Mateo," Evie says breathlessly. Her chest is rising and falling as hard as mine. She has me all kinds of fucked up.

"Let me kiss you," I beg. I feel like this is a pivotal moment between us, and I wanted to feel her lips moving against mine. I don't even let her fully nod before I slant my mouth over hers with a groan. Her hands land on my chest when I drag her flush against me. She's tentative when I stroke her tongue with mine but gets bolder the longer I kiss her, just like she always does. When she moans into my mouth, I'm done. I pull my mouth away and grind my hips against her, showing her exactly what she does to me. "You feel that?" I ask hoarsely. "Let me show you what you do to me."

I know I need to go slow with her; I have no clue what that motherfucker put her through. But right now, she isn't thinking about that. Her eyes are glued to my face, wide open and trusting. For whatever reason, Evie trusts me. And I am going to prove to her that she can. She nods shyly, and I reach for the hem of her shirt, asking for permission with my eyes to take it off; she nods again.

I pull it from her body and have to bite my lip to keep from groaning again. Her huge breasts are pushed up in a white lacy bra, and I want to bury my face in them.

"Take yours off," Evie whispers, and I oblige, quickly whipping it over my head. Her hands return to my chest, spreading her fingers wide, and I can't stop the groan this time. Her finger traces over my Perez tattoo, and I feel like I am going to come in my pants like a damn teenager, just from her touch.

I hook my thumbs into her yoga pants and pull them from her thick hips. I help her step out of them, leaving her in just a bra and panties again. I take a step away to get a better look, and her arms come up, trying to hide.

"Don't do that. Don't you dare hide from me," I tell her sternly. I step back and turn her, so we both face the large mirror on the wall.

"You know what I see when I look at you?" I tell her, running my hands down her sides. "I see a beautiful woman." I move my hands to cup her breasts, my tan skin contrasting with her creamy white skin. "I see big beautiful breasts that I want to bury my face between and suffocate," I say, and she giggles, some of the tension leaving her body. It had its intended effect. I move my hands to her hips. "I see hips I've been dying to sink my hands into." I move my hands down the front of her panties, making her gasp. "I see thighs I want to bury my face between. But most of all, I see you, Evie. Nothing about you is wrong. Everything about you is beautiful. From the tips of your brown hair to the tips of your cute little toes." I kiss up her neck. "Do you trust me?" She nods, and I almost melt with relief. "Get on the bed." I hold my hand out for her and wait with bated breath as she hesitates. When she finally slides her hand into mine, I smile at her.

Taking her hand, I lead her over, helping her get situated. Once she's lying down, I stretch my body over hers and devour her mouth, soaking in every moan she makes when I grind my hard cock against her. I reach under her to unhook the bra and slide it down her arms. Pulling my lips from hers, I do exactly what I said I wanted to do and bury my face between her tits to kiss her chest. She giggles again. Her breasts spilled out everywhere; it was the best thing I'd ever seen. I push them together and suck her nipple into my mouth. Her back bows, pushing it further. I switch back and forth until her nipples are stiff peaks, and she's writhing underneath me. I let it go with a wet pop and look into her eyes. She looks vulnerable with her hair spilling onto the pillow and biting that bottom lip. I peck her lips once and move down her body, kissing each rib on both sides, kiss down her stomach, lick around her belly button, and feel her shiver.

When I get to her panties, I pause and look up at her to make sure she's still okay. She swallows and nods. I peel them down her thighs and almost die on the fucking spot. Her pussy is bare, pouty, and she is soaking wet. For me. "Damn," I whisper, running my finger through the slit. I kiss right above it and lean my head down to dive in.

"Mateo! Wait," Evie says breathlessly, sitting up and taking that delicious meal with her. My eyes snap to hers, and she looks close to panicking.

I sit back on my heels, pissed at myself for taking it that far. "I'm sorry, buttercup. I didn't mean to scare you."

"No! It's not that." She bites that lip again, looking nervous. "I've never done that before." I know my eyes show my shock because she blushes.

"No one has ever eaten that pussy before?" What kind of asshole doesn't please a woman the right way?

She shakes her head. "He was my first," Evie whispers. "And he wasn't always nice."

I close my eyes and count to ten. I am going to gut this mother-fucker. When I open them, I move back up the bed until she has to lie back. "We can stop."

"I don't want to stop," Evie says quietly.

"If we continue, I'm going to make sure you enjoy yourself. None of that half-ass bullshit. This is about you," I say, kissing her lips once.

Her eyes fill with tears. "I want that," she says.

I search her eyes again and make sure she isn't just doing this for me. I see lust staring back at me and maybe a little nervousness, but she wants this.

I start my slow trek down her body, making sure her nipples are stiff peaks again, and when I settle between her thighs this time, she doesn't stop me. I watch her face intently as I swipe my tongue through the slit and circle her clit.

"Oh," she breathes, her eyes latching onto mine. I take two fingers and tease her opening, moving them back and forth until her hips push down. I sink two fingers inside her and suck her clit into my mouth. Crooking them a little, I find that magic spot, and her thighs threaten to close on my head. *Smother me, buttercup.* "Oh god," Evie moans, and it comes from deep in her chest. My cock throbs from the noise. She is so wet, and her body responds just like I thought it would. I watch her cute blush spread from her cheeks and down her chest.

I move my fingers slowly while licking, flicking, and sucking her clit into my mouth. Her breasts are rising and falling rapidly. I continue until I feel her walls starting to clamp down on me and know she's close. She pushes my head away. *What the fuck?* "Why did you stop me, buttercup?" I ask in confusion.

"I felt weird," she answers, confused by my reaction. Has she never had an orgasm before, either?

"Yeah. You were about to come," I explain, still pumping my fingers in and out, keeping her on edge.

"I've never...." She trails off, but she answered my question.

"You're about to," I declare before diving back between her thighs.

"Mateo!" Evie exclaims, then moans again. "Holy shit."

I work my fingers faster, her greedy pussy trying to pull them back in each time I try to pull them out. I start rhythmically sucking her clit into my mouth, watching her face the whole time. She keeps twisting her hips, trying to escape my mouth, so I clamp a hand on one of those thighs and yank her back. "Let it go, buttercup," I say gruffly. "You're right there. Let it go."

"I can't," Evie groans, trying to pull away again.

Keeping my fingers buried in her, I move back up her body, working them against her g-spot, my thumb circling her clit. "You can," I breathe. "You're doing so good, buttercup."

She looks into my eyes, and whatever she sees there has her mouth parting, her back bowing. I push her clit harder with my thumb.

"Mateo!" Evie screams, and I feel her release soak my fingers. I slowly pull my fingers free, sucking them into my mouth to savor more of her flavor. "Oh god," Evie groans.

"You taste so fucking good," I say with a grin. I lean down until my mouth is at hers, giving her the chance to back away if she doesn't want to taste herself on my lips. She slams her lips against mine, and her hand slides down my abs to my cock. I let her massage it a few times through my shorts until I grab her wrist and pull her hand away. I kiss each fingertip. "This was about you," I remind her.

No matter how bad I want to sink into her pussy, now isn't the time.

"But you're...."

"Hard as a rock. Yep," I laugh.

"But won't it hurt?" Evie asks, and it's such an innocent damn question. That asshole filled her head with all kinds of bullshit I would wipe away.

"For a little bit," I tell her honestly. I gather her in my arms and get her head situated on my chest. She lays her hand on my stomach, and I feel the muscles bunching under my skin. "I'll be fine." I kiss the top of her head.

"That was awesome," Evie sighs, snuggling closer, pressing those tits against my side.

"I'm glad you liked it, buttercup," I reply. I've never taken a girl to bed and not gone down on her. A woman has to be prepared, and you are selfish as fuck if you don't make sure they like it and only take the enjoyment for yourself.

We lay there in silence, with me drawing patterns on her back with my fingertips, just enjoying each other's company, when her hand slid down again.

"Buttercup," I warn.

"I just want to see you too," she whispers.

I have plenty of self-control, but can I lie naked in bed with her without this going further than I know she is ready for? For Evie, I can.

Sliding my arm from under her head, I slide my shorts and boxers off. My cock slaps my stomach with a smack, and Evie giggles.

"You aren't supposed to laugh when a man pulls his cock out."

"I'm sorry." She bites her lip. "You're just really big."

I knew I was above average, but hearing that coming from Evie's innocent mouth makes my dick twitch.

"Can I touch it?" *Jesus Christ.*

"Yeah," I reply hoarsely. When she wraps her hand around me, I grunt. "Fuck."

"Is this okay?" she asks, stroking tentatively. I knew she wasn't a virgin, but she is so fucking innocent still.

I wrap my hand around hers, squeezing her hand, showing her how hard I liked it. I move her hand up my cock and swirl her hand around the head. "Yeah, buttercup, just like that." I let my hand drop and slide it between her thighs. She is soaking wet, and the first contact with my fingers to her clit, she moans deep in her throat. I haven't messed around like this with a girl in a long damn time, and it feels good just letting her explore. I turn my head and lock eyes with her. Keeping my eyes wide open, I let her see everything I'm feeling, not hiding a damn thing from her.

My fingers start moving faster on her clit, causing her strokes to speed up. "That feels so good, Mateo."

"You going to come for me again?"

"Yes," she moans, pumping her hand faster.

"Fuck, buttercup," I groan, moving my hips to fuck her fist. "Squeeze harder." She tightens her hand. I'm not going to fucking last. The first jet of come splashes onto my abs and just keeps coming. After my cock is spent, I dive between her legs. No way we are ending this without her coming again. This time, it's going to be on my tongue.

She spears her fingers into my hair, pulling me closer. Fuck yeah, she is feeling it now. I penetrate her with two fingers, rubbing her g-spot, my tongue working relentlessly on her clit. When I suck it into my mouth, she doesn't hold back this time. Her thighs tighten around my head, and her whole body tenses.

"Mateo!" she screams. I lick up everything her body has to offer, savoring the sweet flavor of her pussy.

I kiss her right on the clit when her body relaxes. "Good girl," I murmur against her thigh. "You're fucking amazing, buttercup."

Moving back up her body, I kiss her lips without hesitation.

If I thought I was addicted to her before, it has nothing on it now.

CHAPTER 20
HARTLEY

Ghost dropped me off at Mateo's after he stormed out with Evie and Gray. I had no idea what was up Micah's ass now, but he was a dick through dinner, and it wasn't aimed at me.

We talked to everyone I found on that list, and everyone swore they didn't know where Aaron was, and a few said they didn't even know who they were. So, Micah and I started playing hardball, throwing out threats left and right. I hated to admit how good that felt to be able to say what I wanted without repercussions. All tension aside, we made a damn good team.

I wanted to say something about how he was talking to Evie, but when I got back there, I heard what Mateo said. And it made me realize Mateo cared deeply for Evie. I wasn't sure where that left me.

That question was answered when I heard her screaming his name from my room. I was fucking livid at first. I wanted to rush up there and rip her from his arms when I didn't have any right to. So, I settled against the headboard and let the anger wash over me. When I heard them the second time, I wasn't angry anymore; I was fucking curious. *I was fucked in the head.*

I still don't know what Mateo meant when he told Gray what he did, but I could figure it out. Evie has a way of pulling you in without even realizing it, and Gray isn't immune. Evie is a grown woman, and I needed to remember that. She could make her own choices whether I wanted her involved in this life or not. I wanted to tell her, and in the back of my head, I was hoping it would make her want to leave, but no matter how badly I wanted that, she is safer here.

Would Evie even want what Mateo was suggesting? It seemed far from the girl I grew up with, but I don't know her anymore.

Someone knocks on the door, and I roll off the bed with a sigh. When I pull it open, Gray stands there with the laptop. He shoves it into my chest. "We have work to do." Instead of leaving the room like I thought he would, he walks me backward and shuts the door behind him. He marches over to the desk and folds himself into the small chair. I sit on the edge of the bed.

"What are we working on?"

"I need you to look something up for me," Gray answers.

"Okay. You can't?"

"I don't know how to use that shit. Will you do it?"

With a shrug, I open the laptop. "Yeah."

"This stays between us." I look back over at him. Like I am going to fuck over someone who could make my death look like an accident. I've seen what he can do. Being around him, I now knew more than ever that he was the Reaper, the elusive killer we had chased for a year. Until he just fell off the map, and the killings stopped.

"What am I looking up?" I ask, loading the program Holden had on here. The things you could do on this computer are amazing and could have been useful to the police force. Too bad it's illegal as hell.

"Tessa and Torri Dixon." Not what I was expecting, but okay.

I type the names into the search bar and filter through the results. "What else can you give me?"

"Eighteen. Twins. Last known location was Nashville, Tennessee." I plug that in, and when it narrows down, I walk over and sit the laptop in front of Gray.

"You aren't going to ask questions?"

"Nope," I reply, going back to the bed. "It's none of my business." Why he trusted me with whatever he was trying to find, I didn't know. But I didn't miss the familiar resemblance when the girl's pictures popped up.

The more Gray scrolls, the tenser he gets until he slams the lid closed. "Want to talk about it?" I knew the answer before I asked; I just needed to offer it.

"No."

I lean my head back on the headboard, letting him stew in his own shit. It's finally quiet upstairs, and I am starting to figure out that Gray came in here to block out the noises, too. Probably for entirely different reasons than me.

"What do you know about sealed records?"

"I know that whatever you want is on that computer, Gray. But to answer your question, a lot. Why?"

"Why would the police seal a record of death?" I look at him again, and his face is carefully blank. Is that what he found just now?

"If it was under suspicious circumstances, or the police were involved, they would seal it."

"What about if they were in hiding?"

"That too," I answer honestly. If someone went into witness protection, the actual records would be sealed. I am more than curious now.

Gray leaves the room without another word, and I find myself at the laptop. I'm staring at the first picture, and there's no mistaking that these girls are related to Gray. I wanted to know what the hell he was looking for.

With a sigh, I hit the clear history button before I could dig into it.

THE NEXT MORNING, I walk onto the back patio to get some fresh air. Evie's curled up in one of the lounge chairs with a book in her hands. Right when I'm about to step back into the house, she turns to me with a smile.

Plastering a smile on my face, I sit beside her. "Morning."

"Morning," she replies. She is fucking glowing, and I am going to puke. "I love it out here."

I nod. "Me too."

We fall into an awkward silence when she goes back to reading. Every time I saw Evie when we were growing up, she always had her nose stuck in a book. I picked on her about it, but I envied her for being able to lose herself between the pages sometimes.

"Are you okay?" Evie asks, sitting her book to the side.

"Yeah. Why?"

She shrugs. "I just worry about you." *You were really worried about me last night.* And you sound like a dick.

"I'm fine, Evie. Are you okay?"

"I'm good." That smile stretches across her face again, and even though I know why it's there, it makes me smile in return.

"Where is everyone?" I ask.

"Mateo had some work to do. Gray's in the house somewhere."

I woke up this morning actually worried about the big fucker. Whatever he found last night fucked with his head. I've seen that look before. "Have you talked to Gray?"

"Not this morning. Why?"

Before I can answer, my phone starts ringing. I swipe to answer when I see Mateo's name. How the hell did he get my number?

"Hello?"

"Where's Gray? He's not answering his goddamn phone." Mateo growls through the line. What the fuck am I, his secretary?

"In the house."

"Get him and come pick me up."

"Why?"

"Somebody blew up my fucking car outside of Skyline." Skyline is a nightclub and one of the many places they owned in Abbs Valley.

I jump to my feet, making Evie stand up, too. "What?"

"I'll explain when you get here." The line goes dead, and I look at Evie.

"What's wrong?" My phone pings with Mateo's location, and I'm already walking into the house, Evie right on my heels.

"Gray! We have to go!" I yell when I get inside. "Now!"

"Hartley, what's wrong?"

"Gray! Let's go!"

"What the fuck are you yelling about?" Gray asks, rounding the corner.

"We have to go pick up Mateo. You weren't answering your phone." Gray pulls his phone from his pocket and winces.

"It's been on silent. Let's go."

"Hartley!" Evie grabs my arm to stop me from walking. "What's going on?"

I don't know what to tell her, but she would blame herself, no matter what I said. "Someone blew up his car."

"What?" Gray barks. Then he's moving. I have to pull Evie with me to keep up with him.

I stuff her into the backseat of his truck and climb in. I barely get the door shut before Gray roars down the driveway. I rattle off the address, and he nods.

"Is he okay?" Evie asks, and I can hear the quiver in her voice.

"He's fine," I tell her, turning in the seat. She has tears leaking down her face. "He's just pissed." I didn't want to take her out, but I didn't know what else to do with her and didn't want to leave her alone. I grab her hand. "I promise he's fine."

"This was Aaron, wasn't it?" Evie asks.

"Probably." It wasn't a secret that Frankie Perez left his boys with a fuck ton of enemies. But the chances of someone else attacking right now are slim, especially since the Perez's are aligned with the Italians and the Russians.

"This is my fault."

"None of that shit, angel," Gray says. "This is Aaron's fault."

Evie and I both look at him in surprise. *Angel?* Fucking hell.

We ride past Skyline to get to Mateo's location. The fire is out, but Mateo's Porsche is in pieces and a melted heap. Cops and fire-fighters are everywhere, which is why Mateo isn't with his car. Too many questions.

Gray turns down a narrow alley, and Mateo steps out from a

doorway with his phone to his ear. He gets in the truck, slamming the door behind him.

"I'm fucking fine, Van. This motherfucker just made his move." He listens to whatever Evander is saying. "No shit. I got out before they showed up. I'm going to go." He disconnects the call and jams his fingers through his hair.

"What the hell happened?" Gray asks, backing out of the alley.

"I was going to a meeting, and when I popped the door, I could hear it trigger. He almost blew me all to shit." Evie whimpers, and Mateo's face softens. "Come here, buttercup." He opens his arms, and she dives into them. "I'm fine," he soothes.

"You could have died!" Evie cries.

"But I didn't. I'm smarter than that asshole." He looks at me. "This changes the game."

Gray and I both nod.

"How did he find you?" Evie asks.

"I'm sure the night I was with you; he did his own research. I'm not hard to find."

"You should just let me leave, Mateo."

He tilts her chin up. "You aren't leaving me, buttercup."

"But you aren't safe."

"I'm never truly safe." I can see him trying to find a way to get around the truth. At this point, it might be easier if she knew. "With my status, I'm always at risk." That was as good as it was going to get.

Mateo's phone starts ringing, and he looks at it with a roll of his eyes.

"Hello, Les."

"So, we're blowing up cars now?" she says dryly over the line.

"For sure. Sounded fun. How did you know?"

"Van called Leo."

"Of fucking course he did. I'm fine for the thousandth time."

"That's good to know because we're on our way home." My heart drops right through my asshole. I haven't come face to face with Les in months, and I preferred it that way. But if she is coming back, she would help, and there is no avoiding her. *Fuck.*

"Les! What the fuck? You're on your honeymoon. We can handle this."

"If you think I'm staying in Italy while people are gunning for *my* family, you have lost your goddamn mind." Evie giggles at that. "Evie, I presume?" Les asks when she hears her.

"Uh, yeah."

"I hate to put this on you, but can you make sure they stay alive for like fifteen hours? I know it's hard, and they all suck at taking care of themselves, but I would appreciate it."

"I can't make any promises," Evie laughs.

Les laughs in return. "Yeah, I figured as much. Mateo? Stay the fuck home until we get there."

"Whatever," Mateo grouches. "See you in a few. Love you."

"Love you too, Tay."

"How the hell can she make me feel like an errant toddler in one conversation?" Mateo asks when the line goes dead.

"Because you are," Gray says dryly. "I told you not to go alone."

"What difference would that have made?"

"It doesn't matter," Gray grits out. "We don't go anywhere alone now."

I sit back in the seat and drown out their arguing. I needed every bit of strength to see Les.

And Zane.

CHAPTER 21
EVIE

I had the most amazing night with Mateo. We messed around a few times, but he never took it any further. As bad as I wanted to, I appreciated him giving me time.

I was so embarrassed when he walked into the room when I was changing clothes. I wanted to find the closest hole and hide. But his sweet words seeped into my bones, and when he looked at me like that, I believed every word. Mateo made me feel beautiful, cherished, and safe. Even when he was burying his head between my thighs. Aaron never did that, and he sure as hell never made sure I had an orgasm first. I didn't even know how to get myself off. I was always too shy to try when I was younger. But Mateo has woken up a hunger in me that I don't know how to handle.

When Hartley told me someone blew up Mateo's car, I almost lost it right there. He was close to losing his life because of me, but he ended up comforting *me* instead of the other way around.

So much is starting not to make sense, though. All the cryptic remarks and how he seemed to handle almost dying with ease. I refuse to dive too deep into that, afraid of what I might find. Cowardly, probably. But I already have feelings for him. *There ya go, moving too fast again, Evie.*

I hold Mateo closer on the couch, and he kisses the top of my head. "You trying to squeeze the life out of me, buttercup?"

"No," I mumble against his chest. "I'm just glad you're still here." I look into his green eyes and know already that I can't live without him. How messed up is that?

His lips find mine, and I fall into his kiss, forgetting everything except how they feel against mine. I know I need to be worried about how fast we're going, but when he kisses me, I can't find it in me to care.

Mateo starts kissing me harder, rolling until I'm half under his body. I move my hips to rub against him, and he groans into my mouth. "You're killing me, buttercup," he murmurs against my mouth. I want him to take me upstairs and finish what we started last night.

"Sorry to interrupt." We jerk apart at the sound of Evander's dry tone.

"Fucking shit, Van. You scared the hell out of me." Mateo sits up on the couch, dragging me with him. "Why are you home?"

Evander lifts a brow. "Someone just tried to blow up my brother. I thought that deserves a visit." He says it so casually that my thoughts go back to earlier. Who are these guys? No regular businessman would be that nonchalant about it. "I heard Leo is on his way home."

"Yeah, thanks to you. Why did you call them, anyway?"

Evander sits on the love seat. "Because they would have found out, eventually. It was better coming from one of us."

"Where's Micah?"

"On the phone." Evander lifts a hand when Mateo opens his mouth. "He promised to be on his best behavior."

I don't know why Micah is so cold towards me now. It's a complete one-eighty to how he treated me the night we first met.

"Good, because my threat still stands." I look at Mateo in question, and he shrugs. "I might have threatened to slit his throat if he talked to you like that again."

"Mateo!"

"What? He was out of line."

"You shouldn't go around threatening your friends," I argue.

Evander laughs, and it's a rich sound. "It happens all the time. Nothing to worry about."

Mateo nods. "I threatened to hang him from his empty ball sack once."

"And what was my answer to that?" Micah walks into the living room, and I can't help but be wary.

"That you'd hook me to the back of your Ferrari and drag me down the highway." Mateo laughs.

Micah sits beside Evander and doesn't even look my way.

"You guys are ridiculous," Evander says with a shake of his head.

"You heard anything?" Micah asks.

Mateo shakes his head. "They can't pin it on me."

"Good. That's the last thing we need." Micah gets up, leaving the room. Evander sighs and follows him.

"Is it just me, or are things really tense between them?" Mateo asks when they're gone.

I shrug. "I'm not around them enough to tell." I saw the heat between them in the kitchen the first day, but that was it.

"I'll have to talk to Van about it later." Mateo moves before I can blink and has me pinned to my back on the couch. "Where were we?"

"They're still in the house!" I laugh.

He kisses down my neck. "Do you want to go upstairs?"

As much as I wanted to, I couldn't get Micah's cold shoulder out of my head. "We can't."

Mateo wilts onto my chest with a sigh. "You're right."

I shake my head at his antics. "You remember when I said you were dramatic?"

"I'm not dramatic, damn it. I'm passionate."

I bust out laughing. "That's not the same thing."

"Uh-huh." He rubs his cheek against my breast through my shirt. He chuckles when I suck in a breath. I can't see his face, but I can guarantee that he is wearing that grin that turns me to mush. "It's definitely the same thing."

"It's not," I say breathlessly. His cheek is now against my nipple, and I could feel it harden behind my bra. "You have to stop."

"Why, buttercup? They're awesome fucking pillows." He snuggles his face into them, making me giggle.

"They aren't pillows for your big head."

He pops up. "I don't have a big head."

"Tell that to my titties you're squishing."

"How. Dare. You." He flops back onto the couch on his back, throwing his arm over his eyes. I sit up and get on my knees between his thighs. "No, stay away from my big head."

"But I like your big head."

Mateo moves his arms from his eyes. "Do you now?"

"Yes." When he grins, I smack his leg. "That's not what I meant!"

"Sure, buttercup." He winks. "That's not what you meant."

"Ew, I don't like you anymore."

"Whatever you need to tell yourself to sleep at night." He pounces again, and I let out a high-pitched shriek when he lands on top of me. How the hell does he move that fast? "Shit, buttercup, I'm sorry."

I look at him, confused. "Why are you apologizing?"

"I thought I scared you."

I smooth out the frown line between his brows. "I've never been scared of you."

Maybe I should be, but nothing about Mateo scares me. Except maybe how fast he is taking my heart.

I STUMBLE into the kitchen in the middle of the night, thirsty. I stop dead in my tracks when I see Micah standing at the counter with his back to me, shirtless. I try to backtrack, but he turns slowly towards me.

"Have a seat." He nods toward the stool, and my feet move without my permission. Whatever he is fixing smelled wonderful.

"Sorry, I couldn't sleep," I find myself apologizing.

"All good. Me either."

He doesn't turn around, so it gives me a chance to look at him. The muscles in his back move every time he does. His waist is lean. He turns around, and my mouth goes dry—hard pecs, six-pack abs, and a v-line that disappeared into low-slung grey sweatpants. *Get your eyeballs back in your head!* I knew Micah was hot; I wasn't blind. But his boyfriend and mine are upstairs sleeping while I'm down here ogling him. I keep my eyes locked on the island, so he doesn't know I am seconds away from drooling. *What the hell is wrong with you?!*

"I bake when I can't sleep." My eyes snap to his face, and he's not looking at me. He's staring at the wall over my shoulder. "There's banana bread here if you want it." That's what that delicious smell is. When my brain catches up, he's halfway across the kitchen.

"Micah," I call out and hold my breath when he stops. I had no idea what I would say, but it spills out when he turns those blue eyes on me. "Why do you hate me?"

"I don't hate you," he replies, and my shoulders relax. "I just don't trust you." *Ouch.* I already figured that out, but hearing the words out loud hurt more than I want to admit.

"I'm sorry," I whisper.

He doesn't hear me because he's already gone.

MICAH'S NIECE is more gorgeous than I remembered, with the same black hair and startling blue eyes. She looked radiant on her wedding day, but I never got close to them because they were lost in their own little world. And her husbands? Jesus. Is everyone in Abbs Valley this good-looking? Mateo introduced them all, but I couldn't remember a name to save my life.

She got here over an hour ago after their long flight from Italy, and when Micah tried to pull them to a meeting without me, she put her foot down.

"She needs to be there. She might remember something."

Micah's jaw clenches. "She said she doesn't know anything."

"This is her life, Micah. She goes." Les smiles warmly at me. "Come on." I follow behind her, giving a fuming Micah a wide berth. I know he wouldn't hurt me, but after what he said last night, my feelings are still hurt, and I don't dare tell Mateo.

We get settled around the dining room table. "Holden did some more digging, and we thought it might jog your memory. I know you said he didn't talk in front of you, but he might have said something you didn't even think to listen to," Les explains, and it makes sense.

"This is your new phone. It can't be traced." I take it with a smile. Mateo tossed mine from his window after we were shot at, and I didn't have the money for another one. Curly hair and kind brown eyes. Holden. The one Mateo said worked in internet security. "I'm going to show you some pictures, and I want you to tell me if you recognize anything."

Micah stares at me so hard that I feel my head will explode. "Okay," I answer.

Holden slides pictures in front of me, and I flip through them. Nothing looks familiar until I get to a picture of Aaron, Wraith, Titan, and Screwball. I name them off, and Holden nods. "Anything else?"

I point to another picture. "That's the compound."

Mateo frowns. "The compound?"

"That's where they did everything. I never went inside."

I keep flipping, and the earth drops out from beneath me. There in color is a picture of Aaron and me. My arm is through his, and I'm smiling up at him like he hung the fucking moon. Picture after picture of him and me are stacked together. "Where did you get these?" I feel like I am going to throw up.

"Archives. Aaron had a lot of heat on him from the police. This was in there," Holden answers.

Mateo snatches the picture, and then he looks around the table. "What the fuck is this? You're supposed to be seeing if she remembers anything."

"That's what we're doing," Les says evenly.

"Looks like you're following Micah and accusing her of something." Mateo stands up from the table. "Let's go, Evie."

"Sit down, Mateo." That terse warning comes from Micah, and my eyes snap to his. "We aren't accusing you of anything. We're showing you what we found."

"He wasn't always bad," I say miserably. Fuck, I don't want to talk about this. "This was in the beginning."

"Buttercup, you don't need to do this."

"Yes, I do." I flip through all the pictures and point out everything I know. "Did I pass your test?" I push my chair back and hold my hand up when Mateo goes to follow me.

I run to the bathroom, and everything I've eaten comes out in a rush. Does Mateo think I am up to something? I don't even know what they think I am supposed to be doing here.

I hear the door open and the sink cut on. I don't turn around because I don't want Mateo to see me like this. A feminine hand comes into view. I take the washcloth with a mumbled thanks. I flush the toilet, slam the lid, and sink onto it.

Les slides onto the sink. "I'm sorry we had to do that. I needed to see a genuine reaction. But I know that look in your eyes, Evie; I've seen it in my own."

"I understand," I reply softly. "Micah said he didn't trust me, and I guess he's not the only one."

"Micah doesn't trust anyone. The people you see in this house? That's it. But that's a story for another day. What I'm saying is *I* trust you."

"You do? Why?"

"Call it female intuition or whatever. Your face doesn't lie, Evie. Whatever you think broadcasts there like a neon sign. And more important than me trusting you is Mateo does."

I finally look at her, and she's wearing a soft expression. "I don't know what you went through, but it doesn't define you. You can beat it or let it beat you. I prefer the first option."

"Is that what you did?"

"It took some time, but yes, with the help of my guys. There's nothing wrong with leaning on someone. Aaron sounds like a world-class jackass. Don't let him win."

A shocked laugh escapes. "I don't want him to win."

"Good." Les nods and hops off the sink. "Clean your pretty face, brush your teeth, and meet me in the hallway."

"For what?"

"Self-defense classes," Les answers with a grin before slipping from the room.

When I'm done, she's leaning beside the door. She leads me to the gym, where everyone is sitting around already. She walks over to the mats and turns toward me.

"First lesson, just because they're bigger, doesn't mean anything. Come here, Dex." A guy bigger than Gray steps up in front of her. He towers over her petite frame. Tall, tattoos. Dex.

He grabs her around the waist and hauls her against his chest. She swings her legs up and jerks them back down, breaking his hold easily. *Is Micah's niece a damn ninja?* Dex could crush her with his bare hands.

"Pick me, pretty girl, pick me!" The one with wavy dark hair and equally blue eyes bounces on his feet.

She rolls her eyes. "Come on, Gage." Funny, crazy hair. Gage.

He rushes her, dropping his shoulder into her midsection. I gasp when they hit the mat with a bounce. They grapple for a minute, and she comes out on top. She slams his arms against the mat. "I won."

"Who really won there, *il mio sole?*" I'm pretty sure Mateo called him Ryder. Black eyes, nose rings. Ryder.

She pecks Gage's lips. "Good point." She hops to her feet and turns to me. "You get the point. Come here."

I walk shyly toward her. What would she do to me if she could take down a man twice her size?

But she steps to the side and pulls Micah to stand with me. *What. The. Hell?* "You're too comfortable with Mateo, and Gray might not be the best choice for this lesson," Les explains when she sees my face.

"You got this, buttercup," Mateo encourages from his place, leaning on the wall.

I don't know about that. I can't read anything in Micah's expression, but I'm sure he's as thrilled about this as I am.

"If you get scared, let me know, and we can go again another day.

I just want you to know you can get out of a bad situation with the right tools," Les says. I take a breath and nod. "Grab her."

Micah tilts his head to the side, studying me. When he does move, I can't help the flinch when his arm wraps around my waist, spinning me, so my back is to my front. He has my arms locked like a steel band.

"Breathe," Micah whispers in my ear when he can feel me close to panicking. "Get out."

I try to jerk my arms free, and he tightens his hold.

"Lean forward," Les instructs. "Throw him off balance."

I do what she says, and I can feel the hold loosen. I drop to my knees, and his arm falls away. I jump back to my feet. "I did it!"

We go through several holds, and the more we do, the more aware I am of Micah's body rubbing against mine. I couldn't ignore it. It's like every nerve ending is lit up, and I feel every brush of his fingers. My eyes snap to Mateo's when I break the last hold, and he smiles at me like he knows how Micah is making me feel.

Right now, I feel like shit about it.

CHAPTER 22
MICAH

"What the fuck was that for?" I ask Les, rubbing my arm where she just punched me.

"You said she couldn't be trusted. That is the most trustworthy face I've ever seen."

"Or she's a damn good actress." I sit behind my desk and wait for Les to sit down. She glares at me when she does.

"You are not that fucking blind. What's this really about?" Leave it to her to call me on my bullshit.

"That's what this is about. I don't trust her."

"You don't trust her, or you don't trust yourself around her?"

What?

"I would never do anything like that to Van," I bark.

Les holds a hand up. "Chill out. I didn't say you would. I know you better than this, Micah. You can read people better than I can. You know that girl is telling the truth as well as I do."

I don't know what the hell I feel anymore. I have so many fucking emotions running through me because of what Van said. I thought we moved past what I did, but I was dead wrong. Things have been tense ever since because I don't know how to make it better.

I run my hands through my hair. "Things aren't good with Van," I admit. If anyone could help me through this, it's Les. She cocks an eyebrow, and I tell her everything that's happened.

"You need to give him time, Micah. I went through the same thing with Zane. But Van is still here, trying. It took me and Zane years to get our shit together."

"I'm trying, Les, but fuck, it's hard."

"Welcome to love. No one said it was easy. Is that your deal with Evie? Your issues with Van?" I nod, and Les sighs. "Why?"

"Everyone is so captivated by her." *Including me.* After watching her face with those pictures of her and Aaron, I knew that Evie wasn't lying. She is a victim, and I am so damn insecure with myself that I let their attention to her bother me.

"Okay," Les says slowly.

"I'm fucking jealous, okay?"

"Has he given you a reason to be?"

"No! Goddamnit, I don't want to talk about this anymore."

"Too bad. Spill," Les says unforgiving.

"I pushed Van away constantly because he's too fucking good for me. I knew he eventually would realize he could do better, breaking my heart. So I broke his first."

"Why would you say that? You're the best man I've ever known."

Because my father hated me and told me every chance he got that I wouldn't do shit with my life. He cheated on his wife, and I got blamed for being born. Something I could never tell Les and break her perfect image of her grandpa. "I appreciate you saying that."

"You think I'm saying that to pump up your ego?" Les asks incredulously. "You know that's not my style. Van loves you, Micah, but you hurt him. He sees you as the man I do. The man that stood by my side when Dad died when you could have looked the other way. The man who did everything in his power to protect me. The man who gave me the brother I never had." Only being seven years apart, it was always like we were more like siblings than anything else. "Forget what Grandpa said."

My mouth pops open. "What?"

"You didn't think I knew the shit he said to you? Why do you think Dad froze him out before he died?"

"How did you know?"

"I overheard him talking to you in the gardens one day and told Dad. Dad was livid, but I made him promise not to say anything to you. So, he made Grandpa move out."

I swallow back the emotion. "Your dad did that for me?"

"Your *brother* did that for you. Dad saw the same thing I did. He loved you so much."

I get up and flop down in the chair beside Les. "I miss him."

"I do too. Every damn day. But he would be proud of you."

I nod because I don't know what to say. I would have talked about it sooner if I had known she knew this whole time. My biggest hang-ups about relationships revolved around my father, and that needed to stop.

"You need to slack off on Evie. She doesn't need your shit."

"I know, shithead." I sigh and run my fingers through my hair. "I just need to get my head on straight."

"You do that." She stands up. "I'm going home to sleep, and we can come up with a plan tomorrow."

I pull her into a hug. "You didn't need to come home."

"Yes, I did. I'd do anything for you."

AFTER LES LEFT, I started watching Evie differently. She is on the back patio with Mateo and Gray, laughing at something Mateo is saying. Her laugh is carefree around them. She won't even look me in the eye. Not that I blame her. Les opened a whole lot of shit that I needed to work on, but I needed to worry about Van, not my interest in Evie.

"What are you doing?" I turn to Van's voice.

"Thinking."

"Standing in the door like a creeper?"

"I wasn't being a creeper. I was just lost in thought. Did you take care of everything you needed to?"

Van nods. "Yeah. You can't see anything on the cameras because of the angle. Mateo knows not to park there."

"We don't need proof to know who this was, and you know Mateo does what he wants."

Evie laughs again, and it drags Van's attention to her. *He's just seeing what she's laughing at. No big deal.* But it is a big deal, and I *hate* that she can grab his attention for even a second. *Yeah, and you sound like a psycho.*

Sighing, I walk away from the door. "Where are you going? Micah, talk to me."

I keep walking toward the stairs, and when I get to Van's bedroom door, I can hear his footsteps pounding up the stairs.

"What is your *deal?*" Van asks, throwing his hands in the air. I don't know anymore. I just feel...numb. Even mentioning my father took all the energy from me.

"I don't have a deal, Van."

"I hate when you call me Van. Is this because I said I needed time?" I shake my head. "Then what is it?" I cross to the bathroom, and he grabs my arm before I can shut the door. "Quit walking away and tell me what your problem is."

My control snaps. I don't feel numb anymore; I am pissed. It's all bubbling to the surface, and there is no damn way I could stop it. "I'm fucking jealous! I know that at any point, you will realize how much better she is for you! Or anyone! I'm fucked up, Van. You should have never forgiven me."

"This is about *Evie?*"

"NO! It's about everything!"

"Micah, you're not making any sense."

"You know what my father used to say to me? He used to tell me I would never be the man my brother was. I wasn't smart enough, fast enough, good enough. I was nothing but a bastard that ruined his marriage."

"*He* ruined his marriage, Micah. His guilt kept him from seeing the man you are. You've done things that Alfonso Poletti never thought about doing. You would protect your loved ones with your last dying breath, something he would never do. You are the man Luca was and a thousand times more the man than Alfonso was."

I sink onto the bed and bury my head in my hands. "Why do you even want to deal with this?"

"Because I love you, *mi rey*. Just because I said I needed time doesn't mean I'm giving up on us. I want this. With you."

The bed dips, and I look into Van's brown eyes. "You probably would have run the other way if this came out in the beginning."

"No, I wouldn't have. I saw something in you, and I still see it."

"I pushed you away on purpose," I mutter. "Because I knew I loved you. I knew I'd either fuck it up, or you would get tired of me and leave." I didn't even realize this until I was talking to Les. I always thought it was because he was a man, and I didn't know how to deal with that. That was only a part of it.

"Fuck, Micah." Van pulls me into his arms in a fierce hug, and I wrap my arms around him. "I'm not going anywhere."

Time would tell.

CHAPTER 23
EVIE

I feel the bed dip beside me and want to be annoyed. I told Mateo I needed space after that showdown with Micah in the gym, so I slept in the guest room. I felt so guilty about liking Micah pressed against me.

I roll over with a smile instead of annoyance. But I'm not met with Mateo's green eyes on the pillow beside me; I'm met with Micah's vivid blues. *What the hell?* I could smell the alcohol pouring off him in waves. Where is Evander?

His hand reaches toward me, and I don't move or even breathe. He lays it on my neck, his thumb sitting on my pulse. He rubs his thumb back and forth, causing goosebumps to pop up on my skin.

"What is it about you?" Micah asks, and it's like he's talking to himself. His words are slurred, and his eyes are heavy. I've never seen him so disheveled. He didn't even have a hair out of place when he was beating the crap out of Aaron. Now his thick black hair is sticking up at odd angles like he's repeatedly run his hand through it.

I don't answer his question because he doesn't want an answer. I stare at him with wide eyes.

His thumb rubs across my bottom lip, and I suck in a breath. "I didn't want to see you. I didn't want to notice you. I didn't want to remember you."

"Why?" I whisper.

"Because the first night I met you, I couldn't get you off my mind. Those big brown eyes haunted me until I shut them out. I made myself forget your name. I love Van, and you are a temptation I didn't know if I could resist." He moves closer until I can smell the whiskey on his breath. "Then I have to watch you walk around here and pretend you don't affect me. And pretend you don't have the same effect on Van."

"Micah." I don't speak louder than a whisper, afraid to break whatever trance he is in. Is that why he doesn't trust me? Van's never looked at me in the wrong way, so I'm chalking that one up to Micah being drunk. But the way Micah looks at me right now, I don't know if that's entirely alcohol induced.

His lips skate across mine, not in a kiss but a caress. "I like the way you say my name," he breathes against my lips. My heart starts beating double time; I still can't move. I should be pushing him away, but something is holding me back. Pain is lurking in Micah's eyes, maybe a little sadness, and as stupid as it is, I want to be there for him.

"You're gorgeous, *la mia stella*." His hand goes back to my neck, and his eyelids flutter. "But I won't hurt Van."

"I know," I whisper. I've seen how they look at each other, which is a beautiful sight. But why is he here and not with Evander?

His eyes close, and his face goes slack. I wait until he's fully asleep, pull his hand from my throat, and fold it into mine. Even in sleep, he looks worried. I reach over and softly smooth the line between his eyebrows. He sighs and snuggles more into the pillow. Asleep, he looks younger, less severe. His dark lashes fan across the olive skin of his cheek, and his full lips are parted slightly. I rub my thumb across his bottom lip like he did mine, amazed at how they should look too feminine for his masculine face, but it just makes him even more beautiful.

"What's your story, Micah?"

Everyone has one, and something tells me Micah's isn't a good one.

I WAKE up the following morning feeling like I had dreamt the whole thing with Micah until I catch a whiff of his cologne lingering on the pillow.

I fell asleep with his hand still clutched in mine, and I didn't know what to do.

"Morning, buttercup," Mateo whispers, and my eyes fly open. My head snaps to the side, and my heart sinks. Micah is still there, passed out. It wasn't his cologne I was smelling; it was *him*. "So, I'm sure there's an interesting story here."

I couldn't get words out, and I can't tell if Mateo is mad. "I don't know what to say."

"Why don't you tell me why my brother's boyfriend is sleeping in the same bed as my girlfriend?" Yep, definitely pissed. Micah groans in his sleep and slings an arm over my waist. *Just fucking kill me now.*

"I will tell you everything," I promise. "Just let me up."

Mateo stands up, and I carefully slide out from under Micah's arm. I look back at the bed, and he's frowning.

"I'll meet you in my room." Mateo gives me a pointed look before leaving the room.

I use the bathroom and brush my teeth. When I walk into the bedroom, Micah is sprawled on his stomach, arms tucked under his pillow.

Making my way to Mateo's room, I'm already preparing myself for him to tell me I need to leave. If he doesn't, I'm sure Van will.

I rush into his room and let everything spill before he can say anything.

When I'm done talking, he rubs the back of his neck. "Wow. Okay. Not what I was expecting you to say."

"I'm so sorry, Mateo. I'll pack my stuff and be out before you know it."

"Wait. What? You aren't leaving, buttercup."

"But what about Evander? I can't come between them! I need to go."

"No," Mateo says slowly, pulling me to sit on the bed. "You don't. I know this is confusing, but it kind of makes sense now."

"What does?" None of this made sense!

"It explains why Micah's been an even bigger dick than normal. I knew he was acting funny after talking to Les last night, but I couldn't put my finger on it." I wait for him to elaborate. "He feels guilty for wanting you. But in true Micah form, he blamed it on you instead of taking the blame himself."

"I could have kicked him out of bed last night."

Mateo shrugs. "You could have, but you wouldn't be you if you did. Evie, you aren't the type to intentionally hurt someone."

"What about Evander?" I whisper.

"Evander knows, buttercup. He isn't pissed; he's worried."

"About me? I would never..."

"He knows." Mateo pulls me to his side. "He's worried about Micah. Something is going on because this isn't like him."

"He's hurting," I say, recalling the look in his eyes. I wanted nothing more than to take that hurt away, not hurt anyone else in the process. "I don't know why he came to me, though."

"He feels drawn to you."

"Doesn't that bother you?"

"It should," Mateo admits. "But Micah is my best friend. He wouldn't do anything to fuck me over. If he feels drawn to you, then who am I to stand in the way if he can find peace?"

"But Evand..." Mateo presses his finger against my lips.

"Van feels the same way, buttercup. We think maybe you can help him."

"Me?" I squeak. "How am I supposed to help him when I can't even help myself?"

Mateo chuckles. "Two totally different situations. You have this light around you even after what you've been through. We've been in the dark a long time; we can't help seeking out your light." They've been in the dark? I don't even know what that means. My head is reeling from what he's saying, but he isn't done. "I know this sounds crazy, and I'm not trying to freak you out." He takes both my hands in his. "I think you were meant for me, buttercup, and after seeing you with the others, I think you were meant for *us*."

"Us?" My voice is above an acceptable octave, even to my own ears, but I can't help it. Us? Is Mateo actually insane? Is this the red flag I've been missing this whole time when I thought he was perfect?

"I saw how your body responded to Micah yesterday." I lift my eyes to his expecting him to be disgusted with me, but he just looks... happy. *What the fuck?* "Just be honest with me. Did you like him against you?"

Can I be honest about something like this? It's an enthusiastic yes to that question, but what kind of person does that make me? Micah has been cold to me up until yesterday. He still wasn't particularly nice, but he wasn't cold anymore.

"Yes," I say quietly. Mateo deserves my honesty, even if he calls it quits and kicks my confused ass to the curb.

"Okay," Mateo says, hauling me into the bed to cuddle into his side. "I'm going to be honest here, buttercup. I know you're scared, and this is a lot to take in. But I've always wanted what Leo has with Les and her guys, especially since I've seen it happen."

I wanted to be shocked, but I wasn't. He already has Gray and me. Although he keeps the relationships mostly separate, we are still in some sort of odd relationship with each other.

"Why do you not show Gray affection in front of me?" I know it's off-topic, but I've wondered that since I found out. He flirts and jokes with Gray, but it's not like he does with me. He's very open with his affection for me, no matter who's around. Is it different because Gray is a guy? "I'm not going to get jealous or upset."

"I know. This is all new to Gray, and I'm not sure how he would feel about public displays of affection," Mateo laughs.

"Is your relationship a secret from the others?"

"Not at all. I'm not even sure what Gray and I have *is* a relationship."

"What do you mean?" I cross my arms over his chest, laying my chin on them to see his face.

"We've established that it's not just sex, but we haven't defined anything past that."

"Maybe you should."

"Maybe you should stop avoiding what I said." Mateo rubs his knuckles down my cheek. "I'm not saying you need to decide now, but I wanted to be honest about what I wanted."

"I'm not sure what you're asking me to do."

"I want you to get to know the other guys without worrying if I will be mad." Mateo kisses my forehead. "I want you to have whatever you want."

"I want you," I say honestly. Mateo is more than I've ever wanted, and I needed to stop worrying about us moving too fast. My heart is all in, and it's time for my brain to catch up.

"I know that, and I want you too. You're very important to me, buttercup, and I'm glad you came into my life."

"Me too." Tears spring into my eyes, and Mateo thumbs them away as they roll down my face.

He pulls me closer so he can lay his lips on mine. At first, it's like any other kiss, but something changes. We've fooled around, but I am ready for everything with Mateo. He's been more patient with me than I thought a man could be.

The air charges around us, and Mateo flips us so his body slides against me, his cock pressing against me through my shorts.

I pull my mouth away. "Mateo, I need..." I pant.

"I know what you need, buttercup." He kisses my neck, sliding his hands under my shirt. When it's out of his way, his mouth is on the swell of my breasts. He pops the front clasp on my bra. My tits spill out everywhere, and I always get an attack of self-consciousness, but it evaporates when his eyes heat up.

"Mateo." I try again.

"I got you."

"Mateo." I pull his mouth from my nipple so I can see his face. "I need you."

He frowns. "That's what I'm doing."

"No." I take a breath. "I'm ready."

His frown deepens. I see the minute it dawns on him. His pupils expand, and he's looking at me like I'm his last meal. "Are you sure?"

"Yes, please, Mateo."

He fists the back of his shirt and pulls it over his head. *Why is that so sexy?* His lips seal over mine, and this kiss is harder, showing me Mateo's been holding back. I didn't want him to, I wasn't scared of him, and I knew if I did get that way, he would stop. I slide my hands down his muscled back, and his whole body shudders.

He starts kissing a trail down my neck, stopping to pay attention to my nipples. He sucks and pulls on them until they are stiff peaks. He doesn't waste any time pulling my shorts and panties off.

"God, you have the prettiest pussy." Dirty talk was never my thing, but hearing it come out of Mateo's mouth with his raspy voice makes my clit throb.

Running his fingers through my slit, he leans down and places kisses on the swell of my belly. I hate that part of myself, but he makes me see its beauty. He never seems to mind the cellulite in my thighs, the stretch marks on my hips or breasts, or anything else I found unattractive about myself. Aaron took my self-confidence, and Mateo gave it back.

Mateo's mouth attacks my clit, and my fingers slide into his thick hair. He groans when I tug on it, so I do it again. He loved when I did it, and it always caused him to eat my pussy like a madman. Without warning, he spears me with two fingers, and my back bows off the bed.

"Yes, Mateo, yes!"

He rubs his fingers across that spot inside me that I only thought existed in books, and I can feel that familiar tug in my belly. He sucks my clit into his mouth and reaches up with his other hand to tug on my nipple. Something I found I *really* fucking liked.

"I'm going to come, oh god." He tugs harder, and I shatter. "Mateo!" He brings me down gently and sits up with a grin.

"I fucking love when you come for me." His body slides up mine. "Good girl," he whispers. That's something else I didn't think I would like, but I'm discovering many things about myself. Like I am possibly attracted to multiple men at the same time.

"What were you just thinking about, buttercup?" I can feel my face flush even darker. "Tell me."

"I was thinking about...." I trail off when he starts kissing my neck again. He nips at my neck, making me moan. "I was thinking about the other guys."

Mateo's head pops up from my neck with a raised brow. "If you were thinking about them, I need to try harder."

"No!" I laugh. "I was thinking about what you said."

Mateo nods and jumps from the bed. When he pulls his shorts and boxers off his stiff cock slaps his stomach, and my mouth goes dry. How did I suddenly forget how big he was? He rummages around in his bedside table until he pulls out a foil packet. I am really going to do this. Butterflies are attacking my stomach. I'm nervous, but I am so fucking ready to feel him inside me.

Climbing back on the bed, between my spread thighs, he rips the condom open and rolls it down his length. I watch with rapt attention, transfixed by the sight. "If you want to stop anytime, you tell me, you understand?"

I nod, and he shuffles his knees forward until his cock is notched at my entrance. Lying one hand beside my head, he guides himself with the other until I feel him push inside. *There is no way I can take all of him. Holy shit.* I feel myself stretch around him, and his other hand slams down beside my head.

"Relax," he breathes, and I realize my body is tight as a bowstring. I take a few deep breaths as he rocks his hips. When he feels my body sag against the bed, he pushes his hips, burying himself to the hilt. "Fuuuukkkk, buttercup," Mateo groans, and it vibrates against my bones.

He lays his forehead against mine. "Are you okay?"

I take stock of how I feel, and besides having something that big wedged inside me, I feel amazing. "Yes. You feel so good."

"Goddamn, you do too."

He starts rocking his hips slowly, his eyes never leaving mine. My hands explore his sides and his back.

"Tell me what you were thinking about," Mateo pants. He wants me to talk right now? "Come on, buttercup. I want to know what has your pussy tightening up on me."

"I was thinking about being attracted to the others," I moan when he shifts his hips. He's still moving slowly inside me, building up an orgasm that I know will blow my mind.

"You think they're sexy? You want to know a secret?" I nod. "Van and I have shared before." *Oh my god.* A vision of being between Evander and Mateo flashes through my head. "You like that idea, don't you? You want to be a naughty girl?"

"Fuck, Mateo," I moan again, my fingers digging into his back.

"You want what you read in those books?"

"Oh god, you did read them."

He chuckles breathlessly and swivels his hips. "I read one of them because I wanted to like what you like." That is strangely sweet. "Fuck, buttercup. I don't know how slow I can keep going."

I could tell he was holding back. His arms are locked tight; his muscles are tense. "Then don't."

"I don't want to hurt you."

"You won't. I trust you." That admission makes his whole body shudder. He leans back on his heels, puts his hands behind my knees, and pushes them toward my chest. I feel the way my thighs squash against my stomach, making for an unflattering picture. I'm about to tell him when he pulls slowly out and slams his hips forward.

"Holy shit," I breathe, fingers digging into the sheet.

"Fuck, you feel good." He repeats the movement and groans. "Your sweet pussy likes my cock." *Yes, yes, it does.* "Do you have any idea what you do to me?"

"Harder, please, Mateo." It feels so good; I can't even be embarrassed anymore.

His fingers sink into my hips. "You were made for me. Look how fucking perfect my hands fit here." His grip gets tighter, and he pulls me down when he slams his hips forward.

He starts moving faster, making my tits bounce out of control, his thighs slapping against the back of mine. All kinds of noises are leaving my mouth, spurring him on. I've never felt something this good.

"Play with your clit, buttercup. Come on my cock." I slide my hand down my stomach and circle my clit with my fingers like he's done a hundred times. The moan that leaves my mouth comes from deep in my chest. I move my fingers faster and feel my pussy pulsing around him. "There you go. Good girl."

His eyes lock with mine, and I can't hold back. My fingers are moving at lightning speed. *Holy fuck. This is what I was missing that whole time?* "Mateo!" I let go with a scream that echoes off the walls.

Mateo's thrust stutter, and he slams into me three more times. "Buttercup," he groans. I can feel him swell inside of me, and I watch his face the whole time. He's lost to his orgasm, and *I* made him feel like that. He moves slowly a couple of times before collapsing on my chest, kissing me softly.

"You're fucking perfect, Evie. And *mine*."

"Yours," I whisper, running my hands down his sweaty back.

We lay there until our breathing returns to normal, and our hearts aren't beating out of our chest. "What do you say we have a lazy day? I'll order some breakfast, we can watch some movies and stay in here all day?"

"I'd love that." I smile. "Maybe you can invite Gray?"

His answering smile is blinding. "I think he'd like it too, buttercup." He pulls from me with a groan. "Let's go get dirty in the shower." He waggles his eyebrows, making me laugh.

He pulls me to my feet, deposits the condom in the wastebasket, and leads me to the shower. Once inside, he gently washes my hair and body, kissing random places once the water washes the soap away.

"Are you okay?" Mateo asks in concern, wiping my tears away. I didn't even realize I had started crying.

"Happy tears," I promise.

"I plan to make you very happy, Evie Sinclair."

He doesn't know it, but he already has.

CHAPTER 24
GRAY

When your boyfriend asks you to watch movies with him and his girlfriend, you do. No matter what's going on in your mind at the time. I wasn't sure what Mateo and I were classified as, but I am sticking with what I wanted.

At first, I told him no, that he needed to spend time with her after what they just did. Then he told me it was her idea, so I dragged my sorry ass in here. Now, I am lying in Mateo's bed against the headboard, watching some chick flick with her sandwiched between us. I didn't want to make her uncomfortable, so I stayed on the edge as far as possible. I've spent time with Evie, but not like this.

I look down at her lying on Mateo's chest and can't help the tug at my heart. Not out of jealousy exactly, but I couldn't explain it.

"What even is this?" Mateo asks.

Evie's head pops up to look at him. "You've never seen Twilight?"

"Do I look like a Twilight person to you?"

She looks at me over her shoulder, and I shake my head. "What is wrong with you? This is like the best movie ever," she giggles. "Okay, maybe not the best, but it's good."

"Why does he look constipated?" I ask, making her laugh.

"He doesn't!" She sits in the middle of the bed with her legs under her. "He's a vampire and can smell her blood. It's painful for him."

"It looks like he needs to take a giant shit, buttercup."

"Stop! No, it doesn't. Watch the movie." She zones in on the TV, completely engrossed in this shit. She looks adorable sitting there on her knees, remote clutched in her hand, whispering the words to the movie. How many times has she seen this? Realizing that I'm staring a hole through her, I turn and look at Mateo. His eyes are zeroed in on my face, and I can feel my face heat, making him grin.

"You want her," he mouths. I raise an eyebrow, and his grin widens.

Mateo had called her our girl, and I couldn't get the thought out of my head. I shouldn't even be entertaining the idea. It's already bad enough that I am pulling Mateo into my life, but he could handle it. I'm not sure Evie could. One of these days, my past would come back and haunt me; it's just a matter of time.

I've been waiting for Hartley to ask me about the names I had him look up last night, but he never has. Hartley has turned out to be a nice guy, and I don't have that constant itch to shoot him anymore. Micah has even seemed to let up on him, too.

Something is going on there, too. Micah has always been put together and calm, but I walked into the library last night, and he was hammered. I've seen him drink, but it's usually a two-drink limit, and he's done. He might be a damn good boss, but we weren't close enough to ask if he was okay, so I slipped from the room before he saw me. He was gone this morning when I got up, and all messages to him went unanswered from everyone. I finally messaged Adam, one of the guards under me, and he said he had picked him up to take him to Les' house. That calmed my nerves down, but I wondered why he didn't ask me to take him. That is exactly what I am for. Is he doubting my abilities?

"Gray." My head snaps to the sound of my name, and Mateo's looking at me like I'm crazy. "I've said your name like four times. You good?"

"Yeah," I croak, giving myself away. I give him a look that I hope conveys that we can talk later, and he nods.

"I said we should take Evie shopping."

"And Evie said no," Evie says, not looking away from the TV.

"And I said I don't care what Evie wants. I want to spoil my girl."

I laugh. "I don't think your girl wants to be spoiled."

"She doesn't," she answers, making me laugh again. She turns to look at me. "You should do that more; I like it." My face heats, and she smiles. "I'm glad I'm not the only one that does that."

"We can't go anyway," I say apologetically. "It's not safe."

"Come on. We can put her in one of your enormous hoodies, and no one will ever know."

"Mateo, you don't have to do this. I have everything I need," she argues.

"We can go shop for books," Mateo sings, making her shake her head with a laugh.

"I have books."

"Yeah, that you've read a million times. You need new books for the library."

My eyebrows shoot up. He's talking like she will be staying here for longer than it takes to take down Aaron.

"Evander has plenty I can read in there." She focuses her attention back on the movie.

"Just go online and let her pick them out," I reason.

Mateo scowls but pulls his phone out; Evie snatches it from his hand. "Don't even think about it."

"You can't stop me forever, buttercup. You can pick them out, or I'm going to go fucking wild ordering shit you might not like."

I listen to them banter back and forth and think about what he said. We can take my truck. She could hide her identity, and everything could be fine. I have to admit I wouldn't mind spoiling her a little.

"We can go," I say, making them both look at me. Mateo with a smile, and Evie with a glare.

"I thought you were on my side," Evie huffs. "You guys just don't want to watch this movie."

"You heard the man, buttercup. Let's go." Mateo hops to his feet. Evie shakes her head, crossing her arms over her chest. "Have it your way." Mateo bends down and flips her over his shoulder, striding from the room.

"Mateo! Put me down! I'm too big to carry like this!"

He stops dead in his tracks. "What did you just say?"

"I said..."

"I know what you said, and I told you I never wanted to hear you talk about yourself like that again, didn't I?"

"Yes," Evie says breathlessly.

Mateo lets her slide to her feet. "I meant every word I've ever said." She nods, and he kisses her forehead. "Go get dressed, and we'll get books, okay?"

She nods again but still doesn't look happy about this shopping trip. She slips from the room, and I look at Mateo.

"She always say shit like that?" I ask. I don't like that she talks about herself like that. Evie is built amazingly.

"Not always. But old habits die hard. When I get ahold of that asshole, I will beat him to death."

"Has she told you anything that happened?"

"Not exactly, but I can pick up on most of it."

I nod. "I'll help you hold him down."

Mateo pounces on the bed, straddling my waist. "You're the best."

I slide my hands onto his hips. "Don't forget that."

"Are you getting frisky, Gray?" Mateo asks, wiggling his hips.

"Don't start your shit," I laugh.

"Evie's right. You should do that more." He pecks my lips and slips into his bathroom.

With these two, I might be able to manage that.

BOOK SHOPPING WAS as eventful as I thought it would be. Evie browsed forever while Mateo and I sat on a bench. We never once got bored watching her.

When Evie came to Mateo, and she only had three books in her basket, he went back and picked up every single one that she laid her fingers on. They argued all the way to the register to check out. She eventually threw up her hands and gave up. It was cute as hell to watch.

My bedroom door opens, and I watch Mateo slip inside. He sits beside me on the bed.

"Where's Evie?"

"The library, reading. She said if she couldn't beat them, she would join them and kicked me out," Mateo laughs. "Thanks for doing that today."

"I didn't do anything."

"You took us. I wouldn't have gone without you. You put that smile on her face, too."

"She was happy, wasn't she?"

"As much as she doesn't want to admit it, she was." He pulls his leg up on the bed to face me. "What's been going on with you?" I was waiting for this conversation.

I run my hand over my short hair. "I had Hartley look up Tessa and Torri."

Mateo's eyes widen. "And?"

"They're dead." That lands between us like a brick; it's the first time I've said it out loud.

"Damn, Gray, I'm sorry."

"Something doesn't feel right. Their records are sealed. Hartley said they only do that in certain cases, including if they are in hiding."

"You think they are still out there somewhere?"

"I think so."

Mateo nods. "I can help with whatever you need. I know how important this is."

"I don't think I deserve to find them. They're probably better off without me."

"Gray, what happened wasn't your fault."

He said that every time, but it was. I left them alone when I knew they shouldn't be, and they might have died because of it.

"Do you trust Hartley?" I ask.

"Honestly? Yeah. That would have been a different answer a year ago, but he's different now. Do you?"

"Yeah, or I wouldn't have asked for his help."

"I'm pretty sure he's in love with Evie." That makes my head snap up. Mateo shrugs. "Is it fucked up that doesn't bother me? I want her to have everything."

"What do you mean?"

"Micah has all but admitted how he feels about her. He might have been drunk, but he meant it. I know how you and I feel. I had a long talk with Van this morning. What if we can give her everything she's ever deserved? I'm not saying Evie wants or needs the attention. Because she doesn't. She deserves it, though."

"You want us all to date her?"

He shrugs again. "I talked to her this morning, and she didn't exactly say no. What would it hurt to try?"

"I'd have to think about that."

"No big deal," Mateo smiles.

I lean up and place my lips on his, and he's still for a second before sinking into the kiss. I needed to kiss him like I needed fucking air. Anything to get my mind off of what was sure to drag me under. The more I kiss him, the lighter I feel. I hated talking about my past, but Mateo wouldn't let me hide in my head.

I roll us, so I'm hovering over him, never breaking from the kiss. Fuck, I loved kissing him. It was different from kissing a woman. Their lips were soft and plump. His are rougher and more firm, but I liked it. I grasp his jaw to turn his head the way I want, kissing him deeper and harder. I run my hand down his chest, straight to his hard cock, squeezing him through his shorts.

"Fuck, Gray," Mateo breathes, breaking the kiss and grinding his hips up. This is the first time we've been together again since what happened in the guard house.

I wrap my hand around his throat, squeezing it. I can feel his moan vibrate on my hand. "I want to fuck you," I whisper against his lips. It's all I've thought about.

"Gray, I don't know if now is the right time," Mateo forces out.

"Now is the perfect time," I murmur against his lips. I squeeze harder on his throat.

"Shit," Mateo groans.

I lick his top lip. "We need lube."

"Coming right up," Mateo chuckles, pressing a hard kiss against my lips.

He slips out of the room, and I jerk my shirt over my head. I am hard as a fucking rock, throbbing just thinking about sinking inside of him. Less than a minute later, he walks back in, and his eyes flare with heat when he sees me shirtless. I stand up, my hand going to the button of my jeans. He follows my lead until we both stand there naked, chests heaving. I don't know who moved first, but we meet with a crash of lips, our hands roaming everywhere. I walk him back to the bed, lay on top of him, and slide my cock against his. The past six months have been like fucking foreplay, all leading to this moment. I start kissing down his neck, pecs, and abs. I take his cock in my hand. "I've never done this before," I remind him. I lick the salty pre-cum from the tip, remembering licking his come from his hand. He tastes better than I remember. I suck the head of his cock into my mouth, and his hands fly to my head.

"Oh, shit," Mateo gasps, rocking his hips up. I tease the head a few times before sliding my mouth down onto his cock. "Are you sure you haven't done this before?"

I chuckle, the vibrations making him groan. I test my limits, taking as much of him into my mouth as possible. "Fuck. Stop." Mateo pants. I don't stop. I keep sucking his dick until he's thrusting his hips up to sink further into my mouth. "You're going to make me come," Mateo groans. I let him go with a wet pop.

I grin and slide back up his body. "The only time you'll be coming is when my cock is in your ass."

"Holy shit," Mateo laughs breathlessly. "You're going to wreck me, aren't you?" He reaches down and wraps a rough hand around my dick, stroking hard.

"Goddamn, Mateo," I groan, slamming my lips against his. He nudges me until I'm on my back, breaking the kiss. He straddles my thighs, grabs the lube, and squirts a generous amount into his hand. He massages it onto my cock until I'm fucking his fist.

"I'm going to ride the hell out of this dick," Mateo says with a lopsided grin that makes him even sexier. I had no idea how this would play out when this would happen, but I didn't think it would be this way. Not that I am complaining.

Mateo scoots up until my cock is behind him, lining me up with his asshole. With a tight grip, he starts to push back, letting the head slide inside. My hands fly to his hips, resisting the urge to slam inside him. He slides his ass down my length painfully slow until I'm fully seated inside him. His hands slap down on my chest, his whole body shaking. I'm getting ready to ask if he's okay when he lets out the deepest fucking moan I've ever heard.

"Damn," I grit out, massaging his hips with my hands. "You feel good."

"So do you," Mateo breathes, sliding back up my cock.

Holy shit. He is so fucking tight and hot. He locks those green eyes on me, and his pupils have almost taken over the entire irises.

"Ride me," I encourage. He swivels his hips, making me groan. He grins and does it again. I snap my hips up in warning for fucking with me, and his whole body shudders. Mateo plants both feet on the bed and leans back, bracing his hands on my legs. He lifts his hips slowly so I have a prime view of where my cock is, then slowly slides back down. He starts moving faster, and I'm transfixed by his long cock bobbing between his legs, smacking his stomach each time he moves. *Fuck, that's hot.* I've never seen anything sexier. He is hard as steel, turned on by me being in his ass.

I've never felt anything like this; I am already addicted. I don't think I could have done this with anyone but Mateo.

"Fuck, Gray," Mateo groans, bracing his hands back on my chest and lowering his knees back to the bed. "Wreck me," he pants.

I sit up fast, sinking even deeper, slanting my mouth over his, swallowing the moan that leaves his lips. "Get on your hands and knees."

"Fuck," Mateo says, shuddering. He eases off my cock and gets into position. I get on my knees behind him, running my hands up his muscular back.

"You know how sexy you are?" I ask, my voice raspy. Fuck, I am so turned on. I line up with his back hole again, spread his ass cheeks wide, and watch myself disappear.

Mateo starts shifting his hips backward, trying to fuck himself on my cock; I slap his ass in warning. His whole back bows with a moan. "I knew you were a kinky bastard," Mateo breathes. I slam my hips forward, making him take every inch in one firm thrust. "Fuck-kkkkk," Mateo hisses.

I hook my hand around his throat and pull him to his knees so his back is flush against my chest. His fingers dig into my forearms, but he isn't trying to pull me away. "You like me like this, don't you?" I keep a firm hold on his throat and wrap my hand around his cock; it jerks in my hand. I start stroking him in time with my thrusts. "You want me to wreck you, baby boy?" I whisper in his ear. "Wreck you for anyone else? So it's my cock you always come back to?"

"Fuck. Yes," Mateo moans around the hold on his throat. Something tells me Mateo is usually the one who leads things in bed. Not anymore.

Keeping my hold on him, I start fucking his ass with purpose. Mateo is making all kinds of noises that spur me to go harder. *I* am doing that to him, I'm the one making him moan my name.

"Fuck yourself on my cock," I demand and pull out halfway. He doesn't waste time snapping his hips back, taking what he needs. I could feel my release blazing through me. "You going to come for me?"

"Yes. Oh fuck," Mateo moans again. I tighten my fist on his cock, letting him fuck my fist while he fucks himself on my dick. His movements get erratic, and I know he's about to come. I start snapping my hips forward, meeting him thrust for thrust, my thighs slapping against the back of his. "Fuck," Mateo says. His voice has gone gravely, and my cock jerks inside of him. "Gray," Mateo moans, and I can feel his come hit my hand.

I let go of his cock, grab his hips, and start fucking him so hard the bed is scooting across the floor. Mateo reaches down and starts aggressively stroking his cock. When his ass clenches down on me, I know he came again. I jerk his hips back and groan out my own release. "Baby boy."

We both collapse onto the bed with me spooning behind him, my cock still buried in him, trying to get our breathing under control. Once my heart rate returns to normal, I groan and pull out of him, watching my come leak out. "We're making a mess of your bed," Mateo chuckles, looking at me over his shoulder.

"I don't care," I rasp, sealing my lips over his. He rolls over, slinging an arm over my waist, sinking into the kiss. He pecks my lips and lays his head on my arm. I put my hand on the base of his spine and pull him closer. It just feels so normal.

"You weren't lying about wrecking me, were you?"

I bark a laugh. "You asked for it."

He looks up at me. "Are you feeling better?"

Amazingly, I am thanks to him, and it wasn't just the sex, although that was fantastic. Something about Mateo calmed my mind, the same thing Evie did. And I was an idiot for thinking she couldn't handle me. I run my fingers down his jaw. "I am, baby boy."

Mateo shivers. "I like when you call me that," he whispers, and it's the most vulnerable I've ever seen him. Mateo covers up a lot with his humor, but I've seen through it from the beginning, just like he's seen through my bullshit.

"I like calling you that," I admit and clear my throat. "You're important to me. I don't like putting labels on things, but you're mine."

"Gray, look at me," Mateo says gently. "I've never...felt like this before. You're mine too. And we don't have to label it if you don't want to."

"I just want you to be mine."

"I can do that."

I don't know where this is taking us, but I want to find out.

CHAPTER 25
MICAH

I woke up this morning feeling like complete shit. I was hungover and pissed at myself. I remember what I said to Evie last night, and I meant every word, which made me feel even worse. The guy I begged to come back to me finally did, and I fucked it up.

The night I met Evie, I was hurt and vulnerable. Something about her made me feel better, even if it was just in her presence, because the hurt came back as soon as she left with Hartley. When Van agreed to forgive me, I blocked her from my mind, even if her eyes would haunt my dreams. Was I hoping she would call after I gave her my number? Yes. But as soon as I had Van back, I shut that shit down.

After Van fell asleep last night, I tossed and turned, so I went to his library for a drink. One turned into five, and before I knew it, I was plastered, stumbling to find her. I heard her tell Mateo she was sleeping in a guest room, and like a puppet on a string, I found her. I never drank that much for obvious reasons, and it was a trait I got from my mother. Or so my father used to like to throw in my face. Something else that made me a failure.

"Sir?" I look over at Adam. "We're here."

I didn't even realize we had pulled up. "I'll text you when I'm ready."

"Yes, sir." Shaking my head at the formality, I step out of the SUV. Without knocking, I push into Les' house, praying no one is naked. I have already learned my lesson with that. "Hello?" I call out, walking through the foyer.

"In here!" Ryder yells back.

I follow his voice to the living room and find him with Zane on the couch. Thankfully clothed. I can feel my lips tighten at seeing Zane, but I swallow it down. No use fighting it since he is now married to my niece. I would eventually have to get over him going into the police academy without telling her years ago; she did.

"What's up, man?" Ryder asks, flipping the TV off.

"I need to talk to you."

"I'll leave you guys alone," Zane says, pecking Ryder on the lips and striding from the room.

Ryder raises a brow at me once he's gone. "Okay."

I sit for a minute and gather my thoughts. "What do you get out of your relationship with Zane?" Zane used to be Ryder's number one enemy, and somehow they fell into a relationship of their own after Zane joined their group. "I know the setup you guys have. I just need to understand."

"The setup?" Ryder asks.

"You do know Les talks to me, right?"

"There is no setup, man." Ryder sits up, bracing his arms on his knees. "What's this about?"

"How the hell do you let Zane control you?"

"Zane doesn't control me. I'm still my own person. Zane helps me."

"How? Didn't you submit to him?"

"Yes, but that's not what it's about. I was always so fucking angry at everything and everyone. Zane helps me through that, so I don't take it out on the wrong people anymore. He gives me peace."

"How do you do that?"

"At first, it wasn't easy," Ryder chuckles. "I fought him until he helped me see what he could do for me. And it isn't just sexual. I seek him out when I need guidance, someone to talk to, or if I just need to feel free. I don't have to be the protector or strongest person in the room with Zane. I can just be me. Why are you asking?"

I don't want that type of dynamic with Van. I don't want to submit to him, and I don't want him to submit to me. I just need to know how to be open and honest with someone. I was never that person. Growing up in our lifestyle, you're taught early on that vulnerability can get you killed. My brother Luca chucked that shit right out the window when he laid eyes on his wife, Caroline. Les is living proof that vulnerability with the right people makes you stronger. So why couldn't I be that way with Van? I want to be, but fuck if I know how.

"I think I fucked things up with Van."

Ryder's brows shoot up. "What?"

"Evie."

Ryder nods in understanding. "How did you fuck up? You didn't cheat on him, did you?"

"No! Fuck no, I wouldn't do that." I explain what happened to Ryder, and even though I didn't physically cheat on him, I emotionally did. Drunk or not, it wasn't an excuse.

"Fuck, man. Have you talked to him?"

"Not yet, but I will. I just needed to get my head on straight. I don't know how to do this shit."

"Neither did any of us. Gage was a serial playboy who never had a relationship, Holden was a virgin, I was in love with Les and couldn't tell her, Dex couldn't even get close to someone without freaking the fuck out, Zane pined for Les for seven years, and Leo, well Leo is probably the only one who was ready for this."

I run my hand through my hair. "I don't know what to do, Ryder."

"Talk to Van. You were a miserable fucking bastard without him. Don't fuck it up because you can't handle it. You got him back; now fight to keep him."

"What about Evie?" I couldn't get my mind off how she looked at me last night. She wasn't scared of me, shocked maybe, but not scared.

"Isn't she with Mateo?" And there is the other problem. She is

189

dating my best damn friend, and I confessed to her that I couldn't stop thinking about her.

"I'm a fucking asshole."

"We knew that." I glare, and he grins. "Does Mateo know?"

"I'm assuming she told him what happened."

"Assuming? Micah, did you talk to anyone before you ran away?"

"I didn't run away," I growl.

"Yeah, you did because that's what you do. You skip out before the hard shit, so you don't have to deal with it. That's exactly what you did with Van. You ran."

"Don't hold back, asshole."

"You didn't come to me to stroke your head and tell you everything was going to be okay. You came to me for the truth. And the truth is, you're too afraid of your own feelings to let anyone in. If anyone can handle it, it's Van. As for Evie, you need to talk to Les."

"She's going to give me even more shit than you just did," I admit.

"Good, that's what you need. You need to learn to open up, or you'll lose him for good this time."

I sigh because there's no getting out of this. "Where is she?"

"In Holden's office with him, but I wouldn't just walk in there; they tend to get distracted in there."

I'd rather save my eyeballs from getting burned from my skull seeing my niece naked, so I shoot her a text. Two minutes later, she walks around the corner. Ryder kisses her on his way out of the room, and Les flops on the couch.

"Micah." I turn to Ryder's voice. "I'm going to tell you something Zane told me the first night when I struggled with what I needed from him." I nod for him to continue. "He said that it didn't make me weak. I should never be ashamed to ask for what I want or need. And I'm not now. It's been the most freeing experience for me. All that bullshit we are taught growing up is just that, bullshit. Don't let what they told us get to you because if you do, you'll lose him." He strides from the room, and what he just said hits me hard. I turn to Les, and she's softly smiling.

"Hey, shithead."

"Hey. What are you doing here?"

I take a breath and spill everything for the second time today. It probably would have been easier to talk to them at the same time, but I apparently liked doing everything the hard way.

Les' mouth forms an 'O' when I'm done talking. "Holy shit, Micah."

"I know, I'm a fucking asshole. Ryder already informed me of that." Technically I called myself one, and he agreed, but it's the same thing.

"I can't argue that," Les shrugs, pulling her legs under her to sit criss-cross. "Okay, let's start with Evie. Tell me what draws you to her. Pretend there is no Van and no Mateo. And tell me the truth."

If I can tell anyone the truth, it's Les, and she won't judge me. Ryder said I needed to open up, so this is a good place to start. "She has this thing about her that makes you need to be close to her. She's stronger than what she gives herself credit for. She has the most carefree laugh, and you want to bottle the goddamn sound so you can listen to it on bad days. She's drop-dead fucking gorgeous, and she doesn't even realize it."

"Okay. Wow. What about Van?"

"He's the first person I want to see when I wake up. I crave him more than I need air. He just fucking gets me, no matter how shitty I'm being. He's the perfect balance to the storm always raging inside me. And he's the sexiest man I've ever laid eyes on."

"You know, when I asked you that, I didn't think you'd be honest?" Les laughs. "But seriously. You need to talk to Van first. Get his take on things, then you need to talk to Mateo because I hate to tell you this, Micah, but you sound half in love with Evie."

"What?! I just met her!" Has she completely lost her damn mind? All the lovey feelings in this house have officially driven her insane.

"Love doesn't have a timeline. You love who you love when you love them. Evie's a sweet girl, and I can see how she would wrap you around her finger. But if you hurt her, I will kill you."

"I don't want to hurt her or Van; I need to keep my mouth shut."

"No," she argues. "That's exactly why you shouldn't. I said she was sweet, not a delicate flower. Evie has grit, and if you take two seconds from trying to push her away, you might see that."

"That still doesn't help that I have a boyfriend, and she's dating Mateo."

"Have you listened to nothing I've said? *Talk* to them. It might be easier than you think."

"How the hell do you get that?"

"Let's just say Leo talked to Mateo earlier. And no, I'm not going to tell you about what. You need to take your ass home and fix this."

I narrow my eyes at her. "You already knew about this, didn't you?"

She shrugs. "Most of it. But I wanted to see how honest you would be with me. Now they need this honesty."

"I hate you; you know that?"

"You love me, or you wouldn't have come here."

"Can I hang out here for a little bit? I need to get my shit together."

"You're always welcome here, and I want you to give Evie my number. Tell her I'll be here if she ever needs a friend."

"You don't have girlfriends," I point out.

"I need to find some because I'm surrounded by literal dicks all day, every day."

I laugh. "You have a point there."

"Bring her over one day, and we'll have a girl's day with Bridget."

As scary as it is about Evie hanging out with Les, I think it would do Evie some good.

I needed to think about everything Les just said and think about my revelations about Evie I didn't realize until they flooded out of my mouth.

"How are things with Hartley?" Les asks.

"Not as bad as I thought. We've taken him with us several times to question people about Aaron. He's useful." Hartley is more than useful. He could make one move toward one of those assholes, and they folded at the drop of a hat.

"How does he fit in with Evie?"

"What do you mean?"

"I mean, she lived with him before she ended up at Mateo's."

"They grew up together, is all I know."

Les nods. "And he stuck it out with people who hated him just for her?"

"Yeah." What the hell is she getting at?

"Even though he knew you guys could protect her?"

"Just spit it out, shithead."

"Micah, do you have brain damage? Seriously, like why can you not connect any dots?"

"Why are you being so fucking sarcastic today?"

"Because I can't figure out when you stopped paying attention to those around you. You used to be able to call people on their shit like it was nothing, and now you can't see that Hartley is in love with Evie. And probably has been for a long damn time."

"This got a lot more complicated, didn't it?" I sigh.

Les laughs. "Welcome to my world, Micah."

"Fuck my life," I mutter, slumping down in the chair. "Evie would never go for this shit."

"How do you know? You haven't taken four seconds to get to know the girl. If I've learned one thing, it's that communication is key. When things got complicated with Zane again, the guys and I sat down and discussed it. Was it easy? Fuck no. I thought I would have to lock Ryder in his room at night so he wouldn't kill him. But we made it work."

"What if this isn't something I want?"

"Then I think you need to figure that out before it's too late."

Do I want a relationship like Les has?

The only thing I know right now is that I need to talk to Van and fix the mess I've just made.

CHAPTER 26

EVANDER

I finally got a message back from Micah telling me he was fine, and he was at Les'. He also told me that we would talk when he got back.

When we went to bed last night, I thought everything was fine. He acted like it was, anyway. Some time through the night, I woke up, and he wasn't there. Worried, I went in search of him and found him with Evie. I wanted to be upset and probably should have been, but I wasn't. I was more concerned that maybe I wasn't enough for Micah, and that's why he was with her.

Unsurprisingly, he was gone when I got done talking to Mateo. Micah doesn't handle his feelings well, and it's obvious there is a whole host of them he isn't ready to deal with yet.

My talk with Mateo *was* surprising. Mateo and I have always had a close relationship, and we were each other's confidants. So when he spelled out that he's been wanting a relationship like Les, I was shocked. I had no idea he's even thought about that.

The talk is why I'm standing in the library doorway, watching Evie read what I'm assuming is one of the new books Mateo and Gray took her to buy. I could admit Evie is beautiful, but I'm not necessarily attracted to her; I am intrigued by her. Anyone who could rope my brother is certainly intriguing, and I wanted to know why.

I walk in, finally letting my presence be known. She looks up startled, slaps the book closed, and nearly shrinks back into the chair.

"May I sit?" I ask. She bites her bottom lip and nods. I sink into the chair in front of the one she's curled up in. "I want to start by saying I'm not mad at you."

"You should be," Evie says quietly. "I should have told him to leave."

"Evie, how would you have felt to tell him to leave?"

She thinks about her answer. "Bad. He looked...lost." I was afraid of that, but I don't think it had to do with me. I think it's the doe-eyed brunette sitting in front of me.

"If you haven't noticed, Micah isn't open with expression unless it's anger. The fact he came to you last night means something."

"Like what?" The poor girl looks lost and very confused. I wish I had all the answers for her, but until I talk to Micah, I could only give her theories.

"I don't know for sure. What I do know is that when he was feeling at his lowest, he found you."

"Doesn't that bother you?"

"No," I shrug. "I love Micah at all his highs and lows, and I'll be there for him through them all, and he would do the same for me. But sometimes, we need an extra ear. I have my brothers, and Micah has Les. He also needs *you* if last night proved anything."

"I don't understand why everyone is so understanding about this. Mateo was, and he should have been furious with me, and so should you."

"Would it make you feel better if I was?"

"No! I just...I'm not used to this." Evie runs her fingers through her hair with a sigh. "You know my last relationship wasn't good, but it was more than that. He wasn't just physically abusive; it was mental and emotional." I relax in my chair and let her talk. I don't think she's opened up to anyone yet, and I'm glad she feels like she can with me. "He beat it into my head every day that I wasn't good enough or pretty enough. He pointed out all my flaws and shortcomings. He was just *mean*. For a year, I felt I didn't deserve anything besides what he gave me."

"That's because he wasn't a fucking man, Evie. Men don't treat women like their punching bags, physically or otherwise. And whatever he said to you, I can assure you; it was a lie. His belittling you came from his own insecurities. A real man will tell you every goddamn day how beautiful you are and how special you are to him. He would cherish you; he would never harm you."

Evie smiles, and I see that warmth seeping through like Mateo pointed out. "Thank you for that. When I ran, I had nothing, but I knew if I didn't, I would lose myself to him or lose my life. For eight months, I believed every word he said to me, then I met Mateo. Mateo is everything you described. Not a day has gone by that he hasn't made me feel like I'm worthy. That's why I feel like shit about Micah. I don't want to mess things up for you, either."

I choose my words carefully. I'm not sure if Mateo has talked to her or if he even plans to yet. "I think you're getting ahead of yourself. Micah and I have stuff to work through that has nothing to do with last night. Micah and I have...history together. I want you to be there for him, Evie, no matter what way he needs it; I won't stand in the way of that. I want to be your friend also."

"I'd like that."

I gesture to her book. "I'll let you get back to reading." Her face blooms with color, realizing I saw the cover. "Never be embarrassed about what you read. Come here." I stand up, and she follows me to the corner of my library. I push a button on one of the bookshelves, which slides to reveal my secret stash.

"You read romance?" Evie giggles, running her fingers over the spines.

"Yes, and I'm not hiding them. I just have a shithead for a brother who likes bringing up stuff at inappropriate times."

Evie laughs. "He does."

"He wouldn't be Mateo if he didn't." I push another button; this shelf is empty. "Put your books in here. They deserve their own home."

Evie wraps her arms around my waist in a hug. I didn't think she was very open with affection, so I wrap mine around her neck, pulling her closer. "Thank you for a home for my books and what you said."

"Thank you for trusting me enough to tell me that." She pulls back from the hug with a smile. "Happy reading."

Stuffing my hands in my pockets, I stride from the room.

Evie is intriguing indeed.

"Fuck," I grunt, and my eyes fly open. I look down, and I'm met with Micah's blue eyes, my cock in his mouth. "Holy shit," I breathe, sinking my fingers into his black hair.

My cock slips from his lips. "Hello, *amore mio*," he murmurs roughly, still stroking my cock.

"What are you doing?" I groan, my eyes closing when he twists his hand around the head.

"I want you to fuck me," Micah announces, and my eyes fly open.

"What?" I ask, stunned.

"I want you to fuck me," Micah repeats. "I want to feel you inside me."

My sleepy brain catches up with what he's saying and everything that happened. I push his hand away. "Micah, we need to talk first."

"*Amore mio*. I just need..." Micah closes his eyes, and when he reopens them, I'm struck by their raw intensity. "We will talk, I promise. About anything and everything. I just need to feel you." He swallows. "Please."

I pull him up so he's lying on top of me. "Are you sure?"

"Very sure." He pecks my lips. "I need you." Hearing those words leave his mouth is everything I needed to hear and didn't know. I went to bed early when Micah still wasn't home, but Les assured me he was still there, and they had a lot of eye-opening conversations. Whatever that meant. But I wouldn't betray Micah's trust with Les and ask.

I slam my lips against his, our hips moving to rub our cocks together. I kiss him until he's groaning into my mouth, then roll us so I'm on top. "You want my cock, *mi rey*?" I ask, kissing down his neck.

"Fuck yes," Micah groans, tilting his head to give me better access. He loves when I kissed and sucked on his neck. I kiss down his pecs and abs until I get to his long, throbbing cock jerking on his stomach. I lick from the base of his shaft to the weeping slit. Micah groans long and loud when I slip him between my lips. Grabbing the base, I lick around the head before sucking on the head, just like he likes. His hips buck, trying to force my mouth further on him. I move my hand and slide my mouth down until he bumps the back of my throat. Relaxing, he slides down, and I swallow around the head. "Shit," Micah breathes. He pulls my mouth away. "Please, fuck me."

I reach into the bedside table for a bottle of lube and squirt it onto my fingers. I watch his eyes darken when I slide my hand between his ass cheeks, circling his back hole with the tip of my middle finger. I watch his breathing get ragged as I push my finger forward, breaching the resistance. He was so fucking responsive when I played with his ass, but he never let me take it further than that. I couldn't wait to get my cock inside of him, but I wanted to make sure he was ready. I slide my finger in and out a few times before adding a second. Micah sinks his teeth into that plush bottom lip and moans.

"Fuck, I love that sound," I rasp, working my fingers in and out. When he starts working his hips onto my fingers, I know he's ready. I slowly slide my fingers out and tip the bottle back up, squirting it on my cock. Micah watches my every movement as I slick my dick up, pumping my hips forward to fuck my fist. "You ready?" I ask, and he nods.

I brace my hand beside his head, lining my cock up at his asshole with my other hand. Keeping a tight grip on the base, I slide forward and almost lose it when the head slides inside him. "Damn, you're tight," I groan. I work my hips back and forth. "Relax and let me in, *mi rey*," I say softly, my eyes never leaving his. He takes a shuddering breath, and his body relaxes. I push harder, and my cock pops past the resistance, letting me slide into his tight, hot ass. "Holy shit," I say, half strangled, my other hand slapping the bed beside his head. I feed every inch inside of him until my thighs are pressed against the back of his. "Breathe," I soothe, kissing down his jaw. I stay still, letting him adjust to me being inside him. I shift my hips and drag my cock against his prostate when his breathing slows.

He moans long and loud, making my whole body shudder. "You feel good," Micah pants.

I lay my forehead against his and start to move slowly, savoring the moment because he finally trusted me enough to let me do this. We've been dancing around this very thing since we started messing around the first time.

I can feel Micah's cock twitching against my stomach, letting me know he's enjoying this as much as I am. "You like my cock deep inside you?" I ask, my voice gruff.

"Yes. Sweet fuck," Micah moans again when I slam my hips forward. I lean back, brace my hands on his thighs, and push his hips forward so I can watch myself disappear inside of him. Micah locks his hand around his cock, stroking himself hard.

I start moving with purpose, my thighs slapping against him. Moans and groans are leaving both our mouths, echoing around the room. "You have the sweetest ass," I groan, grunting each time my thighs slap his because of how hard I'm fucking him.

"Harder, *amore mio*," Micah says, stroking his cock in a harsh grip. I sink my hands onto his hips, grab them in a bruising grip, and pull him down to meet my thrusts. "Goddamn, just like that."

Micah's ass clamps down so hard on my cock that it stops my movement and steals my breath. He reaches down with his other hand, squeezing his balls, stroking his cock fast. I watch his abdomen clench. "You going to come, *mi rey*?" I rasp. He nods fast.

"Van," Micah groans long and loud, ropes and ropes of his come landing on his tan chest.

"Hold on," I grit out. I am so fucking close that I know I am going to explode. I slam into him several times, his cock jerks, and more come spurts out, and I finally let go. "Micah," I breathe. My balls draw up, and fire races down my spine. I jerk his hips down, hold myself as far as I can, and come deep inside him. Marking him. I collapse on top of him, not giving a shit about the mess on his chest; both of us are breathing out of control.

Micah runs his hands through my hair and down my back. "I love you," he murmurs, making me shiver.

I look into his eyes. "I'll never get tired of hearing that. I love you, too." He leans up, kissing me slowly. I sit back on my heels and slowly pull out of him, watching my come leak out. "Now I know why you like watching this. It's fucking hot," I say.

Micah chuckles. "Hell yeah, it is."

We both head to the shower to clean up, and I take my time washing him, just like he did with me the first time we slept together. I should have known then how Micah felt about me, but he always fought it so damn hard. Once clean, we go back to bed and curl around each other.

I don't want to break this moment, but so many things are being left unsaid. "We need to talk."

"I know," Micah sighs. "I don't even know where to start."

"Let's start with Evie."

Micah nods. "I'm sorry for going to her last night. I never should have done that, not when I could have talked to you about how I was feeling." Micah scoots up so he's leaning against the head-board; I follow so I can see his face. "The night I met Evie, I was so hurt and angry. When I heard the scream, I didn't think; I just reacted. Before I knew it, I was pummeling some guy's face for daring to hurt a woman, and then I saw her. Something about her eyes made me feel calm. Even though she was the one who was being assaulted, she was worried Gray and I would get hurt for stepping in." He chuckles at that, and I smile. "I dreamed of her that night, and when I woke up, I was so washed with guilt because of you that I tried to block her out. I tried to block out how she made me feel. When I walked into the kitchen that day, and she was sitting there, it was like the world opened up beneath my feet. Van, I would never hurt you. I understand if you want me to stay away from her, and even if I don't want to be away from you, I'll stay at my house while she's here. I'll do whatever it takes not to lose you again."

"I don't want that. I want you to get to know her, Micah. I want you to find out what this is that makes you feel calm around her."

Micah's brows furrow. "But why would you want that after what I just said?"

"Because I would do anything for you, *mi rey*, including this. I know what I said, but I'm all in with you. I'm done holding back because you finally gave me what I wanted." I take his hand. "Your trust."

"What about..."

"We can talk about everything else in the morning. Tonight, I just want to hold you. Tomorrow, we will figure out the rest."

We get settled back on the bed, lying face to face. "I love you, *mi rey*."

"I love you too, *amore mio*."

I know Micah and I have been through a lot in our short time together, but I feel like we can defeat and overcome anything at each other's side.

CHAPTER 27
HARTLEY

I thought I was okay with Mateo and Evie. That was, until I had to listen to them fucking all night long.

This morning I heard them. No big deal, I just slipped outside by the pool. When I came back inside, the only person home was Evander. We talked for a little while, proving to me that I was a judgmental bastard this whole time. They are criminals. There is no denying that, but they are also decent fucking guys.

I came straight to the back patio after breakfast to avoid Evie screaming Mateo's name if they decided to pick up where they left off at three o'clock this morning.

I hear the patio door slide open, and her coconut scent hits me first.

"It's so pretty out here in the morning," Evie says, sitting on the lounger beside mine.

"Yep."

"Are you okay? You didn't say much over breakfast."

"I'm fine."

"Hartley, I know when something is wrong. Talk to me."

"Nothing is wrong, Evie."

"Then why won't you look at me?" I look over at her and raise an eyebrow. "Your mouth might be saying something isn't wrong, but your face tells a different story. You've been avoiding me."

Count to ten. Do not let your feelings show.

"I haven't been avoiding you; you just haven't been around." *One.*

"Oh," she chews on her bottom lip, "I'm sorry." *Two.*

"Stop apologizing. It's fine." *Three.*

"Are you sure nothing is wrong? Because you sound like a grouch right now." *Four.* "I miss hanging out with you." *Five.* "You can come to me whenever you need to." *Six.*

Fuck this.

"You want to know what my fucking problem is? I'm jealous, okay? Is that what you wanted to hear?"

"Jealous? Of what?" Evie asks, shocked. *So much for not letting your feelings show.*

"You really don't see it, do you?" I laugh, but it's completely humorless. "I've wanted you since we were teenagers." Evie's mouth opens and closes a few times, confused. I decide to take pity on her. "Don't worry about it. You have Mateo, and I won't stand in the way of that. You've never seen me; you've only seen what I can do for you." I stand up from the lounger and turn on my heel to head back inside. *Great job spilling that hateful bullshit, asshole.*

"I don't deserve that, Hartley James Cruz!" I spin back around, and Evie is standing up, facing me. "I've always seen you and never once used you for a damn thing. I always told you not to get involved, but you did anyway. So don't you dare act like I've *ever* asked anything of you." She goes to march by me, and I grab her arm to spin her back to face me.

"I got involved because that's the one thing I could be for you, princess," I growl. Her neck is craned back to look up at me since I'm standing so close. Her eyes are huge, her chest heaving. But she isn't scared. Oh no, Evie is pissed.

"If you felt that way, why didn't you ever say anything?" She puts her hands on her hips, her brown eyes narrowing. "You were too ashamed to be seen with the chubby, nerdy girl. Captains of the baseball team didn't go for girls like me."

I advance on her until her back is pressed to the door. I press my body against hers. "You weren't the chubby, nerdy girl to me, princess. You weren't any of those things, period. You were the most gorgeous girl to me, and you never gave me a second look."

Her hands slap on my chest to keep me from moving closer. "How was I supposed to know?! You never said anything."

"Why would I? All that would have done was ruin what we did fucking have."

"But you left! You left me! Left me to deal with Dad dying and Mom drinking by myself! Then you left me with Aaron! And then you have the nerve to tell me all I did was *use* you? You were my best damn friend, and when I needed you, you weren't there!"

Like a punch to the gut, I take a step back. "Fuck, I'm sorry, Evie." I take another step back, and she advances on me.

"No, I shouldn't have said that." Her hand reaches out to me, and I step out of the way before she can touch me. Hurt flashes across her face when her hand drops.

"You should have. I know you didn't use me." Why the fuck did I say that? Out of all the years of our friendship, Evie never asked me for a goddamn thing. I always ran to her rescue when she was bullied, let her sleep in my room when her mom was too drunk to deal with, or she couldn't take watching her dad get sicker, took her to school dances, gave her a shoulder to cry on, and hid her away from her crazy ex. But she is right; when she needed me the most, I wasn't there and left her believing I wouldn't answer the phone when she called. I went about my life like I had planned and left the girl I loved the most to fall prey to a monster. I rake my fingers through my hair. "Just forget I said anything. You're right. I wasn't there, and I should have been."

"I was sixteen, Hartley. You needed to move on with your life. There wasn't anything in Fairview for you; you needed to get out."

"Stop that," I say harshly. "Stop trying to justify what I did." It's amazing to me that she could still do that. She never let me get by with my bullshit, but she always had a way of making me feel better about it. And in true Evie fashion, that's what she is doing now.

"I'm not justifying it, Hart. I'm stating facts. Did I deserve what you just said? No. But you didn't deserve what I said, either. We can't change the past; we move on from it." When she reaches out this time, I don't move. Her hand settles on my chest, right over my heart that's beating out of control. "Why didn't you ever tell me?"

"Because I was afraid you wouldn't feel the same way, and I'd ruin our friendship. I couldn't lose you, Evie." My stepdad was a good man, but he expected no less than the best. Best grades, best at sports, best at everything. He didn't see the toll it took on me in school. Evie was my saving grace. She did more for me than I ever did for her by simply existing and letting me see the side she never allowed anyone else to see.

"I felt the same way, Hartley," Evie says quietly. "But I didn't want to risk it, either." I feel like all the air has been sucked from my lungs. She felt the same fucking way?

My lips are on hers before I can register what I'm doing. Her arms wrap around my neck, kissing me back. Sinking my hands into her hair, I tilt her face to kiss her deeper. Kissing her is everything I thought it would be, and more. Then it hits me like a ton of bricks. *Mateo.*

I pull back breathless, watching her eyelids flutter open. She puts her hand to her lips like she couldn't believe mine were just there. What the fuck am I doing? I told her I wouldn't stand in her way with Mateo, and then I practically mauled her. "I'm sorry, Evie."

I look up from her face and lock eyes with Mateo.

Fuck.

"Will you just fucking say something?" I demand.

After Mateo saw me kissing Evie, he pulled me inside to talk to him. Now we are sitting in the office, and he hasn't said a word, just stares at me. I don't know if he is doing it to make me uncomfortable or if he is imagining all the ways he could brutally kill me. Either way, it's making me nervous as hell.

"I'm trying to think of a way to say this. Hold on." Mateo shrugs. "Fuck it. I'm fine with you kissing Evie as long as she doesn't care."

"What?" What the hell is going on?

"Look, I'm just going to lay it out there. I want Evie to have everything. She deserves to be spoiled. She deserves to be treated right. I think we could do that," Mateo explains. "I've already talked to Gray. I've laid down everything for Van. Van will talk to Micah. I've mentioned it to Evie. All that's left is you."

"Wait. Evie's okay with this?"

"I wouldn't say she was okay with it. Yet. But she didn't say no, either. We're stuck here together for the foreseeable future. What would it hurt to try this out?"

"So, you're saying if I went to Evie right now and fucked her, you wouldn't care?" There's no damn way. Not that I would try, but I wanted to test his reaction. His face never changes from the calm expression he's been wearing since he caught me kissing his girl.

"As long as Evie says yes, then no, I wouldn't care. For whatever reason, I trust you. You care about her. You must trust us, or you would have found a way to leave with her by now." He has me there. When we first got here, I made plans left and right to find a safe house. But in the end, they were the smartest choice, no matter Evie's relationship with Mateo.

"What about when this is over?" Does that mean this stopped? There is no way I can get involved with Evie just for some fun and then go on about my life like it never happened, leaving her with Mateo.

"We cross that bridge when we come to it. All that I ask is she's treated with respect, and I know she will be, or I wouldn't have asked any of you in the first place." Mateo sighs. "I know this is a lot, so go talk to Evie about whatever the hell happened on the patio. Just know that if it happens again, I'm fine. But this is a two-way street, Hartley. You can't get pissed at any of us for being with her. You also need to know I care a lot about her, and I'm not just passing her from friend to friend like you accused me of with Gray. We're all adults, and I think we can do this as consenting adults."

I nod. "I'm not agreeing to anything. I'm just saying that I get it.

But I do have a question. You say you care about her, so when are you going to tell her who you are?"

"Honestly, I want to, but it's not just my secret. A lot is at stake for her knowing, and not just for us. It puts a target on her back."

"That makes sense." I stand up. "I'm going to talk to her."

"Good, because I heard what was said out there." Mateo grins. "She handed your ass to you, so I'm not going to say shit."

I bark a laugh. "Yeah, she did." I get to the doorway and turn around. "I do trust you guys. A week ago, that would have been a different answer."

"We tend to let past prejudices get in the way. Les forgave you, and I don't think you realize what that means. You made it right, Hart; it's time you forgave yourself, too."

I jerk a nod and go in search of Evie. Knowing I need to forgive myself and doing it are two different things.

Finding her on the patio where I left her, I sit beside her. She looks at me with a soft smile. "You knew he wasn't going to be mad, didn't you?"

Evie shrugs. "I figured if he were going to get mad, he would have done it when he caught us."

"I'm sorry I kissed you like that, Evie. I didn't have a right to do that."

"I'm glad you did," she says, lacing our hands together. "I wish you would have told me then."

I kiss her knuckles. "Me too. None of that would have happened..."

"Please don't do that. It wasn't your fault any more than it was mine. I've spent eight months trying to move on, and it's time I do that."

"Is this really what you want, princess?" I haven't called her princess in years, and I've never called anyone that since. Earlier I called her that in anger; now, I mean it differently. Evie was always like the princess in the ivory tower that I could never quite reach. My head is still reeling that I had a chance with her, and I missed that chance because I was a punk-ass coward. Could I have that chance now? I'm not going to make any decision until I know what *she* wants.

"I missed hearing that." She smiles. "Does it make me crazy if I say, maybe? Mateo has helped me find the girl I used to be, and in a way, I think he's trying to make up for all the bad shit Aaron did. He's left this decision entirely in my hands, and I want to reach out and take what he's offering."

"But you're scared," I guess.

"I am, not of you guys but the situation in general. I think too much," she laughs.

"This is something you *should* think about." I sigh. "I also think this is something you want, or you wouldn't have considered it. And to answer your question earlier, no, I don't think it makes you crazy. What's going on with Micah, though? You wouldn't even look at him." But he was sure as hell looking at her.

"Well, Micah drunkenly admitted some things, and we haven't had a chance to talk about it. The last thing he said to me before that was he didn't trust me."

"Maybe you should talk to him."

"I will. I just have to work up some nerve," she laughs. "Micah intimidates me, but in a good way. I think as much as Mateo brings me out of my shell, Micah would obliterate it completely. That's what I need."

"What do I bring to this?" I ask.

"Everything." Evie turns to face me. "One isn't more than the other. But with you, I don't feel any reservations. That kiss, Hartley? Blew my mind. I always used to think about what it would be like to kiss you, but nothing prepared me for the real thing."

"I feel the same way, princess," I say gruffly.

"Will you kiss me again?" *Hell fucking yeah.*

"You never have to ask. Come here, princess." I pat my lap so she would be closer, and she hesitates, making me frown. "What's wrong?"

"You want me to sit there?" Her face blooms with color.

I rub my finger down her red cheek. "I want you close. Come here." I tug her hand, and she stands. Throwing one leg over my lounger, she still looks uncertain, so I take the decision from her hands. Gripping those thick hips, I jerk her down until I feel her ass press against me. I let my hands wander down her thighs and back up again, making her shiver. "Goddamn, princess."

I wrap one hand around her neck and jerk her lips to mine. She opens immediately, letting me stroke her tongue with mine. *I'm finally kissing Evie.* The longer we kiss, the more her shyness disappears. Her hands start roaming over my arms and my pecs. I slide my hands to her ass and rock my hips up. She jerks her mouth away from mine. Her pupils are blown, her blush has traveled to her chest, and her breasts are heaving with each breath.

"You feel that, princess?" I ask, pulling her down to grind on my hard cock. "That's what you do to me."

Her hands spread out on my pecs, and she rubs them down. She pauses, and I hide a grin when she moves over my nipples again. When she pulls my shirt up to look, I can't help but laugh. "Just remember what you do to me, I do to you," I joke.

"Hartley! Are your nipples pierced? Are those tattoos?!"

"Yes," I answer, still laughing.

"When?" she breathes and lets her hands run down my bare skin. "Holy shit, that's hot." My chest and back are covered entirely, and I am working on the arms next. It's my escape from reality when I get tattoos and piercings.

"I got the first one when I turned eighteen; everything else came later." I slide my hands under her shirt and stop at her waist. I just needed to feel her skin. "That's not all that's pierced." I grin this time and watch her mind struggle to catch up. I see the moment she does; she lets out a little gasp.

"Your you know what is pierced?"

"My cock? Yes." Six barbells lined the bottom of my shaft in a Jacob's ladder and two barbells through the head in a magic cross. It hurt like hell, but it was worth it. "You going to pull that out and look at it, too?"

"Hartley!" Evie smacks my chest with a laugh.

"Well, I mean, you just scandalized me by pulling my nipples out."

"Stop," she says, laughing harder. This is what I missed most about her. Her laugh and the carefree way she jokes. I just missed her. "I didn't scandalize you."

"You did. I was enjoying kissing you, and then bam, I'm half naked."

She moves back on my legs, making me groan when her ass rubs against my cock. She runs her fingers over the tattoo that runs down my ribs. "They're so colorful. Do they have meaning?"

Not a conversation we can have yet. I don't want to lie to her, but she isn't ready for that truth yet. "Not really. I just liked them."

"They're so beautiful."

I pull her hands away and wrap them around my neck. "You're beautiful, princess."

This time she doesn't ask before she seals her lips over mine.

I had already made up my mind when Evie kissed me again. I would go through this with them and see where it took us.

I hope we aren't making a huge mistake.

CHAPTER 28
EVIE

Some time throughout the day, I decided that I would give what Mateo suggested a try. That thought both scared and excited me. I have no idea what is in store for me, but I couldn't wait to find out. I am done letting Aaron run my life. It's time for me to live without fear.

I told Mateo, and he seemed just as excited as me. He gave me so many orgasms with his mouth and cock that I blissfully passed out. Now, I am wide awake at two in the morning, dying of thirst. Gently sliding out from Mateo's arm that's anchored on my waist, I turn to look at him when my feet hit the floor. God, he is gorgeous even asleep with his hair sleep-tousled and his mouth slightly parted. Shaking my head, before I wake him up to have a repeat of earlier, I slide a pair of shorts and Mateo's shirt on.

Sex with Mateo was more than mind-blowing. He talked dirty the whole time, explaining in detail what would happen if I agreed to date all the guys. I'm still not sure how this thing with Micah and Evander would work, but I am happy to go along with it. How many chances would I ever get? Zero. Might as well live life to the fullest now.

And that kiss with Hartley? Holy shit. One second we were arguing, and the next, his lips were on me. The second kiss was even better. I'd always had a crush on Hartley but figured, like every other guy, he didn't see me. I've never been more glad to be wrong in my life.

I use the bathroom quickly, wash my hands, and pad quietly down the stairs. I hear a whirring noise from the kitchen and step inside.

Micah is at the island with a mixer in front of him. This time I don't try to back away. Leaning against the wall, I look at him. His hair is a little wild, he was shirtless, and I could see the top of those damn grey sweatpants. As if he can sense me watching him, Micah looks up, and we lock eyes. Everything he said to me comes flooding back, and I don't know whether to turn away or not.

"Want to help?" he asks when he flips the mixer off.

"I'm not much of a cook," I admit.

"I'll teach you. Come here."

"Why are you up so late?" I ask, walking toward him.

Micah shrugs. "I don't sleep well. So I bake." I remember him telling me that the last time I found him in the kitchen in the middle of the night. The night he told me he didn't trust me. "What're you doing up?"

"I fell asleep early." More like passed the hell out. I could feel my cheeks heat at the reason why. "What are you making?"

"Brioche col tuppo." He dusts the counter with flour and pours the mixture from the bowl on top of it. He nods his head for me to step beside him. "You have to knead the dough." At my blank look, he sinks his fingers into it until it starts smoothing out. "Like that. You try." I copy what he showed me. "Faster, or it will stick to your hands."

He steps behind me and puts his hands on top of mine, moving my hands the way he wants. Just from that little touch, I can feel goosebumps pebble my skin, and my nipples harden beneath my shirt. *Good lord, get your shit together.*

"Just like that," Micah says. Did he get closer? I can feel his breath on my neck; he wasn't that close a minute ago. My brain is seconds away from exploding. "Harder." Why does everything out of his mouth have to sound sexual?

Mateo awakened something in me that apparently makes me want all dick within a mile radius, or how many square feet are in this house. I snort a laugh, and Micah's hands freeze on top of mine.

"Something funny?" I can hear the amusement in his voice, and it makes me smile.

"Nope." No way am I telling him what I'm thinking.

He works our hands together in the dough, kneading it and rolling it. I have to admit it was very relaxing until he pressed his body against my back. He helps me separate the dough into pieces of the same size, rolling them into little balls. He sits them on a baking sheet and moves to put them in the oven. I don't look over my shoulder because I don't want to see him when he goes to walk away. I wipe my hands off to distract myself. Now that we are done, the little bubble we were in would burst. I feel him before he ever touches me; he leans his hands on the island beside my hips. *Breathe, just breathe.*

"I meant every word I said the other night, *la mia stella*." And I just stop breathing. I remember him calling me that but forgot to look up what it meant. All I knew was that it sounded sexy coming from his lips. "You're a goddamn goddess wrapped up in an innocent little package. Are you innocent, though?" He whispers that last part in my ear, making my nipples harder. I didn't put a bra on when I came downstairs, so they are showing through the fabric of Mateo's shirt. "It's been fucking torture listening to you with Mateo."

"What about Evander?" I ask once my brain catches up.

"We've talked. A lot. Probably more than I have in my whole life. You know what he said?"

"No," I whisper, leaning further against him.

"He said that if I wanted you, I should go for it. The question is, do you want me, *la mia stella*?" I know there is no slowing this fast-moving train down when I answer this question.

"Yes," I breathe. There's no turning back now.

"Say it," he demands, making me shudder.

"Yes, I want you."

He spins me in his arms, and I look up into those ice-blue eyes I've dreamed about since he saved me, even when he was still nameless. I've never seen somebody protect someone they didn't know so selflessly, and I had to admit I became a little obsessed. Now those eyes are looking at me again, but they aren't looking at me with concern. My hands land on his hips, and he flinches. Thinking I did something wrong, I go to move them, but his hands lock around my wrists and pull them back. "Just give me a second," he murmurs, his face getting closer to mine. I can see the battle he is waging with himself. I'm about to make the decision easier for him and put distance between us when his lips rub against mine. My hands curl on his hips with the sensation, and his lips land on mine.

Micah deepens the kiss with a groan, kissing me hard enough to bruise my lips. I didn't care. At this moment, he could kiss me however he wanted. His tongue licks the seam of my lips, and I open for him. With no real effort, his hands wrap around my waist and lifts, so I'm sitting on the counter. I don't have time to react before he steps between my thighs, cradles my face with both hands, and kisses me with so much passion that I get lost in the sensation. I could feel his hardness rubbing against my shorts, and I couldn't stop the whimper of need that escaped. How the hell have I been with Mateo non-stop and still want Micah? Or Hartley?

He pulls his mouth from mine and pulls back to see my eyes. Both of us are breathing hard, and you could feel the tension pulsing between us. "You do want me, *la mia stella*." His hands slide up my thighs until his fingers tuck under the leg of my shorts.

"It's the grey sweatpants," I joke breathlessly.

Micah looks stunned for a second, then busts out laughing. I've heard him chuckle, but I've never heard him actually laugh. It's a rich, deep sound that I could listen to forever. "So you're saying you won't kiss me again unless I'm wearing them?" he asks, still chuckling.

"Those or the suits."

"Everyone makes fun of my suits," he says with a raised brow. "Are you?"

"Um. Hell no. You could make a nun sweat in one of those. I think they're just jealous."

Micah nods his head like he's taking everything I'm saying seriously. "I want to apologize for saying I didn't trust you. I was trying to find everything I could wrong with you so it would stop the way I was feeling."

I loop my arms around his neck. "I get it. I would have never come between you and Evander. What you guys have is beautiful."

The timer on the oven goes off; he pecks my lips and turns to take our Brioche out. He digs around in the freezer until he finds what he's looking for. Putting one of the rolls we made on the plate, he pulls it apart before putting what looks like ice cream between the pieces. He turns to me and holds it to my lips. I take a bite and moan in appreciation. His pupils dilate, and his eyes stay focused on mine when he takes a bite for himself. The ice cream melts fast on the hot bread and drips onto my thigh.

With a grin that should scare me, Micah bends down and licks it off.

"Holy shit," I breathe when his tongue makes contact. While cleaning one side, he lets the ice cream drip all over the other. This time he doesn't lick it off; he gently sucks it from my skin. *I am never going to be able to handle Micah.*

Feeling bold, I take the bread from his fingers and pull his hand to my mouth. I suck his middle finger into my mouth to get the ice cream, letting it go with a pop. Micah groans deep in his chest, and his lips are back on mine. This kiss is hot and needy, heading exactly where I want it to, and from how hard he is, he wants it too. But we couldn't. Not yet.

"Micah, wait," I pant when I feel his hands slide under my shirt. He starts kissing my neck, making me struggle to remember what I was going to say. "We can't."

When he looks up, I expect anger in his eyes for telling him, no, but all I see is a softness I've never seen from him, and it almost crumbles my resolve to stop this. "You're right," he agrees. He lifts me from the island and sits me on my feet. "It shouldn't have gone this far."

I shake my head. "You didn't overstep some invisible boundary, Micah. I do want you. I just...a lot has changed. I'm still wrapping my head around all this attention, if I'm being honest. And you haven't been...nice."

"You don't have to explain yourself to me. This happens in your time frame, no one else's. And as for the attention..." he trails off and leans in close. "You deserve every bit of it, *la mia stella*. I was a fool to fight it that long."

"Are you sure this is okay with Evander?" I couldn't help but ask one more time.

"Quit worrying about Evander." I turn to the sound of Evander's voice. He pushes off the doorway and walks toward us with a smile. How long has he been standing there? From the answering smile on Micah's face, he knew he was there. "I already told you that I was fine with this." He stops when he's right behind me, trapping me between him and Micah. "I have to admit it was hot to watch."

I gasp and spin around, putting myself right up against him; Micah steps closer, effectively blocking me in. "You were watching us?"

"I was curious, *pequena reina*. You have this whole house tied in knots, and I wanted to find out why." Evander runs his fingers across my cheek, tucking my hair behind my ears. Running his fingers back down my face, he tucks them under my chin to pull my head up. Micah runs his hands down my hips, and the sensation of being between them is almost overwhelming.

"You want to kiss her, *amore mio*?" Micah asks, sitting his chin on my shoulder. "She has the softest fucking lips." *Oh. My. God.*

"Hm," Evander hums, running his thumb across my bottom lip. "They look soft, but I think she's had enough for tonight." I don't know whether to be disappointed or relieved. My chest is heaving, and I am having a hard time not rubbing my ass on Micah. I don't know if I would be able to stop it if Evander kissed me. Every nerve ending is lit up, hyper aware of the two gorgeous men that I am sandwiched between. Evander lays his lips against mine, not really in a kiss, but enough that I feel the softness against mine. "Good-night, *pequena reina*." Evander rubs his thumb across my lips again and strides from the room, leaving me with Micah, who is still against my back.

"Still worried about Van?" he asks, making me laugh.

"No, I think that answered that question."

"We don't want to overwhelm you, so if we ever do, say something." I nod. He tilts my head back and kisses me softly. "I'll walk you to your room."

I giggle. "How gentlemanly," I tease.

He takes my hand and leads me up the stairs, stopping in front of Mateo's room, where he kisses me again. "What I have on my mind isn't gentlemanly. Goodnight, *la mia stella.*"

I slip into Mateo's room, and he's still sleeping soundly. I strip back out of my clothes, dust off the lingering flour with a giggle, and slide into bed. Mateo pulls me against him as soon as my head hits the pillow.

With a smile, I fall into a sleep full of dreams.

Involving five very hot guys.

CHAPTER 29
MATEO

"Mateo," Evie says, stomping her little foot. "I don't need any of this stuff!"

I brought her to one of my favorite stores in downtown Abbs Valley. And I kept piling her clothes higher and higher with everything I could find. She told me she needed necessities earlier, but I thought this was even better. She isn't happy with me right now.

"Yes, you do," I argue, tossing a yellow shirt on the pile for her to try on. It's my favorite color on her. "You have unlimited money. Go crazy."

"I can't," she argues back. "I need shampoo and conditioner, Mateo, not all that." She gestures wildly to the mountain of clothes. "Plus, I don't wear this kind of stuff."

I shrug. "We can stand here and argue all day, or you can go try it on."

She glares but whirls around into the door leading to the dressing rooms, her shopping assistant following behind her.

It's an upscale store that sells everything you could think of, and Evie argued as soon as I pulled over in front of it. Gray coaxed her out of the car and is now stoically standing guard at the main door. Evie doesn't know I paid to have the place shut down so she could shop in peace.

I flop down in the chair outside the door and wait, my mind going a hundred miles a minute. What if Evie is what I have been looking for? I don't believe it was just a coincidence. I believed in fate, and I felt fate had just dropped the delicious package that is Evie into our laps. She's started to open up, and I like what I see. She is smart, with a sense of humor that rivals mine, quick as a whip, and so fucking stunning it's hard to hide what I feel about her.

And it isn't just me. Everyone is feeling it. Micah is finally walking around like he doesn't have a stick shoved permanently up his ass, and after Evie told me what happened last night, I could figure out why. Now that I know Van is starting to come around, we could set things in motion.

Hartley was more of the unknown until he finally grew some fucking balls and kissed her. I heard them arguing and almost intervened until I heard Evie telling him exactly where to shove his nonsense. I wanted to high-five her. I was so damn proud.

I get up and make my way to Gray. Things with Gray are better than I expected. He has some shit in his past to deal with, but I am hoping I can help him with that if he would let me.

"Hey, Gray," I say, sliding to stand beside him.

"What are you up to?" he asks without even looking at me.

"I just came to keep you company," I defended myself, which is total bullshit.

Gray looks at me with a brow raised. "You always have a motive."

"Why does everyone always say that?"

Gray snorts. "Because you do."

"Fine," I grumble. "I think you should take Evie on a date. Just the two of you."

Gray turns to me with a frown. "I don't think that's safe right now."

"He hasn't made a move since he blew my damn car up. Keep it discreet, and you should be fine."

Gray sighs. "I don't think Evie can handle me, Mateo. I have too much baggage for her."

"Like we all do? Come on; I think it will be good for you. And her."

Gray doesn't know I've caught him staring at her, and it wasn't just in a protective way. He wants Evie, but he is holding back. That needs to stop.

"I'll think about it," he answers.

"Nope. No more thinking. Ask her, or I'll ask her for you."

"Mateo!" Evie's voice saves him from having to answer. She has her head sticking out the door, waving me over.

"What's up, buttercup?" I ask when I get to her.

"The zipper's stuck!" she whisper-yells, indicating the dress she's wearing. *Fuck.* It's the light purple one I picked out.

"You're keeping this one," I declare and motion her to walk back to her dressing room. "Where's your assistant?"

"I told her I was fine. I felt bad she was just standing there," Evie answers when she pulls the door to her dressing room open.

"That's her job," I chuckle, shutting it behind me.

Evie sweeps her long brown hair off her back. I get to work on her zipper, watching goosebumps pebble her skin. The zipper comes loose, and the dress falls from her shoulders and gets stuck on her waist. I reach forward and shimmy it down until it pools around her feet.

"Get that look off your face, Mateo," Evie says, watching me in the mirror.

"What look?" I ask with a grin. I slide my hands around her and pull her against my chest.

"Mateo," Evie warns when I slide my hand across the front of her panties.

"Have a little fun, buttercup," I whisper, rubbing teasing circles with my fingers.

"What if someone hears us?"

"So what? They will know how satisfied my girl is."

"Mateo," Evie groans. "We can't do that in here." I push harder against her pussy through her panties and feel how wet she already is.

"Are you sure, buttercup? I want you so bad all the time." I don't want to push her to do something she doesn't want to, but as soon as her hips start rolling, trying to seek the friction from my fingers, I know she is game. "You want me to play with this pretty pussy?"

Evie swallows, her eyes locked on mine in the mirror. "Yes," she whispers.

"Watch me, buttercup," I instruct, pulling her panties down. "Widen your legs." I lock my arm under her breasts as she does what I say. "Good girl," I praise, sliding my fingers between her thighs. The first contact with her clit, her hips buck. I start in slow circles, putting just enough pressure to bring her to her release slowly. Evie sinks her teeth into her bottom lip to keep from making a sound. "I want you to see how beautiful you are when you come."

"Mateo," Evie breathes, grinding back on my hard cock.

I hear scuffing feet, so I look through the gap at the bottom of the door and smile. Those big black boots are unmistakably Gray's.

"Gray is right outside that door, buttercup," I whisper, dipping my fingers down to slide inside her. Evie moans low in her throat. "Does it turn you on knowing Gray is out there?"

"Why do you do this when you're driving me crazy?" she asks breathlessly.

"Because you tell me the truth then." I chuckle. "Answer me."

"Yes," Evie moans.

"Do you want Gray, buttercup?"

"Oh god. Yes." I knew it was unfair to ask her this shit when I had my fingers buried in her pussy, but it was like a truth serum for her. She isn't embarrassed when I am pleasuring her.

"Reach over and open the door." Evie's hips stop moving, and she stares at me through the mirror. "No one else will see. Just Gray."

I watch Evie's hands fidget at her sides. Finally, her hand shoots out and pushes the door open.

Gray is leaning against the wall right in front of the room, and there is no mistaking what we're doing. His eyes widen and then zero in on my hand. I look back at Evie in the mirror, and her eyes are screwed shut.

"Open them. Keep watching." Her eyes flutter open, and I groan at the sight. They are glazed over, pupils blown. "Put your foot on the bench."

Gray moves to lean against the doorframe, giving him an unhindered view in the mirror. Evie catches his movement, licks those pouty lips, and lifts her foot, planting it on the bench.

"You're such a good fucking girl, buttercup."

Sliding my fingers from her pussy, I move around in front of her and drop to my knees. "Put your hands on the wall beside the mirror." She does it without hesitation, and I slide my hands up her ass, jerking her forward. "Ride my face, buttercup."

Her eyes drop to my face. "What?" she squeaks.

I lick up her slit, making her hips drop. "Ride. My. Face." I don't give her a chance to protest before I bury my face between her thighs. Sucking, licking, flicking her clit with my tongue, her hips finally start to move. "Look at Gray," I murmur before going back to the best thing I've ever had my mouth on.

I watch as her head slowly lifts, and she locks eyes with him. I wish I could see his face, but I am going to make her come first. Sliding one hand up the inside of her thigh, I tease her opening with two fingers before I push them inside her. Crooking them, I rub against her g-spot.

"Fuck, Mateo," she pants.

I pull her forward with my hand on her ass, so her pussy is directly over my mouth. A groan rips from my chest as she smothers me between her thighs. *If this is how I go out, I've lived a good fucking life.* Fuck, she tastes so damn good. One of her hands slides into my hair, pulling me closer as her hips buck. *That's it, buttercup. Take what you need.*

Her hand tightens into a fist. "Mateo, I'm going to come," Evie whispers. I make sure her eyes are on Gray, then suck her clit into my mouth hard. She clamps the hand that was in my hair over her mouth to hide her scream, and her flavor explodes over my tongue.

Gray reaches down and jerks me to my feet with a fist in my shirt. His mouth slams against mine, tongue seeking out Evie's flavor on my mouth.

"Oh," Evie breathes. I pull back from Gray's kiss, and her eyes are locked on us.

Gray's eyes flash with heat, and he stalks closer to her until her back is pressed against the wall. *That's it, big guy.* I am chanting in my head for Gray to kiss her finally, and when he does, I want to whoop with joy.

She whimpers when his mouth covers hers, and I step forward, afraid he scared her. But Evie's arms come up around his neck, pulling him closer. Gray's groan echoes through the room, and I know there is no damn way that no one knows what the hell is going on here. Good thing it's just the owner and one assistant, and they know to be discreet.

"Fuck," Gray breathes when he pulls back.

Evie's looking up at him with wonder on her face. "Holy shit," she giggles. God, I love that sound. I was afraid I pushed her too far when I started this, but from the look on her face, she likes it. Evie told me she wanted to try new things, and I am the man for the job. "That was a hell of a kiss, Gray."

I watch Gray's face redden and have to cover a laugh with a cough. He could talk all kinds of dirty shit, but one little compliment and he turns the shade of a tomato.

"I agree, angel," Gray says, taking a step back. "We should go. Micah told us to meet him at his house."

"What's the matter, big guy?" I tease.

Gray turns to me with narrowed eyes, and I know I'll pay for fucking with him later. "We've been here too long. You know that's not a good idea."

He is right, but at least this time, he has Adam sitting vigil inside his truck, so Aaron doesn't try to fucking blow me up again. I nod. "Let's go. We can bring back anything that doesn't fit."

I help Evie back into her panties and kiss her lips softly. "I'm not getting all that," Evie says when I pull back.

I sigh dramatically. "Why do you have to hurt me, buttercup? I made you come on my face, and this is the thanks I get?"

Evie laughs. "That's not how that works. You made me come, so I should be giving you something, not the other way around."

"You are giving me something. *You*. That's all I want," I declare, making her smile. "And all these clothes." Her smile turns into a glare, making Gray chuckle.

"Might as well give in, angel; he's relentless," Gray comments. He would know how relentless I can be.

"Mateo, you really don't have to do this."

"Do you like this stuff?" I ask, and she nods.

"Then accept it. I know I don't have to, but I want to. Let me do this for you."

I watch the inner struggle play across her face. Evie isn't used to people paying attention to her, much less spoiling the shit out of her. Which I plan on doing every chance I get.

"Okay," Evie says finally. "But I still need what we originally came for."

"Already taken care of, buttercup." I grin. I called in a favor from my favorite sister-in-law, and anything Evie would need is sitting at the house, thanks to Bridget, Les' stylist.

Evie rolls her eyes. "I should have known you were up to something."

"Why does everyone always fucking say that?" I grouch.

"Because you are," Evie and Gray say at the same time and start laughing.

"Fine, just for that, I'm getting more shit," I say, pushing out of the dressing room with a smile.

I feel like everything is falling into place. We take care of Aaron, and Evie will be mine without the threat looming over us.

Then she could be ours.

CHAPTER 30
MICAH

Van and I rode over to my house when Evie left with Gray and Mateo. I've been sitting in my office for an hour trying to get some work done, but my mind keeps drifting back to last night. I was thinking about her when she walked into the kitchen, and it was almost like my mind had conjured her up. One minute I was thinking about how I could make up for being a dick, and the next, she was standing there.

I didn't mean to take it as far as it went, and I'm glad she stopped me. With how I've acted, I didn't deserve an ounce of her attention, but she gave it anyway. And I was fucking glad for that. Now that I've finally had a small taste of her, I wanted more, and I am going to prove to her that I won't take it for granted.

Van and I have talked about this new development, and after I talked to Les and Ryder, I've opened up to him. We still have a lot to talk about, but we have plenty of time for the rest. The most important stuff was hashed out, like what we would do about Evie. Mateo's been very clear about what he wants, but he's also said only if that's what Evie decides. In a way, I think she already has; she just has to admit it.

Van told me he wanted to take it slow with her, and that's fine with me. But having her between us last night had him six shades of fucked up when I got back to the room. I've never seen him that turned on, and I was the lucky bastard who reaped the benefits.

My phone rings, breaking me from my thoughts. I snatch up and almost hit ignore when my mom's name flashes across the screen. It's been over a month since I've heard from her, so that could only mean one thing. I consider hitting ignore but decide to get it over with instead. I have been ignoring her calls for a couple of days.

"Hello?"

"It's about time you answer the phone, Micah," my mother huffs. "I've been trying for days to reach you."

I know, and I've been ignoring you. "I'm sorry. I've been busy. Is something wrong?"

"Can't I just call and check on my son?" she answers defensively, and I suppress a snort.

"I'm fine. How are you?"

"I'm not good, Micah," she says. "I need to see you."

I roll my eyes. "How much do you need this time?"

"I'll swing by, and we can talk," she huffs again.

Over my dead body. Evie would be back soon, and no way do I want that blood-sucking vampire around Evie. "Now's not a good time."

"Nonsense. I'll see you soon," she says, and the phone disconnects. I have to count to ten before I launch my phone across the room.

I don't know why I couldn't just cut her out of my life. Les doesn't even know she still contacts me, and she especially doesn't know it's always for money. Mother never has anything nice to say, and it usually dissolves into an argument which ends with me writing her a check so she would leave. No matter what, though, she is still my mom. Even if that makes me stupid.

Van sticks his head in my office, and I wave him in. He sits in front of my desk, and I take a minute to appreciate him before I blow his apparent good mood all to shit. Van doesn't wear jeans often, but when he does, they are molded to him, just like they are today. I let my eyes roam up his chest to the top two buttons undone on his shirt and finally to his eyes.

"My mother is on her way," I say. Van's jaw instantly hardens, and the smile falls from his lips.

"Why?" Van grits out.

"She said she needed to see me," I answer, sitting back in my chair.

"Come on, Micah," Van says harshly. "You know what she's coming for."

"She's my mother, *amore mio*."

"Yeah. And she's fucking using you. Why don't you see that? You don't need her in your life," Van argues.

"I don't know what you want me to say here," I reply.

"How about that you get it?"

I shake my head in denial. "It might be different this time," I say. I always hoped she would just show up to see me one day. It hasn't happened in thirty-two years, but one day it might.

"That's never the case, *mi rey*," Van says softly, standing from his chair and striding out of the room.

Shit.

MY MOTHER COMES into the house like the force of nature she is. Tall, blonde, petite. Obviously, my father's genes were strong. "Micah, darling," she says before kissing both my cheeks.

I close the door behind her. "Hello, Mother," I greet.

When he knew she was here, Van disappeared into the back office with Hartley. Hartley is getting close to a lead on Aaron and has been working nonstop on it since.

I lead her toward the living room and gesture for her to have a seat on the love seat. She sits down, eyes already moving to find something to criticize me about. I sit down on the couch and wait.

"You need more of a feminine touch, dear. It looks like a bachelor pad in here," she remarks.

I lift a brow. "I am a bachelor, Mother," I say, even though I wasn't. She doesn't know about Evander.

"You're thirty; don't you think it's time you settle down with a good woman?" she comments.

I shake my head because she doesn't even know how old I am. "I'm thirty-two. And I will when I'm ready."

She blinks several times, then waves her hand. "I knew that."

I suppress an eye roll. "You said you needed to see me," I say, encouraging her to tell me what she came for.

"I need a loan," she says. And there it is.

"You could have told me that on the phone," I grit out. "How much?"

"Two hundred grand," she replies like it's nothing. "I need it for..."

"I don't fucking care," I interrupt. I just want her out of my house. Why do I insist on doing this to myself? "I'll write you a check."

"Is that any way to speak to your mother?" Her voice is starting to reach that screeching level that I fucking despise. "Is that how your father raised you to talk to a woman?"

"At least he raised me," I say before I can stop myself. This dissolved faster than it usually does; it must be a record. She doesn't need to know how my father actually raised me.

Her face turns blood red. "He had the means to raise you; I didn't. I wanted you to have a better life." That's because you're an alcoholic.

I shake my head and stand up. "Let me get your money."

She follows behind me slowly, her hands touching everything. Her eyes light on the picture of Evander and me on the wall. It was taken at the pool house on his phone when we were staying with Les. You can immediately tell it's more than just a friend picture by how we look at each other. He sent it to me one night when he was drunk in Cabo, and I had it printed. It's been hanging there ever since.

"Who's that?" she asks. Here we go.

"Evander," I answer, still walking toward my office.

"Who is he to you?"

I turn on my heel to face her, and the words fly from my mouth before I can stop them. "My boyfriend."

Her eyes widen, and her mouth pops open. "Your boyfriend?" she squeaks.

"Yes. My boyfriend," I say slowly, enunciating each word.

"What did your father do to you?" she says like she's almost in tears. Or like she gave a fuck.

"He didn't do anything to me. This has nothing to do with Father," I answer, trying to keep from yelling.

"It has everything to do with him! You wouldn't have turned out this way if it weren't for him!" she screeches.

"Turn out like what?" I grind out.

"Turn into a fag...."

"That's enough!" My head whips to the sound of Evie's voice. She's standing at the end of the foyer with Gray and Mateo. Her face is red with anger, hands balled into fists, chest heaving. She looks like an avenging angel. "That is *no* way to talk to your son!"

Van walks up to my other side, probably hearing the yelling. Fucking hell, this is not how I wanted this to go down. I was hoping I could get rid of her before Evie got home.

"And who are you?" Mom sneers, looking Evie up and down.

"Who I am doesn't matter. What matters is you can't see how much you're hurting him," Evie says. Van walks to stand beside me, hand sliding down my arm in support. Mother doesn't miss it.

"What is going on here?" Mom sniffs.

Evie walks over and slides her hand into mine. "I'm his girlfriend," Evie says and squeezes my hand. I look down at her, and she squeezes harder, like she's telling me to go along with it.

"We're all together," I explain when Van takes my other hand. It looks like Mother's head is about to explode, and it's entertaining as hell.

"What...why...I don't..." Mom stutters, then her eyes take on that look that I know I won't like what comes out of her mouth next. "This is the girl you choose to settle down with?" Mom says, looking down her nose at Evie. "You could do much better than her. She's..."

"You need to leave," I interrupt. She opens her mouth. "Now," I demand, pointing to the front door.

"But..."

"But nothing. You think you can come here and spew your hateful bullshit about Evie? You have to be out of your goddamn mind if you think I'm going to let that happen. Get the fuck out of my house, and don't come back. I don't want to see you, and I don't want to hear from you," I say, feeling like there is a weight crushing my chest. "I should have cut you off a long time ago, but I was stupid enough to think you gave a fuck about me. All you cared about was what you could take from me. Get out."

Mother turns on her heels and stomps out of the house, slamming the door behind her. All the anger washes out of me, and I feel empty. Why couldn't I have just listened to Van? Evie didn't need to hear that.

I turn to Evie. "I'm so sorry..."

She places her fingers over my lips to silence me. "You don't have to apologize for her. I've heard worse. I need to know if *you're* okay?"

"It fucking sucks," I say raggedly. "My mom uses me as her personal ATM because I let her. I'm so damn stupid."

"You aren't stupid, Micah," Evie says, placing her hands on my chest. "You have a huge heart. You deserve so much more than what she said to you. You and Van have such a beautiful relationship. Don't let her tarnish that with her hate."

I feel Van slide his hand across my back. I turn to him, and he pulls my forehead against his. "I know what it feels like to have parents that don't care," Van says. "But you have me now, and I *do* care about you. I love you, *mi rey*."

"I love you too, *amore mio*," I reply, pecking his lips. I wasted so much time fighting my feelings for Van that I almost didn't get this with him. The day he forgave me was one of the best days of my life. I hear Evie sniff and look down at her.

"Sorry," she laughs, wiping tears from her cheeks. "You guys are just awesome together."

"Come here," I say, pulling her into Van and me. "Thank you for what you said, *la mia stella*. There is a lot about my mother that I don't talk about, but you stood up for me when you didn't have to." I peck her lips.

"When you're ready to talk, I'm here," Evie says quietly, snuggling into our group hug.

I tip her chin up with my fingers to look into her eyes. "That goes for you too, *la mia stella*," I tell her.

"Oh my god!" Mateo practically squeals. His body hits on our other side, wrapping his arms around us all. We all laugh, and it's the lightest I've felt in a while.

Van told us that she talked to him, but he still felt she was holding something back.

There are many unknowns surrounding us right now, and I don't like it. I want to put Aaron down for what he did to Evie.

That motherfucker will pay for it in blood.

AFTER MY MOTHER LEFT, I returned to my office to get my head back together. Whenever I think I'm making headway from my childhood, the hits start again. But it didn't bother me as much this time. Not with Van and Evie having my back. I am so fucking proud of Evie for standing up for me. At this point, I am officially done with my mother's bullshit. I tried to have a relationship with her, but she only wanted me for one thing.

"Are you okay, *mi rey*?" Van asks, stepping into my office.

I shrug. "Yeah. I actually am." I stand to meet him in front of my desk.

"Evie was a little badass out there," Van chuckles.

"She was," I agree. It was hot as hell to watch. "What made you change your mind about her?" I ask. Van was firmly on the going slow train until last night.

"Seeing you guys together. And I've been watching her."

I pull him to me. "You've been watching her, huh?"

"You know I have. There's something about her."

"I know," I agree, rubbing my lips down his neck. I have a permanent hard-on any time he is around. It's becoming a problem. "She's gorgeous."

"She is," Van agrees.

"Hm," I hum, sliding my hands down his ass. "So, you have been watching her."

"Are you jealous, Micah?" Van laughs, caging me against my desk with his arms.

"No, *amore mio*, I'm not," I tell him honestly. The thought has crossed my mind of how hot it would be to put a girl between Van and me. I don't know if Evie is ready, but I've seen how she looks at me. And the other guys. Something tells me there is more to Evie than meets the eye. "Have you ever thought about having a woman pressed between us? Working her over at the same time?" I ask. Van groans, and I know he has. We talked about it the first time we were together, but shit went south before we could make it happen.

"Yes, I have," Van answers when I nip at his neck.

Now that I brought it up, the scene unfolds in my head of Evie with us. Her big brown eyes closed in ecstasy, and her mouth parted as she moaned. *Shit.*

"You're thinking about it, aren't you?" Van whispers, and I nod. "Me too."

I haven't been with a woman since I made the vow that I wouldn't sleep with anyone else in my efforts to get Van back. That was over six months ago. Something about Evie makes you look at her, even if she tries to hide under oversized shirts.

"Goddamn, I want to bend you over this desk," I groan, my cock jerking in my slacks at the thought.

Van slants his mouth over mine, and I quickly take over the kiss. Grinding our hips together, our hard cocks rubbing against each other.

"Oh," a feminine voice breathes, causing Van and me to break apart, but I won't let him step back.

"Can I help you?" I ask softly. I forgot that the damn office door was open.

"I, uh," Evie stammers, and it's the cutest thing. "I came to see if you were okay."

"I'm fine, *la mia stella*," I smile, finally letting my hold on Van go. He steps to the side, and her eyes snap to my obvious erection. Those expressive brown eyes snap back to my face, and her face blooms with color. I wonder how far that blush would spread?

"Have a seat," I tell her and motion for her to sit down. Van sits in the chair beside her with a soft smile. I sit down and cross my arms on my desk. "Did you get what you needed today?"

"I did." Evie smiles, and it changes her whole face. She seems so damn innocent, and in a way, she is. She has no idea who we are; if she did, she probably wouldn't be as trusting.

"I want you to tell us if there is anything else you want or need," I tell her with a raised brow.

"I don't need much," Evie says, embarrassed.

"I'm going to be honest. I don't know how long you'll be here. You need it, you ask. Money isn't an issue." I tell her, and I wasn't bragging. I need her to know she won't break the bank if she goes wild with my credit card.

"You don't need to do that. I don't even know when I can pay you back..." she trails off when she sees the look on my face.

"I don't want you to pay me back. I want you to feel at home here. Mateo and Gray can take you tomorrow," I say, not leaving any room for arguments. Van hides a smile with his hand.

Evie huffs. "But I already have stuff." I guess she could argue. I liked it.

"It wasn't enough. Go tomorrow."

She narrows those pretty eyes, and I get my first peek at the real Evie. She is still in there, and I would make her come back out. Evie isn't this scared girl that came here; she has a backbone. "You aren't my boss," Evie says, and her eyes widen, and she shrinks back in her chair. "Oh my god, I'm so sorry!"

237

"Don't apologize," I say gently.

"But that was so rude!" Evie exclaims, burying her face in her hands.

Van reaches over and tugs her arm until her hands drop. She is as red as a tomato. "What the asshole is trying to say is you need clothes for when we go out. Go out with Mateo and have fun. Burn a hole in his credit card." I don't miss him rubbing his thumb over the skin on her arm before he pulls his hand back.

"I'm not an asshole," I grumble.

"Yes, you are," Van snorts, and I glare harder. Evie giggles, then claps her hand over her mouth. "Don't hide that sound," Van tells her. I was getting addicted to that sound that only Mateo could pull out of her until now.

"Any more remarks, comments, or questions?" I say dryly, making her giggle again.

I clear my throat and get to the next thing I want to talk to her about.

"Van and I want to take you out on a date."

Her eyes widen. "A date? With both of you?"

"Yes, *pequena reina*," Van adds. "Tonight."

"Tonight?" Evie squeaks. "You really don't have to."

"We want to," I assure her. "I called Les' stylist Bridget, and she'll be over later."

"Oh no." Evie shakes her head. "I don't need all that. Please don't go through all that trouble for me."

"*La mia stella*," I say sternly. "It's not any trouble. I want to do this." Plus, I felt like she could use another friend.

Evie twists her hands in her lap. "I'm not used to this."

"Get used to it," Van says gently. "It will be fun. So, would you like to go out with us?"

"Of course! I didn't mean to make it sound like I didn't want to. I just don't need all the extra stuff you guys do. I mean, it's awesome. I won't lie, and I would be stupid to pass up a date with two hot guys. And I'm rambling, and I'm going to shut up now." She clamps her lips shut, making me laugh.

"We'll leave at seven, okay?" I tell her.

"Okay," she agrees with that damn tempting smile again.

"Shopping with Mateo," I remind her.

She stands up. "Shopping. Mateo. Got it." She gives me a mock salute and leaves with a sashay of those thick hips.

I stare at Van's head, who's also watching her walk away until he turns back to me. He shrugs. "She has a nice ass," he defends.

That she does, *amore mio*, that she does.

CHAPTER 31
EVIE

A date. I am going on a date with two of the hottest guys I've ever seen.

I was still on cloud nine after what happened with Mateo in the dressing room and finally kissing Gray.

"What about this one?" Bridget, Les' stylist, asks. She's holding up a floor-length sparkly silver dress with a split up the thigh. "I think you would rock this." Bridget is sweet and gorgeous, with bright red hair and green eyes. She is tall and skinny.

"I don't know," I say with uncertainty.

"I do," Bridget says, shoving the dress at me. "Try it on."

She came over with a heap of dresses, and my only guess for her knowing my size is Mateo. I don't like that he knows I am a size sixteen, but he doesn't seem to care. His eyes heated when he saw my body; I've never experienced that before.

I pad to the bathroom and run my hands over the dress. It truly is gorgeous. Taking a breath, I take off my clothes and slide it on. The inside of it is silky, so it slides down easily. Bridget knocks on the door a few minutes after I've stood there just staring at myself. I pull the door open.

"I can't wear this," I say miserably.

Bridget's eyes widen. "Oh, honey. You're wearing that." She

reaches over and tugs the zipper up, spinning me to look in the mirror. "You look hot."

It is cut low in the front, and my boobs are practically falling out of it, and it shows off every curve and imperfection.

"Give me something else," I demand.

"Nope," Bridget says, popping the P. "You want them drooling at your feet? Wear this dress."

I can't stop the giggle. "They aren't going to be drooling over this."

Bridget snorts. "Yes, they will. Trust me."

The funny thing is, I do trust her. Her bubbly personality is infectious, and she could work magic with her quick fingers. She curled my hair into big curls, letting them flow down my back; my hair never looked this shiny. She kept my makeup understated with a smokey eye to make my big brown eyes stand out, gave me some color on my cheeks, and light pink on my lips, making them look pouty.

"I'm so nervous," I admit.

"I don't blame you," Bridget giggles. "But these guys are good guys; they will treat you right." She spins on her heel and disappears from the bathroom, giving me time to get my nerves under control. My palms are sweaty, and my heart is pounding out of my chest.

I take a few deep breaths and pull up my big girl panties, figuratively and literally. I walk back into the bedroom, and Mateo is leaning against the dresser.

"Holy shit," Mateo says hoarsely. "You look beautiful, buttercup."

My first reaction is to call bullshit, but I bite it back. "Thank you."

"Damn." Mateo shakes his head. "I got you something to wear tonight."

He opens the lid on a blue velvet box in his hands, and I can't stop the gasp. Lying in the box is a gorgeous silver necklace with a diamond right in the center with matching earrings. "I can't wear this. It's too much." It looks like it cost a fortune; there is no way I could accept that.

"Nonsense." Mateo waves that away, taking the necklace from the box. He doesn't give me a chance to argue before he clasps it on my neck. The diamond nestles right above my cleavage. "Perfect," Mateo breathes, locking his arms around my waist. I slide mine to his neck, still amazed he looks at me like that. "Have fun tonight, buttercup." He kisses my lips with a smile.

"Are you sure you're okay with this?" I ask for the twentieth time. This is still all new to me, and I really like Mateo.

"I'm more than ok with it," Mateo says, pecking my lips again. He smiles and slips from the room. I'm just putting the last earring in when Bridget barges back in.

"Shoes!" she exclaims, clapping her hands. Her enthusiasm is infectious, and I find myself getting excited. She helps me slide on a pair of silver heels and steps back. "If I were a lesbian, I would eat you up."

A laugh bursts out of me, my nerves sinking into the background. "Thank you for doing this."

"No worries." Bridget waves her hand. "It's been fun." It has. We joked and laughed the whole time. I felt like I had a girlfriend. Something I've never had before. "All right, your men are waiting."

And I am nervous again. They weren't my men, but they are tonight, at least. I am going to enjoy myself, grateful that they even wanted to do this. They don't know me. None of them do except for Hartley, but they go out of their way to ensure I have a good time here. I know there is more to them than meets the eye; I'm not oblivious. It's in how they speak about certain things or dance around the truth. I'm not sure what it is, but I am not going to let that ruin my night.

I follow Bridget to the living room, careful in my heels, and almost die on the spot. Evander and Micah are dressed to kill. Evander has on a pair of fitted grey slacks with a matching grey dress shirt, the top couple of buttons undone to show off a tanned, toned chest. His hair is in his usual perfect style, swept back from his forehead. Micah has on a white dress shirt that stands out against his tan skin and black fitted slacks. His hair is messy, deliberately so. Holy shit, they are sexy.

Both of their eyes land on me, and I have to lock my muscles to keep from fidgeting under their scrutiny. What if they changed their minds after they saw me in this dress?

Micah steps forward, letting his gaze slowly crawl over my body. "You look ravishing, *la mia stella*." Micah's normally smooth, deep voice is husky. He takes my hand, kisses the back of it, and I almost fucking faint. I already had his lips on me, but something about the gesture makes me weak in the knees.

Evander steps to my other side. "This dress was made for you," he says and kisses my other hand. That's it. I'm going to die right here.

They tuck my hands onto their arms and lead me to a blacked-out SUV idling in front of the house. "Have fun tonight! Don't do anything I wouldn't do!" I hear Mateo yell before the door shuts, making me giggle.

"God, I love that sound," Micah mutters, and I don't think I was supposed to hear it.

We get in, and they put me right between them. I look into the rearview mirror and meet Gray's hazel eyes; he smiles warmly before shifting the car into drive and heading to the restaurant.

"That's Adam," Micah answers my unspoken question when he sees me looking at the guy in the passenger seat. Adam gives me a polite nod before turning back around. "He's one of my guards. I wanted you to feel safe tonight." What ordinary man would have guards just milling around? You could tell by the size of Micah's house that he is important.

"I feel safe with you guys," I tell him honestly. They have given me every reason to believe that.

Some people might think I'm crazy for going from what Aaron put me through to putting my trust in these guys. That's what got me into trouble in the first place. So maybe I am. But I've lived a year in constant fear about what would set Aaron off next, walking on eggshells around him, hiding my true personality because he hated when I was outspoken, and wallowing in self-pity because he constantly told me to lose weight. Then I spent months trying to escape him when I finally found the courage to leave.

These guys look at me like I'm the only person in the room,

shower me with gifts I did nothing to earn, and I am helpless against them. I could give myself this, even if it is just temporary. I earned it. Right?

We pull up behind the restaurant called Whispers, still hiding me from view, and Gray gets out to open the door. Evander steps out, extending a hand inside to help me out, and as soon as my hand touches his, I can feel electric pulses run up my arm. Micah gets out and slides a hand to the small of my back, and my body goes haywire. *Down girl.* I chastise myself. Since all the sex with Mateo, my libido is going crazy, something I've never experienced.

The maître d' leads us to a table in the back, secluded from the rest of the restaurant. Micah pulls my chair out and waits until I'm seated to take his seat beside Evander. The waiter comes over, and Micah orders a bottle of wine by a name I couldn't pronounce again to save my life. Nerves are attacking me all over again with both their eyes on me. I take a second to appreciate them. Micah's icy blue eyes stand out against his olive skin, his cheekbones are pronounced, showing off his Italian heritage, his nose is proud with a little lift on the end, and his lips are almost too full to fit a guy's face.

Evander is all dark. Dark brown hair and dark brown eyes that look like melted chocolate. His skin is darker than Micah's; his nose is stubborn and thin. His bottom lip is fuller than the top.

They are both so sexy that it almost hurts to look at them.

The waiter comes back and pours us a glass; I snatch mine up to give me something to do with my hands. The taste explodes on my tongue. "This is so good."

"It's my favorite that the restaurant offers," Micah smiles, showing off those perfect white teeth and that little dimple on his left cheek. Jesus. I am not going to make it through this meal without self-combusting.

"What are you doing in my restaurant?" My head jerks up to that voice; it's deep and faintly Russian.

Micah turns around slowly to face two guys with black hair and eyes. They are definitely identical twins. "I can go wherever the fuck I want," Micah replies, his voice dripping with ice. Are we not supposed to be here? Then Micah laughs and stands up, jerking them both into a hug. "What's up, assholes?" He knows them? I almost had a damn heart attack, and he knew them?

The one who spoke laughs. "I saw your name on the reservation list. Thought we'd drop by."

"This is Alexey and Dmitri," Evander introduces after giving them a handshake. He indicates each one. "This is Evie." I smile politely, still trying to pull my stomach from my asshole.

"Evie," the one Evander said was Dmitri purrs, and I could feel my face heat. What is it about Abbs Valley? I have not met one guy that didn't look like they could pose for GQ. "Pleasure to meet you."

"If you don't get your goddamn eyes back in your head, I'll cut them out and serve them to your fucking patrons," Micah threatens, and my head whips back to him.

Evander chuckles, but it sounds dark. "And I'll hold your punk asses down."

"Don't be like that," Alexey grins, making him look scary. Still gorgeous, but scary.

"Unless you want a bloodbath in here, I suggest you two find someone else to harass," Micah says between clenched teeth. I know my eyes are wide as saucers.

Both guys give a mock salute, leaving us alone, and a nervous giggle slips out. Evander and Micah's eyes focus back on me, and I feel it like a caress.

"You don't do that nearly enough," Micah says, tilting his head to the side. Something I noticed he does a lot.

"I haven't had much to laugh about," I admit.

Evander and Micah exchange a glance. "Aaron is fucking scum for not seeing what was right in front of him," Evander says smoothly. Did I just sigh? He grins, and I know I did. Damn it. I couldn't control my mouth or my reactions.

"You guys are good for my ego," I laugh.

"We aren't doing it just for your ego, *la mia stella*," Micah says. That nickname got me every time, and I wanted to soak it in. I still don't even know what it means. "Everything we say is true."

The waiter returns for our order, and Evander patiently explains what's on the menu. I've never eaten at a place like this, but they don't seem to mind helping me out.

"What do you guys do for a living?" I ask, taking a sip of my wine. They exchange another glance.

"I own several properties in Abbs Valley and help Les with hers," Micah explains.

"Same here, except I run them with Mateo," Evander adds. That explains the expensive cars and clothes. That doesn't explain all the guards. They aren't telling me something, but it's none of my business.

"That's cool. How old are you?" I ask.

"I'm twenty-five. He's thirty-two," Evander answers.

"There's no way you're thirty-two," I say, shocked. Micah doesn't look any older than me at twenty-three.

"I'll be thirty-three in a couple of months," Micah says with a chuckle.

"How do you have a niece Les' age?" I ask because I was curious about that. I watch his face shutter and take it back. "Sorry. That was a really personal question."

"No. It's fine," Micah says, his voice clipped, but I don't think it has to do with me. "My father cheated on his wife with my mom late in life." There is a lot more to that story, but it isn't my place to ask.

"What about yours?" Evander asks. I already knew about his parents from Mateo.

I shrug and fiddle with my napkin. "My dad passed away a couple of years ago. My mom is still in Fairview."

"Does she know what's going on?" Micah asks gently.

"I didn't want to involve her," I answer.

"You should call her. I'm sure she'd love to hear from you," Micah says with a smile.

I shake my head. I didn't like talking about this, but I felt I could after the display with Micah's mom. "She probably wouldn't," I admit. "Mom's an alcoholic. We didn't really get along well when I was growing up." I was never pretty or skinny enough for my super-model-looking mom, and it caused us to have a very strained relationship. The only people who kept me sane were my dad and Hartley. Then dad died, and Hartley left.

"Welcome to the shitty parent club," Evander says dryly, raising his glass in a toast. I laugh, and we clink our glasses together.

"Can I ask you guys a question?" I ask.

"Of course," Evander answers with an easy smile.

"Are you guys okay with Hartley now? I know there was a lot of tension at first. It just seems...better now."

"Les told me what he did in the end, and I'm trying," Micah answers. "We've all realized a lot about each other in a short amount of time. It all stems from how we were raised. It's time we stop letting our parents or anyone else dictate how we live our lives." I'm sure he meant more by the statement than he said. I hated the look on his face when his mom almost called him that awful name.

"Damn right," Evander agrees, squeezing Micah's hand.

"Here's to putting the past behind us," I say, and raise my glass. This is my official declaration that I am done with the bullshit and holding back. I am strong, goddamnit, and I am going to reach out and take everything these guys had to offer.

The waiter steps up with our food. I take a bite of my dish and moan in appreciation. It isn't as good as Micah's, but it is delicious.

I look up to two pairs of heated eyes aimed right at me. Micah clears his throat and takes a bite of his food.

This is going to be a long night.

CHAPTER 32

GRAY

"Where are we going?" Evie asks as I lead her to the garage. After breakfast, I sucked up every bit of courage I had and went to ask her to take a ride with me. After kissing her, I was done fighting it.

"I want to take you somewhere," I tell her. It was my favorite place in the city.

"Okay," she says and smiles up at me. I lead her over to my Harley, and her eyes widen. "I've never been on a motorcycle before." I had Mateo take me to pick it up from Micah's last night because I just needed to ride. I couldn't think of a better person to be on the back than Evie.

"We can take my truck if you feel safer that way," I tell her, but I want her pressed against me.

"I want to try the motorcycle," Evie says with a jerk of her head. I grab the extra full-face helmet and get it fitted on her. I made sure she wore jeans, tennis shoes, and a jacket. She looked good enough to eat. I put mine on, push the kickstand up, and walk it out of the garage.

I swing my leg over it to steady it for her. "Hop on." She puts her hand on my shoulder and slides on, her hands landing on my sides. I jerk them around my waist. "Hold on tight. You'll get used to it."

I fire the bike up and smile when she gives a giddy laugh. I make my way to the gate, nodding at Adam when we pass through. Since we've been staying at Mateo's, I brought him over to help keep an eye out. I trusted Mateo's guards, but I trusted Adam more.

I slowly take the winding road off Micah's property until I hit the straighter road leading to where I wanted to go. I open the bike up a little, and her arms tighten. Her breasts crushed against my back, her thighs clamping around my hips.

I loved to ride. I could let my mind clear and just exist. Now I have a beautiful woman pressed against my back, which makes it even better.

What Mateo said about us dating her has repeatedly run through my head. I couldn't stop thinking about it. So, when Mateo took off with Hartley, I took my chance. When she kissed me back, it surprised me. There wasn't any fear when she saw the intentions on my face. I didn't know what I brought to the table with all the other guys, but I was going to shoot my shot.

I take a left onto a dirt road and pull my motorcycle over to the side. I kill the engine, and Evie claps. "That was amazing."

I steady the bike with a laugh while she slides off. I take my helmet off, then help her with hers. "I'll take you on a longer ride sometime," I promise. I had a plan today: to get to know her without everything going on in the house.

I grab the blanket from my saddlebag and tuck her hand into mine, leading her down the path. When we break through the trees, Evie gasps, "This is beautiful."

It's a waterfall hidden deep in the California hills. I found it accidentally while riding one day, and I've never seen anyone else here.

We spread the blanket out and get seated, her snuggly by my side. "Does Mateo know about this place?" she asks, and my head whips to her.

I can feel my face heat, but not out of embarrassment. "No. Not yet." I wanted to bring him here one day.

"I love that," she says, rubbing her hand down my cheek. My blush deepens. She hooks her arm with mine. "Tell me about yourself, Gray."

I couldn't tell her much. "I was born in Tennessee. I went into the military when I was eighteen. Worked security after that."

She turns to face me. "How long have you worked for Micah?"

"Six months."

"Is he good to you?" she asks sternly, making me chuckle.

"He's the best I've ever worked for," I answer honestly. Micah treats me with nothing but respect, and he trusts me with Evie, which means a lot. At eighteen, I didn't think this was where I would be at twenty-seven after serving overseas. My life took several turns leading me here, but I wouldn't change it. I like where I am. It doesn't mean I don't have regrets about my past.

"I like it here," Evie says. "Is that weird? It's the first time I've ever felt at home."

"I don't think it's weird," I tell her. I didn't feel at peace until I started working for Micah, but I think that had a lot to do with Mateo. At first, I wanted to be annoyed that he was always around, but the longer he was around, the more I *wanted* him there. I've never felt that way before. I always lived my life in solitude after I left the service.

"Do you think I'm crazy for seeing all of you?"

I turn to look at her. "Not at all. I don't know what that prick did to you, but I've seen it before. Live your life for you. It's your time now."

She hits me with one of those full smiles, and it always takes my breath away. She is perfect. I don't feel that overwhelming panic around her when she is in my space; I don't feel it with Mateo, either. "That's what I've always wanted to do. My mom hated it. She probably had the right to given what I got myself into."

"Everyone makes mistakes. You learn from them," I say. Getting involved with the Mafia probably wasn't the way to go, though. Until you're in with the Mafia, you have the wrong idea. You think they're all bloodthirsty, and some of them are. But then you have guys like these, and they only deal out punishments when needed. For the most part, they stay to themselves or with each other.

"What's Gray short for?"

"Grayson."

"What's your middle name?" Evie asks, and I can see her eyes dancing with mischief.

"What is this? Twenty questions?" I laugh.

She grins. "Yep. Mateo taught me how to play."

I roll my eyes. "Maverick."

"Yours is cooler than mine. Mines Louisa."

"Evelyn Louisa. I think it's pretty."

Her cheeks bloom with color. "How tall are you?"

"Six-five."

"Mines the exact opposite. I'm five-six."

"Do you have any siblings?" I ask, playing along. She seemed to be enjoying this game, and I'd do anything to make her smile.

"No. It was just me. Do you?"

"I have two sisters."

"Older or younger?" Evie asks, scooting closer.

"Younger. I'm twenty-seven." I answer the question I can see on the tip of her tongue. Said tongue sweeps out to lick her lips, and my eyes are transfixed by the sight. I'm wondering what it would be like to kiss those bee-stung lips again. My eyes snap back to her face, and I know my face is blood red.

I clear my throat. "Besides reading, what else do you like to do?" I ask, trying to move past my fumble of checking her lips out.

Evie shrugs. "I don't really have many hobbies. I've tended to stick to myself. What about you?"

I nod because I understand. "I like working on my bike and music."

"Do you play?" Evie asks, turning toward me.

"No. Just listening," I answer. I could get lost in the music.

She nods. "I like finding bands no one has heard of. There are some gems out there that people overlook."

I look closer at her. "That's what I do. There's a club in downtown Abbs Valley that only pulls in indie artists."

Evie's eyes light up. "Really? That sounds awesome."

"I'll take you some time," I say before I can stop myself. "How was your date last night?"

"That would be awesome!" Evie says, smiling from ear to ear. She hooks her arm back through mine. "I had a really good time. They were perfect gentlemen," she laughs. "They kissed me goodnight at Mateo's door. It was sweet." She turns to face me. "Tell me about you and Mateo."

I bark a laugh. "There isn't much to tell."

"Come on. Mateo just said he followed you around until you just gave in."

I whip my head to her. "He said that?" I wanted Mateo; I just didn't know how to take what I wanted until the day in the guard house.

"No," Evie laughs. "Well, he said it took him six months to wear you down."

I shrug. "Mateo's the only guy I've wanted to take that step with. Do you have a problem with us?"

"Not at all. I think it's awesome when you go after what you want. It's what I've always been too scared to do."

"What about now?" I ask.

"I'm still scared. But I don't want to be like that anymore."

"Is that what this is?" I ask. Are we some kind of test?

"It was at first," she admits. "I don't have any misconceptions about where this will go when Aaron is gone, but I want to enjoy the time I have with you guys." She looks at me. "Does that make me a bad person?"

"No," I say gruffly. I don't have any misconceptions about this either, but the thought of her leaving already makes my heart flip in my chest. I am captivated by this girl, and I don't understand why. Except she needs protection, and that's what my whole life has been about. Protecting those weaker than me. Is that all this is? Making up for the ones I couldn't protect? I push that thought from my head before it takes me to a dark place and look at Evie. She's looking at the view with a sort of wonder on her face. I don't look away when she turns to me like she can feel me staring at her. Her face flushes at the same time I feel mine heating up.

"See something you like?" Evie asks.

"Yeah," I say roughly.

"Me too," she whispers and leans forward, letting me make that decision.

I slide my hand onto the nape of her neck and pull her lips against mine. I tease her lips with my tongue, and she opens immediately. Stroking my tongue with hers, I soak in every moan she makes. If her body is this responsive while we are kissing, I wonder what it will be like when I have her underneath me.

That thought has me groaning and pulling her closer. She wraps her arms around my neck and throws her leg over mine, straddling my waist without breaking the kiss. I grunt when I feel her sitting on my hard cock, unable to stop the reaction.

She pulls away and tries to scramble away; I latch my hands into that delectable ass and hold her in place. "I didn't mean to hurt you."

"You didn't hurt me," I assure her.

"It sounded like I did."

"Angel," I say hoarsely. "Your delicious ass was right on my cock."

She sucks in a breath, then giggles. "Oh."

I slide my hands up to her hips, letting my fingers sink into her flesh. "You might look like an angel, but you're built for sin." I slide my hands up higher, cupping her huge tits. Her back arches, and she rubs against me again. When I make a noise this time, I watch her eyes darken, the pupil taking over the iris. She grinds her hips down, and I groan loudly. Mateo must have worked on her confidence because the Evie that came here wouldn't have done that.

"I like that noise," Evie says huskily. I grab her hips again and pull her down when I lift up, letting her feel every inch of me rubbing against her. Goddamn, I wanted to peel every piece of clothing from her body and worship her for hours, but here isn't the place.

Still using her hips to grind on my cock, I sink into a kiss. This one is a little rougher, letting her know what she does to me. I wanted to know if Evie can handle my demands in bed, but I am nervous to try. Evie moans deep in her throat, and all nerves dissipate.

"Let's go home, angel," I say, kissing her neck, letting her know exactly what I have in mind.

"Okay," Evie whispers.

I help her to her feet; together, we fold the blanket, and I tuck her hand in mine, trying not to drag her out like a caveman.

Once she's pressed against me again, I can't stop the shiver when she slides her hands across my stomach, splaying them wide so she can feel my abs through my shirt.

Yep. Time to get the fuck out of here. I fire up the bike, and her arms tighten on me.

I swing the bike around and head back toward the main road. I see an SUV hauling ass up behind us two minutes into the drive. I slow down, hoping the dick will pass us, but he stays on my back tire. A feeling of unease runs through me, and I've learned to always trust my gut.

"Hold on," I yell to Evie over the rumbling of the bike, and she presses closer. I open the throttle up, and the SUV stays right with me. *Shit.* This isn't good. My Harley is built for the ride; it isn't built for speed.

I hit the side of my helmet to activate the built-in Bluetooth. It rings twice.

"Hello?" Micah answers.

"We have problems, Boss," I say, hoping Evie couldn't hear me.

"Where?" Micah asks, and I can tell he's already moving.

"Two-twenty-two. I have a tail."

"Can you lose it?"

I glance in my side mirror. "No."

"Shit. We're on our way. Five minutes tops." The line goes dead, and I go through my options.

The SUV speeds up behind me, then backs off repeatedly, trying to cause me to overcorrect and turn the bike over. Is this connected to Evie or me?

It backs off again, and I take my chance. I swerve into the other lane and slam on the brake. The SUV flies by me, doing the same. I jerk the bike down what looks like a walking path, following it as far as possible. I see a break in the trees and pull into it, shutting the bike off.

I help Evie pull her helmet off. "What's going on?" she asks with a quiver in her voice.

"Shhh," I say gently, pulling her off the bike. I reach into my saddlebag and pull my Glock out, checking the clip. I grab her hand and pull her down into a crouching position. "Stay quiet."

Her eyes are wide, but she nods, fear shining through. We sit there for five minutes, and just when I think the coast is clear, I hear gravel crunching.

"I saw them go down this way," I hear a guy say.

Evie's eyes swing towards me, and she looks more than terrified. She knows that voice. I put my fingers to my lips, and her eyes start filling with tears.

"I think we missed the goddamn turn," the other argues. There are two of them; that would be easy. I don't want to scare her if I don't have to.

"I'm telling you, dickhead; they're down here. He'll kill us if we come back without her."

I can feel Evie's entire body vibrating with fear. I pull her into my chest just as I see boots come into view outside the trees. If they look in here, our cover is blown. I am going to have to shoot our way out of here. I slide my safety off, slide Evie to a sitting position, and get ready.

"Let's go. We're wasting time. We'll get Spud to check the tracker." Tracker? Are they fucking tracking us? How?

I hold my breath as they turn around, and the gravel crunching fades in the other direction. I wait two minutes and slowly make my way out of the trees, Evie behind me.

She pops out right about the time Micah comes around the corner. She screams at the top of her lungs. "Jesus, Evie. It's just me," Micah soothes.

She launches herself into his arms, big heaving sobs wracking her body. Micah runs his hands up and down her back, whispering in her ear.

"There were two of them that I could tell," I say, tucking my Glock into the back of my jeans. "They said something about a tracker."

"Ho...how?" Evie asks, pulling her face away from Micah's chest.

"I don't know, *la mia stella*, but we will find out."

Evander presses into her back. "We need to go. Now," he says.

Micah meets my eyes over her head, and they are burning with anger.

This motherfucker doesn't know who he's fucking with.

CHAPTER 33
MICAH

I called Ghost and Caden as soon as we got Evie back to the house. She is tucked between Mateo and Hartley on the couch. They came rushing into the house two minutes after we got back. She has a cup of tea I made in her hand, and every once in a while, I see the cup shake. Those sobs that were coming from her made me see fucking red.

"What do you need from us?" Ghost asks, kicking back on the loveseat.

"I want you to find these assholes. Don't leave a stone unturned," I tell him, pacing. I couldn't get my shit together enough to sit down. What would have happened if they hit that bike?

"Did you get a good look at the SUV?" Caden asks Gray.

"Black Mercedes G-Class," Gray answers from his spot, leaning against the doorway. He is tenser than I am, and he is fucking pissed.

"Did you recognize the voices?" Ghost asks Evie softly.

"One of them was Wraith," Evie answers.

"Are you sure you didn't miss anyone in your crew?" I ask.

Ghost turns cold blue eyes on me. "No. I didn't fucking miss anyone. There was only a handful left, anyway."

Caden runs his hand through his blue hair. I couldn't ask for

259

much; at least he got rid of the name Squid. "We'll check the usual spots. See what we can see," Caden says.

I follow them to the front door and step out onto the porch. "Shoot first," I tell them. "You run into trouble; call me."

Ghost grins. "We got this. Wraith was always a piece of shit, anyway."

"Where all have you been with her?" Caden asks.

"Mateo took her shopping at a bookstore and Lala's place, and we took her to Whispers."

"Why not come after her, then?" Ghost asks, leaning against the side of his Dodge Challenger.

"Maybe she didn't have any tracking on her then," Caden muses. "Holden's shit can't be tracked, and I'm assuming the phone she has is his."

"It is," I agree.

"Who else has been here?" Ghost asks.

"Just us. And Bridget came over to get her ready."

Caden's eyebrows hit his hairline. "You brought a stylist to get her ready for a date?" Caden whistles, and I want to throat punch him.

"Pulling all stops, Micah?" Ghost grins. "You like this girl?"

"Shut up," I bark, making them grin.

"If they are around, we'll find them," Ghost assures me before sliding into his car and driving off with Caden.

I go straight to my office, trying to get the sounds of Evie's cries from my head. Jesus. They fucking broke me. Seeing the fear in her eyes absolved every doubt I had about her. You couldn't fucking fake that.

"Micah." My head snaps up at her soft voice, and she surprises me by coming around to my side of the desk. I tug her hand until she's sitting on my lap. I just needed to be close to her. She tries to resist, and I hear a little squeak when I tighten my arm around her waist.

"What did you need, *la mia stella*?" I ask.

"I just..." Evie's voice trails off, wringing her hands in front of her.

"What is it?" I ask softly, squeezing her hip in encouragement.

"I just needed to be close to you," she whispers, and my heart squeezes.

I pull her until she's against my chest and rub small circles on her back until she's relaxed in my arms.

In such a short time, we've become entranced by this woman. She screamed fragile, and all my instincts are screaming to protect her with everything. I don't know where it came from; I've only felt like that about one other woman, my niece. I knew I would do everything in this world for Evander. And even Mateo. They are my family.

I think about when she rushed into my arms when Evander and I found her and Gray. The look on her face was one of relief. She found comfort with me, and I don't know how to describe that feeling.

I am done with all the suspicions and jealousy. Evie's safety is my top priority now.

"Micah."

"What's wrong?" I pop out of bed, instantly alert at Evie's voice.

"I'm sorry," she says quietly. "I couldn't sleep."

I hear Evander shift over on the bed, already preparing for her to climb into bed with us. I look back at the bed as he lifts the sheet in invitation.

"Go on," I encourage.

She climbs onto the bed and snuggles into his side with her head on his chest. "I like your hair like that," she tells Van. It is all mussed from sleep and not perfectly styled like she's gotten used to.

I smile and slide in behind her, molding my front to her back. She lets out a little sigh and wiggles around to get comfortable. I have to count to ten and think of something nonsexual to will myself not to get hard. This goes on a few times before I can't take it anymore. I clamp a hand on her hip.

"Evie," I warn. I was trying to comfort her, but I could only take so much of that thick ass rubbing all over me. She giggles, and my eyes narrow even though she can't see me. "Are you teasing me, you little minx?"

"What?! No! I couldn't get comfortable!" she answers, and I hear Van cover a laugh with a cough.

"Uh-huh," I grumble. "Keep moving like that, and I'm going to make sure you're really comfortable."

Her breath hitches, and I catch Van's eyes over her head. His pupils are huge, and I know she has the same effect on him.

I slide my hand to her stomach, flatten my palm, and jerk her against me. All I've thought about since we took her on that date was her lips on mine. It took everything in me to be a gentleman, kiss her goodnight, and leave her at her door. Especially after the little moan she let out when Van finally kissed her.

Her ass makes contact with my hard cock, and her breathing speeds up. "Is that why you couldn't sleep, *la mia stella*?" I whisper against her neck, making her shiver. I keep repeating in my head to go slow. "Do you need something?" Her ass rotates on my cock, and it twitches in response. "Words, Evie. Tell me what you need."

"I want you," Evie whispers, and I close my eyes. "Both of you." *Holy shit.*

"Do you know what you're asking for?" Van asks gently, running his finger down her cheek.

"Yes," Evie breathes. "Ever since I saw you guys kissing and then the date...it's all I've thought about."

Van and I exchange a glance, silently communicating if we think she could handle us. He nods subtly, and I know he will go slow with her, too.

I nudge her until she's lying on her back between us; I need to see her eyes for this. "Are you sure?"

"Yes. Please, Micah," Evie says huskily. *Fuck.* Hearing her beg for us is my undoing.

I slip my hand under her shirt, and she sucks in a breath when my hand lands on her bare skin. I run it up higher until my fingers brush the underside of her delicious naked tits. With my eyes on her face, I massage one in my hand, and her back arches. Van shifts over on his side, following the same path with his hand.

"Oh god," Evie groans, her mind catching up with two different hands touching her right now.

Together Van and I help her out of the shirt, and I'm struck fucking speechless at her breasts spilling out everywhere.

"No," I say harshly when her arms come up to cover herself. "You don't hide from us. Now let me look my fill." She whimpers but lets her arms drop to the bed. I start rolling her nipple between my fingers. "Goddamn, you have gorgeous tits."

Van chuckles, but it's deep and husky, showing how turned on he is. Fuck, that was hot. I knew it would be explosive when Van and I got a woman between us. "She does," he agrees, slowly lowering his head. His tongue snakes out and licks around her nipple, looking me in the eye the entire time. I lower my head and do the same.

Evie sinks her fingers into our hair, forgetting about her earlier shyness or insecurities. She has no reason to feel insecure. She is built like a fucking sex goddess. Her breasts are huge and full. She has a soft belly, a dip in her hips that your hands get lost in when you grab them, and thick ass thighs that I want locked around my head. Or watch them wrap around Van's. That thought has me groaning deep in my throat.

"That feels so good," Evie moans.

"You haven't felt anything yet, *pequena reina*," Van promises, letting her nipple go with a wet pop. He slants his mouth over hers, groaning as he sinks his tongue into her mouth.

I know what she is feeling. Van kisses like a man starving, and you are his first meal. It consumes you: body and mind.

I take my time exploring the top half of her body with my hand until she's squirming between us. I flatten my hand and slide it under her shorts, straight into her panties.

I circle her clit. "She's wet for us, *amore mio*."

He pulls back from her lips, a dazed look on his face. "How wet?"

"Fucking soaked," I answer, earning a moan from her. The more I rub her clit; the more blush spreads from her cheeks and down her chest. "I need these out of the way," I murmur against her neck.

I pull my hand free so Van and I can work her shorts and panties off her hips. As soon as the offensive material is out of the way, I look back at Evie. Her eyes are squeezed shut, and I can tell it's taking everything in her not to hide.

"Open your eyes," Van demands huskily. Her eyes pop open. "Like Micah said, you don't hide from us. That includes those beautiful eyes," he tells her and then lets his eyes roam down her body, his eyes heating with every square inch he takes in of her creamy skin. "Fuck, you're gorgeous," he says hoarsely, and I know he means every word.

"Open those thighs," I whisper. I see her fighting that internal battle until her thighs part showing off that glistening pussy. Hooking her leg over my hip, I move closer, and Van does the same, spreading her open for us. Perfectly in sync, we run our hands up her calves and thighs. We let our fingers barely pass through her slit, and her breathing kicks up double time.

"Please," Evie breathes.

"Please, what, *la mia stella*?" I ask. I need to hear her say the words.

"Please touch me."

Together, Van and I slide our hands on her pussy again. I tease her opening with my finger while Van massages her clit. Her back arches when I slide two fingers inside her, hitting her g-spot with precision, rubbing it in time with his fingers on her clit, making all kinds of delicious noises leave her mouth. We both bend down and take her nipples into our mouths.

"Oh!" Evie exclaims, her hips fucking herself down on our fingers.

"I need to taste you," Van rasps, sitting up on his knees. I could see his cock, hard as a rock, behind his boxers. He works his shoulders between her thighs and attacks her clit while I finger fuck her.

"Evander!" Evie says, sinking her fingers into his thick brown hair.

"You like his mouth on you?" I ask. "He's damn good with that mouth." She moans deep and throaty. "You like that I know what his mouth feels like?" Evie might be innocent, but she has a vixen buried in there, and I am going to coax it out. "You like knowing his mouth has been on my cock?"

"Oh god, yes!" Evie says, working her hips down on his mouth and my fingers.

"Fuck, Micah," Van groans, working harder on her clit.

"You're a dirty girl, aren't you, *la mia stella*?" Evie moans again. I start finger fucking her harder. "Come on his tongue," I demand, letting the roughness in my voice bleed out.

"I don't...I can't...oh my god! Evander!" Evie screams. Her pussy clamps down on my fingers, pulsing. Fuck, she's beautiful when she comes.

Van sits back on his heels, her wetness glistening on his mouth and chin. "Come here," I say roughly. He leans forward, and I crash my lips against his, sinking my tongue in his mouth to taste her on his lips.

"Oh my," Evie whispers.

"You taste good together," I whisper against Van's lips. His eyes meet mine, and the look almost takes my breath away. Van is holding on by a thread, just like I am.

He leans down and kisses her gently. "You did so good, *pequena reina.*" Her whole body relaxes under his praise.

"I want to be inside you," I say roughly. "Is that still what you want?"

Her eyes snap to mine. Her eyes are darker than her warm brown. "It is," she answers. *Thank fuck.*

I stand up and dig around in the bedside table for a condom. When I find it, I drop my boxers, and my eyes snap back at the slight noise Evie makes. Her eyes are zeroed in on my cock, widening when she takes in my size.

"He feels good," Van tells her, rolling her nipples between his fingers.

"You're so big," she whispers, and I chuckle.

"Second thoughts?" I ask and repeat in my head that I hope not.

"No, I just...wow," Evie breathes.

"Don't make his ego swell anymore," Van says with a roll of his eyes.

I grin, and Evie giggles.

I climb back on the bed, get situated between her thighs, and look at her pussy. It is pink and pouty from Van eating it like a madman. I rip the condom wrapper open with my teeth and roll it down onto my cock, her eyes watching me the entire time. I brace one hand between her head and Van's, using the other hand to notch my cock at her entrance. My eyes not leaving hers, I start to push inside her.

Her eyes widen, her hands fly to my chest, and I'm not even halfway in yet. "Are you ok?" I ask, stopping my movement.

"You're too big," she whimpers.

I work my hips back and forth, letting her adjust. I push forward when her body relaxes again, sinking balls deep into the sweetest pussy I've ever felt. "Holy shit," I croak. I brace my other hand beside her head, and Evie's hands latch onto my biceps. "Fuck, you feel good."

"Tell me how good she feels," Van says, kissing her neck.

"Hot. Tight. Wet," I groan when I slide back out. "She has a greedy pussy. It tries to hold me inside her."

Evie moans loudly. Does my sweet girl like dirty talk? Good to know because I am a nasty motherfucker.

"You like me talking about this pussy like that, *la mia stella?*" I couldn't stop myself from that pet name dripping from my tongue, and the way her pussy clamped down on me, she liked it too. "You like knowing how good you feel on my cock?"

"Yes. No one has ever..." Evie trails off, but I know what she was going to say.

I sit back on my heels, place my hands on her thighs, and spread her wide. I slowly slide out and watch my cock disappear, groaning the whole way back in.

"Fuck, you look sexy," Van says hoarsely, and I expect him to be looking at Evie, but he's got those lustful brown eyes locked on me.

"I want you..." Evie moans. "I want you too," she whispers to Van.

He traces her pouty bottom lip with his thumb. "You aren't ready for that yet, *pequena reina.*" He kisses her slowly, causing her pussy to clamp down on me. "But I can give you something else."

Van rolls from the bed and shucks his boxers. His thick dick stands proudly between his thighs, leaking from the slit.

"Oh shit," Evie giggles, clamping down on me, making us both groan. "You both had to be big."

Van waggles his eyebrows playfully, making her giggle again. "Fuck," I grunt. "Hands and knees," I tell her, and her whole body freezes. "What's wrong?" I ask, stopping my movements.

"I'm too big to be..." Evie's eyes widen when she sees my eyes narrowing.

"I want nothing more than to bury my face in that ass. And if I ever hear you say something like that again, I'll turn that ass red. Are we clear?"

"Yes," Evie squeaks.

I lean down, kissing her gently to soften the blow. "You're fucking perfect. We will spend the rest of the night making sure you believe that. Now. Hands and knees." I reluctantly pull from her pussy and wait until she makes up her mind. She swallows and sits up. I help her get turned over with her face towards Van. I smooth my hands up her glorious ass and can't stop the groan that rips from my chest. "Better than I imagined." I get a handful of both ass cheeks and sink back inside her. This position sinks me even deeper, and Evie moans long and loud, her head dropping forward. "Does that feel good?" I breathe, still massaging her ass.

"Yes. Oh, god."

"Suck his cock," I demand.

She lifts her head, and Van fists his cock, feeding it into her mouth. He teases it in and out a few times until he sinks in, testing her limits. She gags, and he pulls back, letting her get a breath. He repeats this a few times. "Breathe through your nose. You can take it," Van encourages. He grasps her chin between his thumb and fore-finger, pulling her head up more before pushing forward. I know the moment he sinks into her throat. His head drops back on his shoulders with a groan, and I almost come on the spot. "Swallow," Van rasps. "Oh shit."

We start moving again, fucking her mouth and pussy at the same tempo. She's moaning around Van's cock, pushing her hips back on me. I sink my hands into those hips like I've been dying to and start fucking her harder. My control is hanging on by a thread. The need to claim her is clawing at my brain. I've never felt this urge with anyone but Van. I reach down and start rubbing her clit.

"Come on my cock," I demand. "Let me feel you squeeze it." Like a detonator, my words cause her pussy to spasm, and she clamps down on me so hard I can't even move. I breathe through my nose, trying to hold my fast-impending release off. I let her body relax, then start rubbing her sensitive clit again. "Give me one more. You look goddamn beautiful when you come, *la mia stella*." I watch her swallow Van's dick whole, and my control snaps.

I dig my hand into her hip and start fucking her ruthlessly, rubbing her clit in tight circles. My thighs are slapping against hers; her ass is bouncing with each thrust.

"Fuck," Van groans. "I'm going to come." He goes to pull from her mouth, and her hand snaps out, locking on his hip. He sinks to her throat and comes with a shout.

"Shit," I rasp, rubbing faster. I am determined to make her come before me; I'm addicted to it.

Van slips from her lips. "Yes. Yes. Yes," Evie chants, spurring me on. Her fingers ball into the fists on the blankets, and her back bows. "MICAH!"

That's all it takes, hearing her scream my fucking name. I slam into her twice, burying myself as far as I can, and let go with a groan. It felt like it started from my damn toes. I release my fingers from her hips and slide from her. She collapses on the bed with a sigh.

Laying a kiss on her spine, I pull the condom off and knot it, tossing it into the wastebasket beside the bed. Van and I get her rearranged on the bed, kissing her slowly. She snuggles between us with such a sigh of contentment that I feel myself doing the same. I kiss Van over her head, curl myself around her back, and flip the sheet over us.

"You're amazing, *pequena reina*," Van murmurs against her head.

"Fuck yeah, she is," I agree.

Evie yawns. "I feel like that with you guys. You're perfect." Her voice fades off, and I know she's about to pass out.

Van laces our hands together on her hip and squeezes my fingers, telling me silently that he is okay.

I am more than okay. It's like something slotted into place, letting me feel relaxed fully for the first time in a long time.

Van brought that too, but something about this moment made it feel like more.

Waking up the next morning and seeing Evie snuggled into Micah's chest, I waited for the jealousy to kick in. When it didn't, I soaked in how good it felt to be with her last night. I'm glad she felt she could come to us when she was scared, and I wouldn't have been able to turn her away, anyway.

Seeing Micah and her in the kitchen made something shift in the way I looked at her. I was no longer just intrigued by her. I now fully understood the draw she had on the others.

When Micah got the call from Gray that they were being followed, we'd never moved so fast. It was a panic I was only used to feeling with a few people.

"Morning, *amore mio*," Micah says. His voice still had that sleepy gruffness to it that I loved. He peeks down at Evie's head on his chest and smiles.

"Morning, *mi rey*."

"I'm still sleeping," Evie grumbles, snuggling further into Micah, then shoots up in the bed. The sheet falls away, leaving her beautiful tits on full display. "My eyes are up here, fellas," she laughs when she catches us both staring.

"You can't just whip those out first thing in the morning and not expect a reaction, *pequeña reina*," I joke.

"I've never felt so scandalized in my life," Evie says dramatically, making us chuckle.

"I think you'd feel pretty scandalized after seducing us last night," Micah says with a grin.

Her mouth drops open, and her cheeks bloom with color. "I didn't seduce you. I remember someone not being able to control his bottom half."

"My bottom half?" Micah snorts. "You mean my hard cock you were rubbing your ass against?" He pulls her until she sprawls on his chest. "Are you complaining, *la mia stella?*"

"No," Evie says breathlessly. I knew what she felt when it came to Micah, and I couldn't help but laugh.

"Something funny, *amore mio,*" Micah asks with a raised brow.

"Nope." I kiss Evie's shoulder and climb from the bed. "I have some stuff to take care of today at Skyline."

"I'll go with you," Micah offers.

I smile and bend down to kiss him. "No, you stay here today." I look pointedly at Evie. I wanted him to spend time with her.

"At least let me fix you breakfast."

"That I can agree to." I laugh. No way am I passing up anything Micah cooks.

"Come on, *la mia stella*, you can help."

Evie laughs. "You know what happened last time I helped you cook?"

"Oh, I remember," Micah growls, rolling so she's under him, making her squeal.

I shake my head with a smile and head to the shower. I step inside the stall, letting the warm water run over me, and I can't believe how happy I feel. I'm sure a lot of people would think I was fucking crazy for letting this happen after I just got Micah back, but I didn't care. It felt right to me, and that's all I cared about.

I've learned through the years to block out what people say about me. We weren't liked by many because of Frankie, and those whispers followed us around. People always assumed we were just like him, which couldn't be further from the truth. Mateo and I carved our own path through blood, sweat, and tears. Not to prove anyone wrong, but for ourselves. The shit Frankie put us through still lingers over both of us. It was hard for it not to. But I refused to become the hateful, abusive piece of shit he was.

I step out of the shower and dry off. Digging through the drawer for my hair supplies, I stop remembering what Evie said. She said she liked my hair like this, and it's one more way I could say fuck you to Frankie. He wanted us perfectly polished without a hair out of place. But when a woman as beautiful as Evie says she likes your hair, you listen.

After getting dressed, I step into the kitchen and take in the scene in front of me. Micah is behind Evie at the stove with his arms wrapped around her waist while she cooks. Mateo, Gray, and Hartley are sitting at the kitchen island, heads bent together, deep in conversation. It looks so normal that I have to take a minute to appreciate it.

Mateo turns to me with a smile. "What's up, bro?" He takes in my hair, and his eyes widen. I narrow mine in warning before he can give me shit. "Uh, where are you headed?"

"Suppliers will be at Skyline today," I remind him.

"Do you need me to go?" he asks.

"No, you hang out here. I shouldn't be gone long."

Mateo's eyes travel to Micah and Evie, then back to me. He raises an eyebrow, and I nod, letting him know that whatever he is thinking, he's right. He smiles so big it looks like his face will split apart. I've never seen him so fucking happy. I take a seat beside him.

"You good?" Mateo whispers.

"Better than good, brother."

"So, you're in?"

I take another look at Micah and nod. "I'm all in."

"You're not just doing this for him, right?"

"No." At first, it was just for Micah. I would have done anything to make him happy, even if that meant him being with Evie, too. But I want her just as much now.

"I want you to take Gray with you," Micah says, looking over his shoulder. "No arguments. That asshole made his move; we need to be vigilant."

"I have guards," I argue.

"I know you do, but I trust Gray with my life, and that's you, *amore mio*. Take him."

I swallow the lump in my throat and nod. It's pointless to argue with him when he gets that look in his eye, anyway.

Evie starts passing out plates of French toast and takes her place on the other side of Gray. He kisses the top of her head. *Fuck.* That feeling of rightness just keeps intensifying.

Micah slides his hand down my thigh, bringing my attention to him. His blue eyes are bright, none of that usual darkness swirling around like there has been the past couple of days.

"I love you, *mi rey*."

"I love you too, *amore mio*."

Something tells me this is no longer temporary.

"WHAT THE FUCK do you mean the shipment didn't come?" I bark into my phone.

This day is fast turning to shit. Nothing is going like I wanted, and it's working on my temper.

"Sir, it was beyond our control," my supplier soothes. "We will have it here by Friday."

"That's in two goddamn days. You're telling me you can't handle a simple fucking task? Do I need to find someone else?"

"No, sir! We will have it there." I hit end call and sling my phone on my desk. My "supplier" isn't for Skyline, but it's where Mateo and I run most of our other business out of. We wanted to keep everything as legitimate as we could. The drug business is where our money comes from, though, and if we supply it, we keep it controlled to the best of our ability. We don't like it, but it came with this life. This side of the business is Ecstasy.

"Is everything good?" Gray asks, sticking his head in the door.

I wave him in. "Have a seat. You don't have to stand guard out there." I hated that he felt that way, but Gray took his job seriously. But he isn't just a guard; he is involved with my brother.

Gray folds his frame into the chair in front of me. "It's my job."

"I understand, but I can handle myself. I appreciate you coming, though." I sigh and lean back in my chair. "I should have stayed the fuck home."

"Anything I can help with?"

"If you can get a shitload of Ecstasy here by Friday, then sure." According to Dom, my supplier, it's stuck in the middle of the fucking ocean.

"How much?" Gray asks, and I sit up.

"If you're serious, whatever you can get me."

Gray shrugs. "I know a guy. I can get a meeting if you need it. And you need to fire your supplier."

I laugh. "No shit. It's always something. But you know I can't just fire him as well as I do." This part of the job didn't even bother me anymore. If someone fucked up, they paid the price in blood. I've let Dom by with too much shit lately, and that needs to end.

"I can take care of that too," Gray says confidently. I have no doubt. I know all about who Gray is.

"Let's go. I need to let off some steam."

Gray grins and stands from his chair. "Do you know where he is?"

"Only so many places he can be," I answer, messaging Mateo.

> Dom is done.

MATEO
Oh shit. Now?

> Gray and I are taking care of it.

MATEO
Aww 'heart eye emoji' you guys are bonding.

I bark a laugh. Nothing like a couple of guys bonding over bloodshed.

> If that's what you want to call it.

MATEO

Take care of him. He's important.

I look at Gray's large frame and laugh again. If anyone needed protection, it wasn't Gray. But I understand what Mateo is saying.

I got you, brother.

My fingers hover over the keys before I ask the next question after I slide into one of the guard SUVs, Gray behind the wheel.

How's Evie?

MATEO

She's great. She told me what happened last night. 'grinning emoji'

I figured. I'll keep you updated.

MATEO

Be safe, bro.

Oh yeah, I forgot to tell you I liked your hair.

I knew that asshole wouldn't let that go, and he would be digging for the reason why.

I rattle off one of the addresses to Gray that I think Dom might be hiding at. I could tell by his voice on the phone that he knew I would be pissed. We get through the first two places before finally finding him at the third.

Dom's eyes widen when I walk into his bar. "Van, what can I do for you, man?"

"Somewhere to talk. Now," I bite out. His buddies eye me warily and keep shooting nervous glances over my shoulder at Gray.

"We can talk back here." He stands from his chair, and two of the others follow.

"Sit," Gray barks, and even I have the urge to listen.

Dom swallows and nods. He knows why I am here. He may be incompetent, but he isn't stupid.

I shut the door behind us. It looks like he brought us to their meeting room. "Any news on our shipment?" The more I thought about it, the more this shit wasn't sitting right with me. I had backup plans in place for this very reason, so why the hell didn't he tell me before now?

"Yeah. Like I said, it will be here," Dom answers, trying not to look nervous.

I nod and walk around the room, looking. It always puts somebody on the defensive when you invade their space. "What happened again?"

"I told you. The yacht broke down. We're waiting on the other one now."

Gray folds his arms over his chest. "Sounds a little like bullshit to me."

"Who's this?" Dom asks, gesturing to Gray.

"Your worst fucking nightmare," I answer. They don't call him the Reaper for nothing. "Why don't you really tell me what happened? Or I'm going to take your brother down with you, Dom. I'm done with this shit."

"He doesn't have anything to do with this!" Dom exclaims. Dom's brother has everything to do with this. Eric wanted the quick buck, and they really thought they could fuck me over. They've been testing me this whole time to see how much they could get by with.

"Bullshit," I growl. "Where's my supply, Dom?"

"I told you!"

"You lying motherfucker." My fist snaps out, and I hear the bones crunch under my knuckles. Fuck, I haven't been in a good fight in a long time. It felt good. I pull my Glock from my holster and press it under his chin. "Where. Is. It?"

"You're going to kill me no matter what." Dom swallows. "Why would I tell you?"

"Because if you do, your wife and daughter will never find out what a fuck up you are. You want your daughter growing up knowing her father was nothing but a drug smuggler? And he couldn't even do that right? I pay you damn good, Dom. There isn't any room for error. Now, tell me." It's an empty threat. I would never let an innocent know who their father really was. I grew up knowing mine was a monster. It wasn't a good feeling.

Dom closes his eyes. "We were approached a couple of days ago. They offered us double what you were paying to let them hijack the shipment."

"Goddamnit! Are you fucking insane?! Who?" I press the gun harder. "Who?"

"Aaron Rockford." *Shit.* If he knows about my business, he knows too much already, which means someone is leaking information or we underestimated him.

Gray and I exchange a look. I pull the gun away, and Dom opens his eyes cautiously. "Where is he?" Gray asks.

"I don't know."

"How do you get in contact with him?" I ask. "Don't fucking move," I bark when he reaches for his pocket.

"There is a card with a number in my wallet. I haven't seen him since we made the deal."

I dig his wallet out and pull out a plain black card on it with a number in gold. "This it?" Dom nods. "Did you really think I was going to let this slide?" I pull the trigger before he can answer. I already knew it anyway.

"What about his buddies?" Gray asks, nodding his head to the other room.

"Find out where his brother is and then kill them."

"Yes, sir," Gray grins.

"Let's make it bloody. It's time we remind people who we are."

This is the part of myself I never shied away from. It was inevitable when you were taught at the age of thirteen how many ways you could kill a man. Hiding it just made it harder to make the tough calls.

I just don't know how Evie will handle who we really are.

CHAPTER 35
MATEO

"So, what'd you do last night?" I ask Evie the following day. After Van left with Gray, I brought her outside by the pool, which is her favorite spot. Her face blooms with color, and I have to stifle a laugh. I know what she did last night; the whole house heard it.

"I'm not talking about this," Evie says and crosses her arms over her chest.

"Oh, come on. Give me something," I beg.

"We shouldn't be talking about this. He's your brother," Evie hisses.

I grab my chest in mock outrage. "My brother? How dare you?!"

"Stop," Evie giggles. "Seriously, Mateo, I don't even know what to tell you. It's your brother." She whispers that last part, and I know she's struggling this morning. Not because she had sex with them last night, but because of everything that has gone on.

"Hey," I say softly, grabbing her hands and laying them on my thigh. "You know we don't care, right? I'm glad you trusted them enough to go to them."

"That doesn't mean I don't trust you!" Evie exclaims.

"I know that," I soothe. "You needed something you knew they could give you last night."

"I don't know what it was," Evie says quietly. "I was laying in bed, and my feet were leading me to them before I could stop it."

I shrug. "I get it. They have an air of safety around them."

"Don't you think this is crazy?" Evie asks, laying her head back on the lounger with a sigh. "I trust you guys. You make me feel." She swallows. "Safe, protected, pretty."

"Buttercup, you're more than pretty. You're gorgeous. A man should always make you feel that way. If they don't, they aren't worth your time." I tug her chin to look at me. "To answer your question. No, I don't think this is crazy."

I don't know how to explain to her that this is exactly what I wanted. I don't want to scare the poor girl. I knew eventually she would completely let her guard down and have sex with someone else. I'm glad she chose Micah and Evander. Plus, I don't blame her; Micah is fucking hot.

"What are you grinning about?" Evie asks. I didn't even realize I was.

I chuckle. "I was thinking I didn't blame you for Micah because he's hot," I answer honestly.

"He is, isn't he?" Evie says in such a dreamy voice that I laugh. "And Evander? Oh, my god." That makes me laugh even harder.

"I mean, sure, he's my brother. Good looks run in the family." I grin at her when she turns her head, and she blushes.

"How are you okay with this?"

"You know we've shared women before."

"I still don't know how that works," Evie says, looking genuinely curious.

"We don't touch each other if that's what you're wondering. Our soul focus is on the woman between us. Giving her as much pleasure as her body can handle." Evie's mouth forms an 'O' as she takes that information in. "Is that what they did to you, buttercup?" My dick is starting to harden just thinking about it.

"Yeah," Evie answers breathlessly. Her mind had taken her back to last night, and her blush isn't from embarrassment this time.

"Tell me about it," I ask her. My voice is husky, even to my ears.

"They were sweet and slow. Wanting to make sure I was

comfortable the whole time." She smiles at that. "I've never felt like that before except with you."

"With us, buttercup, you always will be."

The patio door slides open, and I look over my shoulder, smiling. Micah walks onto the patio, looking the most relaxed I've ever seen the uptight bastard. He's shirtless with swimming trunks on. I hear Evie's breath catch when she catches sight of him, and I have to fight a laugh. He walks by her with a wink before diving into the pool. Asshole.

"No one should be able to look that hot," Evie grumbles. "None of you. It should be illegal."

I laugh and jump to my feet, ripping my shirt over my head, soaking in how her greedy eyes take in my body. I've never been vain, but how she stared at me made me feel like I was on top of the world. I drop my shorts, leaving me in my boxer briefs. Walking backward with a smile, I dive into the pool with Micah.

"Jesus. Fuck, Mateo," Micah says when I surface right in front of him with a grin. "You scared the shit out of me."

I know Micah's my brother's boyfriend, but that didn't stop me from appreciating that Micah is sexy as sin. All that dark black hair and those weird, almost clear blue eyes. I also wondered what it would be like to press Micah between Van and me. We've done it with women; why not Micah?

"What are you thinking about? You're plotting," Micah accuses.

"I'm not plotting," I defend. "Have you heard from Ghost or Caden?" I ask, changing the subject.

"Not yet," Micah sighs, running his fingers through his wet hair. "I'm on fucking edge now."

"Somebody didn't take that edge off last night?" I tease.

"Oh, she did," Micah chuckles. "I had no expectations when she walked into our room, but she started grinding her ass on me."

My mouth pops open. "She did fucking what?" Evie initiated that? Wait. "Did you just say *our* room?"

Micah's brows furrow. "Uh, yeah? No matter where we are, it's our room."

Holy shit. "You're really serious about this, aren't you?"

"Serious about your brother? Yes. What? Why are you giving me that look?"

"I didn't think I'd ever see the fucking day the mighty Micah would fall," I admit. "Most of all with Van."

"I fucked up the first time. I won't make that mistake again." Micah glances back at Evie, who's kicked back on the lounger with a book. "I'm worried, though."

It's my turn to frown. Micah didn't get worried. "About?" I prompt.

"I saw the way Van looked at her last night."

"Are you jealous?" I ask, dropping all teasing.

"Not jealous. It was fucking hot watching them together. What if he realizes he doesn't want a man? What if he wants a woman?"

"That's where my idea came in," I remind him. "We all enjoy each other and have a woman? It would be the fucking life." I wait for him to catch onto the first part of my statement. I see the moment he does.

"What do you mean enjoy each other?" Micah scoffs. "You've been around Les' crew too damn much."

"Come on. Think about it," I say, floating closer. "That's the perfect setup. As long as we are loyal to each other." I shrug. "It shouldn't matter."

"You do remember I'm dating your *brother?*"

Here goes nothing. I hope he doesn't kick me in the balls. "We've shared before. What would be the difference between that and sharing you?" I let my voice drop an octave, letting him know I am fucking serious. I watch Micah take that in. His pupils expand, and his breathing speeds up. Ah. Micah has thought about that before. He's my best friend, and if Van wouldn't have made a move, I probably would have.

Micah stares at me for so long that I start to get nervous. Then he shakes his head. "You're crazy," he says, swimming to the edge of the pool to pull himself out.

We'll see about that.

"You did what?" I ask, my mouth hanging open.

"We cleaned house, just like I fucking said," Van answers. He and Gray just got back from Dom's and filled us in on what happened. We sent Hartley outside with Evie because although we are building that trust with him, he isn't ready for this yet.

"Aaron Rockford?" Micah sighs. "Aaron fucking Rockford got the drop on your shipment. What else does he know?"

"I was wondering the same thing," I add. "If he knew that, he could know who we all are." Which could spell trouble for Evie.

"What's the plan?" Gray asks.

Van pulls a card from his pocket. "This is the number they used to contact Aaron. It's probably a burner, but I put Holden on it just in case."

"I still don't understand how they found Evie and Gray," Micah muses. "And they mentioned a tracker. We've checked everything she owns multiple times. How would he be tracking her?"

Van sighs. "Micah, I don't want to say this, but the only other person that's been around besides Bridget is your mother."

"My mother?" Micah asks with a frown. "What would she have to do with this?"

"The stuff we found at Evie's apartment is easily hidden. She could have planted something at your house like he did at her apartment, Boss," Gray says apologetically. I've never wanted to punch a woman in her face before. That is until I heard what Micah's mom was about to call him. Before I could react, though, Evie was standing up to her like a fucking warrior.

"You think my mother is working for Aaron Rockford?" Micah asks dryly.

"She's a money-hungry bitch, Micah. He could have approached her just like he did Dom. And it's the only explanation we have."

Micah scrubs a hand down his face. "I want to argue, but it wouldn't surprise me." It sucks that Micah tries so damn hard to have a relationship with that woman, only for her to turn around and betray him.

"What do we do?" I ask.

Micah thinks for a minute, then sighs. "Bring Hartley in here." I pull out my phone and send him a message. Minutes later, he walks into the office. Micah motions for him to sit. "I need a favor," Micah says once he's seated. "I need you to dump some phone records for me."

Hartley raises an eyebrow. "Okay. That laptop should be capable of it. Who's?"

Micah scribbles down a number and hands it to Hartley. "It's my mother's."

Hartley's eyebrows hit his hairline. "Oh." We all exchange looks, and Hartley catches it. "What am I missing?"

"What we're about to tell you doesn't leave this fucking room," Micah says, and the threat is there. You talk, you die. "Not to Evie, not to anyone."

Hartley's jaw clenches. "I'm not going to fucking tattle."

We slowly fill Hartley in on everything from today, including what Van and Gray did afterward. I watch Hartley closely, and his face never changes. Everything he built while he was a cop to take us down, we just laid out for him on a silver platter.

"I'm not exactly sure how everything works, but I'm assuming your supplies are private. Anyway, your supplier was running his mouth to get Aaron to approach him, or do you think Aaron figured it out on his own?" Hartley asks finally. That was not what I thought his first question was going to be.

Micah looks at him hard, and I can tell he's impressed. "We don't know, but we need to treat this like Aaron found out. Once you dump my mother's phone records, we might know how he's tracking Evie and use it to our advantage."

We all nod in agreement, and I decide now is a good time to bring up what's been on my mind.

"I think we should tell Evie who we are. I don't like lying to her."

"I don't think that's a good idea," Micah says.

"I thought you trusted her?"

"It's not about trust, Tay. I do trust her. I was fooling myself by thinking otherwise. It's about her safety. She can't know. Not yet."

"I agree, Tay. I'm sorry," Van adds. "Until she's more permanent, she can't know."

"She is permanent," I say, getting pissed. "I don't care if there's an Aaron or not. I'm not letting her go."

"I understand," Van says in that soothing voice that does nothing but piss me off further. "But I also don't think she's ready."

"And I think you're underestimating her." I look at Hartley. "What are your thoughts?"

He shrugs. "I'm with Mateo. Evie's not the type to go blabbing her mouth, and she's stronger than what we give her credit for."

"I'm not ready to tell her about me," Gray says. "Let us get to know her better."

"Okay. But I'm not going to lie to her much longer. She deserves to know."

Evie needs to know what she is getting herself into so she could decide to be with us for good.

Because I wasn't lying when I said I wouldn't let her go.

With all of us in agreement, we make our way outside to Evie. I stop with a smile when I see her dancing to whatever is playing in her earbuds, and I appreciate the swing in her ass. She spins with a plate of vegetables in her hand from the fridge and almost drops it. She sits it on the island and clutches her chest.

She yanks her earbuds out. "You scared the hell out of me."

"Sorry, buttercup," I laugh. "We were enjoying the view."

"Ha. Ha. I hope you did because now my heart is in my asshole," she laughs. Her phone starts ringing, and she looks at it with a frown. "This number has been calling nonstop."

"Answer it," I demand. Something in my gut doesn't feel right. "Put it on speakerphone."

She does what I say. "Hello?"

"Hello, Evie," a male voice says, and I watch all the color drain from her face. I'm at her side before I can think.

"How did you get this number?" Evie whispers, her whole body shaking. I reach out and grab her hand.

"You know my reach, baby. You thought you could hide from me?" the voice growls, and I have to clench my jaw to keep from saying something.

"What do you want?" Evie asks with a quiver in her voice. This just proved our earlier theory. Someone planted something here or at Micah's. My guess is his house because of his useless mother.

"You," Aaron says simply. "Wraith said he saw you with someone else. I'm not happy about that. Who was he?" That means he doesn't remember Gray from the night Micah kicked his ass.

"Evie," Aaron barks when she doesn't answer. "Answer me, you fat bitch."

Evie's whole face crumples, and Gray snatches up her phone. "You don't talk to her like that," he growls. "Who I am is none of your goddamn business."

"Ah, you're the one I'm going to enjoy cutting the fuck open. Do you know who I am?" Aaron threatens. Evie's vibrating in my arms so hard that all I can do is rub her back and hold her closer.

"I know who you are. You're an abusive piece of shit. When I get ahold of you, I'm going to enjoy beating you to death," Gray says in a deadly tone.

Aaron laughs. "Mark my words. I'll get her back. No one takes what's mine." The call disconnects, and he lays the phone down on the counter, turning Evie to face him.

"Angel," he says gruffly. When she lifts her tear-stained face to him, I almost lose it. With gentleness, I didn't know he could possess, he wipes the tears from her cheeks with his thumbs. "It's ok. We'll figure this out."

This will be the last time my buttercup cries over him. It's time to take this to him.

CHAPTER 36
HARTLEY

"Hey, princess," I greet Evie. I sit down beside her on a lounger by the pool.

"Hey," she says with a smile, laying her new Kindle down that I bought her.

"How are you?" I ask, grabbing her hand.

Evie sighs. "I didn't think he could hurt me anymore. I was wrong."

"You don't deserve the things he said or done. You can't let him win."

"I don't know how to let it go," Evie says, angrily wiping a tear from her cheek. "I can still hear him in my head telling me how disgusting or fat I am. I can still hear him telling me no one would ever want me but him. I can still feel all the things he's done to me. I think I've finally won, and he proves me wrong."

I swallow down the anger and take a deep breath. "Princess, he's an evil piece of shit. None of what he said is true. It would help if you talked to somebody, though," I say gently. "You can't keep that bottled up inside."

"I can't," she whispers, tears starting to fall down her cheeks.

"Please talk to me. I think it would help."

She angrily wipes her tears again, staring into the pool. I don't think she will say anything until she takes a shuddering breath. "When we first started dating, he used to tell me how beautiful I was; I guess that was to pull me in. After about a month, he would hint that I needed to lose weight. And then he started demanding I lose weight. I argued back, and that's the first time he backhanded me across the face." I squeeze her hand for support, but I also do it for me so I would keep my damn mouth shut. "I tried to leave that night, and he begged me to stay, telling me how sorry he was. I stayed. It got worse after that. He would call me names, making fun of my weight in front of the friends I met. After six months, I just let it happen. I was so lost. He would fly off the handle at the drop of a hat and take his anger out on me. He beat me so bad one night that I ended up in the emergency room." Evie chokes back a sob, and I resist pulling her into my arms, sensing that's not what she needs.

"He told them I was robbed and said he would kill me if I told anyone the truth. The nurse knew he was lying, but I couldn't tell her because he would kill her, too. When I got home, he acted like it had never happened." Evie takes a big breath. "Wraith moved in after that so he could watch my every move when Aaron wasn't there. He used to grope me, and I knew I couldn't tell Aaron. It was my word against Wraith's. They both got called away the night I ran, and I knew it was my only chance."

I pull her into my arms, letting her cry into my shirt. I rub her back in soothing circles, letting her get it all out. I have so many questions that I am biting my tongue. I'm glad she finally told someone, even if it makes me fucking murderous.

"You're brave, princess," I say softly. "I know you don't feel like it, but you are. You got away. Some people don't."

"You guys make me feel that way," Evie says. "You make me feel alive again." I've seen such a difference in her since being here. All the guys make her feel special; I don't know what that meant for our future. Would Evie want to stay here? Where would that leave me? They might be agreeing to this while I am here, but I don't think they are going to welcome me with open arms.

Evie lifts her head, giving me a small smile. I smile back, and her eyes drift to my lips. All I could think about anymore is her lips on mine. I heard her with Micah and Evander. I wanted to get pissed, but it turned me on so fucking much that I jacked off listening to them. Surprising even myself.

Evie leans in and presses her lips to mine, tentative and sweet. I let her take the lead, mostly out of surprise but also not wanting to push her. "Kiss me, Hartley," Evie whispers against my lips, and I deepen the kiss with a groan. Kissing her is everything I always dreamed about and more. I drag her closer until she's half lying on top of me. I slide my hand into her hair and stroke my tongue against hers. Her body starts wiggling against me, making her thigh rub my hard cock.

"Evie," I groan against her lips. She has to stop, or I won't be able to stop it.

"I want to know what they feel like," Evie whispers.

"What?" I ask hoarsely.

"Your piercings," Evie says shyly. *Motherfuck.*

"Princess," I say, rubbing my knuckles down her face. "I don't know if now is the right time." I don't want her to think I am taking advantage of her after what she told me. I am an asshole, but I still have boundaries.

"You don't want to?" Evie asks, trying to push against my chest to sit up.

I tug her back. "I want to so fucking bad, princess," I assure her. I take her hand and put it on my hard dick. "You feel that? I want to."

She squeezes me through my thin basketball shorts, and my head drops back on the lounger. "Then why not? I don't want to think about what he said. Make me forget, Hartley."

Fucking hell. I pick my head up so I can see her eyes. "Are you sure? Because if you have any doubt, we don't do this. I want you to be sure what you're asking for."

"I'm sure," Evie says adamantly. "I want you."

I jerk her lips back to mine, swallowing the little gasp she made. I roll to my side, pull her leg over my hip, and grind my hard cock against her. She makes this mewling noise and tries to get closer, almost making me bust in my fucking shorts. I pull back breathless. "Let's go in the house," I tell her, kissing her neck. Evie shakes her head, and I think she's changed her mind. I look into her eyes. Her pupils are blown, her cheeks flushed, and she has this mischievous smile. I raise an eyebrow. "Here?" I ask. Anyone could walk through those doors at any time. She nods, biting her bottom lip. "Fuck, princess," I rasp, slanting my lips back over hers.

This kiss is different from the last. Hot, needy. Her hands are roaming all over my chest, and I sink my fingers into her ass cheek. She starts tugging at my shirt; I sit up and jerk it over my head. I help her get out of hers and take in the yellow lacy bra she has on, pushing her tits up to her goddamn chin. I reach behind her, unhook it, and let it fall from her arms. Her tits are perfect. Big and round, with dark nipples. Leaning in, I pull one into my mouth, sucking hard. Evie moans and sinks her fingers into my hair, pushing my face against her breast. I pay the same attention to the other one until she's panting. I lay kisses all over them and look into her eyes. "Are you still sure?" She nods fast. I slide my hand down her stomach and into her panties. "Are you still sure?" I ask again.

"Yes. Please, Hartley."

I am reeling from the fact that this is even happening. I didn't think Evie looked at me like that, but I am trying not to get my hopes up for anything else other than just a way to make her forget what she just told me.

I stand up and pull her with me. I tug her shorts down with her panties, leaving her bare in front of me. I can't stop fucking staring. She starts fidgeting foot to foot, and my eyes snap to her face. She's chewing on her bottom lip, looking uncertain. "You're fucking gorgeous," I say hoarsely. "Shit, princess. I don't know where to start."

She reaches over and jerks my shorts and boxers down, making my cock slap my stomach. She giggles. "Now we're even." Her eyes widen when she sees my cock. Knowing someone has piercings is one thing. Seeing it with your own eyes is another.

I smirk and advance on her. "Lay on your back on the lounger," I say, my voice rough. She sits down and leans back. "Bring your hips to the edge," I instruct. She swallows and wiggles down. I am going to show her how much she doesn't need to be shy about that body. I throw a pillow from the other lounger on the ground and drop to my knees in front of her. "Part those pretty thighs, princess." She whimpers and slowly parts her legs. She is dripping wet; her pussy is perfect. I slide my fingers through the slit, and she jolts when I touch her clit.

"You're dripping. Is that all for me?" I ask, circling her clit with my fingers.

"Yes," she pants, lifting her hips.

I kiss the inside of her thigh. "I'm going to make you come with my fingers," I say, kissing the other thigh. "I'm going to make you come with my mouth." I kiss each thigh again. "So, I know you're ready for my cock." I kiss directly on her pussy. "Then I'm going to make you come on it."

I start circling her clit again until her hips rotate with me, then slide them down to her opening, pushing two fingers inside her. "Oh," Evie moans, her eyes flashing down to my face. I start working my fingers in and out, twist them, and rub her g-spot with the tips of my fingers. "Oh god," Evie groans, her back bowing. With my eyes locked on her, I lean forward and suck her clit into my mouth. I work her slowly until her pussy is dripping down my fingers, and her hips are moving harder against my hand. I feel her tighten on my fingers and suck her clit hard. "Hartley!" she screams, her hand flying to my head.

Her taste explodes on my tongue, and I know I'm already addicted to it. I work my fingers faster, making all kinds of noises leave her mouth. I wrap my hand around my cock, squeezing it and stroking it. I can't wait to sink into her pussy, but I have to make sure she is ready for all my metal. I look up and almost come on the spot. She's massaging her tits, twisting her nipples with her fingers. Her blush has crept past her chest, and her hips are bucking against my mouth. I suck her clit harder, flicking it with my tongue. Her breathing speeds up, her pussy clamps down on my fingers, and she explodes. "Hartley!" Fuck. I'll never get tired of my name leaving those pouty lips.

Without giving her time to recover, I remove my fingers and throw her legs over my shoulders. I clamp my hands on her thick thighs and jerk her down to my mouth. "OH, GOD!" Evie screams. I suck, lick, and flick her clit. I slide my mouth down and spear her with my tongue. "That feels so good," Evie moans. I don't let up. I'm eating her pussy like a starved man, and this is my favorite meal. Her fingers are in my hair, pushing me away and then tugging me against her. Evie is a fucking wildcat. And I want more.

"I'm going to come! Oh, fuck!" Evie says. "I can't, Hartley!" She tries to push my head away, but I don't let her. I double down, and she screams with her release. I lick back up to her clit, taking everything her body offers. I pull back, and she's dripping everywhere. Her breath is sawing in and out of her lungs.

"You good, princess?" I ask and grin when she looks down at me.

"Holy shit," she breathes.

I stand up, and her eyes zero in on my cock. I wrap my hand around it and stroke it a few times. Her eyes widen, and she sinks her teeth into her plump bottom lip. "Is this what you wanted?" I stroke to the tip and squeeze the head, making pre-cum drip from the slit. She licks her lips at the sight, and I groan loudly. "What do you want, princess?"

"I want to taste you," Evie says, her face blooming with color. She sits up and swings her leg over the lounger, standing up. "Sit, please."

I sit down and lean back, my legs on either side of the lounger. She gets between my thighs on her knees and wraps a hand around the base. It jerks in her hand, and she looks up with the most innocent look on her face. She leans forward and licks the pre-cum from the tip. I have to grab the side of the lounger so I don't grab her head. Sucking the head into her mouth a few times, she slides her mouth down, going as far as she can. It's different sucking a dick covered in piercings, and she is learning fucking fast.

"Fuck," I grunt when I bump the back of her throat. I take one hand and push her hair to one side so I can watch my cock slide between her lips. I gently close my fist in her hair, and she moans against the head. "You like that?" I ask. It sounded like I was pushing the words out.

She moans again, and I tighten my fist, wrapping the strands of her brown hair around my fingers. I watch her face and push her down while I lift my hips, fucking her mouth. She slides her hands up and scrapes her nails down my abs. I need to fuck her. Right now. I pull her off my cock by her hair, and she lets it go with a wet pop. I loosen my fingers and run my fingers down her face. She is so turned on by sucking my cock that she is squirming.

"Ride me, princess," I demand, pulling her up my body. She looks down shyly, and I tip her chin up with my fingers. "What is it?"

"I've never done that," she admits, and my eyebrows hit my hairline.

"You've never rode a cock?"

"He always said I was too..." I press my fingers against her lips before she can finish.

"He was an idiot," I say harshly and lean forward, pecking her lips. "You want to try it?" I ask.

She bites her lip again but nods. I pull my legs back on the lounger so she can put her knees beside my hips. I reach between us and line up at her entrance. As soon as her hot wet pussy touches my cock, we both gasp. It feels so fucking good. "Is it going to hurt?" she asks hesitantly.

"It might feel weird at first. But I promise, princess, I'll make it feel good."

She lets out a shuddering breath, puts her hands on my shoulders, and starts sinking down on my cock. That's when I realize why it feels so damn good. "Evie, I'm not wearing a condom," I say, grabbing her hips to stop her from sliding any further. She stops moving, the head of my cock sitting right inside of her. "I can go get one." I'd walk right into that house butt-ass naked and ask for one. I don't give a fuck.

"You know I can't..." She trails off when I nod. "I always used one."

"What are you saying, princess?" Her pussy is pulsing around the head of my cock, and if she doesn't move, I am going to die.

"You don't have to wear one. I trust you," Evie whispers. "I want to feel all of it."

"I'm clean," I assure her. I always had to get regular physicals for the police department, including blood work, to check for STD's, and I have kept up with them since then. "You want me to fuck this pussy bare?"

"Yes," Evie breathes and starts lowering herself on my cock. I sink my hands into her hips and let her take her time. "It feels funny, but it feels good." I've never gone without a condom before, and now I am sinking into the hottest pussy ever without one.

Her thighs settle against mine, and her breathing is ragged. "You feel so damn good, princess," I groan, kissing those pouty lips.

Now that I am inside her, she looks lost on what to do. I drop my legs back off the lounger and spread her wider. I plant my feet on the patio, sink my fingers into her hips, and start fucking her from the bottom in slow, deep strokes.

She gasps. "I can feel everything."

I purposely drag the barbells of my magic cross against her g-spot, and she moans so deep that I have to remember not to start slamming inside her. I wanted to bury myself so deep inside her that she never forgot I was here.

She starts moving her hips with me. "There ya go, princess. Ride me." Her eyelids flutter, she tips her head back, and the tips of her long hair tickle my thighs. Then she starts to move. "Fuck. Yeah," I say, sliding my hands up her sides. "Make those titties bounce in my face."

She tips forward, so her feet touch the patio and starts riding my cock. She finds a rhythm that has her titties bouncing and has me panting for breath. "Hartley," she moans.

"Does my cock feel good, princess?" I ask, kissing her neck. "Tell me."

"Yes. Oh my god, it feels so good." I start moving my hips, meeting her thrust for thrust. "Harder." Evie moans.

I wrap my arm around her waist, slamming my hips as I pull her down. I latch onto one of her nipples, never stopping my thrusting. I reach down with the other hand and start circling her clit.

"Oh. Oh!" Evie gasps. Her body starts shaking; her fingers dig into my shoulders. "Hartley," Evie groans. "I feel...fuck. Oh god, something's wrong!"

I let her nipple go. "Nothing's wrong, princess," I say, grunting with the force of my thrusts. "Let it go."

"I can't! Hartley," she drags the last of my name on a moan.

"Let it go," I repeat. "Come on my cock." I know what is happening. The piercing on the head of my cock is scraping against her g-spot. My fingers are insistent on her clit.

"But it..." She trails off on another moan. She's shaking out of control now, trying to fight against her body's pleasure. Her fingernails dig into my skin, and her pussy clamps down on me unbearably tight. "What's happening?!"

I keep going until it peaks and jerk her up off my cock, rubbing her clit relentlessly. Evie's making all kinds of noises until she finally lets go, squirting all over me. Her mouth is open in a silent scream, her body completely flushed, and she's never looked more beautiful to me.

I line back up and pull her back down, fucking her hard. I am so fucking close. Evie slams her lips against mine, kissing me wildly. My finger is still rubbing her clit in tight circles. I feel my balls draw up. "I'm going to..." Evie pants.

"Yeah," I groan. "You're going to come on my cock." She clamps down on me again, and I can't hold back. A groan rips through my chest as I empty everything inside of her. She starts pulsing around me, screaming my name.

"Hartley!"

She collapses against my chest, both of us struggling to breathe. I lift her hips and gently slide out of her. "Fuck, you're amazing, princess," I tell her, kissing the top of her head.

"What was that?" she says breathlessly.

"I made you squirt," I say smugly. I fucking love doing that shit.

Evie sits up. "I thought I was going to." She stops and bites her lip. "I thought I was going to pee," she whispers, and I can't help the laugh that busts out of me. She smacks my chest. "It's not funny!" I bite my lip to stop laughing, but it's useless. She looked so damn cute when she said that. Evie starts giggling with me. "Okay. It's a little funny."

"It was hot as fuck," I tell her, pecking her lips.

She smiles and then gasps when she looks over my shoulder. Frowning, I turn my head and come face to face with Micah. I expected anger.

His blue eyes are blazing, but he isn't mad.

He is turned the fuck on from watching us.

CHAPTER 37
EVIE

I'm frozen in place, and I have no idea what to do.

I am staring into Micah's blue eyes while I'm naked, with Hartley's cum dripping out of me. What the hell am I doing? I try to move off Hartley's lap, but he locks his hands on my hips and won't let me move.

I don't know whether to be upset, mortified, scared, or all of the above. This was my idea, but now that we got caught, I have no idea how to act. Micah hasn't said a word; he's just staring. He finally tilts his head in that weird way and steps further onto the patio.

"What do we have here?" Micah asks, and I still can't tell whether he's mad or not.

"I...we...well..." I stammer. I am so fucking flustered! Hartley chokes on a laugh, and my mouth pops open when I look at him.

"Go on, princess. Tell him," Hartley says, grinning from ear to ear.

"We were having sex," I whisper, trying to cover myself up.

"What?" Micah asks, stepping closer. "I couldn't hear you." Why is he doing this?

"We were having sex," I say a little louder.

"I still can't hear you," Micah taunts.

"We were fucking!" I half yell, and Micah finally grins.

"There you go," Micah says, laying out on the lounger beside us like he doesn't have a care in the world. "Own it, *la mia stella*. Don't be ashamed of what your body wants."

"You aren't mad?" I ask hesitantly. I still have the irrational fear of pissing any of these guys off.

Micah looks at Hartley and then back to me. "I mean, I don't like your choice in the dick you choose to ride, but no, I'm not mad." Micah looks down to the wetness on the patio and then back to me. "On second thought, if he can make you do that shit, I'm all for it."

I had no idea what was going on when Hartley made me come like that. I felt the usual tug in my stomach that I'd gotten used to since being with any of these guys. Then it started getting bigger, and I was in full panic mode. I seriously thought I was about to pee everywhere. When that gushed out of me, Hartley groaned so deep that it almost made me come again. I can feel my face flame, and Hartley chuckles.

"Don't get shy now, princess," Hartley says, massaging my hips with his big hands.

"You looked fucking beautiful riding his cock," Micah says gruffly. Hartley's hands tighten on my hips, but I can't get a read on what he's feeling.

I can feel my blush creeping down my neck with the way they are staring at me. I've never had someone look at me like these guys do. It's exhilarating. But I don't have any misconceptions about what this is. This is just a way to pass the time. Aaron would be gone soon, and I would have to move on. I don't want to admit what that thought already made me feel.

"I came out here to tell you lunch was ready," Micah says, standing from the lounger. "And to escape the noises Mateo and Gray were making."

Hartley barks a laugh. "You heard that, too?"

"All of Abbs Valley heard that shit," Micah answers.

I frown. "What are you talking about?"

"Gray owned Mateo's ass. Literally," Micah laughs. Heat flashes through me at that thought.

Hartley runs his knuckles down my cheek. "You like the thought of that, don't you, princess?" he asks.

"I shouldn't," I say, taking a shuddering breath. "But I do."

I never thought I did until I saw any of the guys kissing. And it wasn't just sexual. I loved that they didn't care what people thought, and they didn't hide who they were. There was something so beautiful about the way they moved against each other. And when Micah kissed Evander to taste me on Evander's lips, I almost died on the spot.

"There's nothing wrong with liking what you like," Micah says. "Get cleaned up and come eat lunch. I'm sure you're hungry after that." Micah waggles his eyebrows at me, and I bury my face in my hands.

"Oh my god," I groan while both guys chuckle.

I look at Hartley when Micah closes the door behind him. "I thought you guys didn't like each other," I say.

Hartley sighs. "We didn't, and I still don't know my place here. But if they can make your face light up the way it does, why would I fight against that?" he answers. I don't know what to say to that. "Come on, princess."

After we're both standing, he leads me to a little shower beside the hot tub to rinse the evidence of what we just did. I can feel it running down my thighs, and Hartley's eyes are transfixed by the sight. He swallows and looks back at my face. "That's fucking hot," he says hoarsely. It is. Everything we just did was insanely hot, but the words are locked in my throat; all I could do was nod. He flips the shower on and pulls me under the spray, using his hand to clean between my legs. "You can take a real shower in the house. I just wanted you to be able to put your clothes on." Something about the sweetness of that statement makes tears spring to my eyes. It's fucking sad, too. That something so damn simple could make me want to weep.

I don't know where my life got off the rails or why I let myself stay with Aaron. And I am afraid I'm letting myself be with these guys because they showed the slightest bit of interest in me. They've given me more in the short time I've been here than the year I was with Aaron.

The gifts didn't even matter; it's the way they make me *feel*.

I SPENT the rest of yesterday and all last night thinking about everything that's been happening. I went from beating myself up for letting this happen to beating myself up for thinking this was bad. I am twenty-three years old. Isn't this when I am supposed to have fun? My mind is a whirlwind of different thoughts, and I don't know which way is up anymore.

"They are going to love this dress," Bridget declares when I step out of the bathroom. The long black dress sits off the shoulders and pushes my boobs up. Definitely something I wouldn't normally wear, but Bridget insisted. She did my makeup in a smokey eye, blush, and red lips. My hair is in a twist, with tendrils hanging around my face. All of this again because of my date with the guys tonight. I am nervous as hell because they wouldn't tell me where we are going. They just told me Bridget was coming to get me ready, and that was that.

I look at myself in the mirror and can't believe how the dress fits. It looks like it was made just for me. "I love it," I tell Bridget. She claps and squeals, making me laugh.

While she did my makeup and hair, she peppered me with questions, and I answered them honestly. She is so easy to talk to, and her reactions cracked me up. Bridget would gasp and physically fan herself. But there was never any judgment in her eyes. She actually helped me come to the conclusion that I am allowed to have this for myself, even if it is just for a little while.

She helps me step into a pair of sparkly black stilettos and stands back to survey her work. "If they don't eat you up on the way to your date, they are wasting an opportunity. Because. You. Are. Hot."

"You're good for my self-esteem," I giggle.

Bridget snorts. "I'm not lying. I'd kill for those curves. And those tits? Girl, please."

"Thank you," I tell her honestly.

"No problem, girl," Bridget smiles. "Come on; your men are waiting."

My men.

Bridget and I make our way to the living room, and I'm hit with déjà vu of my date with Micah and Evander. I was so freaking nervous, but we had such a good time. They made me feel at ease with them. My eyes light on all the guys, and my mouth goes dry.

Micah and Evander are dressed similarly in grey button-ups and fitted grey slacks. Micah's is just a couple of shades darker. Mateo has on fitted black slacks and a dark green button-up that makes his eyes stand out. Hartley is in a white button-up and black slacks that hug his legs in a delicious way. My eyes find Gray, and I almost swallow my tongue. His black slacks are also fitted, but he's wearing a deep purple button-up that looks delicious on his skin. The top couple of buttons are undone, and I can see a tattoo peeking through.

Bridget kisses my cheek. "Have fun tonight," she says with a smile, waving at the guys and disappearing through the front door. I couldn't even say thank you; my eyes are stuck on the guys staring at me like they wanted to rip this dress off.

"You look like a vision, buttercup," Mateo says, planting a kiss on my lips.

"You guys look amazing," I say in awe.

"That would be you, *pequena reina*," Evander says, hip checking Mateo out of the way, making Mateo pout. He pecks my lips and steps back. "Are you ready?"

"Where are we going?" I ask, sliding my hand onto his arm.

He leads me to the door, darting a glance at Micah. "That's a surprise, *la mia stella*," Micah answers, sliding his hand to the small of my back. I keep meaning to google what Evander and Micah call me, but something about the mystery of it makes it that much sweeter.

The drive to where we are going is quiet and quick. Before I know it, Gray opens the door for us to slide out. I look at the sign on the front with a frown. "What's New Vision?" I knew we weren't going for dinner because Micah cooked before we left.

Mateo chuckles. "This is a place Van and I own. One of them, anyway." Mateo slips his hand into mine and tugs me toward the door that Gray is holding open.

We step through the door into a foyer where a beautiful blonde girl is standing behind a booth. She smiles politely at everyone. "Good evening, Mr. and Mr. Perez."

"Evening, Whitney," Mateo greets.

"What color?" Whitney asks, holding up glowing green, yellow, and red bracelets. What the hell?

"Red for me and red for this beautiful lady," Mateo answers. He snaps the bracelet on my wrist and then his own.

I hear the other guys answer red, and we make our way through another set of double doors. Mateo pushes them open, never letting go of my hand. My eyes try to take in everything at once, but it's impossible. The place is packed. Two bars sit on either side of a huge dance floor. The whole area is dimly lit, giving it a romantic feel. Bodies are gyrating together on the dancefloor to sexy music. I look around, and my eyes almost bug out of my head. Some people are dressed like me, and others are barely dressed. A woman in head-to-toe leather is leading a guy around with a leash around his neck.

"What is this place?" I whisper to Mateo.

"A sex club," Micah answers, stepping up on my other side.

I have no idea what to say. This is not what I thought they had planned for the night. Obviously, I've never been to a sex club.

"The red on your wrist represents that you're just observing," Evander explains. "We wanted to give you a little taste of our life."

This just confirmed that I have no idea who these guys are. "You own a sex club?" I ask hesitantly.

"We do. We just celebrated our third anniversary of the opening," Mateo says proudly.

I nod slowly, taking everything in. The servers are dressed in evening gowns, walking around with trays. I look at Hartley, and he doesn't look shocked at all. They are all looking at me, waiting for my reaction. I said I wanted to live life; this is one way to do it.

Mateo takes my hand. "Let's get a drink," he says, pulling me toward the bar. "What do you want, buttercup?" I didn't drink, so I shrug, causing Mateo to chuckle. "White wine and a scotch on the rocks," Mateo orders.

I feel a hand slide down my back and settle right on the curve of my butt. I look up into Micah's smiling face. "You are easily the most beautiful woman in this room," Micah compliments.

I look around and can't help the frown on my face. Every girl here is gorgeous. "Don't do that," Micah says, catching the look on my face. He brushes his fingers down my cheek. "I don't say stuff like that just to say it, *la mia stella*. I mean every fucking word."

There is so much sincerity in his voice that I melt into a puddle. "Thank you." I kiss his cheek on impulse and then pull back just as quickly. He isn't mine to be showing any type of PDA, no matter where his hand is. A look passes over Micah's face so fast that I can't identify it. I am getting too carried away and need to remember that this is only temporary. I swallow the lump in my throat, force a smile to my lips, and accept the wine Mateo hands me.

I take a sip and notice several eyes on us, staring with barely concealed shock. I want to say it's because they are wondering what these guys are doing with a girl like me, but that isn't it. I turn around to say something to Mateo and realize they aren't looking at me at all.

Mateo and Gray are locked in one of the hottest kisses I've ever seen. Gray has his hand on Mateo's throat, holding him in place. I can feel my whole body flush and can't look away. I've been curious, and I had to admit I wanted to watch them go all the way together. I could feel my panties getting wet, and my clit is throbbing. I am so turned on that I don't know what to do.

"See something you like, *pequena reina?*" Evander asks huskily in my ear, causing me to shiver.

"Yes," I breathe, answering honestly.

Evander runs his lips over my cheek. "You like watching?" Evander asks. I nod, just now realizing that about myself. "I have something to show you." He slaps Mateo on the ass to get his attention. Mateo breaks away from Gray, both of them breathing heavily. "Let's go upstairs."

Mateo's eyes widen, but he nods. Evander takes my wine glass and sits it on the bar, sliding his hand on the other side of my ass, so I'm sandwiched between him and Micah. We get to a large staircase, and my heart rate spikes with every step I take. I don't have to be familiar with a sex club to guess what happens upstairs. When we get to the top, several closed doors are lining the hallway. Evander walks to a closed door in front of us; placing his hand on the handle, he turns to me. "If you feel uncomfortable at any time, tell one of us. We'll leave. No one will touch you because of that bracelet. Unless you want one of us too," Evander says.

"But only us," Micah adds. "No one else touches this," he finishes, running his hand over my butt cheek. I take a deep breath and nod.

Evander pulls the door open, and I can't stop my mouth from falling open. This room is lit up with red lights, setting a sensual mood. Right in the middle of the room is a round platform that looks like a huge cushion. And people are in varying stages of undress. Some are just touching and kissing, and some are already having sex. My heart starts beating double time, and I can't get a full breath. I'm not uncomfortable with what I am seeing. It's beautiful, in a way. The way they could just let themselves go in a moment of passion without a care in the world.

Evander whispers something to Micah, and I watch a grin spread across Micah's face before he nods. They kiss my cheek and move through the room, leaving me with Mateo, Gray, and Hartley. Mateo's phone pings after Evander and Micah round the corner, and I frown when he chuckles.

"All's good, buttercup," Mateo says, sliding his arm around my waist. "What do you think?"

"I don't know," I say breathlessly. "There is so much going on." I feel like I should look away, but they wouldn't be in the middle of a room if they cared if people stared.

Gray steps up to my other side. "This isn't all of it." I look up at him in question, and he smiles. "You'll see," Gray assures me. I'm surprised Gray is even talking to me. I felt like he was avoiding me since our date, and I didn't know how to ask if something was wrong.

I look at Hartley to see how he is taking all of this, and he's staring at me with a heated look. Our time by the pool flashes through my head, and I have to clench my thighs together to stop the ache.

Mateo shows his phone to Hartley, whispers something to him, and Hartley raises an eyebrow, then shrugs. *What the hell is going on?*

Mateo grabs my hand, leading me to another set of doors. He opens the one to our left and leads me down a hallway. My eyes are shooting everywhere. Down the hallway are different rooms.

"What is this?" I ask Mateo breathlessly.

"Observation rooms," he answers, pulling on my hand.

Each room has different things going on, and you could watch it all through a glass window. I'm overwhelmed, but not in a bad way. I want to know more.

Mateo stops when I do, transfixed by the sight in front of me. It's a beautiful woman with white blonde hair spread out on a table, her arms and legs tied down. A giant guy with a white mask on is holding a vibrator to her clit but pulls away when her legs start shaking.

"What is he doing?" I ask.

"Orgasm denial," Gray answers, stepping up behind me. He's so close I can feel his body heat against my back.

"Oh," I breathe.

"He does that until she gives her safe word when she's had enough," Mateo explains.

"Does it feel good?" I couldn't imagine what it felt like not being able to orgasm.

"It's a different feeling. You get so fucking sensitive to touch that the slightest thing can set you off," Mateo says. "But the payoff is amazing."

We continue down the hallway, and Mateo explains everything that I'm seeing. One was two guys that Mateo said were doing prostate stimulation. All I could see was the guy's cock throbbing and his partner working his fingers in and out of his ass.

The one I watched the longest was a threesome with a girl and two guys. They were working her at the same time, and her face looked lost in so much pleasure that I was almost jealous.

We stop at the end of the hall at a door. Mateo pushes it open, and I have to swallow my nerves again. This is different from the other ones because it's closed off. The lighting is the same here as in the red light room, with a big bed in the back and a couch right in the middle of the room. Mateo pulls back a curtain, and all the air whooshes from my lungs. It's a huge window.

With Micah and Evander making out on the other side.

CHAPTER 38
MATEO

I'm watching Evie closely. Her eyes are wide, cheeks red, and she hasn't looked away from the scene in front of her.

It was my idea to bring her here, and it took me some time to convince the other guys. But I had a feeling Evie would like it here. She had expressed that she wanted to try new things, and I wanted to insert her into my life little by little, so I could prove to them she could handle the truth.

Evander messaged me downstairs saying Evie liked watching, so we brought her to the observation rooms so she could look until her heart was content. I showed Hartley the message and asked if he was down, and his shrug surprised me. I didn't even have to ask Gray. Although I usually bottomed, I've never let someone take over like that in bed, but it wasn't even a question with Gray. He could do whatever he wanted to me.

Evie lets out a little gasp, so I turn to look through the window. Micah and Evander are locked in a heated kiss, rubbing their erections together through their clothes. They look hot as fuck. Evie sits down on the couch, never letting her eyes leave them.

I sit down close beside her. "You okay, buttercup?" I ask.

"They're so passionate," Evie says breathlessly. That's one way to put it.

Evander is pushing Micah's unbuttoned shirt off his broad shoulders while Micah's fingers are working on Evander's buttons; their lips still locked together. My dick is painfully hard, so I shift my hips. Most people would find it odd that I got turned on watching my brother with his boyfriend. But it has nothing to do with Evander. It's two people letting their inhibitions go and giving into their basic desire—each other. Also, Micah is sexy. There is something about the way he moved with such confidence.

Hartley sits on the other side of Evie, and Gray sits beside me, all our eyes glued in front of us.

Evander's shirt hits the floor, and they start working on each other's pants. Evie's breathing speeds up, and she starts squirming on the couch. She is so fucking turned on, and I know if I touched her right now, she would be soaking wet. Like we are on the same wavelength, Hartley and I run our hands up her thighs, and her whole body shudders. I look at Hartley, and we have a silent conversation, and he nods, letting me know he is down for whatever is about to happen. No matter how turned on we are, this is going to be all about Evie, about what she wants.

Evander shoves Micah's pants down with his boxers, and Micah's long cock springs free. *Damn, his cock is nice.* Evie makes a noise, almost like a moan, and I know she remembered what that cock felt like. It is something I've always wondered about myself.

Evander and Micah stop kissing to undress the rest of the way. As soon as they are naked, their lips meet again, and their bare cocks rub together, jerking against each other.

Fucking hell.

Hartley and I work Evie's dress up her thighs so we can touch her bare skin.

"Shit," Gray whispers, adjusting his hips. I reach over and lay my hand on his thigh, squeezing, making him groan.

"What do you want, princess?" Hartley asks. His voice has taken on a deeper husky tone, and it is sexy as hell. Micah and Evander have made it to the bed, with Micah stretched out over Van. Their hips are grinding together, hands roaming everywhere.

"Touch me," Evie whimpers. Hartley and I share another look, agreeing again. Hartley helps her stand, pulls her panties from under her dress, bunches the dress around her waist, and sits her back between us.

We each grab a thigh and put it over our legs, so she's spread wide open. I slide my hand between her legs and circle her clit. Her hips jerk, and she moans deep in her throat. Hartley moves his fingers to the entrance of her pussy and shoves two fingers inside her.

"Oh my god," Evie pants, moving her hips to fuck his fingers.

Micah has Van's cock in his mouth, taking him as far as he can. Van's hips are lifting, begging for more. Their groans start filtering through the room, and Evie gets even wetter.

"You like watching them, buttercup?" I ask her, circling her clit faster. "You want to watch them fuck?"

"Yes," Evie moans. "Are they going to?"

Hartley chuckles. "They are well on their way, princess. Don't worry about that."

"Have you ever..." Evie's voice trails off on another moan. "Have you ever been with a guy?" I knew she wasn't talking to me because, obviously, I have. Gray's hand slides over my cock through my pants, and I start throbbing harder.

"I've experimented before, yes," Hartley answers, and I know the shock shows on my face.

"Did you like it?" I find myself asking.

Hartley clears his throat. "I did," he says. *Well then.*

Van pulls Micah off his cock, slams his lips against his, and rolls them, so he's on top. He doesn't waste any time sucking Micah into his mouth. Micah's deep groan echoes around the room, and I feel it in my bones.

Hartley and I start working Evie faster. Her hips are rolling with us, her breath is heaving, and she's making noises that are driving me crazy.

"Are you going to come for them, angel?" Gray asks, still massaging my dick.

"Yes. Shit," Evie breathes. Her hands latch onto our forearms, fingernails digging into the skin. Her body tightens up, and then she lets go. "Oh my god!" she screams. She drops back on the couch, body trembling. I pull my fingers away, but before I can lick her taste from them, Gray jerks my hand to his mouth. I can't stop the groan when he licks them, tasting her on my skin. "Oh, wow," Evie giggles breathlessly.

"Fuck, *amore mio*," Micah groans, and our eyes snap back to them. "Your ass is so tight."

"Oh, fuck," Evie says.

Van is on his hands and knees with Micah balls deep in his ass. I can't take it anymore. I make quick work of my pants, pulling them down just enough to pull my cock out. I start stroking it in time with Micah's thrusts inside of Van. Van's hands are bunched in the sheet, shoving back against Micah.

Evie hops to her feet, and I think she's seconds away from running from the room. "Unzip me," she demands right when I'm about to ask if she's ok. I guess that answered that question. "I'm not going to be the only naked one in this room." She is so keyed up that shy Evie is nowhere to be found.

Hartley reaches up and pulls her zipper down, letting her dress pool around her feet. Fuck, I'll never get over that body. "You heard her," Hartley says, getting to his feet.

I turn to Gray, asking with my eyes if he is still okay with this. He has some stuff to work out with Evie, but we have some sort of mutual agreement that this would happen no matter what. Gray's eyes stray back to Evie, and he swallows hard. I follow his line of sight, and Hartley has taken her bra off, and she is bare to us. I pat Gray's thigh. "I know, big guy. I know," I say.

Evie's not paying attention to us; her eyes are still on Micah and Van. Van is begging Micah to go harder, his hand stroking his cock rapidly.

We make quick work of our clothes because our lady demanded we be naked, and we are going to deliver. I grab Evie's hand, and her head slowly turns toward me. Her eyes travel down my body to my very hard cock, and she bites her lip. I am dying to get inside of her, but I would let her decide on her own.

"You want my cock, buttercup?" I ask. I stroke my dick a couple of times for her benefit.

"Yes, please," Evie answers. Her voice is husky and breathless, giving away how much she wants this. Gray reaches over in the dish beside the couch and hands me a condom. We had them in every room and everything else you would need. I rip it open and roll it down my length.

I turn her around so she can still watch the show. "Sit on it," I say, tugging her hips backward. She sucks in a breath, braces her hands on my arms, and I line up with her pussy.

She lowers herself slowly on my cock, and I can't stop the groan from sliding inside her.

This wasn't the intention when we brought her here. It was kind of like a test to me, in a way. I wanted to know if she could handle my life, so maybe I could keep her in it.

Evie moans when her thighs settle against mine. I pull her back against my chest. "You feel so good, Mateo," Evie says. I turn her head to me and kiss her slowly, then lay my forehead against hers so I can watch her gorgeous brown eyes. I wrap an arm around her waist and start moving my hips, dragging my cock slowly out of her, watching her pupils expand.

"Get your hand off your cock," Micah demands. "You're going to come just from me fucking this tight ass."

"Micah, fuck," Van groans. Evie and I both turn to look. Micah is hammering into Van, Van's cock throbbing under him.

"I don't know where to look," Evie whispers.

I kiss her neck. "Watch them, buttercup. I'll take care of you."

I sink my hands into her hips and start moving slowly, savoring the feel of her pussy. Gray steps in front of us, and I hear Evie whimper, taking him all in. Which is a lot. He drops to his knees and, surprising us both, leans forward and licks my cock when it slides out of her.

"Holy shit, Gray," I groan, fingers digging harder into her hips when he circles his tongue around her clit, making her tighten on me.

Gray alternates from sucking on her clit and letting his tongue slide down to where Evie and I are connected. I've never been so turned on in my life.

Hartley steps to the other side, and Evie doesn't waste any time sinking her mouth onto his cock, making him suck in a breath. I got an eyeful of all the metal on his cock before it disappeared into her mouth.

"Never took you for the dick piercing type, Hart," I pant, still pumping my dick into Evie.

"It comes with its benefits. Right, princess?" Hartley asks, thrusting slowly into Evie's mouth. She moans around his cock, and his eyes roll back in his head.

I flick his nipple ring. "Or these." Hartley just grins.

"*Mi rey,*" Van moans.

Micah pulls out of Van's ass and rolls him onto his back. Micah lines up again and slams his hips home, making Van's back bow.

Gray locks his hands on my hips and jerks me forward, so my ass hangs off the couch. I feel his slippery fingers slide between my ass cheeks, and a groan rips from my chest, more than ready for his fingers. He pushes his fingers forward, and my head falls back with a moan.

"What's he doing?" Evie asks with a moan, swiveling her hand on Hartley's cock.

"Playing with my ass," I answer.

"I can feel you throbbing inside of me," Evie whispers. *Fucking hell.*

"Fuck, fuck, fuck," I hear Micah chanting and look up just in time to see Van coming all over his chest. Micah stills, locked inside Van as far as he can, and lets go with a sexy groan.

"Oh fuck," I say breathlessly. I grip Evie's hips again and start fucking her hard from the bottom. Gray stimulates my prostate, and I can feel my release racing up my spine. He leans forward and sucks Evie's clit relentlessly, making her squirm all over my cock. Her head tips back. "Mateo! Gray!" she screams. Her pussy clamps down on me, and I can't hold it back anymore. I empty into the condom with such force that I'll be surprised if it's still in one piece.

"Buttercup," I groan in her ear, making her whole body shiver.

When Gray slides his fingers from my ass, I slide from inside her. I knot the condom off and throw it in the wastebasket by the couch.

Gray stands up, still harder than a fucking rock, stroking his cock. I know what he wants to do, but I also knew he wouldn't do it until he talked to her. I tug him to my side and slide my mouth down his cock.

I feel Hartley step between my thighs, where Evie is still spread out. I watch from the corner of my eye, and he kisses her, sinking into her pussy, not giving a fuck that she's still on my lap. I don't give a fuck, either.

While Hartley takes care of Evie, I take care of Gray. And I could feel the rightness of it. I don't want to get my hopes up, but I feel like we all took a turn for the better tonight, and maybe this could work in the long run.

Gray grabs the side of my face and starts fucking my throat, just like I loved. I open for him so he can slide deeper, and his groan rattles my bones.

"Oh, fuck," Evie gasps, and I know she just caught sight of what's happening.

I slide my hand up Gray's huge thigh and grab a handful of his tight ass. He locks a hand on my throat so he can feel his cock there, causing me to moan.

"Hartley," Evie moans, and I can feel myself hardening again.

I've done some freaky shit in my day, but this tops everything I've ever done.

Gray's thrusts start stuttering, and I look up into his eyes. They are locked on mine. He throws his head back and, with a groan, empties down my throat; I swallow around the head, taking everything he has to offer.

He slides his dick from between my lips, and Evie jerks my face to her by my chin. She slams her lips on mine and starts stroking my tongue with hers. She pulls her face away, breathing heavily. "I can taste him," Evie pants.

"Fuck, princess. You just got so fucking tight," Hartley groans, fucking her harder.

I knew I was right about Evie. I wanted to pat myself on the back. Evie could take anything we threw at her.

"Harder, Hartley," Evie begs, grabbing his ass and pulling him to her.

I reach down, grip her thighs, and pull her legs wider. Hartley braces one hand beside my head and reaches down. My eyes widen when his hand wraps around my hard cock. He positions my dick beside his, trapping it between their bodies, and starts fucking Evie in deep, hard thrusts. She starts making these whimpering noises, but I know it's not from pain. It's because of his piercings rubbing inside of her.

The side of my cock is rubbing against his; the underside is rubbing against his groin. It is erotic as fuck.

"Hartley," Evie moans deep.

"Come for me, princess," Hartley pants against her lips. His eyes slide to mine, and I'm locked there, helpless to look away. "Come for me, Mateo," he rasps.

Well, fuck.

Evie's back bows, her fingers sinking into Hartley's thick shoulders. "Hartley!"

I let go, pumping come all over Hartley's abs. He kisses her softly and then slides out of her.

He looks down at the mess I made and runs his fingers through it. With a wicked gleam in his eyes and a grin, he licks it from his fingers.

"Shit," I laugh, and Evie giggles. I look over at Gray, and he's shaking his head with a smile. "You like the way I taste, Hart?" I tease.

Hartley drops on the couch beside us. "Can't complain."

We look back at the window, and I can't stop the smile that spreads across my face. Micah and Van are relaxed on the bed, Micah running his fingers tenderly down Van's face.

I lock my arm around Evie's waist, hugging her to my chest. Reaching over, I grab Gray's hand, lacing our fingers together. Evie holds Hartley's hand, making the connection complete.

I've never been so happy in my life.

CHAPTER 39
MICAH

"We should go check on the rest of them," I murmur into Van's neck.

"Or we could stay here," he suggests, snuggling closer to my chest.

I chuckle. "I like that idea." I kiss his neck, making him sigh.

When Mateo suggested we bring Evie here, I thought he was out of his fucking mind. Ultimately, we decided we would give it a shot, and if she didn't like it, we would leave; no big deal.

Then I saw how she reacted to watching Gray and Mateo kiss and remembered how excited she got when Van and I did. Evie was turned on by the fact that the guys were kissing or watching. Probably both. Van's idea to take her to the observation rooms was a no-brainer. She would get the best of both worlds. I wasn't going to say no to fucking my boyfriend, either.

The thought they might be watching made us so ready for each other that we almost didn't get into the room before we ripped each other's clothes off.

"I love you," Van says, lifting his head.

"I love you too," I reply, kissing him softly.

I never thought I could love someone the way that I love Van. I didn't have a lot of good examples growing up except my brother and his wife.

"Where did you go?" Van asks, running his hand down my cheek.

I kiss his palm. "I'm right here with you, *amore mio*," I say, and Van lifts a brow, calling my bluff. I didn't want to talk about my blood-sucking mother right now. "It's nothing. We'll talk about it later," I assure him, pecking his lips. I just know in my damn gut she is behind this shit with Aaron; I just need proof.

He nods. "We need to go so they can clean this room."

"You own the place. I'm pretty sure you can stay as long as you want," I laugh.

He shrugs. "Probably. But I'm fucking hungry."

"Worked off some calories?" I growl playfully, nipping at his neck.

"Yes. You were on a whole other level," Van chuckles.

"It didn't turn you on that they were watching?" I whisper against his neck, making him shiver.

"Don't start," Van laughs, pushing me away and standing up. "But to answer your question. It did," he answers. His hardening cock is all the answer I need.

"Round two?" I suggest grinning.

He looks at me so long that I think he's going to cave, then shakes his head. "You're insatiable," he accuses.

My mouth pops open. "Me? I remember someone *begging* me to fuck him harder."

Van grins, and I want to drag him back into bed. I slide across the bed to my feet and advance on him. He holds his hands up. "Micah," he warns with a laugh. His back hits the door, and I press against him.

"Get clothes on before I have you under me and screaming my fucking name," I growl against his lips. He lets one of those moans slip free when I rub against him. "You want my cock again, don't you?" I rasp, already hard as steel.

"Fuck, Micah," he groans, letting his head hit the door with a thud. I know I needed to give his ass a break, literally, so I take a step back.

"Get dressed. But later, *amore mio*? I'm going to make that ass mine again," I say, scooping up my clothes. "Then you're going to fuck me." I shove my legs into my boxers, tucking my hard cock into them. I get my pants on and fastened, and Van still hasn't moved. He's watching every move I make. It was like a reverse strip tease. "If you don't stop looking at me like that, we aren't ever getting out of here."

That seems to snap him out of it, and he starts getting dressed. Once we're dressed, we head for the door, but I pull him back to me before he can open it, kissing him one more time.

We make it to the other room, and I knock on the door. Mateo opens it with one of his shit-eating grins, and I roll my eyes. "Hello, *mi rey*," Mateo quips, earning a punch in the arm from Van.

I walk into the room, and my eyes light on Evie. She's laughing softly with Gray and Hartley, looking relaxed and happy. Her hair is no longer up, and her face is completely clear of makeup. I don't even have to ask why; the guy's faces say it all.

"I say we hit up Dolly's," I suggest. "*Amore mio* is starving."

Evie turns her soft smile on me. "No wonder," she jokes, making Van choke.

Mateo loses it and is wheezing with laughter; I can't help but join him. "You guys didn't work up an appetite?" I ask with a raised brow. Evie's face blooms with color.

"Oh, we did," Evie says, making my eyes widen in surprise.

"Getting bold, *la mia stella*?" I ask.

She stands up to face me and shrugs. "I don't see why I should be ashamed of it," she answers.

"You damn right, buttercup," Mateo says, slinging an arm around her shoulders.

I smile at her. "You have nothing to be ashamed of," I say, putting my hand out for her. She slides her hand into mine, and I kiss her knuckles. "Did you enjoy yourself?"

"I did," she giggles. "You guys are hot together," she whispers, like everyone in this room wasn't just watching us fuck.

"Did they treat you good?" I ask, tucking her hand on my arm and leading her to the door. I watch her blush spread to her chest.

She clears her throat. "They did."

From her flushing rapidly, I would say they treated her damn good. I would have loved to see what went down in there.

We get to the parking lot, and Hartley and Mateo are shoving each other playfully; I raise a brow at Gray.

He shrugs. "We buried the bullshit, Boss," he answers.

"When are you going to let him quit calling you boss?" Evie whispers, making me snort.

"I told him to call me Micah when I first hired him. He's always called me boss," I answer with a chuckle. I've told Gray more times than I can count to stop calling me that, but he's never listened, so I gave up.

We slide into the SUV and watch Hartley joke around with Mateo and Gray. I didn't immediately trust him, but I trust Gray's instincts. If Gray thinks he is trustworthy, I would give him a chance. Plus, he makes Evie happy.

I slide my hand into hers once the car is moving, and her smile is the sweetest thing I've ever seen. I don't think anyone has shown her the slightest bit of affection, and I hate that. We would shower her with as much as possible between the five of us. I watch Evander grab her other hand with a smile on my face.

I am getting ready to say something when Gray slams on the brakes, the car fishtailing. "Get down!" he yells before I hear shots fired at us.

I wrap my arms around Evie's head and pull her down, glass exploding everywhere. Van reaches under the seat, pulls out a semi-automatic, and tosses it to Hartley. He catches it one-handed and starts checking the clips. One by one, he hands one to everyone and then looks at me. "Get her out of here!" Van yells, sticking his head out the window and firing off shots. "NOW!" he exclaims when I hesitate. They are mainly on the passenger side. I assess the best option and push the door open.

"When we hit the pavement, run," I yell to Evie over the gunshots. She nods, tears streaming down her face.

I pull her by her hand, and we take off toward the building across the street while the rest of the guys distract the shooters. I could feel my blood boiling and wanted to get out there to fuck something up, but I need to get Evie to safety first.

We duck down an alley, and I slow my stride to match her shorter one. I start checking doors and find them all locked. There is a window at the end, so I heft a piece of concrete and smash the window, hoping the sounds of gunshots block the noise. With my elbow, I rake all the broken pieces away from the window and help Evie step through.

It looks like a consignment shop of some sort, but I don't give a shit. I would send them money to fix the window. Still pulling her by her hand, I find a place in the back and push her inside. "I'll be back," I tell her. I couldn't leave them out there to fight this on their own.

"Please, Micah," Evie cries. "Please don't leave me."

I can still hear the gunfight outside, and I am itching to get out there and make sure everyone is still in one piece. I look into Evie's eyes and push myself beside her, assuring myself they could handle it.

I pull my phone out and shoot off a text.

> Pinned down. Corner of Melrose and Gentry.

The reply is instantaneous, just like I knew it would be.

> LES
>
> On our way.

"Help is on the way," I tell Evie, pulling her into my arms. Her whole body is shaking. I rub my hands up and down her back, trying to calm her down.

We sit there for a solid two minutes, listening to gunfire outside with my guts twisting into knots the entire time. I need to know if Evander is safe; it's killing me not knowing. But somehow, I know he would want me with Evie. Van knows this life, and he could protect himself, but that doesn't mean I wouldn't worry.

"Evie," a voice sing-songs, and her entire body goes rigid. "Where are you?" I pull her closer and move us slowly backward into our hiding spot. I can hear boots crunching over the broken glass. "Come

319

on. Don't hide from me." Is that fucking Aaron? I don't have my Glock on me. In my haste to get Evie out, I didn't grab it from its hiding spot in the SUV.

I look down at Evie, and she's biting her lip to keep from crying out. I would fight with everything before they touched her.

"Come out, you fucking bitch," the voice growls. "I know you're in here."

The boots get closer, and Evie's shaking intensifies. They pop around the corner, Evie gasps, and their head explodes. *What the fuck?* I didn't hear a damn gunshot, but that was definitely a bullet that made his brains splatter on the door beside us.

I hear a bunch of commotion in the front of the store; then the door is splintering open. I look into black masks with a smile. Les jerks her head for us to follow without speaking. Too bad her height gave away who she is. With my arm still tucked around Evie, we walk through the front doors, where the glass is busted out.

I walk around the side of the building where the SUV is and almost wilt with relief. All the guys are standing behind the SUV with several bodies lying around. It looked like everyone else had taken off.

They converge on Evie when I get to them, and she silently cries in their arms. I step back beside Les while they take care of her.

"Meet me back at the house," I tell her quietly. Her head slowly turns toward me, and it's creepy as fuck with the mask. "Please," I add, making her shoulders shake with laughter.

Les and her crew take off the other way, and we bundle Evie into the destroyed SUV. At least it's still drivable.

We make it back to the house, and Evie hasn't said a word. She just clutched mine and Van's hands so tight I lost feeling in it. Once in the house, we are met with a bunch of black masks.

"It's ok, *la mia stella*," I assure Evie, pulling her toward the couch. I know they left them on to protect their identity, but it is scary if you aren't expecting it. Mateo and Gray put Evie between them on the couch, trying to calm her down.

I rush to Van and check him over. "I'm fine," he says softly. "Not a mark." I didn't realize I was holding my breath until it came out in a whoosh. I jerk him to my chest.

"I can't lose you," I whisper.

"You won't," he whispers back, pecking my lips.

I pull back reluctantly and look at Les. "Come on," I say, walking toward my office, Van behind me. I close the door.

Les pulls her mask off, and the rest do the same. I didn't even notice Ghost and Caden being there, so they must have been with Les and her guys. Once Ghost and Caden were officially welcomed into the Poletti family, I had their crews fitted for the same masks that we all wore. I recognize all of them except for one. Ghost sees where my eyes go and gestures to him. "That's Banger. I just brought him on," Ghost explains. Banger? What the fuck is with these guys and code names?

I thrust my hand out. "Nice to meet you," I say. He slides his hand into mine, giving it a hearty shake.

"Who took out the one in the shop?" I ask.

"I did," Zane answers. No wonder I didn't hear the shot. It came from a sniper rifle.

"Thanks," I say sincerely. If it weren't for him, I would have had to fight that guy off, and I knew he was armed. I guess that worked in his favor for me to forgive him, too.

"No problem," Zane replies.

"So, what was the damage?" I ask the room.

"Banger took out two," Ghost answers. "Some of my guys are following the ones who took off."

"We took out three," Van adds.

I nod, trying to gather my thoughts. This is what we wanted when we took Evie out. We wanted him to make a move, but I should have known he would be a coward and not show his face. When we made the plan, we laid it all out to Evie that we were going to let him track her. We hoped Aaron would come for her like he did at Les' wedding reception. We didn't think he would ambush us into a shootout.

"You were right about the number," Les says. "Holden said it was a burner, but he may still be able to get a general location from when it was on." I fill Les in on what theories we had and what happened to Van's shipment. "Shit, Micah, your mom?"

"Yeah." Tomorrow we are going over there to sweep the house, and Hartley is going to dump Mom's phone records. I just needed one more day to pretend that my mother didn't betray me.

"You know what you have to do if it was her, right?" Les asks.

"I do," I snap. I don't want to have this conversation right now. Les' eyes narrow on me, and I take a breath. "Sorry, but this isn't easy."

"You fold so fucking fast," Gage says, laughing obnoxiously.

"Whatever," I gripe.

"You want to tell me what the hell you were thinking taking her out?" Les asks.

"Kind of careless," Ryder agrees.

"We thought he would come out of hiding if he saw her with all of us. Not send a convoy to shoot at us."

"They weren't shooting to kill," Dex adds. "This was a warning."

"We know," Van agrees. "He wants Evie alive."

"What's the deal there?" Les asks. "*La mia stella*?" Shit, I didn't think she heard that.

"We'll talk about it later."

"You bet your ass."

"This sounds like some juicy fucking gossip," Gage says, all ears.

"Shut up," Leo laughs.

"Don't fucking start," I warn.

"I'm not going to give you shit," Les says, surprising me. "She's a sweet girl; she doesn't need your bullshit."

"We aren't doing anything wrong," I defend. Are we?

"She doesn't need you guys leading her on."

"We aren't leading her on," I argue.

"So, she's staying long term?" Les asks, and when I don't answer, she snorts. "That's what I thought. You guys better be treating her with respect, or I'll murder you all in your sleep," Les threatens, and I believe her. She might not know Evie well, but she would go to hell and back to protect someone she deemed worthy.

"We are," I promise. I don't want to get into anything else while everyone is still in my office.

"Uh, Micah?" Mateo says, sticking his head through the door. "Evie wants to thank our friends." He laughs a little on that last bit.

Les shrugs, and they all slip their masks back on, flipping their hoods up. Evie's met them, but it was better to keep their identity hidden after something like that. They probably felt better about it, too.

Mateo leads Evie in, and I watch her shrink back slightly from seeing the masks staring at her. Mateo squeezes her hand, and she straightens her shoulders. She's changed out of her dress into those delicious yoga pants and a shirt I think is Van's.

"Thank you," she says to the group. Les nods in acknowledgment and waves her hand for the group to follow her. They slip out the door, and Evie watches them go with a perplexed look on her face.

We can only do this for so long before she starts asking more questions.

I don't know if I want to lie to her anymore. And that brings up a whole host of questions I have for myself.

CHAPTER 40
EVIE

"I want you to teach me how to fight," I announce to the room the following day over breakfast. Every eye in the room turns to me at the same time, and it doesn't freak me out anymore, which is a miracle in itself.

"To fight?" Micah says slowly.

"Yes," I nod, my decision made up. "I want to be able to protect myself." I tossed and turned all night with the thoughts of Aaron grabbing me, and no one was there to save me. I could have gone to any of them when I couldn't sleep, but I needed to learn to be independent when I left, so I suffered through it.

"I can show you, angel," Gray says, surprising me. I figured he would be the last to agree.

"When can we start?" I ask.

"Finish your breakfast and meet me in the gym," Gray replies, sliding from his stool. He kisses the top of my head and leaves the kitchen.

"The rest of us will be out," Evander says. Instant panic grips my chest. Aaron already threatened Gray; he wouldn't hesitate to kill any of them. "We'll be fine, *pequena reina*," Evander soothes, tucking his fingers under my chin to look into my eyes. "We'll be back later." He kisses my lips slowly, pulls back with a smile, and kisses the tip of my nose.

"Go easy on Gray, buttercup," Mateo teases. He doesn't give me the gentle kiss like Evander just gave me; he kisses me until I'm almost panting, trying to pull him closer. "Hm," he hums when he pulls back. "Save that for later."

"Move, bitch," Micah jokes, shoving Mateo away. I look into his blue eyes, eyes so much softer than when I first met him. "If you need us for anything, even if you want to check in, call." He slides another cell phone in front of me. He tucks my hair behind my ear, sliding his fingers down my cheek. "Are you ok?" he asks.

They've asked me that all morning, and I didn't know how to answer it because the answer to that question is no, but not because of the shooting. "I'm fine," I lie with a smile that I hope is convincing.

Micah, as always, didn't miss it. "I know you have questions, *la mia stella*, and I wish we could answer them."

"I know," I sigh.

"Why don't you work out with Gray and then call Les and Bridget?" Micah suggests. "Have a girl's day."

I smile genuinely this time. That sounds like exactly what I need. "I'll do that."

He kisses me softly. "Have fun today."

Hartley steps up. "Kick his ass, princess," he whispers, making me giggle. He kisses me almost as hungrily as Mateo, and I still can't believe this is Hartley. *I had sex with Hartley.* Who would have thought that would ever happen?

Micah jerks his head, and the other guys call out their goodbyes and slip from the room.

I finish my breakfast like Gray said and search for him in the gym. I stop dead in my tracks at the door, my mouth hanging open. I saw him naked last night but was so distracted by everything going on that I didn't have time to appreciate it all.

He has his back to me doing pull-ups, shirtless. The tattoo I saw on his chest rounds his shoulder and down his back. On the other side are words that I can't read from here but are huge.

I let the door swing shut, and Gray drops to his feet, turning to face me. We still haven't had our talk yet, but I know he hasn't forgotten.

"What do you want to learn?" Gray asks, motioning me to join him on the mats.

"Self-defense," I answer, stepping in front of him.

"All right," Gray nods. "If you get scared at any point, tell me."

"I'm sick of being scared, Gray," I huff. "I can take it."

He slides his knuckles down my cheek. "I know that, angel. I just don't want you to feel what you felt with him with me."

"I never would," I tell him honestly, grabbing his hand from my face to hold it. "You're too good."

Gray's brows furrow. "I'm not good, but I would never hurt you." He pulls his hand from mine and rolls his shoulders back. Why do none of these guys see what I do?

"I'm going to show you basic holds and how to get out of them today. Are you ready?" Gray says all business, so I nod. "We'll start simple."

He goes over several holds, and I listen intently when he explains how to get out of them. Gray doesn't go easy on me, and I appreciate it. It's like he knows I need this, just like they always do. It takes me longer in some holds than others to break free from Gray's massive muscles, but he always praises me when I do, making me work harder.

"Get free," Gray almost barks. He has me pinned to the mat flat on my back, straddling my waist, my hands over my head.

"I can't," I say, struggling in his hold. This is the only one I haven't been able to get out of.

"Yes. You can," Gray says evenly. "What did I say to do?"

"I don't know," I say miserably. I can feel anxiety creeping up the longer he holds me down, but I refuse to tap out.

"I've left myself wide open. That won't always be the case. Get. Free."

"Damn it, Gray," I jerk my wrists that are locked in his big hands.

"There you go. Get pissed because an attacker isn't going to talk you through how to get out."

"I know that," I hiss, jerking harder on my wrists.

"Then why aren't you struggling harder?" Gray taunts. "Head or knee." He reminds me to either headbutt him or knee him in the junk. I jerk my knee up, and he recovers before I can connect with his balls, so I hit his thigh. "Harder," Gray actually barks this time, and I feel anger course through me.

I struggle, moving my body from side to side, jerking my wrists. My breath is heaving in my lungs, and sweat is pouring down my face. I feel his body shift to one side, so I buck my hips up to knock him off balance. His hand slips free from my right wrist, so I use my arm to hook around his back and roll hard to one side, making him hit the mat. I push until he's on his back, and I'm perched on his hips.

"Ha!" I exclaim, excitement coursing through me that I finally did it. I slap my hands beside his head. "I did it."

"You did," Gray smiles, all his gruffness gone when he was teaching me. His hands settle in the dip of my hips. "I'm proud of you, angel." I beam at him, and he smiles bigger than I've ever seen. It changes his whole face, making his features less severe. Gray is beautiful.

The air in the room changes with Gray and I locked in an intense stare-off. Working out with him is like an intense version of foreplay.

We move at the same time, our lips meeting in a heated kiss. His hand slides to the back of my head, holding me to his mouth. Our tongues are sliding together; our hips are rocking together. Gray shifts until I'm poised over one of his big thighs. He jerks my hips down, grinding me against the muscle.

"Oh god," I say breathlessly, jerking my mouth from his. His leg is making direct contact with my oversensitive clit. I can't stop rotating my hips.

"There you go, angel," Gray says gruffly.

"What about you?" I gasp out. I felt how hard he was against me.

"Another time. I just want to see you come again," he rasps, pulling me harder against his leg. "Ride it like you would my cock."

"Oh fuck," I moan. I widen my legs and grind down, riding his leg like I rode Hartley. Thinking about my time with Hartley while I'm with Gray makes me feel guilty.

"Whatever just happened, get out of your head," Gray demands. "Come for me, angel."

I focus on Gray's pretty hazel eyes and start moving my hips back and forth, scraping my clit over his knee. *Oh, shit.*

"Gray," I groan. "More. I need more." Gray reaches up, pushes my shirt to my neck, jerks my bra down, and sucks my nipple into his mouth. When he bites down, my whole body starts shaking. "Yes," I moan. My hips start moving erratically. He flexes the muscle in his thigh, and I go off with a scream. "Gray!" I collapse forward on his chest.

"Fuck," Gray groans. "You're beautiful when you come for me." My thigh rubs his hard dick, and I sit up with a brow raised. He shakes his head. "Not until we talk."

"We can talk now," I suggest.

Gray swallows and looks away. When his eyes meet mine, they are blazing with old memories. "Later. Micah said you are supposed to have a girl's day. Call Les."

I sigh and slide off him. "Okay," I say weakly. I feel like I am taking two steps forward and five back with Gray.

"Angel," Gray says, nudging my chin to look at him. "I promise we'll talk. Just not right now."

I nod.

I don't know what I am expecting from them.

He doesn't owe me anything.

I DIDN'T DRINK. But when someone shows up with alcohol after you've been shot at, you do.

"Let me get this right," Bridget slurs, pointing a finger at me. "They took you to a sex club, and you got to watch hottie one and two bang it out?"

"Oh my god," Les groans, laying her head on the patio table. "Can we please fucking remember one of them is my uncle?"

"Babe, your uncle is hot as fuck. You need to get over it," Bridget says, taking another shot. I lost track a long time ago, and I am indeed wasted. There are currently two of everything.

"He is," I agree, sighing dreamily.

"I'm pissed," Bridget declares, causing me and Les to look at her. "When do I get a group of hot guys to dick me down on the regular?"

We all fall out into laughter, and I've never felt lighter. Not just because of the copious amounts of expensive liquor Les stole from Evander and Mateo. We've talked about everything and nothing. We've laughed, we've cried. Les opened up to me about what happened to her and how her guys helped her through being kidnapped by her stalker. Bridget is hilarious and could make your stomach hurt from laughing so hard. Les admitted to me when she was about six shots in that she's never had this before, either. So Bridget declared she popped both our cherries, and we laughed for thirty minutes.

"I have some guys in mind," Les says to Bridget, taking a shot and shivering from head to toe.

"Ohhhhh," Bridget claps. "Tell me more." Les smiles from ear to ear. "No, stop that right now. Absolutely not."

"Someone want to fill me in?" I ask them.

"Yeah, Bridget. Fill her in," Les says, giggling like crazy.

Bridget rolls her eyes. "It was one time, and we were drunk as shit."

"Who?" I ask, on the edge of my seat.

"Bridget was in the middle of a twin sandwich," Les says, roaring with laughter.

I can feel my eyes widen. "I need details."

Bridget's face blooms with color, matching her hair. "Have you met Alexey and Dmitri yet?"

I run through everyone in my head, and my mouth pops open when I remember. "They are the ones who own Whispers, right?" I ask, and Bridget nods. "Holy shit. They are like creepily hot."

"They are," Bridget laughs. "But it was one time. We haven't talked since it happened."

"At my wedding reception," Les adds. "They broke the fucking bed."

"Shut up," Bridget giggles.

"Why haven't you talked, though?" I frown, pissed off for my friend. "They should have called. You're awesome."

"Thank you for that, but it wasn't like that," Bridget assures me. "It was mutually agreed before it happened that it wouldn't happen again. I just wanted to try it, and they obliged. It was the best sex of my fucking life."

"Oh," I say. "So, they like...did things with you together?"

Les turns to me slowly. "For someone living and messing around with five guys, that was very innocent." My face heats. "Okay, spill. I will pretend that Micah isn't my uncle for five minutes. Were you a virgin?"

I shake my head. "No, but..." I trail off, then shrug. Fuck it. I could talk about this with them. "Mateo was the first to give me an orgasm and eat me out," I say in a rush.

"Wait!" Bridget says, waving her hand around. "You never had that before?"

"No." I didn't want to explain the rest; they could figure it out.

"Have you been with more than one of them at the same time?" Les asks, downing another shot. Probably trying to scrub anything I'm about to tell her from her brain.

"Yeah. Micah and Evander were my first for that." I explain what went down between us and giggle when I see Les' eye twitching. She tunes in completely when I tell her what happened at New Vision.

"So, besides your mouth, their dicks haven't been in you at the same time?" Bridget asks. I shake my head. "Oh, girl, just wait for that because let me tell you." She fans her face. "You won't be the same after." Les high-fives her, and I lose it laughing.

"She's not wrong," Les says. "Mine was with Gage and Leo."

"Doesn't it hurt?" I ask. The thought crossed my mind, especially after seeing the girl from New Vision pressed between those two guys. Her face was one of pure pleasure.

"At first." Bridget shrugs. "But if they do it right, it feels ahhh-mazzzing."

I cross my arms. "I want to do it," I pout. At this point, I was so drunk that I wasn't even sure what I was asking for.

"Then tell them," Les laughs.

Mind made up. When I see any of them, I am telling them. Gray is hiding in the house after Bridget made suggestive comments to him about me. I've never seen him so damn red. So, I wouldn't be asking him.

"Okay," Les says, sitting up. "I need to know something, but no one can tell my husbands I asked this, especially Leo." I nod for her to continue. "Mateo. How's that?"

"You mean sexually?" I ask.

"Yes. I've always wondered," Les giggles.

"He's fucking amazing," I sigh.

"He's big, isn't he?" Bridget asks.

"Oh, yeah." I raise my hands and with one eye try to measure out his size with both hands. "Micah is too," I stage whisper, just for Bridget.

"Oh my god!" Les groans. "Why did my first female friend have to be fucking my uncle?"

Bridget and I die laughing. Les has been a good sport about me dishing about everything, but I knew she had limits. I would too.

"What about Van?" Bridget asks. "He just seems...serious."

"Evander is amazing. In all ways. We haven't gone all the way yet, though," I laugh. "But he makes me feel special, just like they all do."

"I'm going to regret this," Les says, throwing a shot back. "Hartley."

"Hartley's pierced," I say, watching Bridget's eyes widen.

Les chokes on her shot. "Hartley has a pierced cock?"

"And nipples."

"What?!" Les and Bridget say at the same time.

"What kind of piercing?" Les asks after she recovers.

"He said it was a Jacob's ladder and a magic cross."

"Ryder has a Jacob's ladder, and it's fucking epic. The other guys like it too. Now I need to Google the other one." Les picks up her phone and starts tapping. "Holy hell."

"Let me see!" Bridget snatches Les' phone, and her mouth drops open. "Oh my god. I'm still trying to picture the Hartley we know with the Hartley you're telling us about."

"Sex with Hartley is...different," I giggle. "He made me..." Both girls lean in, waiting for what I was about to say. I can't believe I am talking about this stuff, but it feels good to have someone to talk to besides the guys. I'm sure the alcohol was helping with my loose lips. "Squirt."

Les' eyes almost bug out of her head. "So, his dick game is good. Who knew?" We laugh at that. "What about your adorable blushing giant?"

"Gray? We haven't done anything, really. He holds back. I don't know why." That thought makes me sad. Besides me dry humping him in the gym, Gray hasn't tried anything else. He's been avoiding me since the day of our date, and it's starting to make me wonder if he even wants this or if he's doing it for Mateo.

"He has that look." Les waves her hand around. "Something in his past is probably holding him back."

"How do you know?" I was all ears now.

"Dex," Les answers. "No one could touch him for years, including me. He had some bad shit happen to him that caused it. Gray's might not be that, but there's something stopping him. You just have to find out what."

"I don't know if I'll be here long enough to find out," I say sadly. Not only did I find a group of amazing guys, but I also found two friends.

Bridget leans her elbows on the table. "Are you leaving, though? What about Mateo?"

"This is temporary. Mateo and I just started dating. I don't know where our relationship is going. This whole thing with the other guys is just while I'm here."

"You already broke the three-date rule with Mateo. You're in," Les says. "And did he say it was just while you were here, or are you saying it is?"

"Three-date rule?" I ask in confusion.

Les smiles. "Mateo doesn't take anyone out more than three

times. He wants them to have a good time and go about their way without any feelings involved. I've *never* seen him like he is with you. You're it for him, babe."

"Oh," I breathe. Could that be true? If anyone knew, it would be Les. Or it was the liquor she drank. But something tells me she's telling the truth. "You really think?"

Les and Bridget nod their heads comically fast. "Why does it have to end after? Les made it work," Bridget says.

"I don't know," I groan. "I've never seen myself with a guy like Mateo, much less four other guys just like him. They make me feel important, and special, and beautiful."

"Because you are beautiful," Les says. Coming from someone who looks like her, I take that as the highest compliment. Les didn't strike me as someone who says stuff she doesn't mean. "And you should always feel that way. Maybe you should talk to them."

I shake my head. "It's too soon, and I don't want to make things awkward since I'm stuck here if that's not what they want."

"What do *you* want?" Bridget asks, sliding me another shot.

I toss it back. "I want to see where this goes without the clock ticking over our heads."

"I think you would be good for them," Les says. "Who knows what will happen in the future?"

I nod, thinking about what she's saying. I know they are still hiding stuff from me, but could I really expect them to tell me all their secrets? Something about last night is tickling something in my brain. And it didn't until I saw Les again. The black masks flash behind my eyes, with the shortest one standing in front of the group, and I gasp. *Holy shit.*

"It was you!" I say, pointing at Les.

Les raises a dark brow. "What was me?"

"Last night with the mask!"

Les looks momentarily startled, then she sighs. "It was."

"You saved us. But I don't understand." Who the hell is she?

Bridget looks between us. "I'm missing something very important here."

"Shit," Les groans. She looks like she is fighting a war inside her head on what she could tell us. She finally leans her elbows on the table and seems almost sober. "Look, I can't tell you everything for many reasons. It's nothing against you guys; I just can't. But yes, that was us last night. The masks protect our identity when shit goes south."

"Are you guys like vigilantes or something?" Bridget asks with a giggle.

"No," Les laughs. "We aren't the good guys, but we have each other's back and protect who we can." Les looks at me. "You deserve answers. I know you aren't stupid and have figured out stuff isn't entirely as it seems. But I also need you to remember that it's not always safe to know who we are." I've been told so many times that they weren't good guys, but I couldn't accept that. Bad guys wouldn't have treated me like they have.

Bridget nods her head. "She's not wrong."

"You know?" I couldn't help but feel a pang of disappointment that she knew and I didn't.

"Only because my mom works for Les." Bridget stands from her chair. "Okay, enough of the heavy shit. This place have speakers out here?"

"It does, but I have no idea how to use it," I laugh. "Hold on."

I pull up Mateo's contact on my phone, switch it to speakerphone, and dial.

"Well, hello there, buttercup," Mateo answers.

Bridget's mouth drops open. "Buttercup? Fucking swoon."

Mateo laughs. "Are you guys drunk?"

"Yep," I reply. "I need to know how to use the speakers on the patio."

Mateo rattles off instructions to Bridget, and seconds later, music starts filtering through. "Are you guys having fun?" Mateo asks.

"We are," I smile. "You might be a little pissed, though."

"Fuck them," Les declares. "They can kiss your voluptuous ass."

Mateo laughs again, and I hear Hartley chuckle in the background. "Why am I going to be pissed?"

"We raided your liquor cabinet," I say with a giggle.

"What's mine is yours, buttercup. But I wouldn't mind kissing that voluptuous ass."

"Oh my god. Stop." I could feel my face blazing.

"Didn't you have something to ask him?" Bridget says with a grin. I frown until I realize where she's going.

"Absolutely not." I point my finger at Bridget.

"Oh, come on. You can't leave me hanging," Mateo says.

Fine. Fuck it. "I want two of you at the same time."

The line goes quiet, and I have to look to make sure he didn't hang up. Mateo clears his throat. "That can be arranged, buttercup." Mateo's voice has taken on that deepness that he gets when he's turned on, and my pussy takes notice. *Damn it.* "Is that what you really want?"

Both girls are nodding their heads like crazy. "Yes," I whisper.

"Consider it done. But now I'm hard, and Hartley is the only person here to take care of it." I hear shuffling, and then I hear Mateo yell. "Hartley! Come suck my dick!" We fall into laughter.

"Suck mine, and I'll suck yours," Hartley replies dryly. I remember Hartley saying he's experimented before, so I don't know if he is entirely serious. Les and Bridget's eyes are as wide as saucers, making me giggle.

"I'd love nothing more than to choke you with my cock, Hart, but we have shit to do. Get your head in the game," Mateo jokes like he isn't the one who started that.

"I'm going to go," I say, laughing. "Don't choke him too much."

"No promises, buttercup. You know how well I can fill something up."

"Mateo! I'm going to go. Be careful."

Mateo chuckles. "See you in a little while, buttercup." The call disconnects, and I have to remember how to breathe.

"They're friends now?" Les asks.

I shrug. "Yeah, for the most part."

"You know that's for your benefit, right?" Les says. "Does that sound like something someone would do if it were just temporary?"

At this point, I have more questions than answers.

And I want answers.

CHAPTER 41
MATEO

I had a motive for bringing Hartley with me. As always.

I needed to know if he could put aside his prejudice regarding us for Evie. Having sex in front of someone is vastly different from him actually seeing what we do. If we are going to make this happen for real, I need to know he could handle it. Zane went from being a cop to working with Les, but Zane was raised in this life. Hartley wasn't.

"You strapped?" I ask, shoving the car into park. My poor Porsche was no more. I had plenty of other vehicles but we didn't want to stand out so I was driving a guard SUV. We just pulled in front of Evie's apartment, and I'm hoping she isn't about to get pissed at what I am about to do.

Hartley gives me a dry look and pulls his shirt up to reveal a holster with a Glock tucked inside.

"Good. You might need it." I grin and slide out of the car.

I have no idea what will happen here and want him to be prepared. I warned Ghost and Caden that I was bringing him with me. Ghost narrows his eyes slightly when Hartley steps out of the car but doesn't say anything.

"What's up, fellas?" I greet. The group they were talking to took one look at Hartley and me and moved the other way quickly.

"You're late," Ghost says, pushing away from the wall.

"Aw. Were you that excited to see me?" I tease. Ghost rolls his eyes and jerks the door open to the apartment building. "That doesn't fucking lock?" I ask. She was staying here, and the main door didn't even lock? Aaron could have gotten in with no issues, proving my and Hartley's theory that he's been following her this whole time.

"You're in Concrete Row, man," Caden answers. "Not your fancy neighborhood."

Hartley takes the lead, showing us to Evie's apartment. It's on the third floor, the last door on the right, with no escape besides the stairs we walked up. She was a sitting duck here, making acid burn in my throat. Why did he wait until she was in public to make his move? It doesn't make any sense.

I hand Hartley the keys I got from Evie. He unlocks the door and shoves it open. It is all one room with a bathroom in the corner. She has a bed, an old broken-down couch, and a dresser. That's it.

"Damn," I mutter, walking through the small space. I knew she said she didn't have much, but I didn't think it was this bad. "This place is depressing."

"It's not that bad," Caden defends, opening the curtains. "Okay, maybe it is." The only thing you could see through the window is the brick of the next-door building.

"Not all of us can live in million-dollar homes," Hartley says dryly.

Ghost crosses his arms over his chest. "I don't, and I can admit no one should live like this."

"She couldn't afford anything else," Hartley grits out.

"Why couldn't she stay with you then?" Ghost tosses out.

"I offered. She said she wanted to do it on her own," Hartley grinds out, then sighs. "I didn't know it was this bad, or I would have pushed."

I could see that. Evie doesn't know how to accept generosity because she's never had it before. She didn't like that we were paying for her things, but I would make sure she got used to it. I planned on spoiling her as long as she would let me.

"Let's get to work," I suggest. I hand everyone the devices that would scan for bugs to see if Aaron had been back here, hoping to catch Evie. This is just part one of my plan.

"Over here," Ghost says, holding up a pair of Evie's boots. He runs it over them again, and the green light on the device lights up. He starts looking all over them. He pulls the sole on the inside of the boot back and pulls a small tracker out.

We finish searching without talking and find a listening device in an air vent. We put everything back where we found it and leave the apartment.

"Motherfucker," Hartley growls when we step outside. "He really is fucking stalking her."

"For eight months," I add. "I don't understand something, though. Aaron was mean as fuck to her; why the hell would he even care if she left?"

"She was a possession," Caden answers. "He didn't have to care about her. He had the perfect girlfriend. Complacent and quiet. Someone he could control." Caden holds his hands up when I glare at the description. "I don't mean it's right. I'm just saying that's what this guy thinks of her."

"He knew she was getting ready to leave and then tagged her or did it as a precaution anyway." Ghost shrugs. "The dude is level twenty crazy. It's hard to tell. Those guys I was talking to outside said they've seen him around here before but more in the past month," Ghost answers.

"We need to get the rest of the shit from her apartment. She's not coming back here," I announce.

Hartley raises a brow. "What does that mean?"

"It means I'm not done with Evie when Aaron is gone. If she doesn't want to stay with me, then I'll get her something better."

"What about her lease?"

"That's another reason we're here. Her landlord apparently has ties to the Hellraisers. I'm going to buy him out."

"The Hellraisers?" Caden asks. "That's just fucking great."

"Are you still having problems with them?" I ask. The Disciples and the Hellraisers have a lot of history, and none of it is good.

Caden shrugs. "Not for a while." He jerks his head at Ghost. "Not since this asshole follows me around like a shadow."

"Really? I'll leave your ass to get shot then," Ghost says, lifting a blonde brow.

"You wouldn't," Caden replies, making kissy noises. *What the hell was that?* My brain is running wild with possibilities of what they are up to. Add in Alexey and Dmitri's crazy asses, and you have a gang of psychos.

"Let's pack her stuff. I'm hoping the landlord will show his face."

We make our way inside with the boxes I brought and get all of Evie's possessions, talking nonsense so we don't slip up and say something Aaron can use. I hear the stairs creak; I look at the guys, knowing they heard it too.

A big guy with a beer gut and a stained wife beater on shoves the door open. "Who the fuck are you?"

I step forward with Hartley right at my back. "I'm the one who's going to buy out this lease. How much?"

"That's not how it works."

"It does today," I say confidently. "I would threaten you with lawsuits, but you wouldn't give a fuck about that. Look closer at my face. Who the fuck am I?"

He stares, and I see the moment it clicks. "What would a Perez want with something like this?"

"I don't want anything to do with this shithole. I'm buying it out for the tenant."

"We can't all be born with a silver spoon in our goddamn mouth." He jerks his head, and two guys step behind him. This should be fun. "Get lost. The tenant can pay their rent just like we agreed on."

I laugh. "You don't even know who lived here, do you? And do you think your little show behind you bothers me? Fuck off."

The guy's eyes finally light on Caden, and I grind my teeth. "You work with Disciple scum?"

Ghost stands to his full height. "I'd watch your fucking mouth if I were you. Take the money and move the fuck out of the way."

"The big titty bitch lived here, didn't she?"

We all pull our Glocks at the same time, leveling them at this piece of shit standing in front of us. "He said move," Hartley growls. The landlord backs down like a coward, but his friends aren't as bright. The one closest pulls a gun up faster than I can blink. I hear the shot, and I'm being spun around. My back hits the wall with a grunt; Hartley pressed against me. He fires off two shots. One of them screams, and I know his aim is spot on. I hear feet pounding down the steps and know the other guy took off.

"Wow, Hart. I didn't know you cared," I joke.

"Shut up," Hartley growls. "Someone needs to teach you to keep your mouth shut."

I bark a laugh. "So, I've been told."

"If you guys are done making out, we need to move," Ghost says.

I pucker my lips at Hartley, and he pushes off me with a roll of his eyes. We gather the boxes, step over the guy Hartley shot, and get to the SUV. And it's completely surrounded.

"Well, shit," I say, sitting my boxes down. "Why do we have to be like this?"

"You're really fucking brave coming here," Tink, the leader of the Hellraisers, says. "This is Hellraiser's turf."

"Like you give a fuck about turf," Caden laughs.

"You got your goddamn Viper boyfriend, and now you want to be brave?" Tink sneers.

"Wait. Before you start throwing insults, you should know we didn't come alone." I nod my head, and a blacked-out Ford Explorer comes roaring in behind the Hellraisers. Two passengers lean out of the windows with black masks and automatics.

"Shit! Let's roll!" Tink yells, taking off around the building.

Gage raises his mask with a grin. "You good?"

"Yeah. Thanks for sitting lookout."

Holden raises his mask. "You took our wife. What else are we supposed to do for fun?"

"Each other?" I tease.

Ryder laughs from the driver's seat. "That's for later. Call if you need anything."

"Will do. Thanks again."

341

"What are you going to do about this place?" Hartley asks, jerking his thumb at the building.

"How do you feel about arson?" I grin.

Hartley laughs. "If it means he can't rent to any more innocents, I'm down. But what about the other people living here?"

"We'll do some recon, get names of the innocents, I'll make an anonymous donation, so they don't have to live like this, and then we can burn this bitch to the ground."

"Burn, baby, burn," Caden laughs.

With any luck, that landlord will still be inside.

"You're too damn quiet, and it's making me nervous," I tell Hartley on our drive to sweep Micah's house.

"I was just thinking," he answers. He turns to look at me. "I did just kill someone back there for you."

"Thanks for that, by the way," I say. All joking aside, Hartley kept me from taking one to the chest. "You good?"

"Yeah. Why did you really bring me today?" I knew he would eventually ask that. Hartley is fucking smart.

"I wanted to know if you could handle this life."

"Why? You talk like this is long term. When Aaron is gone, so am I."

"Are you, though?" I couldn't believe that. No way is he going to leave Evie now.

"I think it's time for me to go back home," Hartley says.

I frown. "What does that mean? Back to your house or Fairview?"

"Fairview. There's nothing here for me, man. I'll never work here again. Maybe I can join the force there."

"Is that what you really want?" I don't know him well, but he didn't seem all that upset about not being a cop anymore. He was just upset for the *reason* he wasn't a cop anymore. "Because you look like you fit in with us."

Hartley barks a laugh. "I shoot one gangbanger for you, and I'm an honorary member of the Mafia?"

"That, and you've taken all this in stride. Maybe you were on the wrong side all along."

"Can I tell you something without you giving me shit?" Hartley asks.

"I can be serious, asshole. Go for it."

"I never wanted to be a cop. It's what my stepdad wanted, and my whole life was about making him proud."

My eyes widen. "No shit?"

"Yep. That's why I worked as hard as I did to get to Chief, but then I fucked that up. Now, look at me."

"What does he say?"

"He'd never say anything bad, but I can see the shame in his eyes."

"Is there? Or is that your own projection?"

"What?" Hartley asks, turning in his seat to face me fully.

"Is he really ashamed, or are you projecting that on him because you're ashamed of yourself?"

"I guess I never thought about it like that."

"Look, I don't know your home life, but the way Evie talks, it was good. I think you hate yourself for what you did, so you think everyone else hates you, too. Les forgave you. *We* forgave you. It's time for you to let it go. For what it's worth, I don't want you to go back to Fairview. I don't think you'll be happy there. I think you're running when you don't have to."

Hartley falls into silence, staring out the windshield with a puzzled look on his face. I pull in front of Micah's before he looks at me again.

"When did you get so fucking smart?"

I laugh. "I've always been smart. People just underestimate me because I act like a fool."

Before I push open Micah's front door, Hartley grabs my arm. "Thanks for that."

"No thanks needed. That's what friends are for, man." I honestly don't think Hartley had anyone besides Evie, but now he has us. I wouldn't let him run away from his problems. He needs to sort his shit out and be there one hundred percent for Evie.

As soon as I step through Micah's front door, the device starts lighting up. Right beside the front door is exactly what we were looking for. *Motherfucker.*

I did not want to tell Micah that his mom fucked him over.

But it looks like I am going to have to.

CHAPTER 42

EVANDER

I am getting more worried by the second. Evie isn't answering her phone or messages. I suck it up and finally call Gray.

"Hello?" Gray answers.

"Where's Evie?" I ask, making Micah chuckle.

"With Les and Bridget."

"Why isn't she answering her phone?"

"I don't know. She's fine. They are on the back patio." Gray replies and something in his voice sounds off.

"What's wrong?" I demand.

I hear Gray sigh. "They're drunk."

"What?" I ask, making Micah raise an eyebrow. I flip it to speakerphone. "What do you mean they're drunk?"

"They raided the liquor," Gray says dryly. "I've been keeping an eye on them."

I shake my head. As far as I knew, Evie didn't even drink. "We'll be home soon." I hit the end call button, and Micah's trying to hold in a laugh. "What's so funny?"

"You," Micah laughs. I narrow my eyes, but it only makes him roll his. "You're worried about her."

"Of course I am. There's a psycho after her," I defend.

"Uh huh," Micah says, kicking back in his chair. "That's all it is?"

"No," I admit with a sigh. I couldn't stop thinking about her. "Why aren't you worried?"

Micah wiggles his phone in his hand. "Because I texted Gray like an hour ago."

"You aren't worried that she's day-drinking?" I ask.

"No," Micah shrugs. "She needs to let loose some time. Les and Bridget will be good friends for her."

"You're talking like this isn't going to end soon," I point out.

Micah shrugs again, but his eyes shift from mine. "I just meant while she was here."

My phone pings with a message before I can say anything else. Does Micah want her to stay? I don't know if I was there yet, but something twists in my gut at the thought of her leaving.

MATEO

Done. We're headed back to the house. I have some fun planned for later. I'll explain when you get here.

We're headed back too. Talk then.

I lay the phone down. "Micah," I say softly.

"Don't start, Van," Micah warns. "Let's go check on our girl."

With that, he gets up and leaves my office. *Our girl?* I like the sound of that, but she isn't our girl. I've heard Evie say more than once that when this is done, she's leaving.

I have a feeling Mateo isn't going to be the only one crushed when that happens.

We pull up to the house at the same time as Mateo and Hartley.

We make our way into the house without a word, and you can hear the thumping bass coming from the patio. Micah shakes his head, and we follow him to the door. He shoves it open, and we all step outside.

Evie, Les, and Bridget are lying with their heads together on the patio, laughing and singing loudly to the music. Gray is sitting in the corner with an indulgent smile on his face.

"Holy shit," Micah laughs. "They're lit."

Evie's head shoots up at the sound of Micah and waves enthusiastically. "Hello, my sexy lovers!" she yells, causing the girls to giggle.

"Fucking hell," Micah mutters.

Mateo walks over and crouches beside Evie, with us following behind him. "Hey, buttercup," he greets, rubbing his knuckles down her cheek.

"I fucking love that," Bridget says, fanning her face. Her head twists to me. "Hey, hottie number two." That makes them burst into laughter.

"You think buttercup is swoon-worthy? Micah calls her *la mia stella*," Les says, trying to drop her voice as low as Micah's.

Gray shakes his head, walking up. "Holy fuck," Evie breathes when he's standing over her. "Have you always been that tall?"

Gray barks a laugh. "Yes, angel, I have."

"Angel?" Les squeaks. "Holy shit."

"If he's hottie number two, who's hottie number one?" Mateo asks. Evie and Bridget's eyes both stray to Micah answering his question. "What am I then?"

"Baby boy," Micah mutters, and Mateo actually blushes. I don't think I've ever seen the sight.

Evie squints. "Why, baby boy?"

I look at Gray, and his face is blood red. I don't think either of them realized how loud they were the other day.

"Because that's what Gray calls me," Mateo says dryly, causing the girls' eyes to widen.

"That's fucking hot," Bridget declares, rolling to her stomach. She looks behind Mateo, and she tilts her head to the side. "Hello, Hartley," Bridget greets. I'm sure Les has told her the story, and I'm afraid of what will come out of Bridget's mouth when she's sober, much less drunk. "Nice. You're a lucky bitch, Evie."

"I am," Evie says in a dreamy voice. Holy shit, they are trashed.

I run my fingers through Evie's hair. "You need to eat something." It was way past lunchtime, and there was no sign of food anywhere but plenty of empty bottles.

"Oh, Micah," Les sings. "Your girl needs to eat."

Micah raises a brow. "And what would my girl like to eat?"

Evie's face blooms with color, but she doesn't argue with that statement. That's the second time someone has called her ours. "Anything is fine," Evie answers quietly.

"I'm disappointed," Bridget huffs. "When a man looks like that and asks you what you want. You tell him."

"That's right," Mateo agrees, fist-bumping Bridget.

Micah rolls his eyes. "I'll whip up something, *la mia stella*," he says, disappearing into the house.

"What does that mean?" Bridget asks.

Evie rolls to her stomach. "I have no clue."

"I would have googled that shit by now." Bridget grabs her phone from the patio, squinting at the screen. "Oh my god!" she exclaims, clutching her chest. "It means...."

"Shhhhhhh," Evie says, pushing her fingers against Bridget's lips. "I don't wanna know."

"Why?" Bridget asks. The girls share a meaningful look, and Bridget nods once. "Got it."

What the hell was that?

"What time is it?" Les asks, sitting up.

"Two-thirty. Why?" I answer.

"Oh shit," Les says. "Help me up." She reaches up to Hartley, and he pulls her to her feet. She staggers to the table and picks up her phone. "Oh shit," she says again with a laugh. "They are going to kill me." She hits dial on her phone.

"Hello, pretty girl," Gage answers through the speakerphone.

"I need you to pick me up," Les giggles.

"Are you drunk?" Gage asks in amusement.

"Yep," Les says, nodding her head even though he can't see her.

"I hate to tell you, pretty girl, but Holden, Leo, and I just took off for a job. You're stuck with the others."

"Why would you betray me like this, Gage?"

Gage chuckles. "Because I didn't know you were drinking and

would stop answering your phone hours ago. I have to go. I love you."

Les wrinkles her nose. "I love you too." She disconnects the call and scrolls through her phone again while biting her lip.

"A hundred bucks says she calls Ryder," Mateo says.

"I'll take that bet, but it will be Zane," Bridget counters. "No way is she going to call Dex."

"Are they going to be mad? She was just having fun," Evie asks with worry.

"No," I answer. "They'll just be worried."

"*Il mio sole*," Ryder answers, and Mateo grins. "You want to tell me why you haven't answered your phone in hours?"

"Well, you see, I'm drunk," Les explains like he couldn't tell by her slurring her words.

"We're day-drinking now?" Ryder says dryly. I can't tell if he is actually pissed or not. His voice always sounds the same.

"Yep," Les answers, popping the P. "Can you pick me up?"

Ryder chuckles. "Yeah." Les' shoulders relax until he talks again. "*We* can."

While we waited for Ryder to pick up Les, we got them off the patio and seated them around the table. By the time they got there, we had poured enough coffee into them to sober them up. Ryder, Dex, and Zane step out onto the back patio behind Micah. Les gives them a wide smile and digs into the food.

"I need to talk to you," Les says when she's done, looking at all of us. Between the coffee and food, she sounded a lot more sober.

Micah raises a brow. "Okay."

Les hugs Evie. "Think about what I said." Evie nods. "Give me a minute, and we can drop you at your place," Les says to Bridget.

Les leads us into the house and turns around to face us when we get to the office. "She knows it was me last night," she announces.

"How?" Mateo asks.

Les runs her hand in front of her. "She's not stupid. She put two and two together, and I refused to lie. You guys need to tell her the truth."

"It's not safe, shithead, and you know that," Micah answers.

"Yeah, that's what I told her, and it's utter bullshit. She has a right to know who she's getting mixed up with before this goes any further." She levels us all with a look. "Evie doesn't need your shit if you don't plan on making this permanent. I know it's soon, but you need to think about that before anything else happens."

She says her goodbyes and disappears from the office, leaving us to figure out whether to tell Evie the truth or not.

And if this is permanent or not.

AFTER EVERYONE LEFT, we barely got Evie into the house before she passed out. I put her on the couch with her head cradled on my lap, her feet in Micah's lap, while I ran my fingers through her hair absently.

"You think we can trust Hartley?" Micah asks quietly. We've already been through this several times.

"We have to for her," I repeat the same thing I've said every time. "Gray and Mateo trust him, and I trust their instincts."

"Have you been thinking about what Les said?"

"I have," I admit. "But I don't have the answers."

"I don't either. We don't even know what she wants."

Evie starts stirring between us, then sits up with a groan. She looks around, confused, and I can't help but chuckle. "What happened?" she asks groggily.

"My niece got you drunk," Micah replies dryly.

Her frown deepens, then she giggles. "Oh yeah. We had fun, though."

"I can tell," I reply, rubbing her back. "How are you feeling?"

"Okay, surprisingly. My head hurts a little, though," she admits with a wince.

Micah kisses her head. "I'll get you something for it." He's up and off the couch before she can reply.

I am dying to know what is running through her mind. She snuggles into my side, and I wrap my arm around her shoulders, pulling her closer.

"Are you okay?" I ask.

"I have so much going through my head, and I don't know where it stops." She turns to look at me. "I have questions I don't deserve the answers to." I frown at that, and her eyes drop to her lap.

I tilt her eyes up to mine with fingers under her chin. "We're not lying to you just for the fun of it. We aren't good people, Evie. But we would never do anything to hurt you."

"You are good, though, Evander," Evie says, sitting up so she can face me. "No matter who you are, deep in your bones, every single one of you is *good*."

I run my knuckles down her cheek. "You don't know how happy it makes me to hear you say that," I admit.

Micah walks in and hands her some pills for her headache with a bottle of water. She takes it with a grateful smile. "I want to talk about what's next," Evie says, sitting her water on the coffee table.

Micah raises a brow and pulls out his phone. Within minutes, the rest of the guys are rounding the corner.

"You look better, buttercup," Mateo chuckles, sitting on the love seat, Gray sitting beside him with Hartley in one of the chairs.

She smiles at him. "What do we do now?"

We never thought Aaron would send what he did when he realized she was out. All our hopes were that he would show his face.

"What do you mean?" Micah asks, taking her hand.

"About Aaron. I want this over," she declares, making us all frown. She sounded urgent like she couldn't wait to leave, not that she was urgent about getting rid of Aaron.

"We're working on that, princess," Hartley answers. We got word from Ghost that they were able to track one of the shooters to their hideout. Ghost has guys sitting on it, hoping Aaron would show up. We don't want to keep it from her, but we all know what we would have to do to get Aaron's location if he doesn't. "We know who was there from the bodies."

"Do you guys do this a lot?" Evie asks, looking between us.

"More than we'd like sometimes," Micah answers honestly.

"I just want this over," Evie repeats. "I want my life back."

I look over at Mateo, who's being uncharacteristically quiet, and he has one of those looks I've seen before. Everything he is thinking is about to spill out of his mouth. Mateo jumps off the loveseat before I can say anything. "I need to go do something," he says before quickly disappearing from the room.

I squeeze Evie's hand again before following him to his room. I shut the door behind me and watch him pace for a second. "Tay?" I say quietly.

"What if she doesn't want to stay?" Mateo says, spinning to face me. "What if I want her here, but she doesn't want to be? What if she really does leave, Van?"

I knew Mateo was serious about her but didn't realize how much until now. "Do you want her to stay?" I ask. Mateo swallows and nods. "Maybe you should talk to her."

"Does that seem like a girl ready to settle down?" Mateo asks, throwing his hands in the air. "She's already talking about leaving, and this isn't even over yet. Do you want her to stay?"

A lie is on the tip of my tongue, but I need to be honest with him. "I don't know," I say honestly. "I like her, Tay, but I don't know if it's a forever kind of thing for me yet." Even that sounded like a lie to my ears. I know how I felt when Micah called her our girl and when Les said the same thing. It felt right.

"I can't do this anymore if she isn't here for good," he says raggedly.

It hits me like a ton of bricks. "You're falling in love with her," I state. I remember this feeling all too well with Micah. Loving someone you can't have hurts.

Mateo laughs without humor. "Apparently," he says and flops back on the bed, staring at the ceiling. "When the fuck did that happen?"

"We don't get to choose when, Tay," I soothe, laying beside him. We haven't done this since we were scared little kids hiding from our father. "It just happens. We either accept it, or we don't."

"Isn't it too soon?" Mateo asks.

It's my turn to laugh. "No. You know when I knew I loved

Micah?" He turns to look at me. "The first time I kissed him." No one knew that, not even Micah. But I felt like Mateo needed to hear it right now. "I genuinely believe there is someone or *someones* in this life that are made for us, especially after meeting Micah. Never in a million years did I think that my first love would be a man."

Mateo sighs. "I just feel like her leaving would destroy me, Van." He looks back at the ceiling. "I don't think any of us are good enough for her. But together, we might be. Does that make sense?"

"It does," I agree reluctantly. "I don't want to see you get hurt, Tay." Mateo spent the most time with her, so his feelings are fully developed. I believed him when he said it would destroy him if she left.

It would destroy me watching him go through that.

And probably Micah, too.

CHAPTER 43
GRAY

I couldn't sleep. I haven't been able to since the first time someone tried to hurt Evie, and it hasn't gotten any better after last night. Nightmares are a fucking bitch.

So here I am at two thirty in the morning, sitting in the kitchen drinking a beer. This is why I usually prefer to stay alone. I don't want to disturb anyone with my bullshit. But turning down the chance to protect Evie isn't an option.

When she asked us to teach her self-defense today, something else was lurking below the surface of such a simple request. I couldn't put my finger on it, but something was wrong, and her drinking with Les and Bridget today confirmed that. Every time I stepped outside, the conversation would stop, and Evie would give me a guilty look. I just hope she didn't regret what happened in the gym. I wanted nothing more than to sink into her pussy at New Vision and in the gym, but I knew I couldn't until I cleared the air.

I hated how Evie had such a good time at New Vision, and her asshole ex ruined it. She's been through enough with him, and I am ready to take this motherfucker out.

I hear soft footsteps on the floor and turn around to see Evie walking into the kitchen. "You ok, angel?" I ask when she slides onto the stool beside me.

"I couldn't sleep," she answers. "I had a power nap today."

I raise a brow. "You slept for almost three hours."

She giggles. "I'm not much of a drinker," she admits.

"I'm glad you had fun today," I tell her. We were hoping the girls could help her through whatever she was going through. They seemed much closer when they left.

"Me too. I've never had girlfriends," she admits shyly.

"Then we can make it happen more often," I promise her. She smiles, but it looks sad.

We sit in silence for a few minutes before Evie clears her throat. "You've been avoiding me, Gray"

I still wasn't ready to tell her what happened in the past to make me the way I am, but I needed to clear the air about some things. "I'm sorry if I've made you feel like it was your fault I pushed you away," I tell her. "It's not you. I have shit that I'm working through. But I want to try with you."

"I can tell you aren't ready to talk about this, Gray, and that's fine. But I want you to know I'm here when you are," Evie says, sliding her arm through mine.

"I was afraid I overstepped last night at New Vision," I admit. That's something else that is plaguing my mind. None of us have had a chance to talk about what happened.

Evie's cheeks turn pink. "You didn't. I liked what happened. It was...hot. That sounds like an inadequate word for what happened, but it's all I can think about."

"I don't want you to feel pushed," I tell her.

"I don't," Evie sighs. "Honestly, I didn't think this would be my life. I had a hard time catching one guy's attention, and now I have five. It seemed too good to be true, but you guys have shown me what a real man is. And I know you would never push me into something I wasn't ready for."

"All the guys from your past are fucking idiots," I say adamantly, making her laugh. "You're beautiful, angel. Don't let anyone tell you any different."

"Thank you, Gray," Evie says breathlessly.

I lean down until my mouth hovers right at hers, letting her close the distance. When her lips touch mine, I feel that same electricity racing down my spine that I felt the first time we kissed. I deepen the kiss, and Evie moans into my mouth. Needing to be closer to her, I stand up with my mouth still on hers, wrap my hands around her waist, and sit her on the counter so I can step between her thighs.

Evie lets out a squeak, breaking this kiss. "I'm too heavy..." She trails off when she sees the warning in my eyes.

"I could bench press you and not break a sweat, angel. Don't test me," I say. I start kissing her neck. "If I want to toss you around, I will. If I want to carry you around, I will. And don't ever let me hear you talk about your body like that again. Are we clear?"

"Yes," Evie breathes, her hands latching onto my biceps.

I slant my mouth over hers again and drag her to the edge of the counter so I can feel her against me. She wraps her arms around my neck and legs around my waist, pulling me closer. I stroke her tongue with mine, swallowing every needy little moan she makes. I grind my hips against her pussy, and she jerks her mouth away.

"I want to taste your pussy again, angel," I whisper against her lips. I slide my hands under her shirt, pausing to give her time to change her mind.

"Right here?" she asks.

"What better place than here to eat my favorite meal?" I reply. She takes a deep breath and lifts her arms over her head. "That's my girl," I praise, pulling her shirt over her head. I work on her bra, letting those gorgeous tits free. Her hands slide under my shirt, so I fist the back and pull it over my head. Evie's hands slide up my pecs, and I can feel the muscles bunching under the skin at her touch. I place a hand on her chest and gently push until she's lying on the island. I hook my hands in her shorts and panties. "Lift your hips," I encourage and almost groan when she complies. I peel them down her legs.

I place her feet on the counter. "Spread your legs wide for me, angel," I say gruffly. She whimpers, and then her knees fall apart. "Wider," I demand. She spreads her feet further apart and bares her pussy to me.

I slide my hands up her thighs and watch goosebumps pop up on her skin. Leaning down, I grab a handful of her thick hips and jerk her to my mouth.

"Oh," Evie moans, her hand flying to my head.

I lick from the entrance of her pussy to her clit, groaning when her taste explodes on my tongue. I nip, lick, and suck her clit until she's grinding down on my face. Taking two fingers, I slide them inside her, twist them up for that magic spot, and rub it relentlessly. Evie's making all kinds of noises, making my cock throb, begging me to put it into action. Her fingers keep trying to find purchase on my buzzed-off hair to drag me closer. Her hips are rotating, fucking herself onto my fingers. I would never get enough of her taste.

"Gray," Evie moans, her thighs locking around my head. I look up, and her eyes are locked on my face, watching everything I'm doing to her.

Evie's pussy starts pulsing around my fingers, signaling she's getting close. I suck her clit into my mouth hard and gently bite down. "Gray!" Evie explodes with a scream, echoing around the kitchen.

I kiss the inside of her thigh and gently pull my fingers out. She sits up on her elbows, and I grin. "I'm not done with you yet," I say.

Taking the wetness from her pussy, I drag it to her back hole. "What are you doing?" Evie asks breathlessly.

"Anyone ever had you here, angel?" I ask, teasing her asshole with my finger.

"No."

"I'm going to," I declare. "Not tonight because I want to make sure you're ready, but soon."

"I want you to," Evie says huskily, making my eyes snap to hers. "I want…"

"Tell me," I say, rubbing my fingers back over her sensitive clit. Her whole body shudders on a moan.

"I want to be…" she takes a deep breath. "I want to be fucked at the same time."

I lift both brows. "You want one of us in your pussy, and one of us in your ass?" I clarify.

"And my mouth," *Holy fucking shit.* Innocent Evie has left the building.

"We can make that happen, angel," I say. I sit her up on the counter and help her to her feet. I scoop up her clothes, grab her hand, and pull her toward the stairs.

"Where are we going?" Evie asks with a breathless giggle.

"My room," I tell her. I have what we need in there.

As soon as I shut the door, I'm on her again, kissing her like my life depended on it. I get her on the bed and shed my clothes. I stretch my body over hers, letting my chest rub against her hard nipples.

"Fuck me," Evie whispers, rubbing her wet pussy against my cock.

"Damn, angel," I groan, reaching over into my bedside table and pulling out a condom. I make quick work of rolling it down my cock. I notch it at her entrance, lock my eyes with hers, and start to slide inside. "Holy shit, you feel good," I pant. I tease her with just the head of my cock, rocking my hips back and forth.

"Please," Evie moans.

"You want my cock?"

"Yes."

I search her eyes and see nothing but lust there. I slam my hips forward, burying myself in one firm stroke. Evie's back bows on a moan, her fingernails digging into my back.

"Gray! Holy shit."

"I'm going to make you come on my dick," I say. "Then I'm going to put you on your hands and knees. You know why?" She shakes her head. "I'm going to fuck you again from behind while I play with that gorgeous ass."

I start to move in deep, shallow thrusts. Evie's hands are sliding all over my back, her heels digging into my ass, urging me on. I've never felt a pussy like this. She fits around me like a glove, like she was made just for my cock. She is so fucking wet for me.

"Harder, Gray, please," Evie moans.

Bracing one hand by her head and anchoring one hand on her hip, I pull out and slam into her.

"Yes, yes, yes," Evie chants, her eyes fluttering closed.

"Open your eyes. I want to see them when you come for me."

Her eyes snap open, locking onto mine. I start pistoning my hips, setting a relentless pace, my thighs slapping against hers.

"Fuck, angel," I grunt. "If heaven exists, it's between your thighs."

Removing my hand from her hip, I place it on her stomach right above her pussy, and push down, causing my cock to scrape her g-spot harder.

"Oh god," Evie moans, clamping down on me.

"That's it. Come for me," I demand.

Her eyes darken, and she moans so deep I start twitching inside her. I can't come just yet; I need to fulfill my promise to her. Her body tightens up, and she lets go with a scream. "Gray!"

I stroke in and out a few times before pulling out. "Hands and knees, angel," I say, helping her get situated. "Hold on," I warn.

She locks her arms when I line back up and sink my hands into her hips. I jerk her back at the same time as I shove my hips forward, burying myself to the hilt. "Fuck, that feels good," Evie breathes.

I reach over into the table again and grab the bottle of lube. "Are you sure you want to do this?"

"Yes, please," Evie says, working herself on my cock. My palm twitches to slap her ass to stop her, but I don't think she is ready for that. Yet.

I squirt a generous amount onto my fingers, recap the bottle, and toss it on the bed. I run my fingers between her ass cheeks, and her whole body tenses. "You have to relax," I soothe, running my other hand up her back. "I'll make it feel good, angel. You just have to trust me."

She releases a shuddering breath. "I do trust you."

"Good," I say hoarsely, kissing her spine. She doesn't know what that means to me. I slide my fingers back and forth over her back hole until I feel her start to relax. As soon as she does, I push my middle finger past the resistance. Her breathing speeds up, her body tensing. "You're doing so good," I praise, working my finger slowly. I run my other hand underneath her, circling her clit in tight circles. Her hips start rolling with me, so I slide a second finger in.

Her back bows. "Gray," Evie groans. "It feels..." I fuck her back hole slowly with my fingers while she tries to figure out what it feels like. I know the moment she realizes it feels good. Her pussy clamps down on my cock so hard I have to take several breaths to keep from coming.

"It feels what, angel?" I ask. I set a rhythm, rubbing her clit, fucking her pussy in slow strokes, and fingering her ass, making her body feel every sensation at once.

"Good. I feel so full," Evie pants, working her hips back for more.

Goddamn, she is going to undo me. "Wait until one of us fucks this pretty ass. You're so fucking tight, angel," I say raggedly. I pull halfway out of her pussy, watching the whole time. "Fuck my cock."

Evie moans deep in her throat and pushes back against me. I start rubbing her clit faster and letting my fingers sink deeper into her ass while she takes what she needs from my cock. She starts moving faster, and I know she's ready. I slam my hips forward the next time she pushes back, grunting on impact. Evie starts begging, and my control snaps. I start hammering into her, letting my fingers work into her in time with my thrusts.

"You going to come, angel?" I rasp.

"Yes. Oh, fuck, Gray," Evie never lets up, pushing her hips back, taking every hard thrust like she was meant for me. Her fingers curl into the blankets; her head drops back on her shoulders. "GRAY!"

Her pussy squeezes my cock so hard from her release that I can't hold back. I gently pull my fingers from her ass and lock both hands on her hips. I fuck her ruthlessly through her orgasm, causing another to rip through her right on the heels of the first. My balls draw up painfully; my fingers tighten on her hips. I bury myself as far as I can go. "Angel," I groan out my release.

Evie's legs give out from underneath her, almost taking me with her. I stop myself with one hand beside her head and pull my cock free with a groan. I peel the condom off, knot it, and throw it into the wastebasket. I kiss Evie's cheek, slide off the bed, and go wash my hands.

When I come back, she's sitting on the side of the bed, staring at the door, looking uncertain as hell. Was I too rough with her? Guilt slams into my chest before I can stop it. "Angel," I say softly. "Are you ok?"

She turns those brown eyes on me, and I want to fall to her feet and apologize. I knew I shouldn't get involved with her. I wasn't easy in bed; just ask Mateo. But he could handle it. "I didn't know if you would want me to stay with you or not. I didn't know what to do," she finally answers. That isn't what I was expecting her to say.

I climb onto the bed and pull her to lie with me, rearranging her on my chest. "I'm not letting you go tonight, angel. Of course, I want you to stay," I answer. I flatten my palm on the base of her spine and drag her closer.

She looks at me with that blinding smile, gently kissing my lips. "This was amazing," she says, laying her head back on my chest.

Evie traces my tattoo with her finger until her breathing evens out, and I know she fell asleep. I don't sleep in the same bed with anyone due to the nightmares, but no way was I kicking her out.

I would stay awake for the rest of the night just to feel her against me.

I STRETCH my arms out the following day and encounter a body. My head snaps down, and it takes a second for my brain to catch up.

Evie is lying across my chest, her leg is thrown over mine, and she's still breathing softly. And she's still blissfully naked.

Did I sleep all night without nightmares?

I look at the clock beside my bed, and my eyes widen in surprise. It's ten o'clock in the morning. I never sleep this late or for that many hours at a time. Last night slams into me, remembering everything I did to Evie's delicious body. She was responsive, and she took everything I had to give.

I look back at the sleeping girl in my arms, amazed she trusted me so much.

She stirs and looks up at me with sleepy eyes. "Hi," she says softly with a smile.

I peck her lips. "Good morning," I respond.

She snuggles back into my chest. "You make a really good pillow," she remarks, making me laugh.

"Anytime you want to use me as your pillow, angel, you know where to find me," I say. Our stomachs start grumbling at the same time, making us both laugh. "I think we need to go find breakfast," I suggest.

"Five more minutes," she mutters. Two seconds later, her stomach growls again.

I pat her ass. "Okay, breakfast time," I insist.

She sits up with a huff. "Fine, Mr. Bossy," she snarks.

"I'll show you, Mr. Bossy," I growl playfully and lunge for her. She lets out a shrieking laugh, trying to get away. I pull her underneath me, pinning her to the bed. My cock hardens instantly, sliding across her pussy.

"It looks like someone else is awake," Evie says breathlessly. She scrapes her fingernails down my sides, and I slant my mouth over hers with a groan. She widens her legs to accommodate my hips, grinding herself against me.

"Fuck," I gasp, pulling my mouth from hers. Feeling her wet bare pussy rubbing against me makes me think about things I shouldn't. I want to know what she feels like with nothing between us, something I've never wanted with another woman.

"You feel so good, Gray," Evie moans when I slide my cock through her slit.

Fuck it. I reach between us and line my cock up. "I'm clean," I rasp, rubbing the head of my cock against her clit.

"Me too," Evie gasps.

"I'll pull out," I promise and slide home in one firm push. "Oh, fuck," I groan. Fucking her last night was amazing; feeling her pussy bare is a whole other experience. It is so wet and hot, and it feels like she is squeezing me harder. No fucking way am I going to last. I start rocking my hips, letting my pubic bone grind against her clit.

"I can feel everything," Evie moans, rocking her hips with mine.

I put one arm under her head and lock my other hand on her hip. We start moving together, letting our releases build at a slow rate.

We move with eyes locked, sweat gathering on our bodies until I feel the first sign of her orgasm. "Come for me, angel," I say softly.

"Gray," Evie moans, her back arching. Her release washes over her gently. And I realize I've never seen a woman come like that. I always fucked hard and fast; I never made love. But if I could see that euphoric look on her face again, I would make love to her like this again.

"You're so beautiful when you come for me," I whisper, feeling my release building. I thrust in and out a few times before reluctantly pulling from her pussy. I wrap my hand around my cock and stroke hard. "Open for me," I demand, and her mouth drops open. I move up on my knees until I'm straddling her chest. "Stick out your tongue," I rasp. As soon as her tongue drops out, I lay the head of my cock on it, still stroking. I watch jet after jet shoot into her mouth, her eyes locked on me the whole time. "Swallow," I tell her and watch with avid fascination as she does. I lean down and kiss her slowly, tasting myself on her tongue.

"Does that count as breakfast?" Evie asks when I pull back.

I bark a laugh and climb off the bed, pulling her to her feet. Wrapping my arms around her, I kiss her forehead. "No, it doesn't. Let's get cleaned up and go eat,"

I take her by her hand and lead her to my bathroom, turning the shower on. When it's the right temperature, I pull her in with me and spend time washing her body gently. I silently thank her for trusting me with my body because the words are locked in my throat.

I've never spent time with anyone like this except for Mateo. But he has a way of drawing you in, no matter how hard you try not to feel anything.

Exactly like Evie is doing right now.

CHAPTER 44
MICAH

I watch Evie and Gray finally make their appearance. I look closer at Gray and realize it's the first time I've seen him so relaxed. I stand when they enter the living room; Evie squeezes Gray's hand and comes straight to me, wrapping her arms around my waist.

"Morning, *la mia stella*," I say, wrapping my arms around her and kissing the top of her head.

"Morning," she replies, looking up at me. I can't resist tasting her lips, so I seal my mouth over hers, kissing her softly.

Pulling back, I peck her lips one more time. "I left you guys some food in the fridge," I tell her, knowing she would be hungry after what I witnessed last night. I lean down to her ear. "Don't worry, I cleaned the island off," I whisper.

Evie jerks back with a gasp, her face going beet red. "You saw that?"

I push her hair behind her ear. "Yes, I did. You know I don't sleep well. Did Gray treat you good last night?" I can see Gray blushing from here. I have to try like hell not to laugh at the fact that they are both the same shade of red.

"He did," Evie replies, getting up on her tiptoes to reach my ear. "He did dirty things to me," she whispers.

"Like what?" I ask, turned the fuck on that she is sharing information. I love that she feels comfortable enough to do so.

She bites that plump bottom lip. "He played with my ass," she answers.

I jerk back to look at her face and raise a brow. "Did you like it?" I ask, and she nods. I run my hand down her ass, and she shivers. "That's good to know, *la mia stella,* because I have plans for this ass." I peck her lips again. "Now, go eat."

"You're bossy, too," she says, wrinkling her nose. She spins on her heel, flips her hair over her shoulder, and sashays her way to Gray.

"And you're fucking sassy," I retort, making her laugh.

"You remember the last time you called someone bossy, angel?" Gray asks, throwing an arm around her shoulders.

"Oh, I remember very clearly," Evie answers, disappearing around the corner with Gray. I'd love to know what happened.

While they eat, I go to Van's office and get some work done. As soon as I sit down, my phone rings, and I suppress a groan when I see the caller id. I knew if I avoided her, she would know something was up. There is no doubt anymore that my mother was behind the bugs in my house. I had no idea what to say when Hartley confirmed my mother had been in contact with the number Dom had for Aaron. There were multiple incoming and outgoing calls. My question is, how the hell did he even find out who my mother was?

"Hello?"

"Hello, Micah," my mother says softly, and it already has my defenses up. "I want to apologize for how I acted."

"And I told you I never wanted to hear from you again. What do you want?"

"I told you to apologize."

"Bullshit," I bark, done with her shit. "Do you want the money? Is that it? Because I'm done with that shit."

"That is no way to talk to your mother!"

I laugh without humor. "My mother? You haven't been shit to me. You have no idea how Father raised me or what I went through. You didn't give a fuck then, and you don't give a fuck now. All I am to you is money. Don't call me again." I sling my phone on the desk, pissed that I had let her get by with it for as long as I did. Then she turned around and fucking betrayed me. People have died for a lot less at my hands.

"Micah." I look up at Evie's soft voice and wave her over.

"What's wrong, *la mia stella*?"

She surprises me by sitting on my lap and wrapping her arms around my neck. "You just look like you needed this."

I squeeze her tighter and swallow the lump in my throat. "I did. More than you know," I admit.

We stay locked in that embrace for a while, neither of us talking. How in the hell could this girl offer so much comfort just from a damn hug?

I've thought about what Les said since yesterday and have no idea what to do.

Les was right, though. Evie deserves forever.

Could we really give that to her? Would she even want it when we told her the truth? She's openly said she didn't like the person Aaron was. How will she react when she finds out we are worse? No, we don't abuse women and are quiet about what we do, but that doesn't make us any better. We are criminals. And that didn't bother me until I looked into Evie's brown eyes.

Evie pulls back from the hug and cups my face in her hands. "I know how much it sucks to want your mom to love you. And I also know how much it sucks to cut her off. I miss my mom, but the day I left was the best decision I ever made. I'm so sorry for what your mom is doing to you, Micah, and I wish I could make it better."

"You do make it better," I say gruffly. "Just by existing."

I lean in to kiss her, not to start anything, just to feel her lips moving against mine. The more I kiss her, the more I feel my body relax and my mind settles.

If that doesn't spell trouble, I don't know what the fuck does.

"I want Evie to stay, and I want to tell her the truth," I declare to the guys after Evie went outside to the patio. "Les was right." I had already talked to Van because I felt he needed to know where my head was before talking to the rest of them. My time with Evie in the office solidified what I wanted.

"What changed your mind?" Mateo asks.

"Mother called," I answer. Van's jaw tightens even though he knows this part. "Evie heard the conversation and came to me."

"And she made it feel like it was okay?" Mateo guesses.

"Yeah." I run my fingers through my hair. "I won't say anything until we all agree."

Hartley shrugs. "You already know my stance."

"If you think it's best, then I agree," Van says.

All eyes turn to Gray. He seemed the most hesitant to tell her who he was. Gray swallows. "We can tell her."

"What about her staying?" Mateo asks, looking around the living room at us.

"I think we take it one step at a time," Van says. "We need to tell her the truth before we start talking about the future."

"She's going to freak out, isn't she?" Mateo asks.

I shrug. "We don't know that. We've proved we aren't like Aaron."

"Aren't we, though?" Gray asks, voicing my concerns from earlier. "We might not be exactly like him, but we're still fucking criminals. Evie doesn't belong in this world."

"I think we need to let Evie make that decision," Mateo says defensively. "Yes, we're on the wrong side of the law, but no one would ever treat her better than we can."

"Mateo's right," I agree. "She's been here not even two weeks, and she's made such a fucking difference in a bunch of miserable assholes. She's the *good* that we need to balance out the bad." I look at Hartley. "I heard what you did for Mateo. Thank you."

"No thanks needed," Hartley sighs. "I want to apologize for everything I thought about you guys. Mateo said something to me yesterday, and it's time that it fucking happened. I have some shit to work through, but I'm willing to give this a try." Hartley shrugs. "If you still want me here. I know Evie is safe with you guys, and I also know you don't particularly want me here. I would step off if she got what she wanted."

Van gives me a look, knowing I'm the one still holding back from accepting Hartley into the fold. "The past is the past. It won't ever be mentioned again. You're in, but you need to move past it now." I tell him.

Hartley nods. "I know. I'm working on it."

"I say we take Evie out tonight. Show her a good fucking time. Then tomorrow, we tell her," Mateo suggests. We all nod in agreement. They all go do their own thing, leaving me with Van.

"You're still okay with this?" I ask, grabbing his hand.

"I'm fine with it, *mi rey*. Stop worrying."

"I don't want you to think this changes anything between us. I love you, and that will never change."

"I love you too, and I know that. But if you do this with her, you can't hold back because of me. She deserves the full Micah treatment."

I chuckle. "What's the full Micah treatment?"

"The Micah you become when you let your walls down."

"Do you think this is crazy?" I wonder. "We just met her."

"I'm going to tell you like I told Mateo. We don't get to pick the timeline. Sometimes when you know, you just know. I don't think this is any different."

"Are you in the same place?"

Van sighs. "Not yet."

"Maybe *you* should let your walls down," I say gently. I am the reason Van has those walls because when I first met him, he was an open book. The heartbreak I put him through caused him to be cautious, and I hate that I did that to him. I also know that's the reason he hasn't had sex with her yet.

I am excited about this new future, but I would never pick Evie over Van.

No matter how much it would hurt to let her go.

CHAPTER 45
EVIE

I t truly hurt me to hear how hurt Micah is over his mom. He covers it up with anger, but his blue eyes tell a different story.

My feet were moving before I knew what I was doing when I heard what he was saying to her. I just felt compelled to make him feel better. I was getting more and more intertwined with these guys, and I knew when I had to leave, it was going to hurt. I've thought nonstop about what Les and Bridget said about me staying, but none of the guys have hinted at anything more than what it is. Except maybe Mateo, but I'm still not sure about that.

My phone pings with a message, and my heart starts beating double time. Only a few have this number.

I close my eyes and pick up, hoping it's not something from Aaron. I crack an eye open and smile when I see Mateo's name on the screen. I swipe it open.

MATEO

Hey, buttercup.

Hey.

Why are you texting me from inside the house?

Shhh. Don't ruin my fun.

Where are you?

By the pool.

It's the same place I always am if I'm not with one of the guys.

What are you wearing?

Shorts and a tank top.

I bite my lip, trying to work up the nerve to play this game with him.

What are you wearing?

'image sent'

Holy shit. It's a picture of a shirtless Mateo from the neck down, covered in sweat, shorts sitting low on his hips, showing off his v-line. I tug my tank top down, so my boobs practically fall out and snap a picture. Giggling to myself, I load it to our chat screen. I hit send and immediately panic when the bubbles that say he's typing keep popping up and disappearing. What if he doesn't like it? It isn't the most flattering position for me to send a picture.

The absolutely nasty fucking things I want to do to you right now.

These guys have made me want to do things I've never even considered. I never thought I would be naked in front of multiple men or have someone's fingers in my ass. But now that I have gotten a taste, I want *more*. They have awakened something in me, and I want to explore that. With them. My heart starts beating double time.

Like what?

Gray told me he played with your ass last night. Tell me, buttercup, did you like it?

Yes.

378

Good because I got something for you today.

'image sent'

I look at the picture for the longest time and have no idea what it is. When I'm about to ask, he answers the question for me, and my mouth drops open.

It's a butt plug. It's to help stretch you out and make it easier to take one of our cocks. Is that what you want, buttercup? One of our cocks filling that gorgeous ass?

Or do you want one of us in your ass while another is railing that pussy?

I feel my face heat, and my panties are embarrassingly wet from just the image he is creating. Feeling bold since we are messaging, I tell him what I want.

I want that so bad. I want to feel you guys everywhere.

Are you wet thinking about it? Is your clit throbbing, begging for you to touch it?

Yes.

Are you hard thinking about it?

'image sent'

I've never in my life gotten a nude picture of anyone. And to get one from someone as sexy as Mateo couldn't have made my first any better. It looks like he's lying in bed, his fist wrapped around himself. More than a little turned on by this game, I slip into the shower Mateo has by his pool. I shut the curtain, take my clothes off, and sit on the bench. I have to take so many calming breaths that I feel like I will pass out, which is stupid. Mateo has seen me naked in person more than once. What is the harm in a picture? I angle the phone away from my face like he did, so it just shows from my boobs to the tops of my thighs. I lean against the wall, brace my feet on the edge of the bench, and spread my legs wide.

'image sent'

Goddamn, buttercup. Play with your pussy for me.

I slide my hand between my thighs and snap another picture.

'image sent'

I'm so hard for you right now. You want to know my ultimate fantasy, buttercup?

Yes.

My fingers are idly stroking my clit, letting his words wash over me.

I want all of us to take you at the same time. One in your pussy, one in your ass, one in your mouth. We could take turns making you come over and over until you are so worn out, and only then would we let ourselves come.

All over you. Marking you. Making you ours. Is that what you want?

Ours? My breath hitches, and I start rubbing faster, using what the guys have shown me to pleasure myself. The scene plays out in my head, and I have to bite my lip to stop the moan.

I want that, Mateo. Please.

You like begging for cock? Is that needy pussy begging for one of us to fill it up?

It is. Please, Mateo.

Mateo: Please what?

Oh god, he's going to make me say it.

I want your cock to fill up my needy pussy.

While I'm in your pussy, who's in your ass?

The answer comes before I can even think. I could feel my orgasm building slowly just from reading his words.

Evander.

You filthy girl. You want my brother and me to fuck you at the same time?

I want that too. You know what else I want? Picture this, buttercup.

While I'm fucking you, Gray can fuck me.

While Van is fucking that sweet tight ass, Micah can fuck him. Hartley can shove that pierced cock right down your throat. Tell me you want that.

I want that.

My hips are rolling in time with my fingers now. I want that so fucking bad. Mateo just put everything I was thinking but couldn't say into words for me.

'video sent'

I press play on the video and can't stop the moan that escapes. Mateo is stroking his cock in a tight fist, and you can hear his heavy breathing as he does. I watch his abs tighten, and as he comes all over his stomach, he groans out my name. Not giving a fuck anymore, I open my camera, switch to video, and record myself masturbating for him. It doesn't take long before my back arches, and I say his name as I come. It's the first time in my life I've ever gotten myself off.

'video sent'

You're so fucking hot. Did you come just thinking about all the cocks you're going to get?

Yes.

381

Good girl.

You want to be my good girl, buttercup?

I do.

Good. Come to my room.

I pull my clothes back on and make my way into the house. Straight to Mateo's room.

I sɪᴛ down at the dining room table beside a grinning Mateo. When I got to his room, he placed his surprise inside me while he ate my pussy. Now I am sitting at the table with all of them with a butt plug in. It doesn't hurt at all. Every time I move a certain way, it would send aftershocks of pleasure through me, keeping me in a constant state of arousal. After my and Mateo's sexting conversation, all I could see are the images he put in my head about being with all of them at the same time.

My time with Gray opened the door, and Mateo pushed it wide open. I am still slightly sore from Gray's punishing thrusts, but it hurts in a good way. I can still remember the feeling of him sinking in me bare. I didn't use a condom with Hartley by the pool, but all I could feel from him were his piercings. I felt every vein in Gray's cock. They both felt so good like that.

Mateo squeezes my thigh, and his grin widens when I turn to him. I can imagine my red face is giving away everything I am thinking.

"Dude, can you pass me the salt?" Mateo asks. We just sat down to enjoy the meal Micah has prepared. Micah sends Mateo such a scathing look that I want to hide under the table.

"You aren't ruining my food with salt," Micah grinds out, glaring at Mateo. "The only salt you'll get is when you lick it from my balls."

A laugh busts out of me before I can stop it. I slap a hand over my mouth, but it's no use.

"Whip them out, baby. Don't think I won't lick you from your asshole to the tip of your dick," Mateo replies, completely unfazed.

I'm laughing so hard now that I have tears rolling down my face. Evander and Hartley choke on their food at the same time, and Gray's mouth is hanging wide open.

Micah's eyes narrow. "Don't think I won't shove my dick down your throat to shut you up," Micah retorts.

"You think that's a punishment? I've dreamed of what your cock would taste like," Mateo says with a raised brow.

Is it hot in here, or is it just me?

"Are you really hitting on my boyfriend right in front of me?" Evander asks with a chuckle.

Mateo snorts. "Don't act like you haven't thought about us fucking him at the same time."

"This just got really interesting," Hartley comments, sitting back in his chair.

"Oh my god!" I exclaim. "Are you blushing?!" I ask Micah when I see his cheeks get a little pink.

Evander laughs. "He is," he says, getting a closer look.

Micah puts his hand on Evander's face and shoves him away. "I don't blush," Micah grumbles.

"What's the matter, Micah?" Mateo asks, with that signature grin saying he's up to no good. "You thought about it, didn't you?"

"Absolutely not," Micah says. "Shut up and eat."

Mateo winks at me before digging into his food. I love that they can still be themselves around me. Their banter always has me in stitches.

Micah asked me earlier what my favorite food was, and I didn't think anything of it. Now, I am sitting here eating homemade chicken fettuccine alfredo because that's what my answer was.

"We have to run to Skyline after dinner," Evander says once he's done eating.

"Would you want to go, *la mia stella*?" Micah asks.

I frown. "What about what happened last time?" The last time we all went out, we got shot at.

"Let us handle that," Micah says. "You go find something to wear."

"It's casual," Mateo soothes, sensing my nervousness. I didn't know how to do my makeup and hair like Bridget did if it was something fancy. He leans in close. "Wear a dress and your plug," Mateo whispers.

"Okay," I whisper back, already feeling my face heat up.

"Good girl," Mateo says quietly, just for my ears.

My breath catches when I look into his eyes. The pupil has almost completely taken over the iris, showing how turned on he is.

I smile at the guys and make my way to the bedroom. I go into my walk-in closet and dial Bridget.

"Hey, girl!" she answers on the second ring.

"Hey," I smile. "I need your help. We're going to Skyline tonight, and I have no idea what to wear."

"I got you. Show me what you have."

I flip it to a video call and show her all the clothes Mateo bought me that day.

"That one," Bridget declares. "Girl, your tits will look so good in that. Wear it with some white wedges. Do you have a thong? Because that's going to show a serious panty line."

I snort. "Does my ass look like it's made for a thong?"

"Your ass is the definition of who should wear a thong," Bridget retorts, making me laugh. "If you don't have a thong, don't wear panties with it."

"I can't do that," I hiss.

"Why not? It will be like your own little secret all night. You know, unless you want a quickie with one of the five hot as fuck men you're going with. Then all you have to do is flip it up." Bridget says.

"You are so bad," I laugh.

"You love me," she says, making kissy faces.

"I do," I say honestly. I've never had a friend like Bridget and Les. It makes me sad to think about me leaving them. "I have to get dressed."

"Keep your hair down, put on some mascara and that pink lipstick. Send me a pic of the finished product."

"Thank you!"

"You're welcome. Love ya!" Bridget says and ends the call.

The dress she picked out is a dark purple that is long with a split up one leg. It is a tube top style I would never have worn until I met the guys.

I do everything she says and send her a mirror picture.

BRIDGET

OMG! You look amazing. Get some for me tonight.

Haha, love ya.

Love ya too. Have fun!

I have a really good feeling about tonight.

CHAPTER 46
MATEO

We've been at Skyline for ten minutes, and I already wanted to drag Evie out of here. When she walked into the living room in the purple dress, I almost bent her over the fucking couch. I am excited and nervous about tonight because we are going to give her what she wants, what we've all wanted. But tomorrow, shit is going to hit the fan. Plus, I still have to tell her me and Hartley burned down her apartment building.

Getting here undetected was an issue, and I hoped we pulled it off. The last thing we needed was for something else to happen on our watch. We had a couple of our guards drive our usual cars while we left in a nondescript blacked-out limo SUV. The guards usually used it, so we thought Aaron and his gang of assholes would think it was just them.

I am standing to the side, watching Evie order drinks at the bar like a creep, but I couldn't take my eyes off her. A guy walks up beside her, giving her a slow once over with his eyes while her head is turned. Evie turns slowly toward him and says something with a polite smile. I decide to stay back and see how she handles it.

"What are you doing?" Micah asks from behind me.

"Just watch," I answer.

The guy says something else, and Evie shakes her head, gesturing around. He reaches up and runs his fingers down her arm, and her whole body goes tense. *That's enough.*

Micah and I move at the same time. But we don't make it in time.

"Get your goddamn hand off her before you lose it," Van growls, stepping behind her. Micah and I exchange a smile, letting Van handle it.

"Who the fuck are you?" The guy sneers.

Van pulls Evie to his chest with an arm around her waist, and her whole body relaxes. "I'm hers," Van barks, making my eyebrows hit my hairline. *Interesting turn of events.* I look at Micah, and he has the same expression.

"Bitch isn't even worth it," the guy mutters. Van pulls Evie to the side, grabs the guy by the back of the neck, and slams his face into the bar.

"What did you just say?" Van asks in a deadly tone. Van rarely loses his temper, but it's always epic when he does. I pull Evie to my side and kiss the top of her head.

"Aren't you going to stop him?" Evie asks quietly.

"Nope," Micah and I answer at the same time.

"I didn't know she was with you!" the guy insists.

"Funny because I very plainly heard her tell you she was here with someone," Van growls in his face. "She just failed to mention there are five of us, you motherfucker."

Security starts walking up, and I wave them away. Van could handle this.

"Apologize, asshole," I say, egging it on.

"I'm sorry!"

"Get the fuck out of my bar and don't come back," Van says, pulling the guy to stand by his neck. He shoves him forward right about the time Hartley walks up. The guy bounces off Hartley's chest, and his ass hits the floor.

I can't hold the laugh back anymore, and I lose it. I hear Evie try to stifle a giggle, making me laugh harder.

"You heard him," Hartley barks, taking a step forward.

The guy scrambles backward and jumps to his feet, pushing through the crowd.

"Are you okay?" Van says, turning to Evie.

"I'm fine," she assures him. Van nods and follows to make sure the guy really left.

"He didn't have to do that," Evie says, looking at me over her shoulder.

"Yes, he did," I insist. "Have I told you how good you look, buttercup?" I ask, sliding my arms around Evie from behind.

She laughs. "Yes. A couple of times," she answers.

"Did you wear it?" I whisper.

"Yes," she whispers back. It is fucking killing me knowing she has a butt plug in, the one I put there.

When I started sexting her, I never expected her to reply the way she did or agree to the plug. But I was damn glad she did. Before we left the house, I changed it for a bigger one, and this one came with a little surprise.

Gray walks up and props himself against the bar, and I take a minute to check him out, too. He has a black t-shirt stretched across his huge chest, black jeans molded to his thighs, and black boots.

"He looks sexy, doesn't he?" I ask Evie, making her giggle.

"He does," she agrees. "You all do."

Micah and Evander are standing to the side, whispering to each other. Micah has on a baby blue v-neck and stonewashed jeans. Evander wore a v-neck almost the same color as Evie's dress and black jeans. I threw on a pair of faded jeans and a long-sleeved button-up with the sleeves rolled up. Hartley has a pair of jeans on that I've checked his ass out in more than once, and a black t-shirt that looks like his biceps would bust out of.

"None of us compare to you," I tell Evie honestly. We've gotten more than one curious glance when we all walked in, mostly because I couldn't keep my hands off her. I've never brought anyone I've ever been involved with to my place of business, but I wanted everyone here to know she is *mine*.

My conversation with Van made me feel better about my strong feelings about Evie. Because the truth is, I am falling in love with her if I haven't already. When she casually said she would be gone soon, I was gripped with such sadness that it surprised me. One way or the other, Evie is staying with us.

"Dance with me," I say, then grab Evie's hand and pull her to the dance floor.

"I can't dance!" Evie laughs breathlessly.

"Just follow my lead," I encourage, pulling her against my body. She wraps her arms around my neck with a smile. I slide my hands down until the tips of my fingers are resting on her ass.

We dance to several faster songs, just enjoying being pressed against each other. When *Slow Motion* by Juvenile comes on, I spin her so my chest is molded to her back. I grab her hips and start swaying her hips with mine. She wraps one arm around my neck, getting into the music.

"I can feel how hard you are," Evie says, grinding her ass against me.

"All for you, buttercup," I promise, kissing the side of her neck. "I have a surprise for you," I whisper against her neck, making her shiver. I reach into my pocket for the remote to her new butt plug and click it once. I know the second it starts vibrating on the lowest setting. Her breath catches, and she grinds harder against me. "How does that feel?" I ask.

"It feels different," she answers breathlessly.

I slide my hand up the slit in her dress, rubbing her thigh. "I want to fuck you so bad right now," I say hoarsely.

Evie moans low in her throat, and her head hits my chest.

Hartley steps in front of her, and she pulls him closer. "Dance with us," she says.

He raises an eyebrow but starts moving with us. "Why's your face so red, princess?" I was going to let her answer this question with a little encouragement. I flick the remote again, making it vibrate harder.

"Oh fuck," Evie chokes, fingers gripping Hartley's shirt.

"What's he doing to you?" Hartley says, leaning down close to her ear.

Before she can answer, Gray steps to our side with Micah and Evander on the other side, with Micah plastered to Van's back.

"Tell them what I'm doing to you, buttercup?" I encourage.

"I have a butt plug in," Evie says breathlessly. "And it vibrates."

"Does it feel good, angel?" Gray asks gruffly.

"Yes," Evie moans.

"Fuck," Micah groans.

I slide my hand further up her thigh since we have her blocked in, and no one can see what I'm about to do. She doesn't stop me, so I move her dress to the side, and when my hand slides against her bare pussy, I almost swallow my tongue.

"Where are your panties?" I ask, my breathing already speeding up.

"I must have forgotten them," Evie answers, but I can see her smile.

Hartley's green eyes flair. "You've been wearing that sinfully hot dress since we got here with no panties and a butt plug?" Evie nods, and he seals his lips over hers.

While he has her mouth busy, I start rubbing her clit in tight circles. She wanted to explore more, and there is no better way than getting off in a public place where you could get caught at any time.

"You're so wet, buttercup," I say. "Is that from your ass being full?"

She pulls back from Hartley, grinding her hips between us. "Yes," she answers.

"We need to get the fuck out of here," Van says. I look at him and quirk an eyebrow. He nods his head down. I look down and watch Evie's hand massaging him through his jeans.

"I agree," Gray says, just as gruff as Van. Evie's hand is also rubbing his cock through his jeans.

"I'm going to make you come, right here," I tell Evie, kissing her neck. "Then we'll take you home, and you'll get your wish. Is that what you want, greedy girl? You want all our cocks tonight?"

"Mateo," Evie moans. "Yes, please."

I feel a hand slide against mine and look into Hartley's eyes. He slides his fingers inside of her while I rub her clit. We work her together until she gets so loud that Hartley has to seal his lips over hers again. Her back bows against my chest as she lets go.

Hartley and I remove our fingers; I smooth her dress back down.

Hartley rubs his finger that was just buried in her pussy against her lips. "Lick your lips and taste yourself, princess. See how good you taste," Hartley says, and I almost come on the spot. He sucks one of his fingers into his mouth, and I watch as Evie's tongue snakes out and licks her taste from her lips.

"Good girl," I whisper, making her moan. "You ready to go?"

She nods rapidly. I take her hand, turn the vibrations on her butt plug off, and lead her to the back of the bar where we parked. Our security goes out first to make sure the coast is clear before we load back into the SUV. "Make sure we aren't followed," Van orders the guard.

As soon as the backdoor shuts, the sexual tension could choke you. Evie's chest is heaving, and she looks all the way turned on, smashed between Van and Micah.

"This is how it's going to go," Van says, turning to face her. "You don't want this. You tell us anytime, and it stops. No harm at all. This is about you. Do you understand?"

She sinks her teeth into that bottom lip and nods. I watch Van search her face for any uncertainty, and when he doesn't find any, he smashes his lips against hers for a quick kiss.

"We need to get a few things out of the way," Van says, waiting for everyone to nod. "Do you want us leading this, or do you want to?"

"You guys," Evie answers.

"Condoms?" Van asks. "I'm clean." Everyone else answers, and my heart is beating out of control at the thought of feeling her bare.

"I'm clean too," Evie says, looking around the SUV.

"Birth control?" Micah asks. Evie and Hartley exchange a look, making me frown.

"I was told when I was younger that I can't have kids," Evie says quietly. We decide not to push the issue. I'm sure she doesn't want to think about that right now.

"To clarify, you don't want us to wear condoms?" Van asks, just to make sure.

"No condoms," Evie says breathlessly.

Van's hands go to his jeans, and Evie's eyes take it all in when he pulls his cock free. "Ride my cock, *pequena reina*," Van demands.

Evie bites her lip again but swings her leg over Van's. He pulls her dress to one side from the split and bunches it at her waist in his fist. She reaches down and lines Van up with her pussy, then slowly sinks down until her ass is sitting on his thighs.

"Fuck, you feel good," Van groans.

"You do, too," Evie says, throwing her head back. She rotates her hips, making his fingers tighten on her hips.

"That's it, *la mia stella*," Micah rasps, running his hand down her ass. "Show him how good that pussy feels."

Evie starts moving, rising, and falling on Van's dick slowly. Me, Hartley, and Gray have a prime view in our seats across from them.

Micah's hand travels down until it rubs against the diamond on the end of the butt plug, and her whole body shudders. His eyes flash to mine, and I know what he wants. I pull the remote from my pocket and flick on the vibration.

"Shit," Van grunts, feeling it through her thin inner wall.

"Oh god," Evie groans, fingers digging into Van's shoulders. I mash a few more buttons until it's pulsing inside her. She starts riding him faster.

"There you go," Van says, raising his hips to meet hers.

Their heavy breathing fills the car, and I'm painfully hard watching them.

"Goddamn," Hartley mutters, eyes glued in front of him.

"I'm going to come," Evie pants out.

"Come on my cock, *pequena reina*," Van rasps.

She moans low and throaty, signaling how close she is. Micah twists the plug, and she lets go with a scream. "Evander!"

"Fuck," Van grits out. "I'm going to pump this pussy so full of cum, and then you're going to walk into the house with it dripping down your thighs."

Van grabs her hips and starts fucking her from the bottom, making his thighs slap against hers. She lets out a whimper, but it's not from pain.

"Are you going to come for him again?" Micah asks, still playing with the plug.

"Yes. Fuck," Evie pants.

"You want his cum dripping out of you?" Micah asks. Evie nods. "Squeeze it out of his cock with that tight pussy."

"Fuck, Micah," Van hisses, and I know Evie just tightened up on him. She loved when you talked dirty to her.

Van's thrusts get so hard that he grunts each time he bottoms out. Evie lets go with another scream, and he groans, coming right behind her. "Evie."

She collapses forward on his chest, and he runs his hands down her back while they get their breathing under control.

It's time to get her home.

As soon as we get Evie back to the house, Van leads her to his and Micah's room. Micah has her on the bed with her dress bunched around her waist before we even shut the door.

"Tell me you still want this," he rasps.

"I do," Evie groans. Micah's head goes between her thighs, and her eyes widen. "What are you doing? Evander just..."

"Came inside of you? Yeah, I know," Micah says roughly. He licks through her slit and groans deep in his chest. "I wanted to see what you tasted like together."

He buries his face between her legs, devouring her pussy. Evie's thighs close around his head, and he takes his hands and pushes them apart.

I lay beside them and jerk the top of her dress down so her breasts spill out. "Evie told me something today, Van," I say.

Van lies on her other side. "What's that?"

"Someone has a fantasy of us fucking her at the same time," I tell him.

Micah groans loudly again, slides two fingers inside her, and doubles down, eating her pussy faster. You could hear the wet slurping noises he is making, and it's wreaking havoc on my cock.

"Is that what you want, *pequena reina*?" Van asks, rolling her nipple between his fingers.

"Oh fuck," Evie moans, sinking her fingers into Micah's hair. "Yes, oh god,"

Van and I stand from the bed at the same time, taking our clothes off. Evie's head is swiveling between us, undressing, and Micah's head buried between her thighs.

With our clothes out of the way, Van and I slide back onto the bed. As one, we reach down, grab a thigh and pull her legs toward her shoulder, spreading her wide open for Micah. She reaches over and grabs our cocks, stroking them in time with Micah's fingers inside her.

Evie starts panting, and her whole chest flushes. "Micah!" she screams as she comes.

He sits back on his heels, her wetness soaking his chin. I glance at Van, and he raises an eyebrow, answering the question I was asking silently.

I look at Micah. "I want to taste her," I say. He looks at me like I'm an idiot because she's spread out on the bed, ready for whatever comes next. "On you," I clarify.

Micah's eyes flair with heat, the blue orbs burning, then his eyes flash to Van.

Van shrugs. "It's up to you, *mi rey*. We've talked about it," Van says, making my eyes flash to him. They've talked about this? Gray and I have also talked about this; we aren't going to hold each other back if it's something we wanted.

Micah reaches down and jerks me to my knees. Before I have time to blink, his lips are sealed over mine, his tongue stroking mine. Holy fucking shit. I've daydreamed about kissing Micah, but nothing compared to the real thing. He hooks his arm around my waist to pull me closer, his hand laying on my bare ass. My greedy hands rub up his abs to his pecs.

We pull back, both breathless, just staring at each other. Evie's moans catch our attention, and we turn toward her. Van has his fingers buried inside of her, making her hips buck.

"Are you ready?" Van asks, kissing down her neck, sliding his fingers free.

"Yes," Evie moans, long and loud.

"Van's going to get your ass ready," Micah says, rubbing his hands up her thighs before helping her sit up. He pulls her dress off. "Hands and knees, *la mia stella*," he instructs, helping her get situated.

Van rummages around for the lube, then he and Micah switch places. Micah strips, and we lay down on either side of her. My eyes find Gray's, and he's sitting in one of the chairs behind the bed, watching everything. Like a magnet, his eyes pull to mine, and he grins. *Damn, he is fucking sexy.* I search out Hartley and find him leaning against the wall beside the bed, and I can't make out the expression on his face. He is turned on. I could see his erection pushing against his jeans, but I couldn't tell anything from his face. It's carefully blank.

"Goddamn," Van groans. I look at him; he has Evie's ass spread apart, just looking at the plug nestled in there. He pulls the plug out halfway, squirts lube on it, and works it back into her ass. Once her body settles, he starts fucking her with it, stretching her out and getting her used to the sensation.

Evie moans, and I lean close to her ear. "Wait until it's his cock," I whisper. "He's going to stretch that ass open while I stretch your pussy open."

"Mateo," Evie groans, fingers bunching in the blankets.

Van hooks an arm under her and pulls her up until she's on her knees, his chest plastered to her back. "Remember what I said?" he asks, reminding her that she can say no at any time. She nods, turning to look at him over her shoulder. He seals his lips over hers with a groan, making my cock jump. Van pulls back, breathless. He slides around her and lays against the headboard. "You can control it this way," he explains when she looks at him in confusion.

I get on my knees behind her. "I'm going to take your plug out," I tell her. I reach between her cheeks and grab the end. I start pulling, and her greedy ass tries to hold it in. Oh yeah, she is ready.

I toss the plug on the bed when it's free and help her get turned around to face me. I kiss her slowly. "Scoot back," I encourage. I help her shuffle back until Van's dick is right behind her. He nods when he's done lubing up. I take her hands when he scoots down and lines up with her ass to help keep her steady. "Now sit back and push down when he pushes up."

She bites her lip. "Will it hurt?"

"It will burn at first," I say softly, running my knuckles down her cheek. "Van will make it feel good," I promise. She looks uncertain at first, then straightens her shoulders. With a nod, she starts to let her hips drop.

Van keeps his grip on the base of his cock and grabs her hip with the other hand, guiding her back. I see the moment the head pops into her ass; her eyes go wide.

"Breathe," Micah says, rubbing his hand up her spine.

She lets out a shuddering breath and slowly lowers her hips.

"Oh fuck," Van says in a strangled voice. I can't imagine what he is feeling sliding into her virgin back hole.

Her breathing picks up, her chest rising and falling rapidly, and I know he's pushed past the resistance.

"He's too big," Evie whimpers, her eyes squeezed shut.

"Open your eyes," I say gently, making them flutter open. "Do you want to stop?"

"No," Evie groans.

"Are you sure?" Van asks breathlessly. No matter what he is feeling, he won't force her into this.

"Please, just do it," Evie begs, squeezing my hands.

Van places both hands on her hips and lifts his while pulling her down slowly. Her thighs settle against his, and you can see him fighting for control.

"Breathe, buttercup," I remind her. She releases a breath in a whoosh, her body shaking.

Van lifts her hips and slowly drags out of her when she relaxes. She lets out a moan that has us all groaning at the sound.

"Does that feel good, *pequena reina*?" Van asks hoarsely.

"Yes, oh my god," Evie pants.

I help her lean back against his chest, her legs open for me. I grab the lube and make my cock as slick as possible. Her pussy is dripping wet, but I want to make this as easy for her as I could. Van grabs her thighs and spreads her wider.

I start circling her clit with my fingers, getting her even wetter. "You ready for me, buttercup?" She nods rapidly, reaching for me.

I scoot between their spread thighs and slide my cock across her clit, making her back bow. She is definitely ready.

Keeping a tight grip on the base of my cock, I line up and start pushing into her pussy.

"Wait, oh god," Evie whimpers. I stop immediately and look into her eyes. Her hands fly to my shoulders, her fingernails digging into the skin. I push my thumb against her clit and start rubbing in small circles, helping to ease the ache. Her eyes latch onto mine. "Ok, go."

Still rubbing her clit, I start pushing forward, taking shallow breaths to keep from coming before this even starts. I've never been bare inside of anyone, and being raw inside of Evie tests every bit of self-control I have.

"Fuck," I grunt when my thighs settle against hers.

Her breathing is out of control, her face twisted in pain. I give her a minute to get used to the sensation and then slide out.

"Are you ok?" I rasp.

"Yes, fuck. I don't know," Evie gasps. "I feel so full."

Van and I exchange a look and start moving, sliding out of her at the same time.

I feel the bed dip, and a hand slides across my chest. I smile because I would know that hand anywhere.

"Well, hello, Gray."

CHAPTER 47
GRAY

I slide my hand across Mateo's chest with Evie's eyes locked on me the whole time.

"Well, hello, Gray," Mateo says.

Mateo told me about their conversation over text, and I am about to deliver another one of his promises.

I let him and Van find a rhythm pumping their cocks in and out of her while I let my cock rub against Mateo's tight ass.

Evie's whole body is flushed, her lips slightly parted, moaning each time either one of them moves. She's taking this like she was made for this. Made for us.

Hartley lays down on her other side, rolling her nipples between his fingers. I wasn't sure how he was taking this because I couldn't get a read on him. I guess he just needed a minute to accept it.

"Jesus Christ," Micah chokes, taking in all the metal on Hartley's cock. "I didn't see that coming."

Hartley chuckles. "That's always the best part," he says, leaning forward and sucking Evie's nipple into his mouth.

"Oh god," Evie moans, fingers tightening on Mateo's forearms.

Hartley's upper body, front and back, are covered in colorful tattoos. Something I didn't see coming either. He always seemed like

399

he had a stick up his ass. Getting to know him now just shows we unfairly judge each other for the lives we've chosen.

Mateo grinds his ass against my dick when he slides from Evie. I slide my hand up to his throat and squeeze, feeling his moan against my palm. "You want my cock, baby boy?" I murmur in his ear. "You want me to fill you up while you fill her up?"

"Fuck, Gray," Mateo groans, thrusting his hips forward.

I snatch up the lube, get my fingers nice and slick, and slide them between his ass cheeks. His whole body shudders when I slide my fingers inside him. I let him fuck himself onto my fingers every time he slides his cock out of Evie.

Micah gets on his knees, his dick right in Evie's face. He gently nudges her chin toward him, feeding his cock into her mouth. I can feel her moan in my bones when he is buried in her throat.

"Damn, *la mia stella*," Micah grunts. "Is this what you wanted? So full of cock you couldn't move?" She nods the best she can with how far he has his cock in her mouth.

"Fuck me, Gray," Mateo encourages, stilling his movements.

I pull my fingers free, slick my dick up, and line up. I push him forward so his ass is pointing toward me. Not wasting any more time, I slide in until I'm just past the resistance, grab his hips, and slam my hips forward, burying myself to the hilt. Mateo's back bows, and he moans low in his throat.

My momentum slams him into Evie, and my eyes flash to her, thinking I hurt her. Her breasts rise and fall rapidly with each breath, and she's sucking Micah's cock fast.

"Damn," Micah pants. "I think she liked that."

"She's so fucking tight," Van says, fingers tightening on her hips.

Micah pulls from her lips when Hartley gets to his knees, and she turns her head without being told, sucking Hartley into her mouth.

"Fuck, Van," Micah groans. Van has an arm wrapped around Micah's waist, holding him so Micah's cock is buried in his throat.

We start moving in sync, working each other over to the highest pleasure.

"Tell them what else you want, buttercup," Mateo says raggedly. "Tell them where you want us to come."

Evie moans against the head of Hartley's cock. She lets go with a wet pop. "All over me," she answers.

"You want us to mark you, angel?" I ask.

"Yes," Evie moans again and sucks Hartley back in her mouth.

"Goddamn," Hartley grunts, bunching his fist in her hair.

Hartley slides a hand between where Mateo and Evie are connected and starts rubbing her clit in tight circles. She starts bucking between them, letting us know she's close to coming. Her mouth opens around Hartley's cock when she screams, and he pushes forward, making her throat bulge. Evie tightens on Mateo, making his ass tighten on me.

"Holy shit," I gasp.

"I'm fucking close," Mateo groans, his hands tightening on Evie's thighs.

Van lets Micah slip from his lips. "Can't hang, little brother?" he jokes.

"Fuck. You," Mateo grits out, hanging on by a thread. He is getting the best of both worlds, with me thrusting into his ass and fucking Evie. Micah laughs, then groans when Van sucks him back into his mouth. "What's the matter, you old fucker?" Mateo says.

"I'll show you old fucker," Micah grinds, fucking Van's mouth harder. "I need to teach your ass some manners."

"He does need a lesson, doesn't he?" I say, grabbing his throat again. I squeeze, cutting off his air. Mateo's thrusts stutter. "Don't you dare fucking come," I growl. "You come when I say you can."

Mateo whimpers, his whole body shaking, trying to hold off.

"I knew you were a dominant bastard," Hartley says, stroking in and out of Evie's mouth.

I shrug because what else can I say? It isn't something I could control or something I wanted to control.

"Make her come again," I tell Mateo, without letting my hold go. I pull out halfway, and Mateo starts fucking Evie with purpose. Every time he pulls out of her, his ass slams back onto my cock, making me grunt. "Damn, baby boy, you feel good," I groan, running my hand across his abs.

Mateo reaches down and starts rubbing Evie's clit. She's writhing between Mateo and Van and sucking Hartley's cock hard.

Hartley jerks from her mouth and starts stroking his cock hard. The first jet lands on her perfect tits. "Fuck, princess," Hartley breathes, still pumping come from his cock.

"Mateo! Evander!" Evie screams, her back bowing on Van's chest. She is fucking gorgeous when she comes.

"Gray," Mateo moans. "Please."

"Please, what?" I rasp, feeling my release blazing down my spine.

"Please let me come," Mateo begs.

I let him slide free of Evie's pussy and wrap my hand around his dick from behind, stroking hard. His body is tense, and his breath is sawing out of his lungs, but he isn't going to come until I tell him to. I tighten my hand on his throat again and put my chest flush against his back, just like I know he loves. I slam my hips forward, still pumping his cock. I feel my balls start to draw up. "Come, baby boy," I growl, and Mateo lets go with a moan, his come splashing onto the top of her pussy and on her stomach.

I jerk out of him and move to the side, fucking my fist, letting my come land with Mateo's.

"Shit," Van pants. "I'm going to come."

Mateo and I reach down, helping Evie to her knees so Van can slide out of her ass. She lays back down on the bed, wide-eyed, chest heaving. Micah and Van shuffle to her side, stroking each other's cocks, coming all over her tits.

Mateo reaches down, swirls his finger through our come, then sucks his finger into his mouth with a grin.

"You dirty motherfucker," Micah laughs. He leans down and kisses Evie softly. "You did so good, *la mia stella*," he says, making her smile.

"Perfect," Hartley says, running his fingers through her hair. He kisses her slowly and pulls back with a smile.

Van takes his kiss. "How do you feel?"

"Sore," she says with a slight wince. "But not bad."

"I'll run you a bath, buttercup," Mateo says, pecking her lips. He turns to me and kisses me hard. He jumps off the bed and shuts the bathroom door behind him.

Evie reaches a hand out to me, and I go willingly. She kisses me slowly, pulling back with a smile. "You guys are awesome," she declares, making us all chuckle. She looks down at the mess we made, and her face flushes. "That shouldn't be that hot."

"We marked you, *pequena reina*. Do you know what that means?" Van asks, and she shakes her head. He runs his knuckles down her cheek. "It means you're ours now."

I watch emotion after emotion flit across her beautiful face—fear, denial, happiness.

"Yours?" Evie whispers.

Van clears his throat, realizing that he had opened a conversation we weren't sure she was ready for. "Yes," he states matter-of-factly. "We can talk about it later. Go take your bath, and we'll be here when you're ready."

She nods and slides off the bed, padding to the bathroom. We all watch the sexy sway of her ass until she disappears behind the door, shutting it behind her.

"Good going," Micah says with a laugh. "Not only did we just give her a bunch of firsts, you just went caveman on her."

Van grimaces. "It just came out."

"Trust me; I get what you're feeling," Hartley says, running his fingers through his hair and sitting on the edge of the bed.

"It's fine, *amore mio*," Micah says, kissing Van's forehead. "It's past time for us to have this conversation."

We all nod in agreement. We don't know how she is going to react. Sure, she shared her body with us, but would she want to share her heart?

I guess we will find out.

I WAKE with a start to the sound of gunfire, which is not unusual for me after my time in the service. I snuggle in closer to Evie and close my eyes. After her bath last night, she was exhausted. Micah said we could all stay in the room with him and Van.

Van and I tucked her between us, with Micah lying at Van's back. Mateo is behind me with his arm slung over my waist, and Hartley is behind Mateo.

I hear the cracking of the guns again, and my eyes snap open. That wasn't a fucking dream; that is right outside the goddamn house.

I slide out of bed and wake the guys one by one, careful not to wake Evie yet. We pull our clothes back on and step out into the hallway.

"What the fuck is going on?" Micah barks into his phone.

"A couple of carloads drove by and started firing at the guard house," Adam answers. "Motley and a few others tried chasing them down." I keep Adam here with us full time now.

"How the fuck did they even get on the property?" Micah asks, pacing.

Mateo and Van had a gate at the beginning of the long driveway and another one at the main driveway that brought you to the house. They had the second one installed right after I was hired for Micah, on my recommendation.

"The main gate has been tampered with. It wasn't like that earlier, so it just happened," Adam says.

"Get some guards on that fucking gate," Micah grits out.

"Yes, sir," Adam replies before the phone disconnects.

"What are we going to do?" Mateo asks; all business.

"We need to tell her what's going on," Micah sighs. "We need to be prepared for anything." Micah looks at the time on his phone and grimaces. It's only four o'clock in the morning.

"Ghost, we have problems," Micah says when the call connects.

"What's going on?" Ghost asks, and I can hear him already barking orders.

"We just had a goddamn drive-by. Someone tampered with the front gate. Are your guys still on the hide-out?"

"Yeah, they haven't moved. They must have more than one," Ghost answers. "Do we need to ride over?"

"Not yet, but I need you on standby just in case we have to move her in a hurry. I have guys chasing one of the offenders," Micah says when his bedroom door opens, and Evie steps out with the sheet wrapped around her. "I have to go. I'll call you later." Micah disconnects the call and looks at her, looking sleepy and cute as hell.

"What's going on?" Evie asks

"Come on, *pequena reina*," Van says, leading her back into the room. He sits her on the side of the bed and sits beside her, taking her hand. "We had some visitors that shot at the guard house," Van explains gently.

Evie's hand flies to her mouth. "Oh my god, are they okay?"

"Yes," Van smiles.

A ringing phone blares through the room, and everyone looks around. I pluck it from the floor, and the pink case that Bridget bought gives it away that it is Evie's. An unknown number flashes across the screen, and I have to grit my teeth. How the fuck did he get her new number? Everything has been switched since the breach, including ours. I hand it to her, and she stares at it like whoever is calling will jump from the screen. It stops and immediately starts ringing again.

Evie closes her eyes, her hand shaking on the phone. Her eyes snap open; she swipes to answer and flips it to speakerphone.

"Hello?" she says, her voice shaking.

"Hey, baby," a voice drawls. "Miss me?"

"What do you want?" Evie asks miserably.

"You, Evie," Aaron answers and then chuckles. "It's time you came back home. I let you have your fun; that time is up."

Hartley dashes from the room, and I know he's going to get the laptop that Holden got him.

"How do you keep getting my number?" Evie demands, getting strength from Van's hold on her hand.

"You know I have my ways, baby. Did you really think you could move on that easily? I knew you were stupid, but I didn't think you were that fucking stupid."

I want to rip that phone from her hand and tell this motherfucker how badly I wanted to murder him.

Micah steps forward to do just that, and Evie holds a hand up, halting his progress. Van's eyes widen when Micah stops mid-step.

"I'm not stupid, and I'm not coming back. Why do you even want me back, Aaron? You need to move on," Evie says. Mateo gets behind her on the bed and squeezes her shoulders.

Hartley jogs back into the room, already tapping.

"Like you have?" Aaron grinds.

Evie looks around the room, gauging our reactions, and she steels her spine. "Yes. Like I have. I finally found someone to treat me like I deserve to be treated. You were evil, and I don't want anything to do with you anymore. Leave me the fuck alone."

"Don't you mean five someone's, you fucking whore?" Evie sucks in a breath, and her eyes fill with tears. Every single one of us is vibrating with rage. It is taking everything not to interrupt this call, but we need a trace. "Like I said, I let you have your fun. Now come to me willingly, or I start picking them off one by one. You don't want that, do you, baby? Tonight was just a warning. You have two hours to make your decision." The call disconnects, and the phone clatters to the floor when Evie's hand drops.

I crouch down in front of her and take her other hand. "You did good, angel," I say, kissing the back of her hand.

"I don't feel like it," Evie whispers.

"Buttercup, you were amazing," Mateo says, kissing her head.

"Goddamnit," Hartley growls. "I couldn't get a trace."

"What do I do?" Evie asks, tears sliding down her cheeks. "I can't let him hurt you."

Hartley crouches beside me. "Princess, he's not going to get close enough to do that."

"He was just outside the house!" Evie stands up, which causes me and Hartley to stand up. "He is getting that close! Don't you get it?! He's never going to leave me alone!"

She moves past us, ignoring us calling out to her, and shuts the bathroom door behind her.

"Shit," Micah sighs. "We need to regroup. He's getting her number somehow, and we need to find out how."

"I'm going to check on Evie. Let me know the plan," Hartley says before disappearing into the bathroom.

"He said two hours. What happens if she says no?" Mateo asks.

"She's going to fucking say no," Micah growls. "No way he gets his hands on her."

Mateo snorts. "No shit. Do you think I'm going to let her go? I'm asking what you think he will do."

"I don't know," Micah answers, sitting on the bed beside Van. "But we're going to find out."

CHAPTER 48
HARTLEY

"Princess," I say softly when I walk into the bathroom. She's sitting on the floor, leaning against the bathtub, staring into space.

"I can't do it anymore, Hart," Evie whispers.

I sit beside her, taking her hand in mine. "Do what?"

"I can't keep running. I've been running for months, and he's always one step ahead. I was stupid to think I'd ever get away from him," Evie says, angrily swiping tears from her cheeks. "I can't risk you guys."

"What are you saying?" I ask with a frown.

"I have to go back to him," she answers, and before I can open my mouth, she stands up, clutching the sheet to her breasts. "He will keep coming, and he'll kill you. I can't do that! I wouldn't be able to live with myself if something happened to any of you!" Evie reaches for the door, and I'm on my feet. I grab her arm to spin her to face me, and her eyes widen.

"You aren't going anywhere," I grit out. "You really think any of us will let you run out that door and back to him? You're exactly where you belong. Get that through your head now, or I'll remind you that you belong with me every second of every day. You've been mine for a long damn time, Evie. It's about fucking time I start acting like it." Evie's breath hitches, and her bottom lip trembles. I sink my hands into her hair and tilt her face up. "We'll get through this; you have to trust us to do that. No one said it was going to be easy. But we'll finish this. Together," I say adamantly.

I crush her to my chest and let her tears soak into my shirt. I don't need her to say anything back; I just needed her to hear it from me. There is no damn way I will let Evie out of my sight, and I can guarantee none of the other guys will, either.

I let Evie silently cry, rubbing soothing circles on her back. When she finally looks up at me, her cheeks are red, and her eyes are puffy. I wipe the rest of her tears with my thumbs. "Are you ready to go back out there?" I ask, and she nods. I peck her lips. "I'll go get you some clothes."

I kiss her one last time and slip from the bathroom. The room is empty, but some of Evie's clothes are on the bed. Grabbing them, I hand them back to her through the crack in the door. "I'll be downstairs. Come find me when you're ready," I tell her. I turn on my heel, and she grabs my arm.

"I heard you, Hartley," she says. I don't have to ask what she means. She's talking about my admission about her being mine. "And I do trust you."

I smile at her and leave her to get dressed. I find Micah and the other guys in the office already making plans. Micah waves me in when he sees me at the door, and it's weird. We went from enemies to a mutual agreement to make Evie happy. I initially rejected this idea until I saw the changes they've made in her in such a short time.

"We need to sweep this entire house for bugs," Micah says.

"You think it's bugged?" I ask. Who the hell even got in to do it?

"That's what happened with Les," Mateo explains, then shrugs. "Better safe than sorry."

"Sir?" We all turn to Micah's guard, Adam, when he steps into the office. He lays a black box on Evander's desk. "This was on the gate. We must have missed it on our last round before the shooters arrived. I'm sorry, sir."

Micah waves the apology away, turning the box over in his hand. "No need to apologize. What the hell is it?"

"It overrides the code," Gray answers. "I've used them before."

Micah nods. "How the hell did he get it?" Micah muses, then looks at Adam. "Any luck tracking them down?"

"No, sir," Adam answers. "But they're still canvassing the area."

"Good. Tell me when they find something," Micah tells him. Adam nods and leaves the room. "How's Evie?" Micah asks me.

"She's okay," I sigh. "She's terrified something is going to happen to one of us. I think I talked her down, but she said something about trying to leave."

"Over my dead fucking body!" Mateo explodes, looking angrier than I've ever seen him. "She's not leaving my goddamn sight."

Evander slides his hand on Mateo's shoulder and squeezes. "She's scared, Tay. We just need to assure her that she's still safe with us."

Micah sets the bug sweeping devices onto his desk with a pointed look that says don't say shit until the house is clear. We each grab one, and Micah tells us where to go and to meet back in his office when we're done. No one has been in the house that we knew of, but we couldn't take any more chances.

I work my way backward from his office through the hallway, kitchen, and dining room. Not finding anything, I make a second round to be sure and meet them back in Micah's office.

"Report," Micah barks, walking to the desk. Mateo lifts an eyebrow, then shakes his head. We all report that we didn't find anything, and Micah drops into the chair.

"Then how the fuck is he doing this?"

"I don't know, but we need a plan, Boss."

"Jesus Christ, Gray. I just saw you naked; stop calling me boss," Micah grumbles, making Mateo bark a laugh.

"But that makes it even sexier," Mateo says, waggling his eyebrows.

Gray's face blooms with color, and it shocks me every time. I heard the shit he was saying to Mateo, yet the slightest dirty thing said outside of the bedroom, and he blushes.

"Okay." Micah waves his hand around. "Back on task."

"Who's been in the house?" I ask, leaning my hip against his desk.

"Us," Micah replies. "And a few guards."

"Could it be one of them?" I continue.

"No. After Les, we got rid of most of our guards and hired new ones. Gray vetted them all," Micah answers. I don't need to ask what he meant when he said he got rid of them.

"What about the cars?" Mateo asks, looking around the table. "He could have tagged one while we were out with the same shit."

"Goddamnit," Micah sighs. "We should have thought about that."

"You think he'll attack here?" Gray asks.

"Adam said the gate is secure, and he has men on it, too," Micah says. "I still think we need to move her. We need to search the cars and make sure they're clean. Phones need to stay here. I'll get Les to bring us more tomorrow."

"I agree, but how do we get out of here without him following?" I ask.

Mateo grins. "I have an idea."

WE ARE THROWING the last of the bags into the back of Gray's truck when Evie steps into the garage, swamped in a hoodie. Gray pulls her into his side, kissing the top of her head. We found a device on several vehicles and destroyed them. Now it made sense how the hell he was finding us.

Mateo's idea is Fast and Furious style, literally straight out of the movie when all the cars drive out of the garage to lose the cops. It's a damn good idea. Ghost and Caden showed up with several of their guys. And the Russian twins, Alexey and Dmitri, who keep looking at me in the exact same creepy way. So, that makes thirty of us that are going to drive off the property, splitting different directions on the highway so he wouldn't know who to follow. I am taking my truck, hoping that the asshole will come after me. Evie isn't going to be with any of us. She is going to be with Ghost, which I didn't like, but Micah trusts him, and I trust that Micah would protect Evie.

I sling my bag in the back and pause. "Who fixed my truck?" I ask. I haven't been in it and just noticed that the back window is fixed from the shootout at my house.

"I did," Mateo answers.

"Why?" I demand, stunned. I planned on getting it fixed as soon as I could.

"Because I fucking felt like it," Mateo says. He grins and turns to Evie. "You ready, buttercup?" Mateo asks Evie. *Well, hell.*

Evie nods, but her bottom lip trembles. She knows we are fifteen minutes away from Aaron's deadline, and we are damn sure he is going to try to attack us here. We just had to wait and make our move when he made his.

Evie's phone starts blaring through the garage, and Gray squeezes her tighter to his side. I walk closer, so I can hear.

She takes a breath and answers. "Hello?"

"Ten minutes, baby. I can't wait to see you." Aaron's voice filters through.

Micah nods for her to say what we told her to. "I'm not coming with you," she says, trying to keep the quiver out of her voice.

"You really are stupid. Do you have any idea who those guys are? You think I'm fucking bad, baby? You haven't seen anything yet."

Everyone exchanges a look, wondering if Aaron's going to tell her the truth.

"I don't care," Evie says, pulling her shoulders back. "They're a million times better than you, you abusive, sadistic, psychotic, sick son of a bitch. Go to hell, Aaron."

Aaron laughs. "You really have no idea, do you? Their fucking Mafia, baby. You think what I did is bad? They make me look like a fucking angel."

Fuck fuck fuck.

Evie's eyes widen while she looks at us standing around her. She disconnects the call, and her phone hits the garage floor.

"Mafia?" Evie whispers.

"Buttercup," Mateo says in a pleading voice.

Her whole face falls, and she steps away from Gray. *Shit!*

"I hate to do this, but that's our queue. Get ready to move," Micah orders.

Ghost looks around and gently leads Evie to his Challenger. Caden slides into the backseat, and Evie up front without a backward glance.

I share a look with the guys; they know this is worse than bad. We didn't want her to find out like this, but the only thing we can do now is damage control.

I hop in my truck, fire it up, and hope this isn't the last time I see her.

Or them.

CHAPTER 49
EVIE

Mafia.

That word keeps rolling around in my head. I wanted to say Aaron was lying, but I saw the look on their faces. And Hartley *knew* and still let me get involved with them.

Now I am stuck in a car with two guys I don't even know who are more than likely Mafia also.

I look over at Ghost, and he gives me a cautious look. I'm barely keeping my shit together. Talk about jumping right into the fucking lion's den.

Caden sits up between the seats and lays his elbows on the console. "I'm going to say something here, and you can ignore it like most everyone does." Ghost snorts, and Caden chuckles. I nod to let him know to continue. "Those guys back there, yeah, they're Mafia. But they are some of the best fucking dudes I've ever known. I agree you shouldn't have found out like that, but it's not something they can run around telling everyone."

"I'm not just anyone," I say miserably. I take a breath, trying to keep the tears at bay. These guys don't need waterworks when they are trying to keep me and the guys from getting killed. They told me they weren't good guys multiple times, but this never crossed my mind. I don't know how to deal with the information. I gave my body to guys I didn't even know. Tonight should have been the best night of my life, and now it's tarnished by Aaron and finding out they've been lying to me.

"No," Ghost agrees. "But they were going to tell you."

"When?" I demand. "When I was completely in love with them?" I slam my lips shut. Am I falling in love with them? There is no damn way I could do this to myself again.

I watch Caden's eyes widen. "Whoa. Okay, this is out of my wheelhouse. Ghost?"

Ghost sighs, and I swear he muttered pussy under his breath. "You need to talk to them. Demand answers."

"Demand answers from the Mafia?" I say slowly. Is he listening to himself?

"You are probably the only one who can demand anything from them and not face the repercussions," Caden says with a laugh.

Ghost's phone rings, and he hits the button on the steering wheel.

"Get ready." Micah's voice filters through the speaker, and my heart squeezes.

"Got it," Ghost answers.

I watch as Micah's red Ferrari flies by us, with Mateo's new Porsche right behind him. They weave in and out of cars, making me grab the seat in panic. Two SUVs go by us right on their tail.

"Are you buckled?" Ghost asks, looking over at me. I nod.

He stomps the gas, slamming through gears, and it forces me back in the seat. Ghost whips past the SUVs and puts the car right on Mateo's bumper. Mateo makes a last-minute lane change and cuts off an exit, causing one of the SUVs to follow him. My heart can't handle this. I have no idea if he is going to be okay. I haven't seen Evander, Hartley or Gray, and Micah is driving like a madman.

"One down," Ghost reports.

"Drop off. See if they stay with you."

Ghost swerves into the other lane, and the SUV follows us, leaving Micah wide open. "They're tailing me."

"Shit," Micah mutters. "Hold on."

Micah slams on the brakes and swerves over in front of us. He swerves again, almost taking out the back of a car and speeds down an exit. Right at the last second, the SUV follows.

"All clear," Ghost says.

"Take her to the safe house. I don't have to remind you that if one hair on her head is harmed, I'll gut you like a goddamn fish." The line goes dead, and Caden cackles in the backseat.

"Asshole," Ghost mutters, and a giggle bubbles up before I can stop it.

The giggle is short-lived when I feel my throat burning and know the tears are coming. I shouldn't feel betrayed, but I do. They promised me things I know they can't give me.

Caden lays his hand on my arm. "It's okay, Evie," he says softly. I shake my head and let the tears fall. Typical fucking Evie.

Maybe my mom was right about me.

I never could do anything right.

I'VE PACED a hole in the floor. We got to the safe house an hour ago, and there was no sign of the rest of them. It's given me too much damn time to think. Ghost and Caden haven't said a word since I broke down in the car. My mind can't keep up with where my thoughts are going. One minute I'm sad, then pissed, and then I make myself believe it's all going to be okay. It's draining.

A car door shuts outside the house, causing Ghost and Caden to jump to their feet, guns already in hand, pointed at the door. Several knocks have the guys relaxing, and Evander walks through the door.

His eyes light on me, and I'm not sure what my face looks like, but he flinches. I want to run to him, thankful he is okay, but my feet are glued to the floor.

"*Pequena reina,*" he says softly. "Are you okay?" Does he mean physically or emotionally? Surely he doesn't want to have this conversation right now.

"Yes," I croak and resume my pacing.

Evander sighs and starts talking in hushed tones with Ghost and Caden. I wanted to ask about the other guys, but he likely doesn't know either. None of us have a damn phone, and the only reason Micah could communicate with us is because his fancy car had its own phone.

One by one, the guys start pouring in, each asking me the same question. When I look into Mateo's sad green eyes, I almost lose my resolve to demand answers, but I need to know. The last one we are waiting on is Hartley.

Thirty minutes go by before Hartley finally walks into the house. I breathe a sigh of relief. They are all fine, but that's the only thing I let myself feel. Ghost and Caden say their goodbyes, and Micah looks at me with a resigned expression.

"Do you want to talk now, or would you like to wait until morning?" Micah asks.

"Now," I demand and flop down in the chair. Micah, Evander, and Hartley take up the couch, and Mateo and Gray are on the love seat.

They all exchange looks, and I get even more nervous. Micah leans forward and braces his arms on his knees. "Before I tell you, you must understand that this isn't safe information. We work hard to protect who we are. This can't leave this room," Micah says softly, but I can hear the underlying warning in his tone. I nod, agreeing to keep my mouth shut.

Micah sighs. "My brother Luca was the leader of the Italian Mafia, my father before him. When Luca passed away, that title went to Les. We both lead them now, but she's the big boss."

I know the shock shows all over my face. I can feel my heart hit my stomach. *Les?* When I was with Aaron, I heard stories about the Mafia, and they always talked about how brutal they were. I look at Evander and Mateo when I realize Micah only answered about himself.

"My brother and I are the leaders of the Mexican Mafia of sorts in the states. Over the past six months, we have also taken over the Mexican cartel. We got the title when our father died," Evander answers.

No fucking wonder they didn't want Hartley here and why Hartley had such a hard time with me being around them. Why would he bring me here, then? He assured me they would keep me safe. My head is spinning, but I need to get the rest out of the way.

"I was a hired gun when I left the Marines," Gray says before I even look at him. "I did that for years while working security for different organizations. I stopped when I started working for Micah."

"An assassin?" I squeak. Gray nods once in answer. "Holy shit," I breathe, jumping from my chair. "I *knew* there was something about you guys, but never in a million fucking years would I have *ever* guessed this."

"Buttercup..." Mateo starts, but I hold up a hand.

I turn accusing eyes on Hartley. "You let me stay, knowing who they are! You know what I went through with Aaron. You knew I didn't want to be involved in that life."

Hartley shrugs. "I let you stay with the people I knew would keep you safe, princess. That's all I cared about."

I can feel my heart twist painfully. I trusted these guys, and they are worse than Aaron.

"I need..." I take a breath, "I need to be alone."

I take off toward the bedrooms, ignoring the hurt looks. I make it to a room before the tears start flowing again.

I WAKE up the following morning feeling like total shit about how I treated the guys. They have done everything to ensure I am cared for while I'm here. They have shown me things about myself I didn't even know. They made me feel cherished and beautiful. My dreams were full of all the good I've seen in them.

And what do I do? I treat them like they are the scum of the earth because of who they are. Am I still scared shitless that I am in a house with a bunch of criminals? Absolutely. But I'm not afraid of them. I'm scared because I know what follows this life, and I dropped more into their laps. I accused Hartley of not thinking about me when he let me stay here when all he's done is do everything he can to protect me.

I pull my ass out of bed and into the shower. I didn't even get a chance to look at where we were staying when we got here. The house is small but beautiful. I need to find them and apologize. They tried to protect me from this, but I insisted I knew just to throw a tantrum.

Even though I know I had overreacted, I couldn't help but have reservations. Aaron pulled me in with pretty words and promises, then became a grade-A psychopath. Is that what the guys are doing? Lulling me in, getting me comfortable, and then everything explodes in my face? My heart twists painfully at that thought. Would they do that?

By the time I get out of the shower, I am even more tired than when I went to bed. The thoughts swirling in my head are making me dizzy. I take one last longing look at the bed and go to the kitchen, noticing it is too quiet here. There was always some conversation or laughter, especially Mateo's. I see a note on the island and pick it up.

"*La mia stella,*" I read aloud. "We'll be back later. Enjoy. Micah." Did they leave me here alone?

"Hey," I spin toward Les' voice. She smiles tentatively. "They went with the guys to follow a lead and thought you could use someone to talk to." I knew I was staring at her, but I am trying to get my brain to catch up that the sweet girl who talked me off a ledge in the bathroom, taught me self-defense, and got drunk and listened to me ramble about the guys is the leader of the Italian Mafia. She walks by me and slides onto the stool beside where I'm standing. "Micah called me this morning and said you found out. If you prefer I stay out of your hair, I can do that. I'm sure it was a lot to take in last night."

I sit beside her. "It was," I admit with a sigh. "I feel like shit about how I reacted."

Les nods and pulls the cover off of where the note was sitting. There is a freshly baked loaf of Micah's banana bread that I loved.

Did he get up this morning and make that? Where did he get the ingredients?

"I get it. But you reacted how a normal person would. I'm not going to sugarcoat this because you seem like a person who wouldn't appreciate that," Les says, slicing a piece of the bread and laying it on a napkin. She pushes it to me and cuts her piece. "Are we criminals? Yes. There is no other way around it; it's who we were raised to be. Would we change it? No. If I said we would, I'd be lying."

She turns to face me. "Leo didn't know who I was when we first started dating. He knew who his brothers were, but he had only known that life for a year when he met me. He struggled with who he met and who I turned out to be for a while." I met Leo and wouldn't have guessed he was Evander and Mateo's brother until he smiled. "I also had no clue who he was at first. We had a really rocky start."

"What happened?" I ask, fully invested. It felt like two friends talking to each other. I've never had a female friend to talk about these things with.

Les giggles and stands up. "We need coffee for this conversation." She gets everything brewing and turns around. "I have a past with Frankie Perez, their father," she says, and I can tell it wasn't a good one. "He did horrible shit to me when I was a teenager, so you could imagine my surprise when I found out the Leo Janelle I was dating turned out to be Leo Perez. To make a long story short, I found out the hard way, tied him in the basement, and threatened his and his brother's lives."

My mouth drops open in shock. She pours two cups of coffee, sliding one to me. "You guys are married, so it worked out, but how did you come back from that?" I ask.

She leans on the island on the other side. "I was already in love with him when I found out. It didn't come without struggles, but we made it work. I wouldn't change anything that happened that got us to where we are now."

I nod, letting all that soak in. "I know I shouldn't be upset because they aren't mine to be upset over. Once this is done, I'm leaving, so I shouldn't have let it bother me."

"You're so convinced you're leaving. Is it because of what you found out, or you don't want to be here?"

"I don't know, Les," I admit. "One second I want to be here, and then the next, I think I'm hanging on to them just because they make me feel good."

Les shakes her head. "I don't think that's it. You don't seem like a person that would do that. I'm going to be honest here. If they didn't want you here, you never would have found out the truth. No matter what Aaron said. You might have known, but they didn't have to admit to it."

"Where did he get this stuff?" I say, waving my hand toward the banana bread. I know I'm deflecting, but I don't know what to say.

Les smiles. "When he called this morning and told me what happened, he asked me to bring phones for you guys and the ingredients. He made it because he knows it's your favorite."

Tears fill my eyes. "I'm such a bitch."

"No, you're not." Les walks around the counter and wraps me in a hug. "They don't think you are, either. Talk to them, Evie. You'll be surprised about what you'll find out."

CHAPTER 50
MATEO

"Fire in the hole!" I yell before hitting the detonator. Another one of Aaron's hideouts crumbles around the foundation. I usually don't use explosives, but I am just pissed enough to burn everything in Concrete Row to the ground. Usually, blowing shit up makes me happy, but not today.

"You know, it's fucking scary how fast you can build a bomb," Ryder says dryly.

"I had motivation," I grumble.

The look in Evie's eyes when Aaron told her was a punch to the gut. I've never seen so much hurt on someone's face or the anger when we told her everything. She had every right to be pissed. We promised to protect her, and all we did was hurt her in the end.

"Dude, she'll come around," Gage says. "Les said she's talking to her. That's a good sign."

"Whatever," I gripe. "Let's meet up with the other guys."

Gage, Ryder, and I climb into Ryder's Explorer. "You think this is enough to flush him out?" Ryder asks.

"Fuck if I know." I run my fingers through my hair. "He's been unpredictable so far." This crazy fucker took shots at a heavily guarded mansion and chased me for miles last night. The only reason I lost him is that my car could handle curves better than the

SUVs. I don't know if Aaron was the one following me, but something in my gut said it was. It's personal between him and me.

Ryder pulls over in front of Ghost's pool hall. We get out without another word, and the others are already waiting. Dex stayed behind to keep an eye on the girls. Not that Les knew that, but we felt better that way.

After Evie went to bed last night, we talked for hours, trying to figure out how to fix this. And we all came to the same conclusion. We would fight like hell to keep her, but ultimately, it's up to her.

I slide into the chair beside Van. He looks at me, then casts a look at Micah. Micah's pinched expression says he is seconds away from flying off the handle. Hopefully, that happens when Aaron is in the vicinity. I look over at Gray, who's leaning against the wall with a faraway look on his face. He hasn't said a word since last night, and it's starting to worry me.

We wait to see if Aaron will take the bait for an hour. While we were out, we practically waved a red flag announcing our presence.

"Fucking pussy," Micah mutters, looking at the time on his phone.

"He has to know by now that we're here," Hartley says.

"He doesn't want us, though," I add. "He wants Evie. This was a bad plan."

"The fucking plan was to draw him out, so he'd make a move," Micah barks. "What better way to get to Evie than to take us out? The plan wasn't bad; he's just a fucking pussy."

"First off, calm down before that vein in your goddamn head explodes. Second of all, I don't know who the fuck you think you're talking to, but today is not the day."

"Because you're the only one pissed off?" Micah grits out, standing from his chair.

I jump up from mine, ignoring Van's hand trying to pull me back down.

"Will you two calm the fuck down?" Zane yells. "Jesus Christ. I can tell you from experience fighting amongst yourselves don't do shit."

"Yeah," Gage nods. "Listen to Big Daddy."

Ryder barks a laugh when Zane glares at Gage, then Zane's eyes turn to Ryder. "Something funny, love?" Zane asks Ryder.

Ryder chokes back another laugh. "Nah. Just a tickle in my throat."

"He's going to tickle your throat all right," Gage says, laughing obnoxiously.

Zane rolls his eyes. "What's the play? Because this isn't working. If you want my two cents, I think you need to go back and talk to your girl, straighten shit out, and come back with your heads on straight."

"If we leave now, he's going to follow us back to her," Micah says, sitting back down. "And if you ever talk to me like that again, I'll rip your arms off and beat you with them."

Zane snorts. "We've danced that dance before, Micah. Neither one of us came out on top."

My eyes swing between them. "What?"

"Oh, Zane and Micah beat the shit out of each other when Micah found out what Zane did to Les," Gage informs us.

I laugh despite myself. "You're such a gossip queen."

"He lives for the gossip," Leo laughs. He sits in front of us. "I don't need to remind you how I ended up with Les in the first place." Van and I share a sheepish look. "Let us handle this here and go fix things with her."

We managed to get back to the safe house without being followed, which was weird in itself. But I decided I didn't want to worry about that; I just wanted to talk to Evie.

When we walk into the house, Les is the only one in the living room. "She's taking a nap," Les says quietly. "You have a big mess to clean up, but I think it's fixable."

Micah sits beside her on the couch. "Thanks for staying with her, shithead."

"I'm surprised she didn't tell me to eat shit," Les laughs. "She's just confused. This is a lot to take in."

"I know," Micah sighs.

Les stands up. "I'm going to go talk to Dex while you talk to her. She should be getting up soon."

"You knew he was there?" I ask.

"Of course I did," Les snorts. "I know my guys, and they weren't going to leave us here alone. And Dex was the most likely to stay." She grins and slips out the front door.

"You know that's creepy, right?" Hartley laughs.

"That's nothing. If I didn't know any better, I would swear she's fucking psychic," Micah answers. "She knows shit about you before you know it about yourself."

"I can't just sit here," I say, popping up out of the chair. "I need to talk to her."

"Tay, you need to let her sleep," Van says gently. "She probably slept worse than us."

"But this is my fault," I say raggedly. "I had no fucking business pursuing her. I brought her into this mess. I fucked up."

"You didn't fuck up, Tay." Micah runs his hand down his face. "We should have told her before anything else happened. This is on all of us."

"None of this is anyone's fault." I jerk my head to Evie's soft voice. I want to drop at her feet and beg for forgiveness.

"Buttercup," I say, then snap my lips closed when she holds up a hand.

"I want to talk first," she says, looking around the room, waiting for us to nod. She sits down in the chair, tucking her legs under her. She's still in Gray's oversized hoodie, her hair piled on top of her head, and she's never looked more beautiful. "I know why you guys didn't tell me." Micah sits forward, and she holds up her hand again.

"I've thought about this a lot, and I wanted to be pissed off and hurt, but I don't deserve to be. You aren't mine to demand answers from. I know there was no commitment when I agreed to this, and saying you should have divulged a secret like that isn't fair. I want you to know I'd never say anything, and I appreciate everything you've done for me."

"Why does it sound like you're already saying goodbye, angel?" Gray asks, finally breaking his vow of silence since yesterday.

Evie smiles sadly. "Because I am. I can't be in this life anymore. It's better if everything that happened stays back at the house and doesn't follow us anywhere else. When this is done, I'm going back to Fairview so you guys can get on with your life."

"Fuck that," I say harshly, causing her head to whip in my direction. "You aren't leaving. Ever."

"Mateo, it's for the best."

"No, it's not. Goddamnit, I didn't want to do it like this, but I fucking love you. Do you get that? This isn't a game or a fling for me. You're it for me, buttercup. You're the one I've been waiting on. I can't let you go."

Evie gasps and covers her mouth with her hand. Tears flash down her cheeks. "Don't say that, Mateo. Please."

"Why not? It's the truth. I love you, Evie." I get up and crouch in front of her. "I've never felt like this except for..." I jerk my head toward Gray, but he isn't ready for that shit yet for sure. "Give us a chance to prove you can be in this life. You're writing us off before you even hear what we have to say."

"I can't," Evie cries. "You don't get it..."

"No, I do." I stand up, my heart breaking in two. "You don't feel the same way."

Evie opens her mouth, and Micah's phone blares through the room. He checks the display and swipes to answer.

"Get out now!" Les yells through the speakerphone. "Convoy coming your way."

I grab Evie's hand, and we are up and moving before the last word is out of Les' mouth. I help her slip her shoes on and dash out the back door. We parked an SUV back here just in case we needed a quick exit, and thank fuck we did.

We all pile in with Gray behind the wheel and Hartley in the passenger seat. Van and Micah take up the middle seat while I pull Evie into my side in the back. She might not feel the same way, but

I'll be damned if she doesn't get my total protection. He takes off down a rough path behind the house that we scouted out last night that eventually brings you out into Abandoned Hills. We just needed to get to Concrete Row.

"We can only hold them off for so long!" Les says, and I hear her firing off shots.

"Get the fuck out of there, Les," Micah barks into the phone. The line goes dead, but Micah knows damn well Les isn't leaving.

I text Leo, letting him know what's going on, and then Ghost. We need everyone ready.

An SUV roars up behind us, firing shots at us. "Shit," I mutter, pulling Evie's head down and covering her body with mine. Her body is shaking at such a high frequency that all I can do is hold her tighter.

Micah and Van start loading automatic rifles. They both hit the buttons for the window. "On three," Micah says, and Van nods. Micah counts down the three. They pop out of their windows and start unloading their clips. Van jerks back into the window about the time a bullet whizzes past and shatters the passenger side mirror.

"Son of a bitch," Van gripes, rubbing his fingers over his ear. There is blood on his fingers, showing how close they were to taking his head off.

"Van," I say quietly. Good God, I sound like a scared child, but that is my brother.

"I'm fine, Tay," Van assures me.

The SUV speeds up behind us and slams into the back of ours, causing Gray to fishtail on the uneven path. I watch his face in the rearview mirror, and it almost takes my breath away. His eyes look dead, and his face is set in stone. I've never seen that look on him before, but I have a feeling that is what people saw when they met the Reaper.

"We should be coming out in Abandoned Hills in less than a minute," Hartley reports. He turns around in his seat, and I know what he wants to know. I shake my head because Evie isn't okay. I can hear her crying, and her hands are locked over her ears.

We hit the blacktop right about the time the SUV slams us again. This time, the SUV sways to the side from the impact.

"Motherfucker," Gray growls when he corrects again. Even his voice sounds dead.

"We're almost there," I soothe Evie. "Just a few more minutes, buttercup." I already got confirmation from Leo and Ghost that they were in position.

"Hold on," Hartley warns.

The SUV slams the back tail light right when Gray takes a curve. I feel the SUV lift and know we are fucked.

I hold Evie tighter as the SUV tips and slams against the blacktop.

CHAPTER 51
EVIE

My ears are ringing, everything in my body hurts, and I can't breathe. The impact of the crash caused Mateo to rest his entire weight on me. Swallowing down the panic, I push against him.

"Mateo." My voice sounded like I was in the bottom of a barrel, and I could vaguely hear yelling around me. "Mateo!" Oh god, please be okay, please be okay.

He groans and sits up the best he can. The SUV is still on its side, and I have no clue how we will get out.

"You have to get out!" Micah's voice finally breaks through the ringing, and I take a second to be relieved that he and Evander are okay. Where are Gray and Hartley? "Mateo! Get her out!" I hear gunshots and have my answer. They are out there by themselves.

"You have to go out through the sunroof," Evander says, pointing to the hole where it used to be. "We're going to hold them off. There is a path that leads to Concrete Row to the left. Get there."

Evander and Micah slip through the sunroof. "Come on, buttercup," Mateo says, helping me crawl across the seats. "When we get out, fucking run. Got it?"

"We can't leave them," I beg.

"We don't have a choice. Let's go." He tugs on my hand, and I don't have a choice but to follow. Before I can turn around to see the other guys, he's leading me down a path that keeps sloping down. Mateo matches his pace to mine, never letting go of my hand.

"EVIE!" That voice almost freezes me in my tracks, but Mateo keeps pulling. "Baby! Stop running! You're just making this harder on yourself!"

I hear thrashing and know Aaron is right behind us.

"Come on, buttercup," Mateo encourages, starting to move faster.

Buildings come into view, and I know safety is down there somewhere. They have a plan to keep me safe. I just need to believe that. So many things went left unsaid at the safe house.

A body flies by me and smacks into Mateo. I let go of a scream as they tumble the rest of the way down. A hand wraps in my hair and jerks me backward. "MATEO!"

"I got you, you stupid bitch," Aaron growls in my ear, dragging me down the hill. He doesn't slow as I hit my knees.

"Please, Aaron," I beg, clawing at his hands. We reach the bottom, and he pulls me to my feet. I look into his cold dead eyes and wonder how I didn't see that when I first met him.

"You should have listened to me. There is no one left to save you after Wraith takes care of the rich boy. How does that feel? You killed them all just by fucking existing."

No no no. They can't be dead. I try to turn to find Mateo, but Aaron tightens his hand in my hair. Sucking in a breath to scream, Aaron punches me right in the stomach, making me double over in pain.

"Don't you dare," Aaron hisses. "I know you have people down here, but I'll slit your throat before you get a chance to scream, whore. Just like I did the fucker on the motorcycle." Gray? Gray can't be dead. He is too strong and too *good*.

Aaron starts dragging me again, ducking behind buildings. How am I supposed to get away? He had his fist tangled in my hair and was too strong for me. He jerks me into an abandoned building and slams the door behind us, then drags me further inside.

Aaron slams my back up against the wall so hard it knocks the breath from my lungs and pushes into my face. "Was it worth it?" he snarls. "You really think I wasn't watching your every move this whole goddamn time? I let you have your peace thinking you got away. It was a fun little game until you decided to slut it up. Five guys? They must like fucking a dead fish because that's what it feels like with you."

My anger and pain finally bubbles over. I don't care what happens to me now, not if the guys are gone. What kind of life would that be to live knowing I'm the reason they're dead?

"Why do you even want me back then?!" I yell. "If it was that bad, then why?!"

"Because you rolled over and played dead," Aaron laughs in my face. "I knew the minute I laid eyes on you that I could do what I wanted because you're too fucking weak to fight back."

"Fuck. You," I grit out. Flashes of what Les and Gray taught me flash through my head.

"First lesson, just because they're bigger doesn't mean anything."

"There you go. Get pissed because an attacker isn't going to talk you through how to get out."

"Then why aren't you struggling harder?" Gray taunts. "Head or knee." He reminds me to either headbutt him or knee him in the junk. I jerk my knee up, and he recovers before I can connect with his balls, so I hit his thigh. "Harder," Gray actually barks this time, and I feel anger course through me.

I jerk my knee up as hard as possible, making contact between Aaron's legs. His eyes widen in surprise, and he bends at the waist, letting go of my hair and leaving his face wide open. I brace my hands on his shoulders and smash my knee into his nose. Shoving him out of the way, I run as fast as I can toward a door at the end of a big empty room.

Aaron slams into my back, knocking me to the ground. My head bounces off the floor, and all the breath leaves my body. *Don't fucking pass out, Evie.* Aaron rolls me until he's straddling my waist, and my arms are pinned above my head. I have half a second of joy when I see the blood streaming from his nose until he spits it right in my face.

"You're going to pay for that, baby. What happened to the bitch that used to let me walk all over her?"

"SHE'S GONE!" I scream, struggling hard. Gray had me in this same position, and I only got out of it once just because he let me. Aaron's grip on my wrists is so tight I can feel the bones rubbing together, and his thighs are clamped tight to my hips. *Harder!* That voice is Gray's barking in my head to fight harder. I twist, roll, and jerk my arms, but Aaron laughs and tightens his grip.

"Give it up. Or maybe not." Aaron grinds his hardness against me, and I feel the bile rise in my throat. "I kind of like this version. Fight me and let's see who wins," he sneers. He clamps both wrists in one of his big hands and rips my yoga pants down. He starts fumbling with his zipper.

"Stop! NO!" I jerk my hands free and slam my fists into his chest, knocking him off balance. I jump to my feet, but my pants tangle around my legs, causing me to fall back down. "No," I whisper miserably when I feel his body on my back. I feel his dick slide across my leg.

"Yeah, I definitely like when you fight. We could turn this into a game." He shifts, and I know what he's about to do. No. Fucking. Way.

"GET OFF OF ME!" I yell, bucking my waist. He doesn't move the first time, but his body is suddenly gone the second time I do it.

"Get the fuck away from her," Mateo growls. I roll over with a gasp and almost weep with relief. His face is bloody, and so are his hands, but *he is alive.*

Aaron jumps to his feet. "How the fuck?"

"You think that bitch Wraith could take *me* out?" Mateo says, taking a menacing step forward. "All those threats about slitting people's throats open, and I finally made good on one." Holy fuck, that's why his hands are bloody? "You touched my girl, and I'm about to make sure it never happens again."

Mateo leaps at Aaron, and they hit the ground. Fists are flying, and I can't tell who has the upper hand until Mateo rolls and has Aaron pinned beneath him. Mateo rears back with his fist repeatedly, slamming it into Aaron's face. He's muttering something under his breath that I can't understand. I jump to my feet, pulling my pants back up. I don't even want to think what would've happened if Mateo didn't show up.

"Mateo," I say gently when I notice Aaron isn't moving anymore. "Mateo!" I say louder, grabbing his arm. He jerks back to look at me, fist raised mid-air. His eyes are wild, and his chest is heaving. "He's not moving," I say gently.

Mateo's eyes flash down to Aaron, looking at his unconscious form, then I'm in his arms. "Fuck, buttercup. Are you okay?"

"I am now," I cry. "Where are the others?"

"I don't know. I came to you first."

"Let's go," I say urgently.

Aaron groans behind us, and Mateo's eyes flash. "Not this time, fucker," Mateo growls and leaps again.

"Mateo, no!" I yell when I see the glint of metal in Aaron's hand.

Mateo goes stock-still and turns to face me. The knife that was in Aaron's hand is wedged in his stomach, and his eyes are wide with shock. Mateo's knees hit the floor, and I grab the gun from his holster. I run over every lesson Hartley taught me growing up about shooting a gun. I slide the safety off, aim, and pull the trigger. The bullet goes wide, and Aaron laughs weakly.

"Give it up, baby," Aaron groans, pulling himself to stand. Blood is pouring from his face, and his gait is unsteady as he walks to me. "Give me the gun."

I pull the trigger again, and this time it's close enough to make Aaron jump.

"You stupid fat fucking whore!"

Just breathe. I take a big breath and pull the trigger.

The bullet pierces right above Aaron's surprised eyes, and I run to Mateo. I cradle him to my chest, rocking him back and forth. There is too much blood soaking over his hand and dripping from his mouth.

"No, Mateo, no," I cry. "Stay with me, okay? I'll get help."

"Buttercup," Mateo whispers.

"No, don't you dare give up on me," I beg, patting his pockets. I get his phone out, crying harder when I see my picture is saved as his background. I finally get my fumbling fingers to obey and dial nine-one-one. "I need an ambulance. I don't know the address. Can't you track it?!"

"Buttercup," Mateo says again, then starts coughing. It sounds so damn bad.

"Shhh," I soothe. "Help is on the way." I hang up on the operator when she assures me they can. I scroll until I see the number I need.

"Les," I breathe. "I need help now! Mateo's been stabbed, and I don't know what to do."

"Calm down, Evie. You need to put pressure on it. I'm on my way. Holden's tracking your location now. Are you in Concrete Row?"

I flip to speakerphone and lay the phone on the floor. "Yes! Abandoned white building. Les, there's so much blood."

"Just breathe. We're coming. Put pressure on it, Evie."

"The knife is still in there!"

"Don't move it! Take a shirt or whatever you have and put pressure around it."

I jerk Gray's hoodie off and wrap it around the knife. Mateo groans.

"Please, don't leave me," I cry, pushing down against the bleeding. "I love you. Do you hear me? I love you. You can't leave me."

Mateo's eyes open, and he smiles.

"I love you," I say again. "No!" I yell when the smile drops from his face. "No! Please!"

I watch the life drain from his beautiful green eyes.

"Mateo. No," I cry. "I love you."

AFTERWORD

Yikes...that fucking cliffhanger was rough! Have no fear, Part Two is available!

Want to stay up to date?

Join Ames Mills on TikTok, Instagram, and Facebook!
TikTok - author.ames.mills
Instagram - author.ames.mills
Facebook reader's group - Ames Mills' Black Demons

Sign up for my newsletter for announcements, signed paperbacks, merchandise, giveaways, and bonus content at amesmills.com

Comments, questions, or concerns? Email Ames at hello@ amesmills.com

ACKNOWLEDGMENTS

Holy shit!!

This was book three, you guys, three! When I first picked up my computer and started writing Riches to Riches, I didn't know where it would take me. All I knew was that I needed to get Alessa's story out there. I learned some valuable lessons, gained new friends and loyal readers, and learned not to be so hard on myself. I loved writing Alessa and her guys, and they will always be my babies. But Evie and her group found another spot in my heart. I know you guys were excited about Micah (and Evander), and I hope it met what you envisioned. Their story was hard. There were a lot of ups and downs, heartache, and a beautiful relationship formed because of it.

Evie was a harder character for me to write because she was nothing like Les. So, yes, this book is a lot different. But I loved how Evie blossomed with the guys. And Hartley? Did anyone see that shit coming? (lol) He wasn't initially planned for this. I wasn't even going to revisit him, but as I started writing, he had a story to tell. Plus, I really enjoy messing with Micah.

On that note....I killed Aaron; I fucking hated his very existence, so he's dead (go Evie!). But what does that mean for Part Two? You'll have to read to find out. I left a lot of unanswered questions in Part One that will be answered in Part Two. Have theories? Feel free to discuss this in the reader's group! I live for that shit!

To my readers, you guys are literally the best. My girls in the reader's group, you guys make it easier to sit down and make these characters come to life. None of this is possible without you!

Until next time....

Also by Ames Mills

Abbs Valley series

Riches to Riches

(Reverse Harem/polyamorous Mafia Romance)

Part one

Part two

All I Have

(Reverse Harem/polyamorous Mafia Romance)

Part one

Part two

A Very Merry Mafia Christmas Novella

(Reverse Harem/polyamorous Mafia Romance)

The Heart of Psychos

(Reverse Harem/polyamorous Mafia Romance)

Part one

Part two (releasing April, 24th 2023)

About the Author

Ames Mills is an indie author who lives in rural West Virginia with her two beautiful teenage girls. She writes reverse harem/polyamorous romance. She has a soft spot for damaged heroes and heroines that she loves to piece back together, bi-awakenings, and anything in between.

Go stalk her on social media and join her reader's group. She'd love to have you!

Printed in Great Britain
by Amazon

39336007R00260